D0324853

Miracle at Winterville

Beth,

May the Lord bless you!

Miracle at Winterville

Robert Quattlebaum

Heavenly
Light Press
Alpharetta, GA

This is a work of fiction. Names, characters, businesses, places, and events are either the products of the author's imagination or are used in a fictitious manner. Any resemblance to actual persons, living or dead, or actual events is purely coincidental.

Copyright © 2019 by Robert Quattlebaum
First Edition 2019

All rights reserved. No part of this book may be reproduced or transmitted in any form or by any means, electronic or mechanical, including photocopying, recording, or any information storage and retrieval system, without permission in writing from the author.

ISBN: 978-1-63183-696-1 - Paperback
eISBN: 978-1-63183-697-8 – ePub
eISBN: 978-1-63183-698-5 - mobi

Library of Congress Control Number: 2019917857

Printed in the United States of America   1 1 0 5 1 9

∞This paper meets the requirements of ANSI/NISO Z39.48-1992 (Permanence of Paper)

To my wife, Rebekah, who loves this story more than I.

Chapter One

My story starts some sixty years ago. I know that's a crazy long time, but you need to understand what happened back then so everything else will make sense...

* * *

Johnny Jones quit resisting the weight of his eyelids as Ma and Pa tiptoed from his room. And though the doctor whispered to them just outside his door, he still caught every word.

"I'm going to give it to you straight, Pastor." Doctor Fred Snyder's voice carried the deep rasp of a southern gentleman, a voice ill suited for secretive tones. "That boy's body can't take much more. I've done everything I know to do. If he doesn't shake this thing in the next day or so, he probably won't make it. Even if he pulls through, he's likely to be crippled." He grunted a reluctant sigh. "Polio is a killer. I wish I had better news."

"We appreciate what you've done, Fred." Pa's voice sounded higher than normal, evident even through his whisper. "Now it's up to God. We'll just pray harder."

"You do that, Pastor. I'll drop by in the morning to check on him." The doctor's footsteps thudded toward the front door. "I...I'm truly sorry."

Hinges creaked, the door slammed shut, and seconds passed in which Johnny wondered if he'd drifted off to sleep. Pa's voice broke the silence, back to its normal tone.

"Ida, that man needs prayer almost as much as Johnny. I'm not convinced he even believes in God."

"Jeremiah, how can you...?" Johnny thought Ma might be crying. "Is Johnny... is he going to die?"

The thought shocked Johnny from his almost-sleep. Die? In some ways he wished he *could* die to escape the discomfort and pain. But he didn't mean it. Was he really that sick?

"We need to pray." Pa's voice sounded from inside Johnny's room. Johnny played possum.

Footsteps shuffled to Johnny's bed and he felt the mattress droop as Pa leaned close, kneeling, no doubt, as was his custom. "Father God, I've been praying and believing these past few days, but the doctor says there's not much hope. You're the only one who can help Johnny, and I believe with all my heart you can heal him. So I ask you Lord—I beg you—please, heal my boy." Pa sniffed, and shifted his weight against the bed. "I couldn't bear to lose him. I love him with all my heart."

One deep breath, then another. Pa shuddered against the bed. "I want you to know, Lord, no matter what you decide, I'll always trust you." He swallowed hard. "I'm putting my son's life in your hands."

Johnny thought the prayer was over, and a mighty short one compared to how Pa usually prayed. Then the bed jolted as Pa burst into sobs. "Oh, God, please! Please! Spare my boy!"

Again and again Pa pleaded his case. Ma's high-pitched cry joined in. At first the outbursts sent Johnny's adrenaline racing. But as the cries and prayers both quieted and continued unabated, the drone lulled him into fitful sleep.

* * *

Tossing and turning. Half awake. Half asleep. Johnny wrestled with the idea of death, of never seeing his friends, or Ma and Pa again. Well, not *never*. Pa taught that they'd see each other again one day. But even that evaded solid understanding.

Johnny thought of the things he would miss. Playing Indian by himself in the woods behind the house. Games of marbles with friends from school. Ma's apple pies! The many adventures he shared with Pa. Kind of like the one just last month when...

"Come on, son." Pa called to him from the front porch, arm waving. "We're going on a mission."

Johnny jumped up from where he'd been watching a column of ants carry the carcass of an inch-long beetle toward its final destiny. "What kind of mission?" He dusted off his coveralls and squinted into the sunlight.

"A mission of mercy." Pa gripped a basket of apples in one hand and his Bible in the other. He motioned with the Bible toward the truck.

Like a bullet, Johnny shot toward the old Ford. Pa arrived an eternity later, slammed the door shut, and held the key over until the engine sputtered to life. "Hey, Pa—where're we going this time?"

Pa grinned as he shoved the truck in gear. "You'll see."

They bumped along down a number of gravel and dirt roads until the truck ground to a halt in front of a rickety log cabin where weeds ruled the yard. Johnny had never seen the place but he recognized it nonetheless. Old Lady Gritolli—that's what the school kids called her—haunted this no man's land. Rumors circled the schoolyard that the crabby old hermit snatched children foolish enough to trespass, and chained them to trees behind her home.

Pa sprang from the truck and strode toward the house, whistling. "Bring the apples," he called over his shoulder.

Johnny studied the old structure, then grabbed the basket—it was *heavy*—and lugged it in the footsteps of his father. He couldn't imagine what Pa was thinking, bringing them to the very edge of Hell's gates like this.

Pa's three loud raps against the door set Johnny's spine tingling.

"Who's there?" crabbed a woman's voice.

"It's Pastor Jones, Mrs. Gritolli."

"Just a minute, Pastor. I'm coming."

Grunts and shuffling noises sounded from the darkness behind a rickety screen door that squeaked open way too soon for Johnny's liking. The thing that stooped in the doorway bore a vague resemblance to a normal human. He shivered.

Wrinkles. Tons of them, marching across cheeks that sagged into a neck that drooped over the edge of a tattered shawl. Johnny stumbled backward, mouth agape, and fell flat of his backside. Apples rolled all over the porch and, as he scrambled to refill the basket, the old woman cackled at him. Johnny glanced up at her then slinked to relative safety behind Pa where he stole peeks at the strange creature.

"Sorry it took so long, Pastor." The old woman turned toward Pa. "I don't move so fast as I used to. Y'all come on in." She scrunched against the doorframe to make room while holding open the screen.

Pa swung the door wide, and Mrs. Gritolli hobbled back into the darkness, hunched over a cane like a fairytale witch. Pa followed without hesitation. Johnny swallowed hard, then forced one foot in front of the other, apple basket bumping his knees.

An odor of mustiness and dirt and, well, *age* wrinkled Johnny's nose when he crossed over the threshold. He paused, eyes adjusting to the light, then surveyed the room. Clutter. Brik-a-brak. A tattered couch faded to gray.

"We brought you something." Pa pointed the ever-present Bible toward Johnny.

Seconds passed as Johnny studied Mrs. Gritolli, and she him. Pa frowned, and gestured with greater emphasis. Johnny hefted the basket outward.

Squinting, Mrs. Gritolli studied the gift. Then her face lit up. "Bless your soul, young man!" She clasped cold and wrinkled fingers around Johnny's hand.

Time stood still.

Pa waved his Bible at a pile of crumbling timbers serving as a coffee table. Johnny was only too glad to comply. He pulled free of the old woman and unburdened his load atop a yellowed newspaper.

"And God bless you, Mrs. Gritolli. Do you mind if I share some of God's Word with you?" Pa flashed his best pulpit smile. "It'll go right good with those apples."

"Oh, please, Pastor. I got me some reading glasses, but," Mrs. Grilolli's faced sagged, accentuating her wrinkles, "they don't do no good."

"Now don't you worry." Pa squatted, big black Bible flopping open in his lap. He preached a private sermon to the widow while Johnny marveled. His school friends hated this lady, yet Pa treated her like a queen.

Mrs. Gritolli wiped away tears when Pa closed the holy book. "Pastor, would you pray for me?"

"Absolutely. What should I pray for?"

"My eyes, Pastor." More tears filled the ridges lining Mrs. Gritolli's cheeks. "I know I'm old and things wear out, but I miss reading the Bible. Is that too much to ask of God?"

Pa lowered his Bible to the floor. He took both the old lady's hands in his own and squared eyes with her. "God is our Father. He *delights* in the requests of his children."

Tears now a flood, Mrs. Gritolli pulled her hands free and curtained fingers over her eyes. She sobbed, shoulders heaving.

Pa leaned forward. With ever so much care he slid her fingers aside and rested his own giant hands on her brow. "Father God, your beloved daughter wants her sight restored. She hasn't asked selfishly, Lord—she just wants to read your Word. So, Holy Father, I ask you to grant her request in the blessed name of Jesus. Amen."

Would it happen? Johnny glued his gaze on the old woman. Pa's prayer sure was shorter than the ones he said in church. Was it good enough?

Mrs. Gritolli blinked opened her eyes. She turned side to side, looking all about the room. When her gaze returned to Jeremiah, she squinted at him for the longest time.

"Well?" Pa's voice conveyed quiet confidence.

"Can't say I can tell any difference."

Pa smiled and patted her on the knee. "That's all right. It's in God's hands now." He clapped both hands on his thighs and pushed upward. "You just have faith."

"Thank you, Pastor." Mrs. Gritolli smiled back at him, somehow less frightening than when Johnny first laid eyes on her.

Questions burned in Johnny's mind. He sprinted for the truck after the obligatory goodbye hugs and well-wishing.

"Pa?" Johnny's question started before Pa slammed the truck door shut. "Why didn't God heal Old...um, why didn't God heal Mrs. Gritolli?"

A whir of the starter, and the truck sputtered to life. Pa shifted it into gear before answering. "Can't say for sure, son. God has his own ways—and his own time."

Johnny stared out his window as the truck lurched into motion, thoughts running wild. "Was your prayer good enough?" He stole a sideways glance to catch Pa's reaction.

"Ha!" Pa banged his palm against the steering wheel. "How do you measure a prayer? I had faith—that's what counts." He shifted into second and eased out the clutch. The truck lurched ahead, puttering away while woods and pastures glided by. "God does *what* he wants *when* he wants, son." Pa divided his attention between Johnny and the road. "Just because we ask for something, well, that doesn't mean it's God's will. And even when something *is* God's will, sometimes we have to pray over and over before it comes to pass. The important thing is that we never lose faith because of what God does or doesn't do. He knows what's best. It's our job to trust him, no matter how it looks to human eyes."

Pa fixed his eyes back on the path ahead. He adjusted his fading black fedora and whistled a tune Johnny hadn't heard before. Johnny looked at him long and hard, wondering where faith and trust like that came from.

And as Johnny continued to toss and turn back in the reality of his sickbed, he wondered just what it took to have faith as strong as Pa's.

* * *

The morning sun peeked through Johnny's bedroom window, warming his cheek. His eyelids fluttered, and he squinted away from the light. Then he jerked upward at the sight of his parents lying in a heap on the floor.

"Ma? Pa?"

Ma woke first. She raised up on her knees and pointed. "Jeremiah! Look, he's...he's—"

"Ma? What's going on?" Johnny scooted full upright and swung his legs to the floor.

Ma sprang to his side. "Johnny!" She hugged him tight but loosed him just as quick. "Lay down, son. You'll strain yourself."

"How are you feeling, son?" Pa had roused himself and joined Ma by the bed. He reached for Johnny's forehead.

"I feel fine, Pa."

"Hmm. The fever's gone."

Johnny thought back to last night and remembered Pa's prayer. "God healed me, didn't he, Pa? I mean, you helped by praying, but God did it. He really healed me."

A tear formed in Pa's eye. "Yes, son, that's exactly what happened." He hugged Johnny, then pulled Ma in, too. "God healed you, all right, and it's nothing less than a miracle. You always wanted to see a miracle, Johnny. Now you are one."

* * *

Doc Snyder dropped by the Jones' residence late morning to check on Johnny. No sooner had he stepped out of his old green sedan than Johnny whizzed by, chasing a squirrel and yelping with delight. The boy had an odd sort of lilt in his run, but Doc couldn't see as it hampered his zeal. Johnny disappeared into the woods behind the house while Doc stared after him.

"Good morning, Doctor!"

He turned to see Ida waving from the porch.

"It's a pleasure to see you this morning. What do you think about Johnny?"

Doc blinked. He raked off his hat and ran his fingers through his thinning hair. "What happened, Mrs. Jones?"

Ida hopped off the porch and joined the doctor beside his car. Her eyes twinkled. "We prayed, and God answered."

Doc raised his eyebrows. "That's all?"

"That's all."

He flicked his gaze back toward the woods where an occasional yelp echoed from among the trees. He scratched his head. "I've never seen anything like it."

"We serve an awesome God, Doctor." Ida smiled as Johnny bounded back toward the house, sans squirrel, huffing. "I know he's limping, but other than that you would never know he was sick."

Doctor Snyder slid his hat back on. He studied Johnny another minute, then shook his head. "That beats all, Mrs. Jones. Maybe I *will* see you in church this Sunday." He creaked open his car door and settled into the seat.

They both watched Johnny pick up steam again. He ran past them, tripped on a root, caught himself, then scrambled into the house on all fours like a wild dog.

"I expect so, Doctor." Ida stared at him wearing the oddest sort of smile. "Jeremiah's got quite a sermon worked up over this. I reckon you'd be a fool to miss it."

Chapter Two

A looming ninety degree bend dared Trevor McIntire to keep up his breakneck pace. His fire-red Honda eased past eighty-five, blurring cattle and farmland on either side. The car jinked left, then right as human appendages jutting from all four windows rocked to the WHUMP, WHUMP, WHUMP of the thousand-dollar stereo, a collegiate party on wheels.

Locks of hair danced across Trevor's forehead, tossed about by the gale-force wind whipping through his window. Grinning in wild anticipation, he feathered back on the gas pedal. The speedometer swung below eighty just as the car broke into the curve, tires screaming, clawing for traction in a valiant effort to fend off the road's soft shoulder.

"Get on it, Trevor!" A shout from the back seat. "Whatsamatter—you chicken?" A chorus of clucking noises erupted in Trevor's ear.

In the rear view mirror, Kenny and Brent head-banged to the gut-pounding beat of the subwoofer planted in the trunk. Trevor yelled back. "Hang on, ladies. I'm getting that Century Badge—do or die!"

A chant pierced the air, just audible over the manic stereo. Trevor's girlfriend, Lisa Dawson, joined in from the passenger seat. "Trevor! Trevor! Trevor!"

A smile of satisfaction parted Trevor's lips. He turned his full attention back to the road in anticipation of the curve mellowing out.

At seventy miles per hour the squealing tires quieted. Trevor barely noticed. Wind roared like a lion, bass notes pounded his chest, and the little Honda sang at a fevered pitch. The din intoxicated him.

"Rule number one!" bellowed Trevor above the radio.

"Push it past a hundred!" screamed the other three in unison.

"Rule number two!"

"Somebody's gotta see it!"

"Rule number three!"

"Do it again!"

The four friends lifted a deafening cheer, "Century! Century! Century!" then beat drums on various parts of the car's interior. Each let go with a favorite curse then burst into laughter. It was their ritual. It was their creed.

The Century Club had sprung from the antics of their senior year in high school, so recently passed. Heck—the little town of Winterville was so boring, they had to do *something* to keep from going crazy.

Now free of the curve, Trevor stomped the gas pedal. He rolled his head back against the seat and laughed, adrenaline making him giddy. When he focused back on the road he recoiled in horror. A hundred yards ahead a cow straddled the yellow line. He yelped a single expletive before involuntary reflexes took over.

Trevor stood on the brake, pushing his head against the roof, knuckles white on the steering wheel. The car nose-dived and flung its occupants forward. Trevor felt something—or someone—slam the back of his seat. Three empty soda cans and a leaking beer bottle rolled up the floorboard.

The anti-lock brakes clacked staccato under Trevor's foot. He thought the brakes had failed so he pumped them. The car slowed in fits and jerks, fighting Trevor, fighting the road.

No time to steer clear of the danger—the cow filled the windshield. Someone screamed, a horror-movie howl. Trevor uttered one final curse before the car crunched into the cow, spun forty-five degrees, and shuddered to a stop with a metallic screech. The airbag exploded in Trevor's face.

For several seconds the world spun while the airbag deflated.

Moans, groans, and swearing filled the air. Trevor's hands fell from the steering wheel in slow motion. "Unnhh!" He rolled his head side to side and grimaced at the sharp pains racing up and down his spine.

Seconds passed as Trevor rubbed his eyes and waited for his thoughts to congeal. The world faded in, then out, in, then out. When his vision steadied, Trevor's gaze moved to the cow–or what was left of it. The head had twisted sideways onto the middle of the hood, mouth cracked open, dripping blood. He wondered what Lisa would think of the mess. Lisa...

Trevor twisted sideways to find Lisa staring toward the floorboard. Blood traced a thin line down her arm. One hand caressed the seatbelt where it dug into her shoulder.

"Hey, Lisa...you all right?"

Then Trevor remembered his cell phone. He groped his pants pocket and, finding nothing, fought against the seatbelt to search everywhere within reach. "Anybody seen my phone?"

Something smacked the back of Trevor's seat. "Ow! Man!" Kenny's voice. "I think my finger's broke." He then explained in no uncertain terms what he thought of Trevor's phone.

Trevor yanked at the seatbelt but it refused to budge. Face flushed, he slapped his chest where the seatbelt crossed, then banged the door. "Somebody get me out of here!" One more failed attempt at releasing the belt produced a string of expletives. "Yahh!" He vented his frustration then slumped in his seat, staring toward Lisa, but focusing far away.

"Trevor?" Lisa's voice trembled.

"Hey, Brent! Brent?" Kenny's voice again. "Trevor—Brent don't look so hot. I think he's…Oh, man! It looks like somebody beat his head with a bat! Brent, you ok, dude?"

Lisa stretched, first one shoulder then the other. She winced, then swiveled toward the back seat. "Oh, no. Brent? Hey—" Lisa's eyes went wide. "I'm bleeding! Oh, wait—it's just a scratch."

Trevor popped up, squirmed, and yanked like a madman at the seatbelt. Still trapped, he grimaced and banged both hands on the steering wheel.

Lisa raised an eyebrow. She leaned over and clicked his seatbelt release.

Trevor glanced at the latch, flipped the seatbelt out of the way, then shrugged. He creaked open the door until it halted with a metallic pop at the halfway point then scrambled from his seat and surveyed the damage.

"Should I call your mom?" Lisa swiped her contact list, then paused. "Or 9-1-1?"

Trevor heard the words but they didn't process. He gawked at the entanglement of cow and car where wisps of smoke rose from crumpled metal seams and dissipated over the new hood ornament. The front of the Honda reminded him of an accordion.

Kenny piled out of the back seat and jogged over to Trevor. "Oh, man! That's some serious hamburger!" He backslapped Trevor and chuckled.

"Trevor!" Lisa banged her door. "I can't get out."

"Crawl out my side!" Trevor huffed, then turned back to the carnage.

"Ha!" Kenny pointed to a quivering hoof. "That thing's still alive!"

Lisa wormed over the console and out the door, then joined the guys in time for Kenny's remark. She paled upon sight of the cow and backed away, one hand to her mouth. "I think I'm going to be sick."

Trevor reentered the car and poked around for his phone. Nothing under his seat, nothing in the floorboard. He cursed as he leaned across the console, then caught a glimpse of something metallic poking out from under the passenger floor mat. "Found it!" He scooped up the phone and waved it through the cracked windshield at Lisa. Then his gaze drifted to the back seat where Brent lay crumpled and moaning against the C-pillar. "Uh, oh..."

Someone leaned on Trevor's shoulder. "Hey, Brent," Kenny said in Trevor's ear. "You OK?"

The sight of Brent pumped more adrenaline through Trevor's veins. He whipped out his phone and pecked through his contact list. "I gotta call Mom—she'll know what to do." Slap! He canceled the call before it connected. "I can't call Mom—she'll tell Dad." He turned to where Lisa stood several feet away and yelled past Kenny at her. "Can you call somebody? I need to figure this out."

For a moment Lisa only stared. After Trevor waved his phone at her, she focused on him, nodded, then punched at her screen.

Trevor ran trembling fingers through his hair. He looked the car over again. "Dad's going to freaking kill me. He hasn't stopped harping about insurance since my last wreck—and that was three years ago."

"Don't sweat it, man," Kenny offered. "It wasn't your fault that stupid cow was in the road."

"Yeah…" Trevor brightened. "It was an accident. I can't help it somebody's heifer got loose." He fist-bumped Kenny. "Thanks, dude."

"Hey, no problem. That's what friends are for."

* * *

"Hey, Trev! I heard about that wild ride, man."

Trevor searched past Lisa for who had called him amid the gaggle of students shuffling to their next class. There, waving. What was the guy's name? Mitch? Trevor barely knew him. How did *he* find out?

Word must be all over campus. Kenny running his big mouth, no doubt. A smile brightened Trevor's face. This could be great publicity.

"Dude!" Jenson Jerrat appeared in front of Trevor, flashing a big thumbs-up. He extended a hand for a quick shake, then his smile faded. "Hey, man, how's Brent?"

Trevor found Jenson's somber look somehow out of place, even amusing. Spiked electric-blue hair and countless facial piercings on a three hundred pound body didn't exactly exude an image of compassion. Besides, the guy was usually high on something. In fact, maybe he didn't really care at all. Maybe Brent owed him money.

"Um, I don't really know the latest." Trevor admitted to himself he hadn't given Brent much thought since he disappeared into the ambulance. The confrontation he'd had with his dad, and his lack of personal transportation, had occupied most of his thoughts.

Lisa shoved Trevor. She frowned, then turned to Jenson. "The doctor said he has a slight concussion. And he's pretty banged up. But he should be home soon."

"Oh, man."

Trevor shrugged. "Did you hear about my car? I smashed the whole front end off." He whipped out his phone and flipped through some pictures.

Jensen cackled when Trevor got to the cow. "That's too much, man." He gazed a moment longer, then hefted his backpack. "Hey— Gotta go. If you see Brent, tell him I said to get well soon." Jensen cracked an odd sort of smile then ambled off.

Lisa jabbed Trevor in the ribs.

"Hey!"

"You haven't gone to see Brent once."

"So? He's OK. Just some bruises."

Lisa huffed, then marched away. Trevor started after her, but another student wanted to hear about the accident. He was only too happy to oblige.

At first Trevor relished the attention. But by afternoon he was ready to move on. His after-school plans centered on finding a replacement for the Civic. It had to be something really cool this time, Dad and his insurance be hanged.

When Trevor's last class let out, he and Kenny piled into Lisa's Mazda convertible. She lowered the top and chauffeured them to the part of town where car salesmen swarmed like sharks circling a shipwreck.

"Let's go to Taylor Chevrolet," Trevor directed as he leaned back and adjusted his sunglasses. He'd been eyeing new Camaros off and on for months.

Besides, Trevor knew exactly where he stood at the Taylor dealership. He knew the sales staff had it figured out, too. Mr. Taylor owned several dealerships in town, including the one where Dad bought his Mercedes. Sometimes the salesmen switched stores. They all knew Mr. McIntire, and anyone who snagged him for a deal had it made because he never haggled price. Because of this Trevor and his friends had the run of the lot, jumping in and out of everything that caught their eyes.

Despite shiny paint and flashy interiors, Trevor found most new cars boring. He sauntered back toward the Camaro SS he'd picked out earlier, paused to admire its lines, then moved in close and ran his hands over the fenders front to back. Over four hundred horsepower just waiting for him to let loose on the street. He flagged down a salesperson.

The test drive produced three massive smiles and one horrified scream. Sharon, the saleswoman, got way more than she bargained for. Trevor romped the accelerator right out of the parking lot, sending up raging white smoke plumes from both rear wheels.

Two parallel black marks materialized behind the smoke as the car fishtailed thirty feet up the road. Trevor missed sideswiping a semi truck in the opposite lane by inches.

Excitement built from there. Trevor doubled the speed limit, slid sideways through a curve, and rode the bumper of a minivan that got in his way. Sharon's escalating protests finally irritated him enough that he headed back to the dealership.

"Have it ready Saturday morning," Trevor commanded when he whipped the car back into the dealer's lot. "My dad'll be here first thing with a check." He jerked the Camaro to a stop in front of the main doors, hopped out, and tossed Sharon the keys.

For a moment Sharon could only stare. Then she composed herself. "Um, sure thing, uh…Mr. McIntire." She exited the car and made her way around to offer a handshake. Trevor pumped once, then leaned over and helped Lisa out of the back seat. He wrapped an arm around her waist and steered her back toward the Mazda, Kenny trailing behind.

"Pleasure doing business with you," Sharon called after him.

* * *

"I am *not* buying that Camaro, Trevor." James McIntire, Trevor's father, stood arms crossed, peering down to where Trevor lay sprawled across his bed, several of his college texts scattered about him. "Do you realize that last accident is still on your record? And now this thing with the cow." Mr. McIntire shook his head. "I checked the rates. They want six thousand dollars a year to keep you on the policy. Six thousand dollars! You can *walk* to school before I drop that kind of money on car insurance."

Trevor opened his mouth to protest but Mr. McIntire slammed a fist against the wall. "I said I'd pay your way through college because you were making good grades, but now things have changed." He shook a finger at Trevor. "Did you know Brent's father is threatening a civil suit? This has gotten way out of hand."

Trevor raised his eyebrows. It was just an accident, and Brent would be fine. Whatever happened to "boys will be boys" as he'd heard all his life? Why so serious all of a sudden?

"Dad, this is crazy. It was an *accident*. There's no way I could have prevented it. There's no way *anyone* could have prevented it." Trevor felt his face flush. "Why are you taking this out on *me*?"

"Seriously, Trevor? If you had paid more attention—or if you hadn't been driving so fast—" Mr. McIntire shot him a knowing look, though Trevor hadn't mentioned speeding, "—then maybe this could have been prevented. No, I've made up my mind—it's time for you to grow up." He tossed up his hands in resignation. "I'm done with this conversation." Then with an abrupt about-face, Mr. McIntire marched from the room.

Trevor jumped up and ran after him. "Yeah? Well, fine! We'll see what Mom says when she ends up driving me to school every day. You'll find out how insane this is." Mr. McIntire was already halfway downstairs. Trevor trudged back to his room and slammed the door so hard that Lisa's picture fell off the wall.

* * *

Next morning in the math building of Winterville Community College, Trevor met a subdued Brent Bohannon at the doorway of their first class, looking lost. "Brent, old buddy!" Trevor clapped him on the back.

Brent grimaced.

"Oh, yeah—sorry 'bout that. Anyway, it's good to see you back in the saddle." Trevor lowered his voice. "You understand about me not coming to the hospital, right? Just not my scene."

"Hey, no problem." Brent cursed. "I wasn't exactly thrilled to be there myself."

Trevor broke into a smile. "Say—you gonna make the party tonight?"

The school bell sounded nearby, muffling Brent's answer and signaling the beginning of class. Brent winced and rubbed his temple. "I don't know, man. The doc said no drinking until all the swelling's gone."

"Come on—one beer never hurt anybody. Besides, he didn't say you couldn't have any *grass*, did he?"

Brent's features scrunched in puzzled thought. "Well, I dunno... I guess beer and weed are totally different, huh?" He cracked a smile. "So, yeah, maybe I'll be there. But, ah—"

"Good. You can pick me up."

"Wh—huh? No, sorry, man—I can't drive. I—"

"Mr. McIntire, Mr. Bohannon. All in, or all out, please." Professor Thomas, the algebra teacher, motioned from behind his lectern.

"Sure, Prof." Trevor flashed a Hollywood smile and sauntered into the room. Time for his morning nap.

* * *

The four friends sat together at a concrete table outside the cafeteria, picking at the last of their lunch. A light breeze tickled

Trevor's curls. They hadn't been together as a group like this since the accident.

"Hey, guys," Trevor said. "I need a plan."

"For what—gettin' rid of your ugly?" Kenny cackled at his joke. Brent and Lisa joined him.

"Real funny, dog butt." Trevor shot Kenny a dirty look. He followed the insult with a string of "friendly" expletives. "I need a new set of wheels. My old man's being a jerk, and I'm stuck with Mom as chauffeur."

"I can pick you up, Trev," offered Lisa.

Trevor made a face. "That's like, forty minutes out of your way. Besides, I want my own ride. I feel like a freakin' middle schooler without a car."

"You *look* like a middle schooler," said Kenny.

An obscene gesture served as Trevor's response. He turned to Brent and Lisa. "There has to be *some* way to get the old man on board. Any ideas?"

"Eh, give him a few days to cool off." Kenny leaned forward, interjecting himself into Trevor's vision. "He'll come around. My dad blows his top like five times a day but it never lasts more than fifteen minutes."

Lisa peered around her last handful of sandwich. "Yeah, give him 'til the weekend. He'll have so much on his mind by then he won't even remember why he was mad."

"A few days, a few weeks, a few months—who knows how long it'll take? I need something *now*."

"Hey, I got an idea." Kenny banged the table. "Let's take up a collection and buy Trev a bike!" He and the other two laughed.

"Yeah!" said Brent. "We could hang out at the mall with signs–Dollars for the Dummy." He guffawed, then winced, reaching for his temple.

Lisa bit her lip, suppressing a smile.

"We might get enough to buy a Yugo!" exclaimed Kenny. "Fifty bucks and you'll be stylin'!" He slapped his thighs. "Your dad'll be so freaked out by the yard ornament he'll give you anything you want."

"What *he'll* want," Brent piped in, "will be for you to get the Yugo off his lawn. I bet he'll give you a blank check on the spot."

They all laughed—even Trevor. His dark mood lifted as he warmed to his friends' theme. "Hey, listen guys—if you can't get me a Mercedes, forget it. In fact, let's *steal* something worth having—like a Ferrari. *That* would impress the old man."

They fired back and forth, each suggestion zanier than the last.

"Hey, we're working *way* too hard," said Kenny. "Let's just ask the wizard to conjure Trev a car."

Kenny, Lisa, and Brent laughed. Trevor's smile, however, faded. Kenny might as well have spoken Japanese.

"Say—what was that?" The other three might understand Japanese, but Trevor sure didn't.

"We'll get the wizard to zap a car for you. While he's at it, he can conjure up some girls for me and Brent. I haven't had a kiss in over two weeks!"

If Kenny had said *a* wizard, Trevor might have let it go as just another ridiculous statement like the others. But Kenny said *the* wizard. A subtle difference, but something about it piqued Trevor's curiosity. "Hey, dude—what am I missing here?"

Kenny zeroed in on Trevor's confusion. "The wizard, dum-dum. You know—The Wizard of Winterville."

Chapter Three

Being a preacher's boy, I learned the seriousness of God's calling early on. Things really hit home about the time I was fourteen. I guess if I had taken those early lessons more to heart, I wouldn't be where I am today.

* * *

Johnny stared out the truck window at the half-moon following him and Pa home. He yawned. It had been a late night—or morning. He had no idea the exact time. Only the truck's rattling and bouncing over innumerable ruts and potholes in the old dirt road kept him awake. Well, that and the ever-present aching leg.

"So, what do you think, Pa—will she get better?" Johnny twisted toward the driver's seat to find Pa stone rigid and either lost in thought or half asleep. Johnny waited, sucked in a breath to ask again, then cut himself short as Pa stirred.

"You mean Mrs. Ornden? Hmm. Well, I don't know." Pa kept his eyes glued to the road while he spoke. "You ought to know by now God does as he pleases. Sometimes he heals. Sometimes…" Pa shook his head. "Sometimes, I just don't know. But the important thing is we did our part. The rest ain't up to us—it's up to him."

Johnny knew. He'd been told dozens of times. But since Pa had actually heard from God before, shouldn't he have more insight into God's intentions?

They rode in silence for endless minutes. Johnny wondered if it was ever possible to know what God would do. If it *was* possible, did anybody know God well enough to understand his intentions?

"Will she die?" Johnny asked the question as they drew close to home.

Again it took Pa a moment before he answered. When he did, Johnny heard weariness in his tone. "I don't expect so—at least no time soon, anyway. But the important question is, whatever happens, how will it affect your faith? If she dies, does that mean you stop trusting in God? Is your faith dependent on her being healed?"

Johnny wasn't sure if Pa expected a response. He hoped not because he didn't have the answers. He did, however, ponder the questions until Pa brought the truck to a stop in front of their house where the light in the living room window told him Ma had waited up for them.

In fact, Ma met them at the door. "Come in, you two. I've been praying for both of you—and Lydia as well. How is she?"

"Eh, it's hard to tell. I want to say she was doing better, but you know how it is—sometimes people get all excited about prayer when God hasn't done his work yet."

"Then we'll just keep praying 'til we *do* get an answer. Now, get on inside. Do either of you want a snack before bed? There's hot coffee on the stove."

Pa raked off his hat and stepped through the door. He pecked Ma on the cheek and drew in a deep breath. "That coffee smells wonderful, but I don't need anything standing between me and a good night's sleep."

"I'm tired, too, Ma. I'm going straight to bed." Johnny slipped past his parents and limped to his room where a smothering drowsiness overshadowed him the instant his head sank into the pillow. The last thing he remembered was pulling the sheet up to his chest.

Sleep arrived with a jumbled dream. Swirling mist. The rattling truck. Mrs. Ornden's face in place of the moon. In the midst of it all, a voice called for him. "Johnny!" The sound pricked him, darkening the images. "Get up, Johnny!"

A jackhammer beat Johnny from his sleep. Someone at the door. Only halfway to his senses, Johnny croaked a raspy, "Huh?"

Light like the sun burst into the bedroom. Johnny covered still-closed eyes. The voice called him again. Pa. Frenzied. "Johnny, I need you! Come quickly!"

The bed whispered a soft invitation. Johnny rolled away from the light and buried his head beneath the sheet. *So* tired. So sleepy. Slumber soon lulled him back into its lair.

Bam! The door banged the wall and Johnny jerked awake to find Pa standing in the doorway.

"Why are you still in bed?" bellowed Jeremiah. "Get up *now*! I can't wait any longer."

Johnny rubbed his eyes. Was this a nightmare? The thought crossed his mind about swinging his legs out of bed, but they disagreed. That was OK since he didn't really want to move. He just wanted sleep.

The sound and smell of bacon sizzling on the stove drifted into Johnny's room sometime later, tickled his nose, and filled his waking thoughts with pleasure. He tumbled out of bed and, rubbing his eyes, staggered into the kitchen where Ma darted about the stove, fussing over three pans at once.

He glanced at the grandfather clock ticking away in the corner. Almost nine. Odd for breakfast to lag this far into the morning—even for a Saturday.

"Hi, Ma." Johnny sidled up and gave her a quick hug.

"Good morning." Ma pecked him on the cheek then turned back to the stove. "Did you rest well?"

"I dunno." Johnny stretched and yawned, then scratched his head. "It's kind of late for breakfast, ain't it?" He took a seat at the table and glanced around the house. "Where's Pa?"

The front door opened as if on queue. Johnny turned to see Pa shuffle in and hang his hat on the wall. "Hi, Pa. You're just in time. Ma made your favorite—eggs and bacon."

"Leave your pa be, Johnny. He's had a long night."

Johnny eyed Pa as he dragged through the living room toward the kitchen. His shoulders sagged and his face was drawn. He appeared ill.

"What's wrong, Pa? Where ya been?" Johnny had forgotten the voice in the night.

Pa jerked to attention. He slapped his thigh and glared at Johnny. "I've been out doing the Lord's work! A lazy boy like you wouldn't know anything about it."

The outburst stunned Johnny. He couldn't remember Pa *ever* having shouted at him like that before. He turned to Ma in bewilderment.

"Your pa's been at the Ornden's all night. Jesse came and got him not an hour after you two dragged into the house. He said his ma was worse and needed help." Ida patted Johnny on the shoulder. "Now, you give your pa time to rest. No more questions."

"Why didn't you take me with you, Pa? I thought we were a team."

"A *team*?" Pa's face turned beet red. "Don't think for a minute I didn't try! But you couldn't get out of bed. Why would I want someone like *that* on my team?"

Pa roared on in the tone usually reserved for fiery sermons. "What good are you if you're not there when I need you? If you can't handle something as simple as getting out of bed, how do you ever expect to be of any service to God?"

Johnny cowered under the advance. "I'm sorry, Pa. I didn't—"

"Sorry! I'll tell you who's sorry—the Ornden family is sorry. She's dead, Johnny—dead! I was the only one there praying. Maybe if I'd had some help the Lord would have listened. Maybe there'd be rejoicing this morning instead of tears. But, no—I had to spend my time apologizing to the family! Where are God's people when I need them?" Pa banged his fist on the wall and stomped off to his bedroom. He slammed the door behind him.

Johnny reached back to the night's fading memories. The voice in the night. The light. Being so tired and just wanting sleep.

He had let his father down. He had let God down.

Was Mrs. Ornden's death his fault? The thought cut him like a knife. Tears flowed. He sprinted out the front door, pajamas waving in the breeze.

Pa didn't find him until early afternoon. Johnny sat on a mound of pine needles, leaning against a tree a good distance into the woods beyond the back yard. Legs tucked under his chin, hands covering his face, tear stains circled his knees. Overhead, birds called to each other from high branches, the only sounds accompanying Johnny's occasional sniffle.

"Son..." Pa hesitated, staring into the distance. He squatted, bringing himself to Johnny's level. But Johnny covered his eyes. "What I did was wrong—not fair at all. I lost my temper and said some things I shouldn't have. I asked God to forgive me, but I really need you to forgive me first."

A lone tear rolled down Johnny's cheek, quivered at the edge of his chin, then pattered to the ground. Spasms shook him.

Pa raised a hand to Johnny's shoulder. "Look at me, son."

Johnny shook himself free and buried his head between his knees. "I don't want to. Leave me alone."

After an unbearable time without Pa responding, Johnny peeked one eye at him. They stared at each other for the longest time.

"I understand you want to be alone, son, but there's something I have to say first." Tears filled Pa's eyes. "I was wrong—dead wrong. I hurt you, and it hurts me that I did it. It's no excuse, but I was tired and frustrated. I lost a dear friend last night. My prayers weren't answered and I felt like a failure. I let it out on you, and I need you to forgive me for how I treated you."

"It's all my fault!" Johnny burst into tears. "I let you down and I let God down. I killed her!"

"No, Johnny, it wasn't your fault. If anyone's to blame, it's me. I set out to do God's work without having my own house in order."

Pa breathed a deep sigh. "I should have set a better example for you."

"But if I had been there, we could have put twice as much faith to work—as a team. God's mad because I did the same thing the disciples did. They were supposed to stay awake and pray, but they fell asleep. Mrs. Ornden died because of me."

Pa tugged on Johnny until they were face to face. "Now you listen to me. You might have missed an opportunity to serve God, but God didn't punish Mrs. Ornden on your account. God didn't punish the disciples for falling asleep, did he? No. Jesus rebuked them, and he told them to do better next time, but he didn't hold it against them.

"You can't blame yourself for every unanswered prayer, son. You can't stop every death, heal every disease. If you hold yourself to that standard, you'll live a life full of disappointment.

"People die, Johnny—that's just a fact of life. It was Mrs. Ornden's time. This wasn't your fault, and..." Pa sighed, "it wasn't mine, either." For a moment Pa just stared at the ground. Then he turned back to Johnny. "This isn't something to lose your faith over, son. I'm sorry I made you feel that way. God forgive me."

Johnny soaked up Pa's words and pondered them at length. At last he nodded agreement.

"That's my boy." Pa smiled and, rising, clapped him on the back. "Now, why don't you head back inside, get yourself some food, and put on some clothes? There's work yet unfinished, and I'd sure rather have my partner around than face it alone."

A weight lifted from Johnny's shoulders. He stood, managed a half-smile, then squeezed Pa in a hug.

Still, the memory of Mrs. Ornden's death haunted him. He resolved never to miss God again.

* * *

"Hey, Johnny—wait up!"

Back along the dusty trail leading to the schoolhouse, Caroline skipped toward Johnny, ruffled skirt billowing in her wake while locks of dark brown hair danced about her head.

Johnny breathed a silent prayer. He knew she was sweet on him. Everyone at school knew it. They also knew he had no interest in her. Everyone, it seemed, knew these things, except Caroline. And now that she'd spotted him he would never get away.

It had nothing to do with her looks—she had as much going for her as any other fifteen-year-old. And it didn't really matter that she was two years his junior. Johnny simply didn't have time for romance. He reserved all his affections for God.

However, Caroline *was* one of God's children. That meant God loved her, and it followed that Johnny had to love her, too—the way God did, anyway. So he waited for her to catch up while leaning on the cane he had carved from an old hickory limb.

Caroline wore a broad smile, flashing the pearliest whites money could buy. "Hi, Johnny!" She sidled up close and giggled like someone half her age. "I heard you're preaching on Sunday. I think that's *wonderful!*"

"Um, yeah," Johnny took a half step back, "that's right. You'll be there, won't you?" He really did want her there. It didn't take a lover's interest to care about someone's soul.

"Oh, Johnny, I wouldn't miss it for the world!" She closed the gap between them and reached for his hand.

Johnny yanked away, and flushed. "OK, well, uh, I'm glad. It's important you're there." He straightened. "I have a message God wants everybody to hear. You'll bring some friends, won't you?"

"Of course!" She batted her eyelids. "I made Sue and Mary Beth promise to come. They can't wait! It's so...fabulous! Imagine—you in front of the whole congregation. I bet you're the youngest preacher to ever stand behind that pulpit!"

Caroline rambled on, falling in step beside Johnny as he resumed his journey. She babbled until Johnny tuned out the drone, lost in his own thoughts about the upcoming sermon.

The schoolyard had just come into view when Caroline jumped in front of Johnny, halting him in his tracks. "Why are you so quiet, Johnny? Are you worried about Sunday? I'm sure you'll do just fine. I bet half the town will be there! But don't you worry—you'll be great."

Johnny blinked. "Half the town?"

"Sure they will! *Every*body's talking about it."

He stared into the distance, mulling the implications.

"Are you OK?"

"What? Oh, sure—it's just that, well...half the town's gonna miss out."

* * *

The Jones family sat together at the dinner table. Jeremiah fidgeted in his chair. What could be more exciting than his own son preaching behind *his* pulpit? What more could a pastor ask from life? It was a dream come true.

"Son, I'm proud of you." Jeremiah beamed. He knew he'd said the same thing a half dozen times since Johnny got home from school. But he just couldn't contain himself. "You're going to do great, Johnny. I just know God's hand is on you."

"I think so—"

"Ha! And this is just the beginning. God is going to use you mightily before it's over with. I've known that since the day he healed you. It's in the blood, son. It's in the blood!"

Both Ida and Johnny shook their heads at Jeremiah, wearing smirks. He grinned back at them while his food grew cold. Johnny shrugged and went back to eating.

"I guess you're a little nervous, huh? But that's only natural. Heh, I remember *my* first sermon. I was sweatin' bullets—didn't sleep a wink the night before. But there's no reason to get all worked up. We've been gettin' you ready for this your whole life. God'll be with you and everything'll be just fine. So, don't you be nervous—not one bit, OK?"

"Jeremiah, aren't you going to eat?"

"Mm-hmm." Jeremiah nodded, eyes glued to Johnny. "Just remember, son—go over your message every day. Make sure you got one main point, and keep yourself focused on it. Try standing in front of the mirror and preaching out loud. It helps to see yourself like that, and hear what you're saying. You won't be as worried that way when you have a crowd in front of you."

Sure, he'd told Johnny all this before. But it was important—the biggest moment yet in Johnny's budding career. And who was better to get him ready for it?

"I guess I'm a little nervous, Pa. Not much, though. God will see me through."

"He sure will, son! That's the way to go at it!" Jeremiah gave in to his excitement, stood, and bounced from one foot to the other.

Ida heaved a deep sigh then turned to Johnny. "Well, son, I guess you'll be needing the rest of the evening to study?"

Johnny shoveled a man-size bite into his mouth. He talked and chewed at the same time. "Oh, no, Ma—I'm all done."

Jeremiah stopped bouncing. "Done? But—"

"If it's not too big a secret," Ida shot Jeremiah a quick glance, "could you give us just a hint what you're message is about?"

"Sure, Ma." Johnny shrugged. "I'm going to tell everybody how God loves 'em and wants 'em whole." He stabbed a huge chunk of boiled potato with his fork and stuffed the entire thing in his mouth.

"That's a *great* topic, son." Jeremiah resumed his seat, but couldn't stop himself from fiddling with the lace along the bottom of the tablecloth. "Tell you what—how 'bout you show me your notes and I can help you polish things up a bit. I can check your scripture references, too."

"Thanks, Pa, but I'm ready."

"You..." Jeremiah twisted a string of tablecloth thread into a ball. "You mean...you don't need any help?" He planted an elbow on the table and rested a cheek on his balled fist. "How about I just peek at your notes—you know, just to make sure everything flows all right?"

"I didn't make any notes, Pa. Don't need any." Johnny tapped his temple. "It's all up here."

"Umm, son...?" Jeremiah searched for the right words. "You've got a really good theme there, but, ah, I think maybe you should consider more preparation. An old hand like me can get away with a message off the cuff sometimes, but this is your first time preaching—first time in front of a crowd, in fact. On a Sunday morning, there's going to be a lot of folks watching."

Johnny's fork halted halfway to his mouth. He squared eyes with Jeremiah. "I'm not worried, Pa. God'll see me through."

"Of course he will. But we have to do our part, too, remember?" Jeremiah tapped an uneven rhythm on the table. "Do you have all your Bible verses memorized?"

Johnny nodded.

"OK, well, make sure you keep things simple. Children are a big part of the church and they need to be able to understand things, too." Jeremiah chewed his lip. "Yessir, a big part of it, them kids."

Again, Johnny nodded.

Jeremiah found himself frowning, digging deeper for something Johnny would latch onto. "You have to really put your heart in it—bring down fire and that kind of thing. They won't believe you're speaking for God if you don't raise your voice. Can you do that, Johnny? Can you get a little excited—shout a little, maybe?"

"I know what I need to do, Pa."

An uneasy feeling settled in Jeremiah's stomach. "Son, are you *sure* you've heard from God? I mean, you can't just get up there and say whatever you want. It's an awesome responsibility taking God's Word to the people. If the message isn't his, he'll take you down right quick, and…well, you might embarrass yourself." He might embarrass Jeremiah, too.

Once again, Johnny locked eyes with Jeremiah. "I know this message is from God." His tone carried a new air of authority. "Besides, Pa, the whole point of the Bible is how God loves us, and how he wants us whole. Isn't that right?"

Jeremiah blinked. He sent Ida a questioning stare. She shrugged.

"Now, son…" Jeremiah's voice trailed off, thoughts churning. The Bible had a *whole* lot more to say than that, but still… Johnny summed it up pretty good.

For the first time at that meal Jeremiah found his food. He stabbed a fork at his plate, poked a bite in his mouth, and stared at Johnny while he chewed.

Chapter Four

"He hasn't heard about the wizard!" Brent sounded as though he had just watched Trevor sprout three heads.

"You don't know about the wizard?" Kenny's mouth wrinkled in surprise.

"He's only lived here a few years," said Lisa.

"Ha! That's right!" Kenny punched Trevor on the shoulder. "You're the new kid in town." His smile faded. "Still—I can't believe you haven't heard any wizard stories."

"I have no idea what you guys are talking about." Trevor looked from one friend to the other. "The only wizard I know lives in Oz."

Brent and Kenny seized the revelation, both talking at once. Trevor blinked. He couldn't make any sense of their co-mingled babbling. "HEY!" His sharp bark gave them pause. "One idiot at a time, ok?"

Kenny charged ahead, rattling off one wild rumor after another. "There's this wizard, see? He lives in the mountains above Winterville. He's got these magical powers, and sometimes he grants people wishes. People only see him on the mountain because he's afraid of something in town. He only comes out at night and—"

"You have to offer a sacrifice or he won't come out at all!" Brent's interruption drew only a temporary glance from Trevor.

Kenny shot Brent a frown, then went on. "Yeah—a sacrifice. Only, he doesn't like city people. He'll kill you on the spot if you're not one of those mountain weirdos. He even kills mountain people if it's not a full moon. But," Kenny grew animated, gesticulating with both hands, "on a full moon he grants their wishes." He glanced at Brent. "*If* they offer a sacrifice." For a brief moment, he paused, staring off into the distance. "They say you hear weird music when he works his magic."

"You guys believe this stuff?" Trevor cocked his head.

Kenny nodded, serious as could be. "Sure, man. Everybody believes in the wizard." Two seconds of dead silence followed, then he and Brent burst into laughter.

Lisa shook her head. "It's a local legend, Trev. Kind of like Santa Claus. Every town has its crazy story. In Winterville, it's the wizard."

"Forget *her*." Kenny made a face at Lisa. "She probably doesn't believe in Santa, either. There's a wizard, all right, and all it takes is a trip to the mountain to come back a believer."

Brent snickered.

"You guys are nuts." Trevor dismissed them with a wave. "You've been smoking bad weed."

"Yeah, well, don't ask *us* for help again." Kenny screwed up his face in mock indignation. "I try to be nice and get you a car, and you throw it back at me. Some friend *you* are."

Everyone chuckled. Trevor shoved Kenny. And that was the end of it.

* * *

"All right, Trev, let's go." Mr. McIntire called to Trevor from the kitchen door that led into the garage.

"You bet, Dad." Trevor leapt from the couch, pulled on a pair of tennis shoes and, leaving them untied, quick-stepped through the kitchen with the TV still blaring behind him. He shot past his dad, grabbing a spare set of keys from the wall along the way. Once in the garage, he yanked open the driver's door of the sleek, black Mercedes SLK Mr. McIntire had purchased six months earlier. Nestling into the soft leather, he clicked open the garage door with the built-in opener. Not happy with the seat position, he fiddled with the controls until the car molded itself to his backside.

Mr. McIntire appeared next to Trevor's still-open door. He tapped on the window, but Trevor focused on the touch-screen controls. He was searching for the setting that would let him play the songs on his phone through the stereo.

"Trevor—"

"Get in, Dad."

Mr. McIntire rapped on the window again and pointed to the passenger seat. Trevor glanced right, then back with a questioning look. He reached to close the door. "Come on, we don't have all day."

Mr. McIntire caught the door and held it open. "Move over."

"Come on—"

"MOVE OVER!"

Trevor jumped. A protest rose in his throat, but he swallowed it. He'd been waiting for this day *forever*. No sense stirring up trouble by risking the old man's wrath. He held up his hands in surrender and blurted a conciliatory, "OK, OK," then climbed over the console and dropped into the passenger seat and drummed his fingers on the armrest.

Mr. McIntire lumbered into the car, squirmed for a second, then frowned at Trevor. He fiddled with the controls until he got the seat back to its original position, then frowned again as he reached for the stereo control. A moment later, Beethoven's Fifth filled the car.

"Dad, please—let's have some *real* music." Trevor reached for the console but Mr. McIntire shoved his hand away. "Hey!" He reached again.

Thwack! Mr. McIntire locked Trevor's wrist in a vise grip. He pulled Trevor toward him until they were nose to nose. "*My* car. *My* music."

"Hey, all right." Trevor shook himself free, then settled back in his seat. "But keep it down, will you? I've heard that stuff turns your hair gray." He shot his dad an evil grin.

Mr. McIntire fired up the car, stabbed the volume control five notches higher in quick succession, then slammed the shifter in reverse and kicked the accelerator so hard it barked the tires. Once out of the driveway, another kick at the accelerator shot the car forward—and Trevor back in his seat, his continuing protests drowned out by both classical and mechanical music as the Mercedes flew out of the neighborhood and onto the main road.

When they neared the small shops and commercial enterprises of downtown Winterville, Mr. McIntire slowed the car and jabbed down the stereo volume. "You've got your mother to thank for this." He spared quick looks at Trevor while guiding the car through thickening traffic. "She nagged me to death about taking you to school every morning. If it was up to me, you'd be walking to school *and* a job until you could afford your own transportation."

At a dilapidated shopping center, Mr. McIntire braked abruptly, whipped the wheel right, and squealed into the parking lot. The Mercedes jerked to a stop and the driver's door flew open before Trevor realized what was happening.

"Hey!" Trevor fumbled with the latch and threw open his door. "What are we doing *here*?"

Mr. McIntire reached the entrance of a small grocery, stepped halfway in, and called back over his shoulder. "Your mom wants me to pick up a couple of things. I'll just be a minute."

"Can't this wait?" Trevor slammed his door and bounded over the sidewalk. "We're supposed to be buying me a car—remember?" But his dad had already disappeared inside.

Trevor quickened his pace and banged open the old wooden entry door. An explosion of color filled his vision. Every imaginable fruit and vegetable spilled from boxes stacked floor to ceiling along the store's walls. Dozens of fragrances mixed into a single olfactory overload that wafted up Trevor's nose.

Two paces ahead, Mr. McIntire scrutinized an end cap showcasing Vidalia onions. He rolled one about in his hand, sniffed it, shrugged, then dropped it in a plastic bag.

"Dad!"

Mr. McIntire turned, raised an eyebrow, then crossed his arms. "Why can't I have five minutes of peace?"

"Dad—the *car*."

"If you really want a car," Mr. McIntire's voice ratcheted up in volume with each syllable, "you'll shut your mouth and march right back outside." He finished with a choice expletive that drew stares from the small shop's nearest customers.

Trevor wanted *so* bad to respond. He felt he would bite off his tongue choking back a few choice words of his own. Instead, he muttered a heartfelt, "Urh!" and stomped toward the door.

Next to the lone cash register, he passed a gray-haired sales clerk having an animated discussion with a patron half-hidden from view.

"I keep telling ya, Mike," the customer said as Trevor reached for the exit, "the wizard don't take just any ol' apples. If it ain't Red Delicious, it won't work."

The conversation was gobbledygook as far as Trevor was concerned. Except—

"Ed, hush!" The clerk's tone turned guttural and muted.

Trevor halted just as his fingers brushed the cool metal door handle. He paused, waiting for his conscious thoughts to catch up with his subconscious ones. Then he swung back toward the counter, this time getting a good look at the customer who had remained hidden before—a rough old goat with a scraggly beard, polyester pants, and a torn flannel shirt. All he needed was a holster and a set of spurs and he'd be ready for a B-list Western.

For a split second the clerk met Trevor's stare, then he found something intensely interesting near the floor. The cowboy wannabe's eyes grew wide, flicking back and forth between Trevor and the door.

"What did you say?" Trevor cocked his head sideways, attention divided between the two.

The clerk reanimated as if by a switch. "Beat it, kid! This is a private conversation."

Trevor stepped toward them. He caught a whiff of cowboy Ed and wrinkled his nose. "What was that about a wizard?"

By this time Ed had turned downright skittish, balance shifting foot to foot, eyes rollicking between Mike and Trevor.

"You deaf, kid?" Scowling, Mike pointed at the door. "Get out of my store."

Ed scampered backward and out of sight.

Trevor got in the clerk's face. "Not 'til you tell me what you said. What's the deal with you people? You don't seriously believe there's a wizard, do you?"

Trevor felt his cheeks flush. "Didn't anybody tell you hicks that Santa's not real? There's no Easter Bunny, either. No Tooth Fairy, no God, and there sure ain't no wizard." Trevor shook his head. "Do you really tell your kids some magic maniac is going to grant their wishes?"

The clerk cringed. His gaze traveled all around the store then back to Trevor. "Hush up, kid! Get out of here before you stir up more trouble than either one of us can handle."

A blur whipped past Trevor's periphery. He turned just in time to catch sight of Ed through the front window as he high-tailed it across the street. Trevor swiveled back and eyed Mike, thoughts swirling. "Hmm…I get it. You push this wizard legend for the extra cash, don't you? So where are all the wizard dolls and magic potions? Do you sell snake oil, too?"

"Shh! Keep it down, will ya?" Mike's tone turned desperate, pleading. "You've got to stop before there's serious trouble. Now, please—just go."

Trevor huffed. "No way, man—not 'til you spill the beans on this wizard nonsense." He jerked a thumb toward the door. "There's got to be a law against brain-washing people like your nut-job friend there."

"Listen," the clerk's tone softened, "Ed's just a crazy old mountain man. Those folks have some pretty odd superstitions, and they do business with me because I go along with 'em. They get real nervous when outsiders talk about their secrets. I don't want any trouble here, so why don't you just move on?"

Trevor mulled it over. It made sense, but...

"Hold it." Trevor narrowed his eyes. "For a minute there you were as freaked out as Mountain Moe. I think you believe this wizard nonsense, too—like Mr. Hocus Pocus himself might whip in here and slit your throat just for mentioning his name."

Mike hesitated, then sighed. "Like I told you, kid—the mountain people make up a lot of my business. I don't need you scaring 'em off." He planted both hands on the counter. "Now you've got old Ed worked up pretty bad. It might be another month—maybe two—before he comes around again. He's going to tell everybody on the mountain what happened today, and none of them are going to be thrilled about it. Your little tirade is going to cost me, and *I'm* not too thrilled about *that*. It's time for you to leave, and I'm telling, not asking. You got about ten seconds to clear out before I call the police."

Trevor gritted his teeth. The whole thing smelled fishy. But he didn't doubt the threat, and he had no wish to tangle with cops.

"All right, dude. You win." He turned to go, but called back from the door. "There's more to this than you're letting on. One day I'll figure it out, and the whole thing's going to blow up in your face."

* * *

James McIntire made his way from the back of the store to the front counter. Mike—the grocery clerk—stared out the window, oblivious.

"Ah, excuse me?"

Mike startled. "Oh. Yeah, sorry—ready to check out?"

"Yes, please." Mr. McIntire set down his purchase. He pulled a twenty from his wallet and held it ready.

Mumbling, Mike ran his fingers over the register keys.

"Sounds like you had a little excitement up here," Mr. McIntire ventured, drumming his fingers.

"Yeah," said Mike, intent on the register.

"I thought I left that kind of stuff behind when I got out of the city."

Mike looked up. "Eh, it was just some crazy kid." He pulled a paper bag from beneath the counter and flung it open. "Bit of a jerk, ya know? Acting like he owns the whole town."

"Heh." Mr. McIntire glanced out the window. "Believe me—I know the type. Probably has a troubled home life."

Mike bagged the purchase and handed Mr. McIntire a receipt. "Yeah. Wouldn't surprise me one bit."

* * *

"Say, Dad—do you know anything about the wizard legend?" Trevor stared out the side glass, tapping his fingers on the sill while Mr. McIntire secured the groceries in the back seat.

Mr. McIntire settled in behind the wheel and started the car. "Did you say 'wizard' legend?"

Trevor swiveled to face his dad. He shrugged. "Kenny told me a story about a magician that lives on the mountain. He called him the Wizard of Winterville."

"That's the first I've heard of it, Trev." Mr. McIntire shifted the car in reverse and backed out of his parking spot.

"It might be some kind of cult. The locals act all weird when you mention it."

Mr. McIntire held his foot on the brake. He turned toward Trevor. "You stay away from those religious nuts. They're not just full of nonsense—they're downright dangerous."

Trevor smirked. "Come on, Dad—you know me better than that." He shook his head. "I'd never fall for something *that* stupid."

"Hmph." Mr. McIntire slammed the car into gear. "Well, see that you don't." He romped down on the accelerator, and the Mercedes leapt into the street.

Chapter Five

I thought I was ready. I thought it would be simple. The truth is, I had no idea what I was getting myself into. It's funny looking back on it today, but back then I thought my world would end.

* * *

"J-J! How's the preacher boy?" The shout rang out across the schoolyard, rousing Johnny from his inner contemplation. Skip Jefferson sauntered toward him, hand raised in salutation.

Randall "Skip" Jefferson was an anomaly among the laid-back and countrified students at B.L. Kenwood High School. He stood half a head taller than his peers, and his hair frizzed in every direction except down. His eyeballs bulged from their sockets under bushy brown eyebrows peeking over the top of thick, black-framed glasses that dwarfed his face. He wore the same striped and faded cotton slacks every day, sometimes rolled above his ankles, but oft as not dragging the ground and causing him to stumble every other step.

Only a dozen boys made it to their senior year at B. L. Kenwood. Most dropped out early to work their family farms. Skip had told Johnny flat out on more than one occasion that *he* stayed in school just so he could *avoid* work.

Skip's family attended Mt. Carmel with Johnny, but Skip liked playing hooky. In fact, his nickname arose from his innumerable absences both at church and school. Not that Skip had anything against church or religion. He just liked doing his own thing—just being Skip. It made little sense to Johnny, but like most everyone else, Johnny found Skip's easy-going personality irresistible.

"I'm doing great. How about you?" Johnny rose from the bench where he had been resting, and extended a hand. Then he wrinkled his nose and took a half step back. From the smell of him, Skip hadn't taken a bath in a week.

"Fantastic, buddy." Skip slapped Johnny on the back. "And with a preacher friend for good luck, I've got it made."

Johnny planted his hands on his hips. "There's no such thing as luck with God. You're either—"

"—for him or against him. And he's always for *you*. I know, I know. You've said it a million times." Skip flashed his toothiest smile. "But I still think it's good luck having you for a buddy."

What could he say? Skip would always be Skip. Johnny shook his head and moved on. "Say—you going to be at church this Sunday? God gave me a message I'd love for you to hear."

Skip shrugged. "How about a preview? That way, if I don't make it, I won't miss anything."

"Uh, uh. You have to come. God wants you there."

"If God *really* wants me there," Skip's eyes twinkled, "then why doesn't he tell me so himself?"

"Hmph." Johnny stood taller. "He sent *me* to do just that." He retrieved his cane from the bench. "Do me a favor and think about it, will ya? It sure would mean a lot to see you there."

"Well... maybe." Skip grinned again. "I'll be listenin' to see if God gives me direction."

Johnny nodded. He knew Skip was being facetious. But Johnny also knew God.

* * *

It didn't hit him until late Saturday night. Johnny had spent much of the week inviting friends to church. He hadn't thought about the practical aspects of his sermon until the stillness of night sent questions running rampant through his mind. He kicked off the sheet and rolled over for the umpteenth time.

What would it be like standing behind the pulpit? What if he stuttered like Moses? What if he got so nervous he couldn't talk at all? Worse yet, what if he didn't say exactly what God wanted?

Pa had drilled him all week on how to deliver a sermon. He had given him all sorts of advice about avoiding nervousness, making eye contact, and speaking clearly. But when he stood behind the pulpit, would he remember Pa's advice?

"God, is this really what you want?" Johnny's words landed soft against his pillow. "Will you really be with me?"

He thought about failure. Would they laugh at him? Or would they be polite and tell him it was a "nice" sermon? Would anyone even show up?

"Did you really put this message inside me, God, or do I just *want* it to be from you?" The thought frightened him. After all, no audible voice had told him to preach—he just felt deep down inside he had a message people needed to hear.

Johnny spent the rest of the night tossing and turning, questions racing round his head. If God had any input on the matter, Johnny never heard it.

* * *

Johnny rose early for prayer Sunday morning, not from piety but from inability to sleep. Two hours later, tired and excited, frightened and peaceful, he slipped on his clothes and padded out of his room.

The aroma of home-made sausage patties, poached eggs, and toast would have made Johnny's mouth water any other time, but today it nauseated him. But despite not being hungry, he knew attempting his first sermon on an empty stomach could mean disaster. So he plopped down at the kitchen table and picked at his food until he choked down a few bites.

Pa, at the head of the table, was beside himself. Never had Johnny seen him so high-spirited—talking, and talking, and talking, all the while gesturing wildly. In one exaggerated motion he bumped a pitcher of orange juice sitting near the table's edge. Fortunately, the pitcher settled back into an upright position. "Remember, son—face your audience. They need to see your eyes, and you need to see theirs…"

Johnny went back and forth between listening to Pa and thinking about his sermon. After a half-dozen iterations of "take a deep breath" Johnny tuned Pa out altogether and drummed his fingers to match the rattling and scraping noises Ma made at the stove.

Pa finally smacked the juice pitcher dead on and knocked it over. It rolled to the table's edge where Ma rescued it from the floor. Johnny eyed a puddle of juice that first grew, then receded as it slipped between the boards of the wooden tabletop. Ma grabbed a cloth from the sink and wiped away the mess. Pa paused long enough to give the spill a curious look before continuing with his speech and wild hand motions.

Johnny sighed. It wasn't that he didn't appreciate Pa's advice. But he knew what he was going to say, and he wasn't interested in public speaking lessons. He also didn't want to wear orange juice to church, so he pushed away from the table before another mishap ruined his suit. "I think we ought to get going, Pa."

"Already?" Pa glanced at his watch then stood so fast he banged his thighs on the table. He grabbed his Sunday jacket off his chair with one hand and steered Johnny with the other out the door and onto the porch. Pa would have let the screen door slam in Ma's face if Johnny hadn't reached back to catch it.

On the way to the truck, Johnny studied the little beads of dew that spattered on his shiny black shoes while Pa continued his monologue. When the truck sputtered to life, Pa raised his voice above the clatter and accelerated his speech to match. Neither Ida nor Johnny was able to get a word in edgewise on the way to church. Three times Johnny reached past Pa to steer them back toward the road as the truck wandered aimlessly, freed by Pa's gesticulations from human control. Thankfully, being Sunday, the streets were almost deserted, so Jeremiah's inattention to driving did no more harm than fill Ma and Johnny with adrenaline.

When they finally reached the church, Johnny cocked his head at the extra people milling about the parking lot and in front of the building. A number of cars Johnny felt sure he'd never seen before nestled here and there among the regulars. He squinted at them, curious, then returned a half-wave to a stranger that passed by his window.

The Jones family piled out of the truck and immediately found themselves surrounded. Women wearing dresses that scraped the ground beamed at Johnny. Men, most of them in coveralls, nodded and offered handshakes.

A wrinkle-faced woman in a feathered hat shuffled to the front of the group. "How's the little preacher today?" she said through false teeth that slipped out of place every other word.

"Good, Mrs. Grindall." Johnny shook her hand awkwardly. It felt strange being called a preacher.

After completing the required social graces, Johnny followed Pa up the concrete steps and through the double doors into the church. Pa's office, no more than eight feet to a side, opened up to the left of the foyer. A desk and two wooden chairs consumed half the floor space. Books took up the rest of it, overflowing from a built-in bookcase on the left, and spilling onto the floor and up most of the adjacent wall. The room smelled of Pa, a mixture of home and starch and the barest hint of sweat. Jeremiah dropped to his knees upon entry, and changed straightaway into the special language of his Sunday prayers.

"Father, I thank Thee for this day that Thy hand hath made."

Johnny called this "preacher language." He kept the term to himself.

"With an overflowing heart, I beseech Thee on behalf of my son. I ask for Thy grace and Thy mercy to be upon him. I ask that Thou wouldst show special favor to Johnny as he steps forth in obedience to Thy command."

Pa's colorful prayer continued long enough for Johnny's thoughts to wonder. How did Pa find time to breathe in between all those long sentences that ran together like a song? Johnny wondered for the first time if *he* needed to pray like that for God to hear him.

Most Sundays, anywhere from thirty minutes to an hour passed while Pa prayed. Johnny guessed fifteen minutes had gone by when Pa changed course.

"And Father God, I pray that Thy children would be touched this day, knowing the fullness of Thy Grace—"

When the silence grew long, Johnny peeked and found Pa staring at the ceiling. Soon, his gaze came to rest on Johnny, eyebrows raised.

Pa stared for what seemed an eternity while Johnny wiggled in his seat. "Ah, Johnny... God says it's your turn."

Johnny gulped. Pa *never* changed his prayer routine.

"Uhhh... Lord God, I ask Thee to grant me...uh, Thy servant, favor this day. You know...uh, I mean Thou knowest..." Johnny muddled on, navigating the odd vocabulary for several more sentences before giving up. The language just wasn't his own. He heaved a long sigh, then started over. "God, you know I just want to do your will. Please help me get this message right." Johnny stole a glance at Pa, then uttered, "Amen."

* * *

A tear ran down Jeremiah's cheek as he watched Johnny pray. The youngster said such simple prayers, yet they held such innocent truth—and power. Now the fulfillment of all the dreams he'd had since hearing the words "it's a boy" so many years ago knelt beside him.

Memories became a flood. The tiny, naked bundle he held in a single hand. Those first tentative steps that ended with a tumble to the floor. Johnny's snaggletooth smile the day of his first bicycle solo. The look of horror when he thought he had killed Mrs. Ornden.

The sickness, polio, the most painful memory of them all. The devil tried his best to take Johnny, and had almost won. But God came through in the end.

And then there were the times he spanked that behind to line it up with the Word of God. Jeremiah cried, remembering the pain of discipline. Yet here was Johnny, kneeling before God, proving it had all been worth it.

Now Jeremiah saw not a boy, but a young man. Lacking maturity and bereft of experience, but in the throes of adulthood nonetheless. Here was the fruit of many laborious years, and Jeremiah felt proud. Not pride like the Bible warned against, but the satisfaction of a job well done.

Jeremiah laid a hand on Johnny's shoulder. "Amen," he added to Johnny's own closing. Then he rose and left the room. His job was done.

* * *

Johnny sat alone on the floor of Pa's office until he heard the music start. He pushed up using his cane and instinctively started for the door, the pattern Pa had set for him every Sunday as far back as he could remember. But he stopped when his hand brushed the knob. Sweat dampened his palm, and his collar. A righteous fear of representing God settled over him. So this was what it felt like to be the preacher, the point man for an entire congregation. There was no glory in it as far as he was concerned.

Out of the office and across the empty foyer, Johnny paused again at the sanctuary entrance where muffled organ music swooned. After a deep breath in, then out, he swung open the door and placed one foot over the threshold—and froze.

Twice the regular crowd filled the pews. Johnny hadn't seen so many people in one place since the Christmas pageant. He swallowed, throat dry.

Dozens of heads turned as Johnny strode down the aisle. He reached the pastor's bench just behind the pulpit Ma had lined with lilies the day before, and turned toward the crowd. Pew by pew, Johnny examined the many newcomers. He had invited people his own age, but the vast majority of unfamiliar faces belonged to adults. He stole a quick glance at Pa. Did *he* have something to do with it?

Skip was there, sitting with his parents, a look on his face that said he'd rather be anywhere else. Caroline and her friends occupied the third row back. Several of Johnny's classmates clustered on the two benches nearest the entrance. The regular attendees were there, of course, scattered among the visitors. And every last one of them, it seemed, stared at him.

During the second hymn, Johnny finally joined in. He found himself off key more than once, thoughts wandering from the music.

The songs, announcements, and prayers passed in a flash. Johnny felt like he was dreaming when Pa took to the pulpit and, instead of the usual turn-with-me-in-your-Bibles, introduced a new speaker, someone Johnny knew all too well.

"Today, I have the honor and privilege of presenting to you a young man of God. Most of you know him already, but a few of our visitors might not. I've watched him grow and mature in the Lord since the day he was born. Now, he's taking that next step of obedience in following God by delivering his first sermon today.

"I know you'll make him feel welcome, and you'll pay close attention to what he has to say. It's my distinct pleasure to introduce to you my son, Johnny Jones." Pa ended his speech with a gesture that queued Johnny to rise.

When his cane smacked the floor behind him, Johnny jolted back to reality. He glanced behind at his fallen aid, chose to ignore it, and limped to the pulpit where he grabbed hold of the lectern with both hands and held on for dear life.

He studied the crowd. Expectant faces stared back, some curious, some questioning, but most friendly. Though Johnny knew the building's capacity wasn't much more than a hundred, the horde seemed endless. Regardless of it being a hundred or a hundred thousand, the gravity of the task he now faced drained his remaining confidence.

The multitude grew restless while Johnny hesitated, shuffling in their seats. Someone coughed. A couple of people cleared their throats. The time had come to act and, though he had prayed all week, and prayed before the service, Johnny felt the need to pray some more. Whether the urge was from God or from his own anxiety, Johnny wasn't sure.

"Let us pray," he said, bowing his head. Lacking a sound system, the church's poor acoustics absorbed much of what Johnny somehow forced through dry lips. Perhaps only God heard his whispered words. When he finished, it took a second and louder "amen" before heads lifted.

"I've come to bring you a message," Johnny began, eyes roving to and fro. "It's a message from God." He paused, unsure what reaction to expect.

A couple of teenagers snickered in the back. A baby cried. One of the strangers to Johnny's left wheezed the cough of a lifelong smoker. Everyone else sat polite and attentive.

Johnny thumbed through the notes he had scribbled on stray bits of paper that morning after a last-minute panic. One sheet slipped off the podium and floated side-to-side until it kissed the floor. Johnny blinked at it, detached. He fumbled with the remaining sheets until he found a reference he could actually read from his chicken-scratch markings. With something solid to latch onto, he resumed his message with fresh vigor and a mite of confidence.

"In First John, the eighth chapter, the Bible tells us in verses ten and eleven that God loves us." He flipped through his Bible to First John, paper crinkling under his fingertips. It struck Johnny for the first time how such delicate parchment contained solid enough truth to save the world.

About half the congregation floundered with their own Bibles, seeking the reference. The other half continued to stare. Whether they didn't have Bibles or just didn't bother to use them, Johnny didn't know.

"If you look through all the gospels—Matthew, Mark, Luke, and John—you'll see time after time how God brought healing to all sorts of people for every kind of disease. And since the Bible tells us God loves us, God must have healed all those people because he loved them. He wanted them whole."

Johnny paused again. Shouldn't they do more than just stare at him? They seemed to be listening well enough, but there hadn't been a single amen. Pa usually had an amen by now. Didn't God's love excite them?

Desiring a better response, Johnny tried imitating his father. He sprinkled a few Thee's and Thou's in his speech, and stuttered over some longer words he'd heard Pa use. He even tried raising his voice, but he squeaked instead of shouting.

Several minutes of awkward shenanigans passed before Johnny ran out of steam. He scanned the room, trying to figure out what to do next. At least nobody had fallen asleep. Well, OK, so Grandpa Jenkins was snoring, but even Pa had to deal with that.

Now what? He lifted his eyes heavenward for inspiration and whispered so only he could hear. "Lord, I've done all I know to do. I said what you wanted me to say. I need your help. I just can't do this like I thought I could."

His thoughts drifted back to the night he had been healed. Maybe if he told them his story, they would understand how much God loved them. It must be the right thing for him to do.

"I almost died when I was twelve." Johnny spoke in such a low tone that even those on the front pew strained to hear. "You might have heard Ma and Pa talk about it. I had polio—before the vaccine came around."

Muted shushes brought dead silence to the room.

"At first Ma thought it was just the flu. But I kept getting worse and they finally called the doctor. By the time he figured out what was wrong, I was really sick."

"Ma and Pa prayed a lot, but I didn't get better. If anything, I got worse, so they asked the doctor to come see me again."

Johnny watched tears rolled down Ma's cheeks.

"The doctor didn't give my parents any hope. He said I probably wouldn't live, and if I did, I'd be in a wheelchair the rest of my life. But Ma and Pa got down on their knees and prayed with all their might. They poured out their hearts to God and told him how much they loved me.

"When I woke up the next morning, the polio was gone. Ma and Pa couldn't hardly believe it. They knew they'd seen a miracle, and I," Johnny said, pausing for effect, "am that miracle."

He waited for it to sink in, looking from face to face along every pew. "And I believe it was because Pa told God how much he loved me that I was healed. I think it reminded God of how much *he* loved me, and he wanted the best for me. Sure," he tapped his leg, "I have a limp to show for it. But I think of it as a reminder— kind of like a rainbow."

An overwhelming sense of God's love welled up inside Johnny. He felt like God's personal representative, bringing the special message of God's love to every single person before him.

"God loves you, and he wants you whole." Johnny folded his notes and closed them in his Bible. He clasped his hands on the lectern, heart at peace, satisfied.

As he looked over the crowd, seconds ticked away with every last person returning his gaze. The thought struck Johnny that he didn't have *anything* else to say. His message had been short. He sensed them expecting more.

Johnny glanced at his watch. It showed exactly seventeen minutes had passed since his sermon began. Pa's shortest message had been nearly forty minutes—and that was at Christmas when he had to share the stage with the annual play.

Sweat beaded Johnny's brow as panic revisited him. Nowhere during his preparation had he given any thought to how he would conclude his message. He turned to Pa in desperation.

Pa leapt from his seat and managed a single step before the stampede began. A horde rushed the altar, near trampling each other in their determination to reach the front. Johnny stared in open-mouthed astonishment as seventeen teary-eyed parishioners—one for each minute he spoke—knelt just below the pulpit in prayer.

Last down the aisle, Skip Jefferson stepped on toes, bumped elbows, and tripped repeatedly over his own pants. Johnny had never seen Skip shed so much as a single tear, but now he bawled like a baby.

A long moment passed while Johnny held his breath, finally releasing it in a gasp. Sure, he had expected God to move. But this...this simply astounded him. It was too much. The surprise, the relief, and perhaps the oven of heat from a hundred bodies overwhelmed him. He fainted dead away.

Chapter Six

Only a few car dealerships bothered to set up shop in tiny Winterville. Mr. McIntire sped through the part of town where they clustered. He passed the Chevrolet dealership at full speed.

"Hey!" Trevor whipped his head back toward the receding and hoped-for Camaro, then to his dad. "What are you doing? We're not going on another lame errand, are we?"

Mr. McIntire kept his eyes on the road. The Mercedes gobbled up another hundred yards of pavement, then jerked into the center turning lane. A hard jab at the brakes and a quick left turn landed the black convertible in front of the Taraton Ford-Mercury building. Three salesmen—coming from three different directions— made beelines for the car the instant it stopped.

Trevor scanned the lot, digesting this turn of events. "What are we doing here? I said I wanted a Camaro." He scowled, then a smile sprang to his lips. "A Mustang! A Mustang GT. That'll work!"

Mr. McIntire exited the car and tramped past the flock of salesmen. He reached the main entrance before Trevor got a foot on the ground.

"Hey, Dad!" Trevor sprinted from the car and caught Mr. McIntire just as he pushed open the door. "This is great. I never thought about a Mustang." He spotted a shiny red GT a few feet into the showroom, and gawked at it while his dad pressed on.

"Hi! Harold Goldman. My friends call me Harry. You wanna take one of these babies for a spin?"

Trevor tore his gaze from the car long enough to size up a salesman not much older than himself. Harry stood inside Trevor's bubble space sporting a toothy smile, one hand extending a business card.

"I want this one." Trevor pointed at the Mustang, ignoring the outstretched arm and its proffered card. He made a face as burly fingers of cologne threatened to choke off his air supply.

Harry winked while making an odd clucking noise. "Yes, sir. You'll look great cruising around in that thing. And that's a special edition—leather seats, performance suspension, the works. Give me a sec," he jerked a thumb toward the back of the room. "and let me grab the keys."

After Harry disappeared, Trevor surveyed the showroom. Bright lights, shiny cars, and the scent of new, new, new attacked Trevor's senses. Harried sales staff rushed to and fro, glances occasionally cast Trevor's way. A couple of pre-teen girls, one blonde and one brunette, lounged in a diminutive waiting room off to one side, eyes glued to their phones.

When Trevor's gaze raked back toward the Mustang, he caught sight of his dad settling into a chair behind the glass walls of a nearby office. Trevor rushed past the cars and poked his head through the doorway. "Dad! You wanna ride with me?"

"Excuse me," said a voice behind Trevor.

Up, up, up went Trevor's gaze. He found himself at eye-level with the newcomer's shirt pocket. Good grief—the monster had to be almost six and a half feet tall, and thin as a rail.

"This is Mr. Taraton, Trev," Mr. McIntire said. "He owns the dealership."

"Ah, that's great, Dad." Trevor tore his gaze away from the man. "Are you going for a ride or not?"

"Why don't you have a look around the showroom? We have some business to take care of."

"Business?" It took a second, but then a light clicked on in Trevor's head. "Ohhh, I get it—you're on it already. Sure, Dad. Catch you in a few." He stepped out of the office and bumped straight into Harry, upending a cup of coffee down the poor guy's shirt.

"Whoa!" Harry jumped backward while staring at the fresh stain. "Ooh-ee!" He fanned his chest. "That's hot!"

"Sorry, dude." Trevor shrugged. "Hey, listen—my old man got the jump on you. I'll be driving it home in a few minutes. Maybe next time." Sidestepping Harry, Trevor jaunted over to his prize, slid behind the wheel, and fiddled with the seat controls while Harry stared after him, keys dangling from his hand.

Sometime later Mr. McIntire sauntered into the showroom. He lingered at the window sticker of a hulking SUV. When Trevor saw him, he tossed aside the Mustang owner's manual he'd been poring through and leapt out of the car just as Mr. Taraton appeared next to his dad.

"Everything is ready." Mr. Taraton handed Mr. McIntire a set of keys. "Come back to see us any time." They shook hands, and the giant lumbered away.

Trevor dashed over to his dad. "All right! It's about time." He held out a hand for the keys. "I can't wait to show Lisa."

"Hmph." Mr. McIntire turned opposite Trevor and headed toward the door.

"Hey, wait up!" Trevor sprinted after him, slowed for a longing look at the Mustang, then spurred on.

Outside the showroom, Mr. McIntire stood next to an older model Ford Explorer. He dangled a key from an upraised hand. "Here you go, son. See you at home."

"Yeah, sure—thanks, Dad. Don't wait up for me." He reached for the key, then squinted back at the showroom. "Um, how am I supposed to get it out?"

"This is your ride, son." Mr. McIntire gestured toward the Explorer.

Trevor swiveled his head back and forth. "Where?"

"Here." Mr. McIntire pulled open the truck's door, wearing an odd smirk. "I thought you deserved a nice, safe, *inexpensive* vehicle. You know—something that matches your level of income."

The realization of what his dad had done crept into Trevor's mind, then hit him like a brick. He felt his face grow warm. "You had this planned all along!"

Mr. McIntire raised an eyebrow, continuing the smirk.

"You never had any intention of getting me the Camaro—*or* the Mustang! What possessed you to pull this kind of stunt? Wait 'til Mom hears about it!"

Rage boiled inside Trevor until he thought he would explode. He snatched the key with trembling hands and heaved it at the ground with a grunt. "I will *not* take that thing home. I can't be seen driving around in a truck like some freakin' redneck. You go right back in there and tell them the deal's off."

Mr. McIntire ignored the key. He ignored Trevor. The smirk now gone, he spun on one heel and strolled toward his own car, humming.

Trevor followed, mounting a verbal assault. "You said you'd take care of me. All I had to do was keep up my grades and you'd get me through school. I kept my end of the bargain and now you think you can jerk me around? Well, I have news for you—I'm not playing that game!"

A stream of profanities and insults ensued. The tirade attracted a mixed crowd of customers and salespersons who watched from afar. An attractive young mother examining a nearby CUV snatched up her toddler daughter, tucked the blonde package under one arm, and scampered away from the commotion.

Mr. McIntire arrived at his car. He clicked the remote once, unlocking the driver's door. Trevor, on his heels, reached the opposite side of the car, verbal sandstorm unabated. The passenger door refused to open for him.

"If you'd like to come home tonight," Mr. McIntire said when Trevor drew a breath, "bring the Explorer with you." He slipped into the driver's seat, shut the door, and manually locked it all in one smooth motion.

Trevor tried his door again to no avail. He pounded the window as the engine started. "Let me in you stupid jerk!"

The Mercedes bumped into gear and eased backward. Trevor kicked the front tire as it passed. A mechanical click sounded and the car started forward, missing Trevor's shoes by inches. He rushed toward the receding bumper and gave it a solid kick before the car made it out of the parking lot.

Fury consumed Trevor. It was as if every insult he'd ever suffered welled up at once. He pounded into the street, screaming at the top of his lungs. As the Mercedes whisked onto the main boulevard, Trevor stooped down and scooped up a handful of stray gravel. He lobbed the rocks at the receding car, but it was already too far away.

Traffic whizzed by. A horn honked. Trevor yelled obscenities at the driver. Then he stomped back to the Explorer, still seething. He stared at the beast then, in sudden release, he kicked the door with all his might. A paradox of pain and satisfaction lanced through his toes.

"Piece of junk!" Trevor cursed the vehicle, then paced to and fro, weighing his options. In his peripheral vision he noticed a good portion of the sales crew gathered at the showroom window.

Near his feet, a glint of sunlight. Trevor reached down and grabbed the key he'd discarded earlier. He clutched it tight, then loose, tight, then loose. A satisfying feeling of pure evil welled up inside him. He clenched the key between two fingers, then scraped it the length of the vehicle. A dull and uneven silver stripe followed the key's path.

"Ha." Trevor tossed the keys back to the ground. "Let's see what he thinks of that."

After surveying his handiwork a moment longer, he turned, sneered at the group of salesmen still watching from the window, and trekked off the lot, destination unknown.

* * *

Late Sunday night Trevor banged open the front door of his parent's house, stomped over the threshold, and kicked the door shut behind him. Mr. and Mrs. McIntire—James and Olivia—relaxed on the sofa, wine glasses in hand, TV images flashing over them in the soft light of the living room. Trevor trudged past them.

"Trev," Mr. McIntire called as Trevor passed by.

Trevor tromped up the stairs. He made it halfway to his room before the next summons reached him.

"Trevor!"

In no mood for conversation, Trevor plodded into his bedroom and slammed the door behind him. He flopped down on the bed and stared at the ceiling, brooding. Moments later a knock sounded at the door.

"Trev, we need to talk."

"Hmph."

"Come on, Trev—open up. You're acting like a child."

Trevor swore.

The door clicked open and Mr. McIntire eased into the room. He stared at Trevor, expressionless. Trevor scowled.

Mr. McIntire exhaled, then looked toward the window. "The Ford dealership called last night."

Trevor tensed. He wasn't looking for a fight, but if Dad pushed the issue of that stupid truck...

"It seems they're still holding an Explorer for me." Mr. McIntire's tone was even, emotionless.

Trevor held back. He played a game of picking out individual ceiling fan blades as it made wobbly circles above his head—until its breeze dried his eyes and he had to turn away.

"I've been doing some thinking, Trev. It's been a while since you and I spent any time together—just the two of us."

"Yeah." Trevor snorted. "Not since you pulled me around the den in my little red wagon."

"Hmm." Mr. McIntire caught Trevor's eye. "I thought we could go camping. Maybe hike around the mountain—see what the place has to offer. What do you think?"

Trevor twisted upright and stamped his feet on the floor. "Sure—like *that's* really going to happen." His gaze wandered toward the door. "You couldn't leave work five minutes if your life depended on it."

Mr. McIntire grunted. "I made the arrangements already. Have your bags packed Friday when I get back from the airport. We're going camping—just us two men."

Promises like that had been made before, and Trevor couldn't remember the last one that had been kept. But he had to admit Dad sounded convincing. Did he dare trust him?

The last time Trevor went camping was before they moved to Winterville, and that had been with a friend's family. A weekend in the woods sure would break the monotony of life in this hick town. It sounded like fun, but...

"So...why should I believe you *this* time?"

"I told you, Trev—it's already arranged. José will cover anything that comes up while I'm gone. Are you interested?"

Trevor's mind went into overdrive. "You're really serious?"

Mr. McIntire nodded.

"That's way cool, Dad. How about we really rough it?" Trevor gestured at random while he spoke. "We could live off the land—no food, no water, nothing we don't find ourselves."

"All right, I'll take that challenge." Mr. McIntire patted Trevor on the shoulder. "But you'll be the one whimpering for cheeseburgers before the weekend is over."

"Cool!" Trevor stood. "I'll dig out the fishing gear and stock up on shotgun shells, and," he rubbed his chin, "let's see—what else do we need?"

"One other thing, Trev—I thought it might be fun to do some four-wheeling while we're there."

"Huh?" Trevor thought of his old ATV that hadn't run in years. And even if it did, Dad had long ago sold the truck they used for hauling it around.

"It just so happens I purchased a four-wheel drive Explorer recently. What better way to go slogging around those mountain trails?"

Trevor's excitement drained. He tilted his head and squinted. So *that's* what this was all about. Dad thought he could sucker him into accepting that piece of junk in exchange for a weekend in the woods. His face flushed. He was nobody's fool.

Still, banging around the woods in a full-size SUV did sound like more fun than his old four-wheeler. His enthusiasm ratcheted upward. "OK, Dad. I guess we can do that. But just for the record, I'm not that stupid. I know what you're doing."

"I know how smart you are, son. I also know you're not above a bribe."

Trevor leaned over and pulled a can of soda from the dorm refrigerator he kept beside his bed. He popped the top and took a deep swig. The mixture of cold liquid and burning carbonation felt almost as good as alcohol going down. "Lucky for you I just happen to think crashing a car through the woods sounds like fun." A sly grin parted his lips. "It's a little boring on the open road."

"It's a date, then. I just hope they have the paint repaired before we go. It seems there was some vandalism on the lot overnight, but you wouldn't happen to know anything about that, would you?"

"Uh-uh." Trevor flashed a broad smile. "Why would anybody waste their time messing up an old truck?"

"Hmm."

Mr. McIntire turned to go and Trevor called after him.

"Hey, Dad—*I'll* do the driving."

* * *

Trevor picked up the repaired Explorer Thursday afternoon. He spent the evening alone getting to know his new ride. It was no Camaro, but with a V8 under the hood the truck had enough pep that it probably wouldn't embarrass him. He even managed to lay a short black mark when he goosed it on a right turn from a dead start. The blocky beast might even have enough power to make it into the Century Club, but there was no rush on that—he needed to lay low until the cloud hanging over his last crash blew over.

Throughout every class on Friday, Trevor mentally worked on his sales pitch. There were probably enough good points about owning an SUV that he could sell it to his friends. But in case anyone raised a stink, waiting until just before going home for the big reveal would allow him to simply drive away from any jokes.

The Century Club members shared the same English Literature class—their last subject of the day. Professor Litchfield's lecture, as usual, was a sleeper. Trevor and Kenny sprawled headlong over their desks, Kenny snoring sporadically. Lisa nudged Trevor in the ribs a few minutes before the last bell. He jerked sideways, head shooting up. "Unh?"

Lisa pointed toward the front.

"The instructions I'm passing out," Professor Litchfield said, shuffling through a stack of papers, "are for an essay each of you will write." He marched up and down the rows, handing each student a set of instructions. "This project will count as two test grades for the semester, and I'll also be taking several homework grades along the way. Your performance on this one assignment could mean the difference between passing and failing the class. I suggest you pay careful attention to this handout and not fall behind on the individual assignments."

Kenny, still groggy and having missed half the speech, frowned in indignation. "Here it comes. They warned me not to take this dude's class." He further expressed his opinion with a few choice words.

Trevor guffawed.

Professor Litchfield, having returned to his desk, frowned first at Trevor, then at Kenny. "Gentlemen—and I use that term loosely—I shouldn't have to remind you that you're no longer in high school. I realize it taxes you to the limit, but I must insist you display the decorum associated with an adult while in this classroom." His remark drew snickers from the class. He quieted them with a wave of his hand.

"At the top of the second page there is a timetable. As you can see, this is an extensive project. Though creativity and presentation will both be important parts of your grade, don't neglect the initial research. I'm a stickler for proper research.

"On the last page you will find a list of suggested topics. I only allow one person to present each topic, so first come, first served. I will entertain alternate ideas, but be warned that I only accept legitimate themes. Your subject must be serious, and interesting. As the schedule indicates, your choice must be made by the beginning of class on Monday."

The teacher droned on regarding the project's details. Trevor's eyelids drooped, flicked open, then closed. He fell asleep just as the final bell rang.

A chaotic shuffling of papers, closing of books, and excited conversation ensued. Many students—including the Century Club members—lingered in the classroom. Rushing wasn't cool.

Once they left the building, Kenny rolled his eyes skyward. "What a drag! I can't believe that guy. Everything's such a big deal with him."

Brent nodded in agreement.

"You heard the man." Lisa put on the motherly look she'd adopted more often lately. "It's not high school any more. You guys have to be serious sometimes."

"Whose side are you on?" Kenny shot back.

"Mine." Lisa flashed an innocent smile. She grabbed Trevor's arm and tugged him toward the parking lot. Kenny and Brent fell in step behind, cackling over one of Kenny's raucous jokes.

Trevor slipped on a pair of dark sunglasses to ward off the afternoon sun. He felt a tinge of nervousness as they approached the parking area. Kenny would deride him without mercy if he couldn't put the right spin on his new ride.

At least the Explorer wasn't a just a pickup truck. Newer SUV's sometimes substituted for a Lexus or Mercedes, so Trevor thought he had a good starting position for his arguments. At least, he hoped so.

"Hey, dudes." Trevor pumped as much enthusiasm into his tone as he could muster. "I'll handle the driving today. I finally got the old man to let go of his purse strings."

"Awesome, man! Where's the new bike?" Kenny chuckled, and his remark drew laughter from Brent and Lisa.

Trevor played it cool. "Yeah, right. I'll keep that in mind while the *three* of us go for a ride."

Kenny clutched his heart and staggered. "I'm hurt, man—*so* hurt." He straightened back up and rolled his eyes.

Trevor stopped in front of the Explorer. "Here you go, kiddies." He waved a hand over the truck. "Step up to riding in style!" He struck a pageant pose, toothy smile and all.

Kenny didn't skip a beat. "You got a *truck*?" He slapped his knee and guffawed. "You *can't* be serious. Come on—really," he searched the lot, "where's the new wheels?"

"Is this really yours, Trev?" Lisa eyed the Explorer with suspicion.

"Sure is. *Every*body's gonna move to SUVs. I'm leading a wave."

"Ha!" Kenny smirked at the Explorer. "Next thing you know, you'll be driving a tractor!"

Brent moved in for a closer look. "Hey, man, does this thing have four-wheel drive?"

"You bet it does. Four-wheel drive, leather seats, and best of all a V8. SUVs are the hot ticket, and I won't be the one playing catch-up." He searched their faces, uncertain of how he would fare, except possibly with Brent.

"What are you waiting for?" Lisa headed toward the passenger side. "Take me for a spin."

Trevor raced ahead of Lisa and made a show of opening the door for her. He peeked over the hood at the other two. "Any more takers?"

Brent didn't hesitate. "Sure, man." He yanked opened the door behind Trevor's seat and hopped in. "Let's go."

Kenny stared at the ground and shook his head. "All right." He heaved a long sigh. "But if you get the sudden urge to milk a cow, I want out."

Chapter Seven

Back then I had no idea what I was getting myself into. All I had was faith—blind, naïve faith. I would have done anything he asked me to. In fact, that's exactly what I did.

* * *

"Johnny, what a pleasure to have you in our humble home!" Ma looked up from the peaches she had been peeling. She set down her knife, eyes sparkling. "I was beginning to wonder if you remembered where to make your bed at night."

Johnny limped through the front door and leaned his cane against the wall. "Aw, Ma." He shed his boots next to his cane, then shuffled toward the kitchen and into Ma's open arms. After a protracted hug she let him go, stepped back and eyed him up and down, then settled into her work again.

"Where've you been this time, son?" She ran the knife through another peach, adding to both the sweet aroma in the room and the gooey mess on the table. "Have you been chasing churches—or girls?"

"Ma!" Johnny scowled. He jabbed her in the ribs just hard enough to elicit a teensy yelp. "I have more important things to do than chase after girls." He flopped down in the chair next to her, big black Bible rattling the bowl of peaches as he dropped it on the table. He stared at the bowl, then reached for a fruit. Ma slapped his hand but he still won his prize.

"Every preacher needs a good woman behind him." Ma shoved the bowl left, beyond Johnny's reach. "There's nothing wrong with a man of God socializing every now and again. Ask your pa—he'll tell you how good marriage has been all these years."

Johnny rolled his eyes. "If you must know, Ma, I've been talking to people about God's love and inviting them to church. *That's* what God wants me to do. He hasn't said anything about marriage." He opened his Bible and buried his head in the pages, the hunger for God's Word never being satisfied lately.

A few minutes later the front door banged open. Johnny startled at the sound, gaze rising from his studies. "That's my boy!" Pa's voice bellowed through the house. "You can't pour it out if you don't pour it in, I always say." He tossed his hat on a wall peg and swept across the room toward the kitchen.

Johnny braced himself as heavy hands came down hard on his shoulders. Pa squeezed until Johnny winced. He waited until the pressure eased, then breathed deep. If only Pa would learn to love him with a little less force.

Pa leaned over and planted a kiss on Ma's cheek then turned to face Johnny. "Well, son, have you made a decision?"

"As a matter of fact, I have." Johnny closed his Bible and met the stares from two pairs of eyes. "There's no doubt what God wants me to do. I'm going to take this message," he thumped the Bible, "out to the world—to everyone who'll listen."

"I just knew it!" Pa clapped Johnny on the back so hard it knocked the wind out of him.

Ma smiled. "Well, I don't suppose we really had any doubt."

"So where's your first stop?" asked Pa.

"Do you know Reverend Charles?"

Pa cocked his head and squinted. "The Methodist preacher on the far side of town? Sure, I know him. Bit of a stick-in-the-mud, if you ask me."

"Jeremiah!" Ma frowned. "That's not like you."

"Well, it's true."

"He asked me to preach next Sunday."

Pa raised an eyebrow and gave Johnny a long, sideways look. "I'd say you've got your work cut out for you, son. That place has a reputation for being dry as a bone."

Johnny grinned. "God has *his* work cut out for him. All *I* have to do is preach."

* * *

River Woods Methodist Church nestled right next to the street on a cramped lot three miles east of downtown. A petite wooden structure, it boasted stained glass windows and a fresh coat of white paint. The steeple housed a working bell that, at the moment, clanged loud enough to wake the dead in the adjacent cemetery. Small clusters of parishioners milled about outside the building, making leisure of their journey inside.

Ornate, hand-carved pews with green velvet upholstery rested on the wood plank floor. Placards, behind and to either side of the pulpit, indicated attendance, offering, and announcements. Forty people made it to Sunday School last week according to the sign on the left. The right side advertised an upcoming picnic on the grounds.

Pa sat on the front pew with Ma, arm draped over her shoulder. They had left Mt. Carmel in the hands of the deacon board this Sunday so they could experience Johnny's first sermon on the road. Skip Jefferson sat next to Pa, continuing his new tradition of avid church attendance since his turnaround at Johnny's hands a few weeks before.

Even with the addition of Skip and the Jones family, less than fifty people came to hear Johnny preach. The small number came as a surprise because Reverend Charles had said the house would be full. But Johnny wasn't disappointed. He would share with one or a thousand—whatever God set before him.

During the worship music Johnny felt God stirring his heart. He steeled himself against emotion so he would have a straight head when it came time for his message. Nevertheless, he wiped tears from his eyes when Reverend Charles made his way to the podium.

"This morning I'm pleased to introduce a special guest speaker." Reverend Charles punctuated his words by waving his hands in wide arcs that billowed his robe. "No doubt some of you heard about the commotion this young man caused over at Mt. Carmel." A few in the crowd nodded. Others whispered.

"I witnessed the effects of his preaching when I sneaked over to Mt. Carmel a couple of weeks ago." The minister winked at the crowd, drawing muffled laughter. "I can't wait to hear the message God has given him for us here at River Woods. I believe with all my heart that lives are going be changed." He made a final grand sweep toward the young preacher. "Please join me in welcoming Mr. Johnny Jones."

Johnny couldn't quit staring at Reverend Charles' robe. With its fancy purple inlay and gold-laced collar, it lent an air of formality, of regality to the man. Why didn't he wear a suit like he and Pa? Or—the thought troubled him—maybe he and Pa needed robes.

Jeremiah elbowed Johnny and, stern-faced, nodded toward the pulpit. Johnny sprang from the pew and cleared his throat. He glanced back and scanned the congregation, not a little sheepish, then made his way to the podium where Reverend Charles grabbed his hand and squeezed so hard it went numb. Then the reverend patted Johnny on the back and, for good measure, wrapped him in a bear hug. Johnny dropped his Bible with a thud in the confusion.

Once free, Johnny caught his breath and managed a warm-faced smile. He scooped up his Bible and laid it atop the pulpit, then drew a deep breath and looked the crowd over once more. Something rattled against the pulpit, and Johnny glanced down to find his cane trembling in his hand.

"Let us pray." Johnny bowed his head. "Father God, thank you for this opportunity to serve you. I pray that I would speak your words and not my own. I ask that you open everyone's ears, and let them hear the special message you have for them today. Let them feel your love, Lord. Amen." He raised his head to find Ma and Pa beaming.

Johnny tried to catch every eye as he opened with what had become his signature line. "God loves you, and he wants you whole." From there he tossed out a few Bible verses to back up his statement, then dove right into the story of his polio fight. The crowd sat spellbound.

Skip had heard the message no less than half a dozen times already, but still he bawled like a baby. Ma and Pa wiped tears from their cheeks. Reverend Charles, red-faced and blurry-eyed, honked into a handkerchief.

When the sermon ended, Johnny simply stood and waited. He had yet to given an altar call any time he spoke. He smiled a little, just knowing. Then as if on cue, every soul present dove for the front.

* * *

"God wants me to fast." Johnny announced this to Pa immediately upon swinging open the front door. He limped over to where Pa sat reading a Bible at the kitchen table.

"Hm?" Pa glanced up from his studies. "Oh, yeah—that's great, son. There's no better way to strengthen your trust in God."

"Well...it's not about building trust. I'm just doing it because that's what God wants."

"Obedience is better than sacrifice, eh? Well, I'm warning you—you'll need God's strength for fasting. If you do it on your own, well...you'll be miserable, that's what. But if you rely on God, he'll take care of you. Just make sure your heart's in the right place."

Ma waltzed into the room just then and swung an arm around Johnny. "Hi, sweetie. I sure have missed you." She reached up and kissed him on the cheek. "How have you been?"

"Good, Ma. Tired, though." Johnny returned her hug, then flopped down beside Pa and pulled off his shoes. Ma's fragrance lingered on him, a hint of roses.

"The boy says he's going to fast."

Ma cocked her head. "Too fast for what?"

"No—he's gonna *fast*. From food."

"Oh, Johnny." Ma hinted at a frown. "I wish I'd known. I cooked enough to feed an army."

"Don't worry, Ma." Johnny reached up and patted her. "My fast doesn't start 'til morning."

"Well in that case," Ma turned toward the stove, "let's eat while it's hot."

"All right!" Pa pushed his Bible aside. "Beef stew! Mmmm!"

Ma laughed, then filled three bowls and brought them to the table. Pa said grace, and they all dug in.

"If you don't mind me asking," Ma blew across her spoon to cool the stew, "how long do you plan to fast?"

"Two weeks," Johnny said between bites.

Ma cut her eyes toward Pa, who met her gaze. They both fixed serious looks on Johnny.

"I'm going to camp on Helmut Mountain. Just get away from everything so it's easier to hear God." He looked from one to the other, then shoveled in another mouthful.

"Son, have you thought about starting with something easier?" Pa set down his spoon and clasped his hands together. "You've never fasted before, and two weeks is a mighty long stretch for a beginner. A mighty long stretch."

"Listen to your pa." Ma returned her spoon to her bowl. "We're proud of you for wanting to fast, but like he said, you need to work your way up to it. God won't be offended if you take one step at a time."

Johnny stopped chewing. He gulped down what was left in his mouth. "God told me to fast. I have to obey Him."

"Johnny," Pa began, spreading his hands on the table, "listen to me real good, now. You be careful about saying God told you something. It's all right to say you *believe* he spoke to you, or you *think* something would be God's will. But you're heading for dangerous territory when you say God told you what to do."

Johnny stiffened. He set down his spoon and gripped the seat of his chair with both hands. "You hear from God, don't you, Pa?"

"Sure I do. Sometimes. But—"

"Pa, I didn't make this up. God told me to fast for two weeks, and he said if I obey him, he's going to show me great and mighty things. Those were his exact words—'great and mighty things.' Besides, you always told me I need to listen for God's voice. I'm just doing what you taught me. Don't you believe I know how to listen to God?"

"Well…" Pa scratched his five o'clock shadow. "It's not that, son. I just want you to be careful. A lot of good people have gone down the wrong path because they thought God spoke to them. A two week fast isn't something you want to be wrong about."

Johnny didn't bat an eye. "God spoke to me, Pa. I didn't hear him with my ears, but I heard him with my heart. I *know* it was him."

Ma locked eyes with Pa. "I reckon we shouldn't be surprised. He sure does have a gift for preaching. Maybe he has a gift for hearing God, too."

Pa drummed his fingers on the table. "Maybe so." He shifted his gaze from Johnny to Ma and back. "Maybe so."

* * *

Johnny glanced back over the mound of his hiking pack when he reached the mailbox, squinted past the rising sun, and waved to his parents one last time. Arm in arm on the porch, they waved back.

He turned right and headed down the dusty road slinking past the front of their house. At a steady pace, he figured he could reach the foothills of Helmut Mountain within the hour. Three more hours uphill would take him to the family's favorite camping spot.

Cool morning air tickled his face. He breathed deep, and exhaled slowly. "Ahh." The hike would be a pleasant one. He planted his cane in the dirt and pushed forward, setting tiny plumes of dust whirling at his feet.

"I feel you all around me, Lord." Johnny stole glances at the sky, smiling at the sparse, wispy clouds. "I can't wait, God—just you and me. I love you so much. I love you, Lord Jesus. I'm so glad you chose me. You're the reason for my whole life."

When he reached the foothills, Johnny picked out one of several narrow trails, shifted his load, and set a slower pace as he headed up the mountain. A bird rustled in a nearby bush and took flight as Johnny passed. Just off the trail to his right, a rabbit stood tall on hind legs, peeking at him through the underbrush. He smiled at the sights of God's creation. He served an awesome God.

Hours later, babbling water signaled the campsite's imminent appearance. Soon the trees thinned, then parted into a two-acre meadow that bordered a wide freshwater stream. A wall of thick hardwoods stood guard on the opposite side of the water, daring the bright noon sun to cross their boundary.

Johnny's stomach growled. "Oh, no you don't." He patted his belly. "It'll be two whole weeks before you get your way again." A deep rumble answered him.

He sauntered over to the stream and knelt by the bank. Water danced over and around smooth stones of every shape and size, spattering the occasional foot-long blades of grass that stood against the flow. Cupping his hands, Johnny gulped mouthful after mouthful of cool refreshment. The hunger pangs faded. "Mmm. Can anything under heaven taste better than this?"

Johnny plopped down on the embankment, crossed his legs, then flipped open his Bible and read aloud. He started with the Twenty-third Psalm, devouring chapter after chapter with insatiable spiritual hunger. The afternoon sun hung low on the horizon when he finally grew tired of reading and looked up to find long shadows cast from the nearest trees.

"Holy smoke!" Where had the time gone? "It felt like minutes, God. Thank you for your Word. Don't tell Ma, but it's better food than anything she ever put on the table."

Rowwlll.

"You again?" Johnny rubbed his mid section. "I didn't even know you were there when I was reading." He leaned toward the stream for another drink. The water refreshed him, but his stomach rumbled again. He laughed it off. "Heh, this ain't nearly so bad as Pa said it would be."

Brilliant red-orange streaks of sunset lit the mountainside, turning pink, purple, and blue as Johnny watched, mesmerized. "You're an amazing artist, Father God."

With the fading light, crickets warmed up for their evening chorus. One by one, stars blinked into existence until they swarmed the sky. "Oh, Lord, I just can't imagine a better paradise than this." He shook his head. "What is heaven really like?"

Forgetting all else, Johnny gazed at the stars for hours. Then, eyelids drooping, he unfurled his sleeping bag, snuggled inside, and zipped it up tight. No need for a tent in such a utopian environment.

Eyes closed, Johnny soaked in the crickets' sweet symphony. The private concert soothed his spirit. It lulled him to sleep, the tightness in his stomach temporarily forgotten.

* * *

Hunger woke Johnny the next morning. A trip to the stream did nothing to settle his anxious stomach. "Lord, please help me keep my focus on you. Give me strength to resist these fleshly desires."

He prayed off and on much of the day, speaking, then listening, speaking, then listening. Despite his attentiveness, no great revelation struck him and no words of wisdom formed in his mind. If anything, God seemed farther away. Maybe his flesh was the problem. The constant complaining from his abdomen distracted him almost every waking minute.

"I'm following you, God." He patted his stomach. "Do you hear that, flesh? You can't have me—I'm following God."

Three days into his fast, Johnny frequented the stream multiple times an hour. Even so, his stomach tormented him without ceasing. The water, once a refreshing friend, transformed into an enemy, a vicious reminder of everything his body craved. He forced it down despite the bitter taste that had taken up permanent residence in his mouth.

Something changed the morning of the fourth day. Hunger only teased him, its talons no longer forming a death grip. "Lord…" Johnny grinned, sensing victory. "Thank you for your strength."

He lifted his eyes heavenward and raised weak hands in praise. "Father, I love you, and I'm going to follow you the rest of my life."

For three more days, Johnny followed an established routine. Pray, then drink. Nap, then drink. Read and meditate, then drink. Last of all—sleep. The cycle threatened to become a religion of its own.

Late one afternoon, Johnny dipped into the stream and found that a sickly yellow tint now covered his hands, crept up his arms, and snaked past his elbows. He wiggled his fingers, turning his hands back and forth. The skin seemed to cling tighter to his bones than he remembered. He shook his head, resolute. "I will obey you, Lord. No matter what."

During the second week, Johnny's strength faded. His weakening muscles became the greater enemy. "Lord, this is hard. I don't even feel like reading the Bible any more. I must be doing something wrong. Shouldn't I be getting closer to you by now?"

He buried his head in his hands, tears streaming. "I just want to quit. Please give me strength."

No heavenly voice boomed an answer. No burst of energy revitalized him. Only hunger and weakness, preying on his flesh, preying on his mind.

Wind whisked in cooler weather on the ninth day while the mid-morning sun played hide-and-seek with gray clouds. The strong, steady breeze had chilled Johnny out of his slumber, and now a dull ache radiating from the pit of his stomach enticed him to full wakefulness. The darkening sky threatened rain.

Sleeping under the open heavens had been no small pleasure. But soon he would need shelter. His hunger-born weakness made even the simple task of pitching his tent a chore, though it was just a tiny one-man affair. Somehow he managed to secure the pegs in the ground before collapsing. Then, panting, he tossed his sleeping bag ahead of him and crawled inside.

Adding insult to injury, when he lifted the canteen to his lips, only a handful of drops trickled out. Not again. Not another trip to the stream. "Father, help me! I can't do this anymore. I should have listened to Pa." Johnny clamped tight his eyes, fighting tears. Soon fatigue overcame him, and he slept.

Jagged lightning ripped opened the sky in the early morning hours of the tenth day. Thunder boomed seconds later, jolting Johnny to consciousness. "God? Is that you?" He rubbed crusty sleep from his eyes. "Will you talk to me now?"

White brilliance flashed horizontal across the sky, lighting the world brighter than day. Whether God's response, or nature running its course, Johnny couldn't tell. Then bolt after bolt electrified the meadow, boom after boom pounding the ground in a deafening crescendo. Leaves, driven mad by the howling wind, panicked across the clearing, littering top to bottom the trembling sides of Johnny's tent.

Rain! Gumball-size drops pelted the ground with relentless fury. Johnny cowered and pulled his sleeping bag over his head. Wind chased the downpour under the tent flap, creating a river that soaked Johnny to the bone.

A gale-force wind smashed through the trees. Twigs and small branches cracked loose, lodged in the tent canvas, tore jagged holes. The humble dwelling put up a brave fight, but succumbed to overwhelming force. It collapsed inward in a tangle of fabric and poles, one lone rail jutting upward in laudable defiance.

For three days and nights the storm played havoc on Helmut Mountain. Occasional breaks in the tempest raised Johnny's hope for relief. But the miserable drizzle evaporated each time, replaced by a squall more furious than anything before.

"God! Please—help me!" Johnny repeated his cry again and again, barely able to hear his own voice above the din. Hunger returned, wracking his entire body with agony while thirst cracked his lips and parched his throat. Lacking both strength and willpower to reach the stream, Johnny poked his head from the crumpled shelter and, mouth wide, caught what he could from the downpour. The water brought minimal relief.

"I'm not worthy, Father! Just help me—*please*, help me."

Ma's words echoed in his head: "You'll need your strength when this is over, Johnny. Let me send something with you for the trip home."

His response and subsequent refusal haunted him. "Ma, God will provide." The scene played in his mind like a circular movie clip. If only he had listened to Ma. He would gladly abandon the fast now, but he hadn't so much as a crumb to fall back on.

Had God failed to provide? Or, had *he* failed God? His strength had failed him—that much was certain. He had reached the end of his rope and, quite possibly, his life. He couldn't even lift himself to crawl. How would he ever get back home? Where was God when he needed him most?

Johnny tossed and turned, shivering and trembling. Water sloshed from his sleeping bag with every move. Adding to the misery, dreams reminded him of happier times. Playing in the back yard, his recent sermons, Caroline's smile and bouncing curls. His time in bed with polio flashed before him. He would trade those days for his current misery in a heartbeat.

He thought of Ma and Pa. Would he ever see them again?

Sheer physical exhaustion overtook him somewhere in the midst of the images, and he slept. But still he had no peace. First dozing, then waking, he drifted in and out of consciousness while the storm raged on.

* * *

On the fourteenth day the sun peeped above the tree line. A mockingbird chirped in a nearby pine. Forest creatures rustled the bushes. A squirrel dashed about at the edge of the clearing, scrambling through mounds of fallen branches, leaves, and various and sundry debris. A crumpled lump of saturated canvas lay among the remainder of the storm's chaos, unmoving.

Somewhere deep inside Johnny's waning consciousness, a voice cried out. "Awake!"

Johnny mumbled.

"Awake!"

Johnny shifted, tried to answer, but his lips stuck together.

A pinpoint of white light detached itself from the rising sun and meandered toward Johnny. Eyes closed, he saw it clearly. The light loomed larger and brighter, growing, growing until it took the form of a man—a brilliant, light-covered man—advancing toward Johnny from the far end of the meadow. Was it his imagination?

"Favored one!" The light-man sounded at once near and far. "To obey is better than sacrifice! Yet today the Lord sips both obedience and sacrifice from the same cup, and a pleasing aroma has arisen to heaven."

Johnny wrinkled his brow in puzzlement.

Is that you, Lord?

He studied the apparition, its long flowing hair, and its glowing and indistinct face. It was beyond anything he had ever imagined.

Am I in heaven?

"Your journey is not over and your mission is not complete." The light-man floated closer still.

What do you want me to do?

"Seek the Lord always. Obey his voice whenever you hear him, and hear him you shall, for you have been called to touch many in this life." The light-man approached close enough now for Johnny to distinguish facial features, all glowing bright white.

"Show them love, and share with them the gift now placed in your hands."

Johnny felt warm inside for the first time in days. *What gift, Lord?*

"Arise. Eat. Gather strength for the journey."

Johnny's eyelids fluttered. The light-man faded, darkened into the visage of a running man, a shadow man, arms stretched forward and approaching fast.

"No!" Johnny found his voice. "I need you, Lord!"

"Johnny!" The shadow called with a different voice, a familiar voice. It rushed him, all vestiges of angelic appearance completely gone. "Johnny! Oh, God! How could I let this happen?"

Now upon him, the shadow engulfed him, caressed him, held him tight. "Johnny! Oh, Johnny!"

The fuzzy image coalesced at the edges, blurred into focus. Johnny squinted. "Pa, is that you?"

Pa howled like a woman in childbirth. "Oh, God Almighty! Thank you, God! Thank you for sparing my son!"

Chapter Eight

The Century Club had a blast in the Explorer the day before Trevor's scheduled camping trip. Trevor shifted into four-wheel drive and steered off the main road. He tore through the edge of a farm bordering the highway, ears of corn bumping and swishing past the truck's windows, husks and tassels pelting the occupants as the Ford bounced up and down among the rows. Trevor cackled with delight.

When Trevor had exhausted himself with this particular type of mayhem and steered back onto the road, Brent leaned forward and planted both elbows over the front seat. "Hey, man, what's the plan for the weekend?"

"How long since we went on a good drunk?" This from Kenny, who slouched low against his window.

Trevor held up a beer. "Uh, well…"

"No, man!" Kenny sprang forward and jostled Brent out of the way. "I don't mean a couple of beers. I mean falling down, can't-get-off-the-floor, good-for-nothing drunk. Let's go get a fifth—each—and see who's the last man standing."

"I'm in," Brent deadpanned.

"Me too!" Lisa pulled a strand of corn husk from her hair, giggled at it, and tossed it into the wind.

"Well, don't let *me* rain on the parade!" Trevor grinned wide. "And I tell you what—I'm buying. Just let me run by the house and grab some cash."

"Cool," said Brent. "My parents are gone for the weekend. We can hang out at my place."

"It's settled!" Trevor whacked his palm on the steering wheel. "Hang on to your hats, kiddies." He floored the gas pedal, and the Explorer lunged forward, throwing them back in their seats.

In less than fifteen minutes Trevor whipped into the wraparound driveway of his parents' red brick McMansion where a big black Mercedes perched in the driveway. "We're in luck—Dad's home early. It must be pay day." With a wink at his friends he jumped out of the truck. "I'll wring an extra hundred out of him. Be right back."

He jogged across the manicured lawn, ignoring the custom brick walkway. Mr. McIntire met him at the door in a T-shirt and blue jeans, a getup so diametrically opposed to his normal attire that Trevor raised both eyebrows.

"Hey, Dad. I need some cash." He eyed his father up and down. "And what's with this? Mom got you working outside?"

"You don't need cash where we're going. Do you have your bags packed?"

"Come on—quit fooling." Trevor held out a hand. "I'm running low. Help me out, will you?"

"Did you forget? We're going to the mountains. Just you, me, and the great outdoors." He gestured toward Trevor's room. "Better pack quick. We're burning daylight."

Trevor blinked, then his eyes lit up. "Dad! Seriously? We're really going? I can't believe it!"

"I told you I took off. Now get a move on. I expected you here hours ago."

"You *really* got off work? Man! Hang on—I'll be right back!" Trevor sprinted through the door and dashed for the stairs.

Once in his room, he rushed about like a madman, yanking clothes at random from four different drawers and cramming everything into his backpack until it bulged at the seams. He stood racking his brain for anything else he might need when Kenny and Lisa appeared at his bedroom door.

"What the heck are you doing, Trev?" Lisa stared, head cocked, wearing a quizzical expression.

"I think," Kenny said, "he's lost his mind and he's desperately trying to find it. What's with you, man?"

Trevor snatched a ragged orange T-shirt from the floor and gave it a sidelong look. He sniffed it, shrugged, then shoved it in with the rest. Only then did he notice his friends. "What are you guys—?" Everything clicked. "Lisa! Oh, man!"

"We've been waiting for*ever*. I thought you just came for money." Lisa frowned at the backpack. "What's *this* about?"

"Yeah, dude." Kenny backed into the hallway. "I'm not so big in the patience department. Let's get moving."

Trevor breathed an expletive. "Sorry, guys. I forgot." He rammed a fist in the backpack but failed to make more room.

"Forgot?" Kenny poked his head back through the doorway and scrunched his whole face into a frown. "You've been gone, what—ten minutes? You're mental, Trev. Seriously."

Ignoring Kenny, Trevor eased up beside Lisa and rubbed a hand down her cheek. "Hey, listen—I'm really sorry. Dad's taking me camping. He told me last weekend, but I didn't believe him. We're really going, though, and I can't pass this up—I might *never* get another chance."

Lisa nodded and sighed. "I get it, Trev. It's OK—go ahead." She held his eye a moment. "I'm kind of jealous, actually."

"Traitors!"

Trevor shot Kenny a nasty look, then took Lisa's hand and squeezed it. "Thanks." He kissed her forehead, then resumed packing. He shoved a cap in the backpack, wrestled a pair of sneakers through the opening, and fought the zipper to within six inches of closing.

Kenny harrumphed. "Suit yourself. But you're gonna miss a mighty fine drunk." He disappeared from the doorway and tramped down the hall.

Trevor hefted his pack. "You're not mad at me, are you?"

"No." Lisa managed a half smile. "Like I said, I'm kind of jealous."

"Good—about not being mad, I mean. Come on." Trevor took her by the hand. "Let's go."

In the living room Brent stretched out on the sofa, snoozing, stained Nikes sinking deep into soft Italian leather. Kenny hunched in a recliner, chin in hand, vacant eyes toward a sitcom screaming from the six-foot TV hanging on the wall.

"I'm heading out, guys. We can try again next week."

Either Kenny and Brent didn't hear him, or they ignored him.

Lisa joined Trevor on the marble foyer where a crystal chandelier hung overhead like mistletoe, showering them with splotches of gold and rainbow. "Bye, Trev." She pulled him down for a kiss.

"Have fun, Trevor." Mrs. McIntire called from somewhere in an adjacent room. "Keep your dad out of trouble, OK?"

Trevor pressed his lips hard against Lisa's until she melted in his arms. Then he pulled away. "Behave yourself." He kissed her once more, then popped her on the rump and sprinted out the door.

* * *

Trevor drove the Ford like a cowboy drove cattle, foot heavy on the accelerator despite the curving mountain roads. Wind roared past the window and whipped his T-shirt sleeve over his shoulder. The fresh air felt *good*. Air conditioning was for sissies.

James McIntire, in the passenger seat, had yet to mention the breakneck pace. In fact, he'd hardly said anything at all since the journey began. As rolling green meadows whizzed by his window, something sparked him out of his blank-faced stare into worlds unknown. "I brought the fishing tackle." He spared a glance at Trevor. "I heard there's trout in the foothills."

A permanent grin fixed itself on Trevor's face—a grin built on visions of a perfect weekend. His thoughts drifted back to reality just long enough to incorporate his dad's words into the dream. He imagined a father and son casting lines into a cool mountain brook, a cooler filled with fish on one side, a cooler of beer on the other. A full-fledged smile replaced his grin.

Miles of asphalt raced beneath the truck. Trevor envisioned himself holding up a string of fish while Dad snapped a picture of the catch.

"Your Grandpa and I went fishing all the time when I was a kid." Mr. McIntire stared out the window as he spoke. "We'd get a fire going on the beach, and talk about all sorts of nothing while supper cooked." He laughed at the memory. "I used to stuff my belly so full I'd almost throw up."

Trevor wrinkled his brow and spared a quick glance at his dad. "You never told me you and Grandpa went fishing."

"What?" Mr. McIntire turned raised eyebrows toward Trevor. "We fished all the time—I mean *all* the time." His countenance fell. "I quit going when I was old enough to have a say in things. Dad cared more about fishing than he did about me." He stared back out the window. "He used to set a quota and yell when I didn't meet it."

"Yeah, well no quotas *this* weekend." Trevor shot his dad a mischievous grin. "But, I bet twenty bucks I catch more than *you* do."

Mr. McIntire glanced away from the road again. "You're on. But let's make it a hundred bucks." He paused for effect. "Because *you're* going to lose."

* * *

The weekend started on a fantastic note when Mr. McIntire spotted a seldom-used path leading away from the popular campsites. Trevor shifted into four-wheel drive and floored the accelerator. The engine roared, and the Explorer bit into the trail, spewing chunks of dirt from all four wheels as they careened through the woods, narrowly missing trees, cackling like schoolchildren.

Eventually the way grew more challenging as the path narrowed and sported more upward-jutting rocks. Trevor slowed to accommodate the change, but still kept a swift pace as they wound their way upward for miles and miles. For anyone else it might have been enough to just enjoy the scenery, but Trevor steered for every stone and pothole. The truck bucked and shuddered, tossing Mr. McIntire about like a rag doll—to Trevor's utter delight.

"Hey, Trev—stop."

"What for?" Trevor snorted. "You seasick?"

"I think there's a stream." He pointed left. "And that break in the woods might be a good place to set up camp."

Trevor backed off the accelerator and let the truck coast. He scanned the area. "Yeah, this is cool." He hit the brake and the truck slid to a halt. Both men stepped out. The stream, only a few yards away and clearly visible, appeared to be about twenty feet wide. Overhead, trees crowded out much of the sun's rays.

"This'll be fine," said Mr. McIntire. "Let's get the tent up while we still have daylight."

Father and son worked together on the Bibler all-season tent that had been used exactly once in the ten years they'd owned it. When their new home stood erect, they retrieved their belongings from the truck and tossed them inside as the sun's last rays handed off the baton to twilight.

"Tonight, we cheat." Mr. McIntire pulled a package of beef franks from the cooler, grinning. "See if you can get a fire started."

Trevor found plenty of leaves and twigs for kindling. He lugged a dozen smooth stones from the creek and placed them in a circle within spitting distance of the tent. A fledgling fire soon crackled within the ring of rocks. From this crude beginning, Trevor scavenged for larger pieces of wood and soon conjured a respectable bonfire.

Mr. McIntire straightened a couple of metal clothes hangers and stuck two franks on each. He handed one to Trevor, who shoved it into the fire and stared, motionless, until the meat blistered and tinges of black streaked down the sides. It wasn't exactly the fresh game he had imagined but, he had to admit, the open flame gave the dogs quite a savory flavor.

"Let's try fishing tomorrow," suggested Trevor, mouth full and smacking.

"Sounds good to me. But we'll need to turn in early to be up at first light. Are you willing to give up your night owl schedule for that?"

Trevor laughed. "Sure, Dad. Going to bed early just once won't kill me."

Bellies content, they slid into their sleeping bags. Trevor couldn't get over how peaceful the crickets' chirping made him feel. He lay awake listening to them for what must have been well over an hour. What a day. Tomorrow, he thought, promised to be even better.

* * *

"Hey, sleepy head—get up. It's time to make good on that hundred bucks you owe me."

Trevor blinked opened his eyes and rubbed crust from them. What the heck time was it? He could barely see his own hands it was so dark. Then the awareness of cold cheeks, nose, and forehead made its way to his brain. Camping. Saturday. A rush of adrenaline slammed his mind to full wakefulness. He struggled to set himself free from the clutches of the sleeping bag.

"Here's your breakfast." Mr. McIntire tossed him a package of Pop-Tarts.

"So much for roughing it, huh?"

"There's plenty of time to live off the land. No sense starving before we find the right fishing hole."

OK. Dad had a point. Trevor ripped open the silver wrapper and shoved half a pastry in his mouth.

Mr. McIntire swung the beam of his pocket-size Maglite over the fishing gear, grabbed a rod in one hand and the tackle box in the other. Trevor snatched the remaining rod, wolfed down the other half of his Pop-Tart, and trotted behind his father to the brook. He swallowed hard, near gagging from dry throat. When they reached the water, Trevor leaned down and dipped his hands for a drink. Ice-cold water stung his throat. He coughed.

"Let's head downstream a bit," suggested Mr. McIntire. "I think that big rocky area we saw yesterday might be the perfect place to set up."

With a twist of his flashlight to wide beam, Mr. McIntire made his own trail beside the creek bank. Trevor followed. A good ten minutes passed before natural light sneaked into the forest and revealed a point where the stream widened and split around two enormous moss-covered rocks lording over the water.

Trevor stopped and grabbed his dad by the arm. He knew instinctively this was the spot. "Extra twenty for the first catch?"

Mr. McIntire nodded. He pulled a round plastic container from the tackle box, opened it, and scrounged until he found a wriggling earthworm. Trevor snatched away the container and dug out a worm for himself. They baited their hooks, cast their lines, and cranked slowly at the reels.

Trevor felt a tug immediately. He pulled back on the rod and set the hook, then cranked the reel until a flopping five-inch brook trout sprang from the water.

Mr. McIntire frowned. "Better throw it back."

"Are you kidding? This baby's worth twenty bucks!"

"I hardly think that counts—no meat on it."

Trevor grabbed the fish with one hand and unhooked it with the other. "We said first catch—nothing about size." He beamed. "Pay up, old man!"

Mr. McIntire sighed. "All right. But throw it back anyway, will you?"

"Heh." Trevor held the fish close and stared in its eyes. "Thanks for the twenty, baby." Then he flicked it back with a grand sweep and baited another worm.

Late morning the score stood at ten each. Less than half were keepers.

"Let's knock it off, Trev. We have more than we need."

"Aw, come on—how about a tie-breaker?"

"We've got the rest of the weekend for that. Let's get these cleaned up and on the fire. It'll be lunch before you know it."

Trevor scowled, but acquiesced. Back at camp, the aroma of frying fish soon made his stomach rumble, and he was quite happy they hadn't fished longer. As it was, he could hardly wait to eat.

With the fish almost ready, Mr. McIntire rummaged around in the cooler and pulled out a couple of beers which he placed on the ground between himself and Trevor. "I thought we could split a six-pack." He gave Trevor a serious nod. "Just you and me...us men."

Trevor snorted. Dad acted like he was introducing a teenager to alcohol. "Fine." He popped open a beer and downed it in one drawn-out gulp, then tossed the can into the fire. He smirked. "Thanks for the six-pack, but what are *you* going to drink?"

Raised eyebrows met Trevor's cocky stare. Mr. McIntire glanced at the burning beer can, then back. He cleared his throat.

Trevor pulled out his pocket knife and stretched toward the sizzling fish pan. He sliced a chunk from one of the filets and tossed it into his mouth. The trout melted like butter on his tongue. He snatched another beer and popped it open. This time he only guzzled half of it before setting the can down and smacking his lips. "Ahh."

Mr. McIntire shook his head. "I don't know, Trev. I guess...I guess things have changed. I don't know where the time has gone."

A great deal of eating and drinking followed, with Trevor doing most of the drinking. Conversation was sparse.

After the two finished the last fish—and Trevor tossed away the last beer can—Mr. McIntire scrubbed the pan in the creek and packed their cooking gear. He stored everything that might carry the hint of food in the truck and, finally, snuffed out the fire with melted ice from the cooler. Trevor sat through the activities with palms pressed against his cheeks.

By mutual unspoken agreement, they lounged in an extended food-stupor until Mr. McIntire grunted, and stood. "Let's go for a hunt," he said, heading for the truck. Trevor ambled after him, and they both pulled their guns from the back hatch.

They struck out at a right angle to the stream, marching in silence. Hours passed seeing no more than the occasional squirrel or chipmunk. Trevor reflected on the incredible beauty of the multicolored leaves, and the majesty of towering oaks. It dawned on him how much he loved the woods, though he'd never thought of himself as a nature nut.

"Time to head back." Mr. McIntire had stopped a few feet ahead, examining the sky. "If we keep at it any longer it'll be dark when we try to find camp. Maybe we'll have better luck tomorrow."

Trevor started to protest but took his own reading of the sky and thought better of it. They headed back the way they'd come.

About an hour into the return trip, Mr. McIntire startled a small flock of wild ducks hiding behind a thick, green bush. They squawked loud enough to be heard in the next county, and continued the noise as they took to the air with a mad flapping of wings. Mr. McIntire, himself surprised, raised his rifle. Crack! Crack! Both shots went wild. But Trevor had better luck—and the advantage of a shotgun. Boom! Boom! He let go with both barrels and a single duck hit the ground.

Mr. McIntire nodded approval. "Nice job, Trev. I had no idea you could shoot like that."

"Yeah, too bad we didn't have a bet for dinner." Trevor stepped off the trail and retrieved his prize. He led from there the rest of the way back to camp.

With the afternoon sun sinking low, the stream finally came into view. Trevor glanced down at what little shadow he cast, looked back up at the creek, and decided to go left. He guessed correctly, and they found the Explorer in about twenty minutes.

"If you want to get the fire going, I'll clean the bird." Mr. McIntire shot Trevor a sheepish grin. "I guess that's the least I can do for the champion hunter."

"Sure, Dad." Trevor poked around the outskirts of camp for several minutes and soon found just what he needed. A couple of Y-shaped branches made the perfect spit. He had his get-up in place and a fire going well before his dad prepared the bird.

Minutes after Mr. McIntire speared the duck and mounted it on the spit, an electronic rendition of the William Tell Overture intruded on the camp. Mr. McIntire reached for the holster on his belt. He pulled out his cell phone, glanced at the display, and poked a finger to answer it. "Yeah, Matt, what's up?" After listening for several seconds, he squatted on one knee and went back and forth several times with Matt regarding things that had no meaning to Trevor.

When the phone first sounded, Trevor froze. He thought he had Dad to himself for once. And for a few hours, he had forgotten the outside world existed. Now the world had found him—and Dad.

Mr. McIntire cut his eyes toward Trevor and caught his stare. He raised a finger, indicating he would only be a minute. Trevor knew better. There was no such thing as a quick call when it came to Dad's work. The evening was now officially on hold.

Muttering a curse, Trevor shook his head and stood. He trudged to the cooler, yanked it open, and snatched a fresh six-pack. Then he stomped into the woods, following the flow of the stream.

"What? Yeah, Matt, I'm still here. The connection's a little sketchy…" Mr. McIntire's voice faded as Trevor continued on.

He swore. Not loud, just a quiet curse of resignation. "You can take the monkey out of the jungle," he said, "but you can't take the jungle out of the monkey." He cursed again and popped open a beer.

* * *

Sunset burst onto the mountainside in brilliant orange. Trevor sat in a tiny clearing where the trees parted just enough for him to see the colors low in the sky. His thoughts, however, drifted far from the awe-inspiring view. His fifth beer, almost gone, hung from one hand.

"I shoulda stayed home." His words slurred, and he knew it. And he didn't care. "At least I'd had a good friens for gettin' drunk."

The cricket orchestra commenced its nightly chorus as the sun disappeared below the trees. Darkness enveloped the land and Trevor relished the change. The beer had mellowed him, but darkness didn't concern him even when he was sober. Parties started after dark. Nighttime was fun time. Why should it be different here?

But, it *was* different. This drunk was no fun at all. Even five beers couldn't chase away thoughts of Dad and his all-encompassing job.

How long had he been sitting here, anyway? An hour? Two? The night dragged on with no sense of time.

Somewhere in the far stretches of his imagination a sound impressed itself on Trevor's consciousness. More than sound—music. Faint and distant, but definitely music. Strangely familiar, the tune teased his memory. He couldn't name it, couldn't remember where he'd heard it. It was mournful ...like funeral music. Well, maybe. He never went to funerals but it sounded like what he would hear at one.

The tune floated about in Trevor's head, seeking meaning, and at the same time captivating him.

Wait a minute! He sat bolt upright and searched the darkness. He wasn't dreaming, and he was convinced it wasn't the beer. He really did hear music coming from somewhere on the mountain. But who was playing it? And what kind of instrument was it? It was unlike anything he'd ever heard before.

Minutes passed as the song played on, repeating itself in what must be definite verses. "Bagpipes!" A rustic sound, deep and mellow. "No...not bagpipes." Trevor rubbed the growing stubble on his chin.

The music played with his imagination. It spoke his name. "Treeeevvvvoooorrr." That was weird.

"Trevor!"

Wait a minute. That was no bagpipe—someone had really called him. To his left, a bouncing light approached from the direction of camp.

"Over here." Trevor motioned despite the darkness. The bagpipes either stopped playing or he stopped imagining them.

"Trev!" Mr. McIntire closed the gap in a run. He breathed a hearty oath on reaching Trevor. "You had me worried, son. Did you get lost?"

"Huh? Oh, heck no—I'm jus' fine." Trevor tossed his beer can toward the nearby stream. Seconds later there was a distant splash which Trevor punctuated with a belch. "Have a beer." He tossed the one remaining can toward his dad. "Ya hear the music?"

Mr. McIntire caught the beer despite the limited light. He glanced at it, shrugged, then popped it open and took a swig. "Music? Out here?" He shone the light on the four crushed beer cans at Trevor's feet. "I think you're drunk."

Trevor felt mellow, not drunk. He hadn't the gumption to argue, though. But he *had* heard music. Hadn't he?

"Whaddya say, Pop?" Trevor wobbled to his feet. "Time ta go home so's you can finish up your business?"

"I'm sorry, Trev. It was an emergency. It won't happen again."

"*Sure.* Sure thing." Trevor turned to go. He stumbled, flung his hands out to catch himself, then did a wiggly dance until he was sure of his balance.

"Hang on there." Mr. McIntire reached for Trevor's arm. "Let me help you."

Trevor frowned and shook himself loose. "No problem. I got this." He staggered off in the general direction of camp. "Don't worry 'bout me." On his next step he fell headlong in the grass.

* * *

Trevor dreamed of bagpipes. An old Scotsman marched around a tombstone while playing a nameless melody. A man in a dark business suit chased away the Scotsman with a giant cell phone that morphed into a Samurai sword. Atop the mountain, a shadow appeared, grew appendages, and became a magician wearing a star-studded pointy hat. The magician stood beside the wrecked Honda, extended a wand, and zapped the man with the sword, making him disappear.

On Sunday morning Trevor woke with the dream fresh in his mind and an idea bubbling to the surface of his thoughts. The Scotsman. The music. The magician. "The wizard!"

Mr. McIntire stirred in his sleeping bag. He moaned, rolled one way, then the other before settling back down to sleep.

"Ha! That's what I'll write my report on—The Wizard of Winterville."

Not that he believed in the wizard. But it sure sounded like a great story.

Chapter Nine

It really wasn't such a big deal. I never doubted God would do what he said he would do. I'm not so sure it even took faith on my part. I mean, everything just came naturally to me. That's the way it is, I guess, when you're still just an innocent boy at heart.

* * *

Jeremiah hefted Johnny into both arms and strained to stand, but not nearly so much as he expected—the boy had lost considerable weight since leaving home. Abandoning Johnny's scant belongings where they lay, Jeremiah shuffled toward the rocky path leading down the mountain.

After an hour's walk, he ground to a halt, exhausted. Though in good shape for his age, the extra weight taxed Jeremiah's muscles and endurance to the limit. He lowered Johnny to the ground and leaned him against a tree, then rubbed his biceps until the aches subsided. Relieving his back took more effort. He stretched side to side, back and forth until he had new pains from doing *that*.

After a few deep breaths, Jeremiah fell to his knees "Oh, Lord! Give me strength. Keep Johnny alive 'til I can get him home."

No time to pray longer. Jeremiah hefted Johnny back into his arms and continued his journey. He asked the Lord repeatedly for strength and favor on the way down, even as his breathing turned to gasps.

The trail just never seemed to end. Heat from the late morning sun slowed him further, coaxing rivers of sweat from his back. Jeremiah despaired at the distance remaining to the truck.

He paused yet again and set Johnny on the ground, then lay beside him until the jackhammer inside his chest quit pounding. Jeremiah placed his ear next to Johnny's mouth to make sure he was still breathing. He was.

"Oh, Lord. Give me strength. Set your angels around us—and please keep Johnny alive." He ran a hand across his brow and slung sweat to the ground.

After five more minutes of panting, Jeremiah's breathing steadied. With a deep sigh and a glance toward heaven, he hefted his burden and trudged on down the trail. Pain returned within seconds. Despite it he pressed on, but minutes later he ground to a halt again, dropping to his knees, head down with Johnny still in his arms.

His body was through. He saw no way to continue.

But at the sound of approaching hoof beats Jeremiah stirred, lifted his gaze. A rider on horseback appeared from behind the first bend in the trail, charging full tilt.

"Jeremiah!"

The horse's mad pounding made it impossible to recognize the voice, but an instant later, pawing and snorting, the animal reigned up beside the two prone figures.

"Daniel." Jeremiah's voice barely rose above a whisper. "Thank God you're here. But—how did you know?"

"Ida showed up at my place not long after you left. She told me about Johnny, and where you were going." Daniel dismounted and patted his stead. "I thought a horse might come in handy."

"Bless that woman." Jeremiah let Johnny slip to the ground, closed his eyes, and sucked in a deep breath. "And bless you, too, Daniel."

Daniel adjusted his hat, roped the horse to a nearby branch, and leaned over Jeremiah. "Let's get that boy on old Sally here and you can be on your way."

Working together, the two lifted Johnny onto the horse where he landed face down and limp behind the saddle. Daniel formed a sling of sorts from a length of rope and tied it to the saddle horn, then wound it over and around the boy's legs, shoulders, and arms. When he finished, Johnny looked more like the victim of cruel and unusual punishment than a rescue effort. But the contraption held him fast.

"Thank you, Daniel." Jeremiah grabbed his Good Samaritan by the neck, clasped him tight, let him go. "You're a friend indeed. Now, hurry. Get him back to his mother."

"I won't hear of it. Here—mount up." Daniel stepped aside. "Just tie her to a tree near your truck. I'll be on down in my own time."

Jeremiah eyed Daniel but a moment. He wanted to protest, but saw the wisdom of the offer. He lifted a foot into the stirrup and tried to mount, but his weary legs failed him and he slipped back to the ground. Daniel grabbed him by the belt to keep him from falling, then heaved Jeremiah into the saddle.

"Thanks again," said Jeremiah, glancing down. "May the Lord bless you for your kindness."

"God bless you, Pastor. I'll be praying."

Jeremiah double-checked the rope holding Johnny. Satisfied, he tipped his hat, clapped his heels against the horse, and was off in a cloud of dust.

* * *

"Johnny, you've hardly touched your food." Ma, hands on hips, scolded him half-heartedly. She hovered over Johnny while he sat at the kitchen table picking at his plate.

"You need to eat, son." Pa frowned from his chair. "How do you expect to get behind the pulpit Sunday unless you build up your strength?"

Johnny stared into space. He half-processed their words, but his thoughts were on the images running wild through his mind. The bright light on the mountain. The voice. The shadow that became his father. The gift.

He pushed steamed carrots around his plate until they turned to cold rubber, none reaching his mouth. Hunger pangs rumbled his stomach, but served only to remind him of what he had faced on the mountain. He could eat, or not eat—it just didn't matter. Food no longer had a hold on him, its power depleted somewhere along the mountain stream.

"I'm worried, Jeremiah." Ma furrowed her brow. "It's been three days now. He's not acting like himself and he's not eating like he should. Maybe you should call the doctor."

"Eh, I don't see the use in it. He looks a sight better than he did when I first brought him home." Pa reached up and patted Ma on the shoulder. "Maybe his stomach needs to stretch back to proper size."

Johnny listened, and wondered. Why were they so concerned about eating? He'd heard the voice of God. Didn't they realize the significance of that? All they seemed to care about was how much he shoveled down his throat. Why didn't they understand?

"Son, how about you finish up your supper and we'll have some study time together?" Pa clapped Johnny on the arm. "I could help you with Sunday's sermon."

"I have food you know nothing about." Johnny whispered the words, only half focusing on Pa.

A broad grin spread across Pa's face. "You see, Ida? The boy's all right. He's remembering Bible verses." He turned to Johnny. "Come on, son. Let's get to studying. You can worry about food later."

"Yeah." Johnny nodded. "That sounds good."

The two rose as one and stepped out to the front porch. Pa sat in his rocking chair and motioned for Johnny to take Ma's beside him. The rockers fell into a creaking duet on the wooden planks. "You never told me what God showed you on the mountain, son. I'd love to hear about it."

Johnny's gaze swept the front yard. He rocked several more minutes, thinking. Then he halted the rocker and leaned forward. "Pa." Johnny waited for eye contact. "God talked to me. I heard him—with my ears."

Pa loosed the Bible he'd been holding ready. It dropped in his lap. He squirmed, ran a hand over his mouth and down his chin. Fingers drummed the side of his chair.

"You have to believe me, Pa."

More finger drumming. Pa searched the sky for the longest time, glanced at his feet, then let his gaze wander back to Johnny. "What did he say, son?"

"Well, he said he was proud of me for obeying him." Johnny glanced beyond the front yard toward the road and back. "And he said he was giving me a gift."

Pa's rocker creaked to a stop. He gripped the chair arms and cocked his head sideways. "What gift is that?"

Johnny shrugged. "I don't know yet. I got the feeling he would tell me when the time was right."

"Hmm, I don't know." Pa shook his head. "This is all a bit hard to swallow. I'm not convinced God talks right out loud to people any more. That stopped with the apostles, near as I can figure. I'm afraid you're setting yourself up for a fall."

"You don't believe me?"

Jeremiah chewed his bottom lip. "I *want* to believe you. But you're young in the Lord. We get all sorts of crazy notions when we're young. I don't want you losing your faith if it turns out you're wrong."

"I'm not wrong, Pa." Johnny set his jaw. "Just wait. You'll see."

* * *

Johnny couldn't take three steps without someone in the crowd stopping him, asking questions, shaking his hand. He pushed toward the church every chance he got. All he wanted was to get inside and pray.

"Johnny! It's good to have you back." Caroline tossed her head and twirled a lock of hair.

A well-fed woman in a bright red dress pawed Johnny's shoulder and shook him. "I'm so glad you're OK, Johnny."

"Are you gonna tell us what it's like to not eat for two weeks?" This from a wide-eyed little girl tugging at his knee. She stared up at him in wonder as if meeting Santa the week before Christmas.

"I'm going to say just what God wants me to." Johnny leaned down and patted her head, but spoke loud enough so everyone around would hear.

When Johnny finally reached the church, Daniel waited at the door to greet him, a glowing smile adorning his face. He tipped his hat and extended a hand.

"I heard what you did for me, sir. Thanks for your help."

"Just glad to see you back, Johnny."

Only a few minutes remained for prayer as Johnny made his way inside. He found Pa already on his knees in the office, fervently seeking God. Johnny kneeled beside him in silence, a bit curious. Even now, God had yet to reveal the mystery gift.

When music from the service prelude sounded in the office, Pa touched Johnny on the back. "Ready, son?"

Johnny opened his eyes and nodded, then rose. They strode together down the aisle to the seat behind the pulpit. The crowd, larger than ever, shuffled and whispered. Some of them pointed. The noise reminded Johnny of the babbling brook that had sustained him. When the worship songs began Johnny heard only crickets that had been his companions for nights on end. The light-man's words rang in his head. "Show them my love. Touch them with the gift I now place in your hands."

The time for his message drew near, and Johnny's thoughts drifted back into the sanctuary. Well over a hundred people squeezed into the little building, all stealing periodic glances at him. The young ladies giggled when they caught his eye. Older women invariably smiled, while the men simply wore curious expressions. To a person, they all waved paper fans in a futile attempt to chase away the mounting heat.

Every face told a different story, and Johnny wanted to hear them all. He wanted to know them, to know the love God felt for each one. And what about the gift? What wonderful thing did God have in store that would display his love better than it had already been shown?

Johnny stared at Pa as he belted out the notes of every hymn with gusto, his deep baritone vibrating against Johnny's chest. Shame settled over Johnny momentarily. Here he sat, lost in his own thoughts while Pa showered the Lord with praise. Why didn't God choose Pa for the gift?

In her spot on the front pew, Ma sang with more fervor than anyone else in the room, smiling, eyes rarely leaving Johnny. Some said she had the voice of an angel—and Johnny believed them. Why didn't God choose her for the gift?

Daniel Holland and his family—five children in all—took up an entire pew. His two oldest girls sat straight-backed and pretty next to their mom. The three younger boys punched and shoved each other every time their father looked away. Johnny smiled. Where would he be if Mr. Holland hadn't come to the rescue? He had been so foolish to get stuck on the mountain without food. Why did God love such a foolish person?

Skip was there, lost in the multitude on the right-hand side, scraggly hair making him look like he'd lost a fight with an egg beater. On Skip's face rested the answer to every question Johnny might have about serving God. His peculiar friend's miraculous transformation meant the world to Johnny.

Aunt May—the heaviest woman Johnny had ever seen—sat beside Skip, her head adorned with an old straw hat wrapped with a yellow ribbon. She loved the Lord as much as anyone Johnny knew, but she rarely made it to church. Arthritis crippled her knees and filled her joints with pain. Her heavy cane—thick as a baseball bat—leaned against the pew in front of her.

Row after row, tales of triumph and woe, hope and defeat. Many folks Johnny knew, some he didn't. Judging from their embarrassed yawns, a few wished they were still in bed. Johnny loved even these, and knew God did too. He had preached about love in every sermon the past several weeks, but now a new feeling struck him, a deep feeling of love he'd never imagined before. And there was warmth in this feeling—warmth like the light from the angel on the mountain.

Tears streamed down Johnny's cheeks. He knew now. He understood just how much God loved his children, and it overwhelmed him. He covered his eyes.

Pa placed a hand on Johnny's shoulder. Johnny wiped his tears, sniffed, and met his father's gaze.

"It's time, son." Pa cocked his head, indicating the pulpit. The music had stopped.

Johnny nodded, dried his face along his jacket sleeve, and limped to the lectern, cane in hand. A hush fell over the crowd. Every eye clung to Johnny as he gripped both sides of the pulpit— and tried to get a grip on himself. He sucked in a deep breath.

"I can't get over," Johnny began, wiping away one last tear, "what an incredible God we serve." His voice carried softly through the air. Those in the back leaned forward to hear. "In the past several days I've been closer to the Almighty than I thought was possible. And yet, every day I find there's more to God than I knew the day before.

"Today, God gave me a glimpse of how much he loves each of you." Johnny raised his voice now, confident, secure. "He's given me a love for all of you that I can hardly contain. God wants everyone here to experience that love. It's free. All you have to do is reach out and take it." He raised a hand and grasped air symbolically.

His simple words mesmerized the crowd. Even the young sat still and quiet. It had to be God, he thought—God, speaking through him.

This wasn't the message he'd prepared, but he felt it was the message God wanted him to preach. He continued expounding on love for several minutes, then felt compelled again to tell of God's desire to see his people whole.

The concept burst upon him anew. God wanted everyone whole! Words burned inside him, fought the limitations of his vocal cords, rushed to find their intended marks. Johnny's voice rose in a fever pitch as the message of love and wholeness burst forth.

"God doesn't cause sickness! God *hates* to see you sick." He raised a fist in the air. "The Lord wants nothing more than to see you set free from every ailment and every disease!"

He no longer controlled the words—they gushed forth like a raging river, eliciting gasps from every part of the sanctuary.

Johnny extolled the virtues of God's love and healing power just shy of half an hour, the crowd hanging on his every word. He built to a thundering crescendo. "You must have faith! Faith is—" A tingling deep in the pit of his stomach stopped Johnny mid-sentence. He lowered his head and stood in silence, listening, then gazed toward heaven.

Now he knew.

When he focused back on the congregation, Johnny's words flowed at a gentle pace. "God gave me a special gift." Heads nodded all about the room. "And he's asked me to share it with you."

Johnny reached for his cane then did something he'd never seen a preacher do before. He stepped down from the pulpit and made his way into the midst of the people. Flitting from pew to pew, he studied each surprised face. When he neared the front again, he clacked his cane against the floor, then whirled to face the assembly.

"You!" Johnny pointed at a heavyset farmer on the second row. "God loves you." The man burst into tears. He lifted a hand and shouted thanks to God.

"You!" Johnny pointed to Daniel, five rows back on the left-hand side. "God loves you!" Daniel jerked as if punched. He broke down and wept, face in his hands.

Johnny moved side to side down the aisle. "You!" he said over and over, pointing as the Lord prompted him. "God loves you!"

They laughed. They cried. They shouted. One lady fainted in her husband's arms.

Then for an eternal moment, Johnny paused, head down, hands entwined. When he finally raised back up, he was already in motion toward the pew where Skip sat next to Aunt May. He searched the row face by face until his eyes came to rest on the old woman. She stared back at him, eyes wide as saucers.

Johnny pushed his way into the pew, bumping knees and stepping on toes, until he reached Aunt May. He placed a hand on her quivering shoulder. "You," he whispered so only a chosen few could hear. "God gave me a special gift when I was on the mountain. He wants you to have that gift, Aunt May." Then Johnny leaned down until he was nose to nose with the old woman. He rested both hands on the straps of her faded gingham dress and locked eyes with her. "God loves you, Aunt May. And in the name of Jesus, he wants you whole."

People debated what followed for years. Some claimed a bolt of electricity shot from Johnny's hand and engulfed the old lady. Others said Johnny commanded her to get out of the pew. A few insisted that he pushed her. These and a hundred other rumors and tall tales followed Johnny for the rest of his days.

Truth be told, even Johnny wasn't certain of the details. He only remembered two things. First, Aunt May jumped from her seat and screamed at the top of her lungs—and she had some mighty fine lungs. Second, to everyone's amazement, she kicked her cane to the floor and danced past him into the aisle—all two hundred and eighty-five pounds of her—while shouts of praise pierced the air with every swing of her billowing yellow dress.

Chapter Ten

When Trevor's phone rang, he glanced at the screen, saw it was his dad, and answered right away. Dad *never* called during the week. "Yeah, Dad—what's up?"

"I forgot to tell you the dealership called. They said the Explorer needs new tires and they didn't have the right size in stock when they sent it home with you. They've got them now, so I need you to go take care of it as soon as you can."

"OK, sure. Is that all?"

"Yes. I've got to go now, but get those tires taken care of—they made it sound urgent."

The call ended before Trevor could respond. He pocketed the phone, then jogged down the hall to English Lit.

"Good afternoon, class." Professor Litchfield issued the greeting in his usual dreary tone, leaning forward over his old wooden desk, chair creaking behind him. "I trust everyone had a restful weekend. I see from your eager faces that you can't wait to get started, so without further ado, it's time to choose the subjects for your writing projects. I'll try to keep this as simple as possible. As I call the roll, please respond with your selection."

While Professor Litchfield churned through the list of students and recorded their answers, Trevor slinked down in his seat and doodled along the edges of the paper containing the research subjects. The writing project had slipped his mind. His weekend had been full with the camping trip, and various scenes from the outing still reigned at the forefront of his thoughts.

"Mr. McIntire."

Trevor heard his name, but kept doodling. He pushed his pen in circles until a dark blue cloud formed at the top of the paper. Then a desk took shape under the cloud, and a teacher behind it. A fat bolt of lightning sprang from the cloud and turned the teacher into a puddle of grease. His pen ran dry.

"Mr. McIntire, your subject, please."

Darn pen. Trevor banged it on the desk, knowing he had to make a decision. Just as the teacher rose to call a third time, Trevor looked him in the eye and cut him short. "The Wizard of Winterville."

Half the class erupted in laughter. Some gave him curious looks. Trevor pulled a spare pen from his backpack and resumed scribbling.

"I don't believe I see that on the approved subject list, Mr. McIntire."

Trevor aimed his pen at the professor. "You said we could pick our own subject if we didn't like what we saw on the list."

Mr. Litchfield peered over the top of wire-rim glasses. "What I said is that I would entertain other ideas. I did *not* say I would consider *entertaining* ideas. Now," he tapped a finger on the subject list, "I suggest you pick something with a bit more literary appeal—something serious, and scholarly."

"No!" Trevor's face grew warm. "This *is* a serious subject." The professor drew a breath to speak, but Trevor beat him to it. "A lot of people in this town believe the wizard legend. I think researching their beliefs is a legitimate project. I'll find out what started the legend, and I'll prove it's all fake."

Kenny snorted. "Woohoo!" He pounded his desk. "You get 'em, Trev!"

Professor Litchfield's face turned to ice. "That is quite enough, Mr. Jackson." He turned back to Trevor, arms crossed. "I accept your proposal, Mr. McIntire." He flicked his gaze to Kenny and back. "However, you will treat this with all the seriousness that a scholarly work deserves. You will not use this as an opportunity to make light of this class, or this assignment." He unfolded his arms and leaned forward across the desk. "Do we have an understanding, Mr. McIntire?"

Trevor met the teacher's piercing stare with a smirk. The challenge excited him. "Yeah." He stole a quick glance at Kenny. "You're on."

* * *

The storekeeper shook his head. "You're asking for trouble, kid." He scanned the entire store, then looked back at Trevor. The clerk—Mike—was the same man Trevor had the confrontation with the week before, just prior to his camping trip.

"Please, mister." Trevor conjured up every ounce of humility and charm he could muster, and thrust it into a smile. "I'm not trying to cause trouble. Like I told you, this is for a research project. If you don't believe me, you can call my professor—Mr. Litchfield. He'll vouch for me. I've got to write a paper on the wizard so I can pass the class."

"Now, you listen to me." Mike shook a finger in Trevor's face. "Last time you were here, you got all the information you're going to get. The mountain folk take serious stock in the wizard, and I go along with them. In turn, they do a good business with me. But when somebody like you shows up asking all sorts of questions, they get nervous. And when they get nervous, they stay away. When they stay away, I don't make money. And when I don't make money, I ain't happy. So, I'm telling you to drop this." Mike flipped a thumb toward the door. "Now, get along your merry way."

Trevor just knew he was being stonewalled. He wracked his brain for a craftier approach. "OK, mister. I understand." He drooped his shoulders and hung his head. "I know it's a sensitive subject." He raised up just enough to catch Mike's eye. "But forget about the project for a minute. Think about how I feel. I never know when something I say is going to offend somebody. One wrong word and the whole town is mad at me. I don't even know what I said that made your friend so upset.

"If I could just find out what's going on, maybe I could stay out of trouble. As it is, I never know when somebody's going to fly off the handle. I'd *like* to be more respectful, but I don't know how. Can you at least tell me what I shouldn't say? If you can do that, then I'll be out of your hair." He made the puppy-dog eyes that always worked on Lisa.

Mike lifted a hand to the back of his balding head and scratched while he studied the ceiling. Then he squinted at Trevor, sighed, and stared out the window.

"All right, kid." Mike turned back to Trevor. "I'll tell you everything I know. But you gotta promise you won't come back with any more questions. This is it, OK?"

Trevor shrugged. "No problem." He swallowed a smile.

Mike went behind the counter and flopped down on an old barstool. "This is what I know. The locals believe a wizard lives somewhere on the mountain. They say he mostly stays hidden, but he comes out a few times a month to work his magic. The wizard is crazy sensitive—he don't like nobody talking about him behind his back. You bring him up in public, and you might just find yourself under a curse.

"Now, on the other hand, if you have a special need and you're willing to pay the price, sometimes the wizard grants you a favor. But he only helps people that respect him, so they don't like anybody talking about him for fear of making him mad." Mike shrugged. "That's all there is to it. You see—not much different from what I told you last time."

Trevor started to ask a question, but formed his own answer. "I get it. All the talk around town is just a big joke. Everybody is really just making fun of those mountain goofs." He nodded. "Makes sense."

Mike maintained a poker face. "Yeah. You got it, kid. Now, will ya drop this thing and stop scaring my customers away?"

"Hmm. You sure there's nothing else?"

Mike rolled his eyes. "You got the whole thing. The end. OK?"

"You wouldn't be holding out on me, would you?"

Now Mike frowned. He planted both hands on his hips. "What good would *that* do? You'd just keep coming back, pestering me to death until you got what you wanted." He rose from the stool. "Now, if you don't mind, I have a business to run."

Trevor looked him up and down. "Well, OK, dude. I guess that's good enough." He turned to go, but stopped and looked back as his hand brushed the doorknob. "But if I find out you're lying to me, we're going to have us another little visit. And if I have to come back, you're never going to hear the end of it."

* * *

"Come on, man—you have no idea how much time I put into this." Trevor kicked the floor near the leg of Professor Litchfield's desk. "Everybody clams up as soon as they hear the word 'wizard.' They know something, but they're not telling. It's like there's some deep, dark secret spooking the whole town out of their wits."

The professor glanced once more at Trevor's paper, shook his head, and tossed it on his desk. "I sympathize, Mr. McIntire. Truly, I do. But I hardly see how two paragraphs in two week's time could be considered due diligence. I happen to know how backwards the locals can be. For that reason—and that reason alone—I'm willing to let you pick another subject, and—"

"No!" Trevor banged his fist on the teacher's desk. "This hick town's *not* going to get the best of me. Somebody out there's willing to talk, and I'm going to find him if it kills me. I just need a little more time. That's all I'm asking."

Professor Litchfield pursed his lips. Was he hiding a smile? Trevor glared at him.

"I see. Very well—I'm impressed by your fortitude. You have a week to catch up with the rest of the class—"

Trevor started to speak, but the teacher kept right on going.

"—including turning in your final draft on time. Otherwise, I'm afraid you're going to be quite disappointed with your grade."

Gritting his teeth, Trevor clamped back on what he *really* thought, and stalked back to his desk.

Kenny held his fist out for a bump, but Trevor ignored it. Kenny winked. "Way to tell him, boss man."

Trevor glowered at Kenny. He collapsed into his desk with a grunt of satisfaction. It felt good to win a battle, even a small one.

The minute class ended, Trevor charged straight for Lisa and Brent. "Hey, guys—I need your help. Tell me about the wizard."

"What do you mean?" Lisa wore a puzzled expression.

Trevor crossed his arms. "Don't start with me. I need information."

"Why are you asking *us*?" Brent looked just as confused as Lisa.

"Yeah." Lisa shrugged. "We don't know anything. Except like, you know, just the dumb stories we told you."

Trevor's cheeks grew warm. "Well tell me more dumb stories! Where'd you hear the stuff? Give me *something*." He huffed, then pulled a notebook and pen from his backpack.

"It's just a joke, Trev." Brent shook his head. "It's kind of weird you're taking it so serious."

Trevor frowned at Brent then turned back to Lisa. "You said he could make things magically appear, or something like that. What else? I don't care how stupid it sounds."

"You want to know all the legends?" Lisa scrunched up her face. "They're just crazy stories. How's that going to help you write a research paper."

"I don't *care* about the paper." Trevor let fly a vulgar curse. "I want to know *every*thing."

Lisa just cocked her head and stared.

"Hey, I know *all* that stuff," said Brent. "The wizard is *awesome*. He makes gold coins out of rocks, and has a whole dungeon full of treasure. He zaps people he doesn't like with his wand and turns them into frogs. And—get this—when it's a full moon he plays a magic organ that hypnotizes everybody on the whole mountain. They turn into zombies and he makes 'em his slaves." Brent went on for several minutes, with Trevor wondering how he managed to take a breath. According to Brent, there wasn't anything the wizard couldn't do or hadn't done.

Kenny wandered up to the group just in time to catch the tail end of Brent's speech. "You're not filling that innocent boy's head with wild tales, are you? Feed him too much of that stuff and you'll make a believer out of him." He slapped Trevor hard on the shoulder, laughing.

A not-entirely-friendly shoving session ensued when Trevor flung out a hand and knocked Kenny off balance. Lisa pulled Trevor away before things went too far.

"For your information," Trevor said, after peppering Kenny with a few choice expletives, "I got Brent to talk about the wizard. At least *some*body around is good for something."

"Heh." Kenny lunged at Trevor just enough to fake him out. "Can't get the local yokels to talk, so you put the squeeze on your friends, huh? Say, Trev," Kenny's face lit up, "I think I know what your problem is. It's your face, dude. You're scaring everybody away."

Brent and Kenny laughed. Lisa's eyes twinkled, but she covered her smile.

"They don't even *look* at my face!" Trevor felt his temperature rise. "You guys wouldn't believe how crazy things are. A barbecue joint locked the doors on me when I was walking down the sidewalk. It's like these people know who I am and they know when I'm coming."

"Ha!" Kenny snorted. "Maybe they're gettin' inside info from the wizard."

"Come *on*, man. Enough of the jokes. I need help." A grin eased its way onto Trevor's face. "I'll buy you a drink if you tell me what you know."

Kenny lifted a hand to one ear and played Groucho Marx with his eyebrows. "I think I hear someone playing my song."

Trevor readied his pen. "So tell me what you know."

"Uh-uh." Kenny's smile turned devilish. "You get me that drink—*then* I'll talk." He gave Trevor a friendly shove toward the parking lot and motioned for the other two to follow. "I'll drive now. Somebody else can drive later."

* * *

Trevor cut school Friday. He woke at his normal time, but packed his bags instead of his books. With his mom still in bed, and Dad not due in until late, he planned to be long gone before anyone noticed.

On a whim, he retrieved his old acoustic guitar from its resting place at the back of his closet where it had been accumulating dust next to an old PlayStation and three jumbled stacks of CD's. Maybe it would help him relax before turning in at night.

He slung his backpack over one shoulder and tucked the guitar against his other side. Halfway out the front door, it struck him that it would look awful suspicious when he didn't show up for a few days. The last thing he wanted was a frantic call from Mom, so he grabbed a stray piece of paper from the kitchen counter and scribbled a quick note on it. *That* should keep everyone off his trail.

Driving through the back roads in the Explorer brought back bittersweet memories. Some of the time he had spent with Dad had been wonderful. If only the weekend had ended on the same good note which it began. That call from the dark side, though, showed him where Dad's true loyalty lay. Mom always said that's why he brought home the big bucks. Trevor cursed silently. Big freakin' deal.

Many miles and long minutes later, Trevor pulled into the same campsite where he and Mr. McIntire had spent their weekend together. The truck lurched to a halt and Trevor hopped out. He hefted his backpack, strapped the guitar onto it with bungee cords, and pulled the whole affair over his shoulders.

After a moment's contemplation, he checked his watch and compass, then headed toward the area where he'd had his private beer-and-pity party. It was there, while drowning his sorrows, that he'd heard the eerie music. If he found the musician, he might also find out something about the wizard.

The music seemed to emanate from somewhere far beyond the stream. So, after reaching the clearing where he'd spent his drunk, he slogged across to the other side. Searching the tree line, he found no clear trail, so he simply set off through the middle of the woods. A thick canopy of leaves and branches shielded him from the sun, making the journey an easy one. An hour passed while he navigated the gentle incline without breaking a sweat.

A pathway soon appeared at a right angle to Trevor's direction of travel, just before a wall of thick underbrush that blocked further progress ahead. To his left, the path led up a steep incline. To the right, it sloped away. He chose the downhill route.

After following the path for almost hour, Trevor found the first sign—other than the trail—that intelligent life had been this way before. A rusted and ramshackle mobile home squatted about twenty feet off the side of the path. Kudzu crept over everything but the door—and the door looked like it might lose the battle soon.

Trevor breathed an expletive. He scratched his head as he looked up and down the trail. "How the heck did they get that thing up here?" Any clues had been lost to time—and kudzu.

Fresh-trampled greenery formed a walkway to the door of the old relic. Curiosity got the better of him. He stepped off the path and approached the trailer.

The door hung half open on rusty hinges. Trevor swung it wide, and it screeched like fingernails running down a chalkboard. He peeked inside but it was too dark to see.

Pulling himself in by the sides of the doorframe, Trevor waited for his eyes to adjust. A one-room pit materialized before him. Girlie magazines, dishes, and filthy rags covered the floor, making it difficult to walk. Miscellaneous and unidentifiable knickknacks hung suspended from the ceiling. A rotting couch, chair, and loveseat hugged three different walls, sagging under the load of dozens of unsealed trash bags. A coffee mug and a broken food-stained plate rested on a small footstool. Well-worn combat boots hung on a strap near the couch, just above a straw pallet matted down thin enough to indicate someone might have slept on it recently.

Trevor wrinkled his nose at a strange mixture of sweat, dirt, and...urine? All of a sudden his stomach's contents felt insecure. And though he'd never considered himself claustrophobic, the walls felt like they were closing in on him. "And Mom says *my* room is a mess." Finding nothing wizardly, he turned to go. He set one foot out the door and...

KABOOM!

"Yiiiaah!" The explosion startled Trevor such that he lost his footing and, eyes not yet adjusted to the sun, stumbled face first to the ground. The world spun for a moment, then Trevor pushed up on his elbows. He coughed out a mouthful of vegetation and a lungful of dust just as another blast set his ears to ringing.

"Get outta here, ya thief!"

Trevor searched left and right, but couldn't find the source of the voice. He tried rolling into the foliage to get out of the open, but the backpack made the maneuver impossible so he scrambled up on all fours and skittered back toward the mobile home. With one foot in the doorway, Trevor spared a quick glance over his shoulder and came to an unconscious halt.

A monster crashed out of the bushes at the far end of the trailer. The giant towered seven feet or more in the air and had to weigh at least three hundred pounds. Muscles bulged from the sleeves of his tattered T-shirt, stretching the fabric to the breaking point. A carpet of dark hair clung to his neck. Trevor thought him more animal than human.

Twin barrels of an over-under shotgun leveled in Trevor's direction. If he hadn't heard the blasts, Trevor would have believed the gun a toy, appearing so small as it did in those hulking arms.

But knowing the weapon was real failed to thaw Trevor's legs. Oblivious to the danger, he continued to stare.

The titan snarled. "What's wrong wid ya?"

His accent, Trevor decided, suggested an aversion to proper schooling.

"Get outta here afore I blow your head off, ya no good thieving rascal."

Something in the back of Trevor's mind suggested the giant either was a poor shot, or wasn't all that interested in killing him. He found his voice and took a chance on the latter. "I'm not a thief." He faced the giant straight on and displayed open palms.

"You were stealin' my food. That makes you a thief." The gun waggled sideways toward the trail. "Now get."

Trevor shook his head. "I don't want your food." He patted his backpack. "I have my own. I'm looking for the wizard. Have you seen him?"

The big man raised the gun and sighted down the barrel. "I don't need the likes of you runnin' round here. I'm gonna count to three."

Though it would be entertaining to find out if the oaf could actually make it that far, Trevor chose caution. He raised both hands and eased away from the home. "OK, I'm going."

The gunsight tracked him.

Several feet up the trail, Trevor turned and looked back. The giant eyed him like prey, gun following his every move. Trevor shifted the backpack off his hip where it had started to chafe, frowned in resignation, and resumed his trek.

"So much for the friendly mountain folk."

* * *

Saturday morning, after an uneventful night on the mountain, Trevor resumed his quest. He skirted the giant's home, giving it a wide berth by way of a circuitous route through the trees and brush, and continued exploring the downward leg of the trail. That stupid trailer had been hauled in from somewhere, and there was no way it came from the up side of the path. There had to be civilization somewhere down near the valley.

An hour and a half of planting one foot before the other landed him in a place where the path widened to reveal a small shantytown. A dozen rotting homes sagged in random spots on either side of the pathway. Clapboard shacks made up the majority of residences, but a mobile home that couldn't have been thirty feet long, and a hut—complete with thatched roof—added variety to the mix. All the "houses" showed various signs of occupation, from clothes drying on lines, to shady characters milling about performing various tasks.

Just the kind of freaks who'd believe in a wizard.

A wrinkled old woman in a bonnet perched on half a whiskey barrel in front of the first shack, shucking corn with shriveled hands. She looked up when Trevor drew near, eyes full of nothing.

"Hi!" Trevor donned his brightest smile.

The woman dipped her head in the barest nod of acknowledgment, then tore off a handful of husk and tossed it at Trevor's feet.

"I'm writing a paper about people on the mountain. Can I ask you a few questions?"

The old lady lowered the basket to the ground, stood, and hobbled into her shack. Trevor stared after her. "I feel like I'm in a cartoon."

He turned to the next home just in time to come face-to-face with a white-bearded oldster poking his head out a ragged hole that passed for a window.

"What do *you* want?" The growl barely sounded human. At least he didn't have a gun.

"Um…I'm writing a paper about life in the mountains. I was wondering if I could ask you a few questions."

The guy spat, missing Trevor's boots by inches. "Ain't got time for no questions, boy."

"I'll only take a minute…" But the man had already retreated into his shack.

Scratching his head, Trevor scanned the other homes. He sighed, trudged to the next one, and the next. Every response either rivaled the first or made it look pleasant in comparison. The less hospitable inhabitants convinced him to leave with various weapons. At the last home—the straw-roofed hut—a maniac with a foot-long beard chased him away.

"Waaahhhh!" The wild-eyed hillbilly sounded like a dying mountain lion. "Outsider! Outsider! I'll teach you, pokin' round here!"

Trevor's heart skipped a beat when the crazy old coot lunged at him. He took off running with his aggressor right on his heels. Fortunately, the lunatic ran out of steam a half mile from the village, and Trevor got away. He paused a minute later, panting, and stared back up the trail to make sure he was safe.

Sweat dripped down his forehead and into his eyes. He swiped an arm over his brow, then cursed the loon for all he was worth. Eventually, Trevor's panting transformed into normal breathing and he started back down the trail at a restrained pace. "Well," he muttered, "I might not find the wizard, but I've got a *ton* of material for a stand-up routine."

* * *

"Hello?" Mrs. McIntire laid her Cosmopolitan magazine beside the couch.

Lisa's voice came through the speaker. "Is Trevor there? He's not answering his phone."

"No, didn't he tell you? He's spending the week at Kenny's."

"He won't answer my texts or calls. I was getting worried."

Mrs. McIntire frowned, tapping French manicured fingernails on the couch. "It's odd he doesn't answer. But, you know Trevor."

"I haven't seen him at school all week, either. But Kenny was there."

"The whole week? I had no idea he was skipping school. But I shouldn't be surprised. He's always doing something crazy like that."

"Should we call the police?"

"Oh, heavens—I don't think so. Let me see if he'll pick up for me, and I'll ask James what to do. You keep trying, too, and let me know if you reach him."

"OK, I will. You do the same, OK? Bye."

Mrs. McIntire clicked off her phone and exchanged it for her magazine. She sighed. "That boy. If playing hooky affects his grades, James will never let him hear the end of it."

* * *

"Trev! Where *are* you?"

Trevor looked around. Pretty much, he was nowhere. He shrugged, though no one could see it. "Umm... somewhere on the mountain."

"*What?*"

Trevor winced and pulled the phone away from his ear.

"You mean you spent the whole week on that mountain and didn't even tell me?" Lisa cursed him. "Why didn't you answer my calls? You could have at least texted."

"Reception's kind of spotty up here. Sorry."

"Sorry? I've been worried sick."

Trevor glanced at the sun. It would be dark in less than two hours. "Yeah, well. Sorry. I'll make it up to you when I get back."

"When you get back! How long are you planning to stay up there?"

"I don't know. Maybe through Sunday."

"Trevor! Get off that mountain and come home *now*. We have *got* to talk."

"OK. See you soon."

"Trevor, I...Trevor?"

The cell phone slid back in its clip. He could argue with Lisa another time.

A short ways up the trail gray wisps from a smoldering campfire beckoned him to explore. Trevor trekked in that direction and, as he drew closer, a four-man army tent in desert-themed camouflage came into view. The door flap hung loose, and rustling noises emanated from within.

Exercising a fresh appreciation for caution, Trevor stood back a safe distance from the tent and cupped his hands. "Hello?"

The rustling stopped. A thin, brawny man a good three times Trevor's age appeared outside the tent so fast that Trevor blinked. Dark splotches mottled the fellow's wrinkles. A sweat patch covered the belly of his muscle shirt. For several seconds the two stared at each other.

"Whaddya want, boy?" The old guy folded his arms high across his chest, just below a tuft of white hair poking past the neckline of his shirt. He spat a wad of tobacco in the dirt and squinted at Trevor.

"I'm from the other side of the mountain." Trevor pointed left. He tried to slur his words like the natives. "It's my sister. She's sick— bad sick. I, uh, came to get some help."

"So?" Another wad of tobacco splatted the ground. "I ain't no doctor."

"I heard you have a way around here—a special way when the doctor can't fix it. I heard people around here know how to take care of things. Is it true? Can you help me—uh, my sister?" Trevor did his best to look desperate.

The man continued squinting for the longest time. "Maybe," he said at last. "But not now. I got me some huntin' to do. Come back in two weeks. Then we'll talk."

"But—"

"If yore sister lived long enough for you to hike halfway round the mountain, she'll live long enough for me to get fresh meat. Now, you best leave me be 'til then." The man dismissed Trevor with a wave and disappeared back into his tent.

Trevor stared after him. Two weeks would be forever long. But this might be his lucky break.

Chapter Eleven

I'll never forget that day. It was the beginning of everything. Sure, some pretty spectacular things had happened already. But nothing else compared. My whole life changed. In just one day.

* * *

Trinity Pentecostal Church couldn't hold them all. Ten rough-lumber pews each had room for eight parishioners in the tiny whitewashed frame building at the opposite end of the county from Mt. Carmel. And every seat was filled. Another forty or so squeezed shoulder to shoulder along the walls while dozens more crowded the foyer and outside the front door, pushing, shouting, and carrying on like it was New Year's Eve.

Pastor Frank Martin, seated next to Johnny and Pa in a chair to the left of the pulpit, leaned over and spoke just loud enough to be heard above the din. "Can you believe this?" His wide-eyed gaze never left the crowd. "I've never seen anything like it."

"Yes, but that's a good thing, don't you think, Frank?"

"I'm not sure *what* to think." Pastor Martin let his gaze circle the room. He straightened his tie. "I mean, I always wanted to pack the church, but what are we supposed to *do* with all of 'em?"

Reverend Johnny Jones—his official title these past two months—also eyed the throng. He'd never seen so many people fill a church and he'd never seen such energy in a crowd. He had to admit it was a bit of a circus, but Johnny chose to view the bedlam as hunger for God.

Though he usually felt nervous before a sermon, today a supernatural peace permeated the chaos. It could be that Johnny's senses had dulled after standing in front of so many congregations and witnessing countless miracles firsthand. Or, this special calm could be another of the Father's gifts.

The pianist kicked off a lively tune Johnny hadn't heard before. Some of the chatter quieted as people began to sing. Most of the regulars—at least, Johnny guessed they were the regulars—swayed in time to the music, clapping their hands. This was something new. Nobody at Mt. Carmel or the other churches he'd visited worshipped with such vigor. He didn't know people were even *allowed* to move like that in church.

Johnny bowed in silent prayer. He asked God to help him with the sermon, and to show him which person should get the special healing. After listening for a moment, he raised his head and searched the crowd. Lately, he had made a game of guessing who God would pick.

Several in the congregation caught him looking at them, and this set up a commotion of hands waving, faces smiling, and fingers pointing. They had heard the rumors—only one person got the touch. And it was true. Though Johnny wished he could help them all, so far God had never allowed him to heal more than one person on any given day.

When the choruses ended, and Pastor Martin introduced him, Johnny limped to the pulpit and opened in prayer. The pianist continued a gentle prance upon the keyboard. Johnny peeked open an eye. Didn't she understand he was praying? She saw him, and smiled. It wasn't until Johnny pronounced "Amen" that the music finally stopped, at which point Johnny couldn't help but sigh.

The congregants leaned forward, gripping their seats, whispering to each other while he spoke. He knew they all wondered—just as he did—who would be the lucky one. But Johnny had more than miracles in mind. He wanted them to know God's love.

"Turn your lives over to God, my friends." Johnny extended his hands in a perfect Billy Graham pose. "Don't look for the gift, but look to the giver. *He's* what's important—not the things of this world." Johnny paused, praying under his breath. He wanted them to truly receive the message. How could he remove the distraction of the miracles?

Commotion somewhere near the back of the room disrupted Johnny's train of thought. Heads turned and a low murmuring grew louder. A voice beyond the doors—a woman's, perhaps— yelled over the growing disturbance. Johnny couldn't quite make out what she said, but the sound grew louder, and closer.

A young lady more or less Johnny's age burst into the sanctuary, shoving men twice her size out of the way. "Step aside! Move, I tell you!" She pushed toward the altar, rippling the crowd sideways.

When she burst into the open, Johnny gaped at her. Fiery red hair rolled past dainty features down to her shoulders, marking her like a rose in a sea of daisies. She flung a hand at the strands of unruly curls covering her eyes, exposing rosy cheeks. Johnny couldn't determine whether nature had colored her face, or if she was flushed from battling her way through the sea of worshipers.

A hush fell over the crowd.

Johnny froze, a statue of granite. She stamped to the base of the altar. And he watched her. She glanced behind her, glaring at those who stared. And he watched her. She whipped back around toward the pulpit and fixed her gaze on him. And he watched her.

She was the one.

"I've come for a miracle." She announced it chin forward, eyes full of fire, defiant. Her voice—oh, her voice. It tickled the air like a whispering angel, yet carried the same authority as a crack of thunder, strength and beauty fused in a tantalizing package, all tinged with an Irish lilt. "Is this the right place?"

Until this very instant, Johnny had never given a woman a second look. But she—she captivated him. And at the same time, deep in his spirit, he again recognized God's prompting for the gift. She was the one.

"What's the matter?" She planted both hands on her hips. "Cat got your tongue?" When Johnny didn't respond, she huffed, then turned to the onlookers. "And just what are you gawking at? Does anyone have their wits about them?" She raked back her hair and turned to Johnny.

Pa recovered first. "You've come to the right place, ma'am." He stood, motioning her closer. "We'll be glad to pray for you."

"It's not myself what needs the praying—it's my mother. She's on her death bed this very minute, and..." Her tone softened and her countenance fell. "She's far too young to die."

For a moment the young lady appeared as though she might cry. Then the fire returned. "So is it true—can you help her?"

"We'll certainly pray, miss." Pa sounded hesitant. "Johnny?"

"Wha...?" Johnny tore his gaze from the captivating face. He shook his head at Pa. "No—not here. I have to go with her." He reached for his cane and stepped toward the choleric angel.

She snorted at him. "So—this one's not dumb after all."

Johnny shuffled forward, studying his shoes. "Um... Lead the way, miss."

"Hmph." She wheeled around and the crowd parted for her like the Red Sea before Moses. Her scent struck Johnny for the first time—not perfume, but the natural fragrance of a beautiful woman. He glued his eyes to the ground and followed her skirt.

Don't let her distract me, Lord. Help me focus on you.

As Johnny watched his shoes, the wood church floor turned to concrete steps, and then to the dirt of the parking lot. The young woman stopped beside a pickup truck. Johnny raised his head just enough to see that it sported more rust than paint, and its fenders appeared they might fall off at the least provocation. The young woman creaked open the driver's door, hopped inside, and slammed the door after her. "Get in," she called through the window. "It's not far."

Johnny swallowed. It wouldn't be appropriate for him to be alone with her. What should he do?

"Hurry!"

"Um..." Johnny studied the ground. "You go ahead." He strained to speak above a whisper. "I'll follow."

"Suit yourself." She cranked over the engine until it caught, then yelled out the window as the vehicle lurched into motion. "I hope you drive faster than you walk!"

Johnny jogged, best as his leg let him, over to Pa's truck. It sputtered and shook when he keyed the starter, then chugged out an eager rhythm.

Movement in the corner of Johnny's eye drew his attention. A dilapidated Chevrolet lurched out of the parking lot, rear wheels spitting dirt, engine roaring. It screamed bloody murder every time the gears changed.

Johnny eased out the clutch and crept through the rows of cars. A glance left showed the old Chevy a half mile away already. He shifted through second and into third, then put the gas pedal on the floor. Just when he built enough speed to keep his quarry in check, it dropped out of sight behind a rise.

When the truck began to roar, Johnny glanced at the speedometer and his eyebrows went up. That crazy girl would get them both killed if she kept up this pace. But there was nothing for it. If he slowed down he would lose her.

Wary of his speed, but settling into the chase, Johnny peeked in the rearview mirror. He did a double take. "Oh, dear Lord—no." Dozens of vehicles stretched out behind him as far as he could see.

Johnny had no idea how long he'd been traveling when, far ahead, the Chevy's one working brake light popped on and the truck veered left. Johnny slowed and, seconds later turned onto a gravel drive where he found himself bumping along toward a ramshackle wooden farmhouse a hundred yards ahead. The girl's pickup sat beside the front porch, empty.

He rolled to a stop, set the parking brake, and hopped out. A cursory glance over the property caused him to wonder what kind of people lived here. Gray cedar planks, perhaps a hundred years old, crawled up the side of the house and hung tenuously by rusty nails. Every single board warped so far away from the structure, and rippled with so many cracks, that Johnny honestly didn't understand how the building remained standing.

When he reached the porch, Johnny had to pick his way over exposed joists where numerous boards had rotted away. He tested every footstep before trusting it with his full weight. Even so, the wood creaked and popped underfoot, and he prayed for protection with earnest fervor. Curiously, what remained of the porch had been kept free of debris and clutter.

As Johnny neared the door, his gaze came to rest on a petite pair of dark brown shoes, one of which tapped steadily on the threshold.

"Hurry!"

The shoes disappeared with the whirl of a skirt. Johnny hesitated, then stepped into a room illuminated solely by natural light—of which there was plenty, what with all the ill-fitting boards conspiring with their brethren outside the house. Here and there a sparse collection of keepsakes rested on a shelf or table, or hung on the wall. The sum total of furniture consisted of a couch and a wooden chair.

"In here." An arm waved from the second of two doors on the left wall. Johnny limped toward the vanishing arm as the rumble of automobiles crept into the room.

In the modest bedroom—at most ten feet to a side—Johnny found the young lady kneeling beside a rough-hewn bed that held a small, motionless figure enveloped in a hand-sewn quilt. Johnny drew near the bed and absorbed the scene for several seconds until he detected the slight rise and fall of covers, and a hint of labored breathing.

He leaned in for a better look. The woman, pale and of gaunt complexion appeared as a corpse. Johnny would have guessed her to be in her eighties but for the fiery orange hair hinting at youth. He shivered. An unnatural cold, reminiscent of death, permeated the room.

The young woman pulled a bony hand from beneath the quilt. The older woman croaked, "Sarah?" Her lips barely moved when she spoke, and her sunken eyelids stayed closed—not so much as a flutter.

"It's me, mother." The young lady—Sarah—whispered with such genuine tenderness that Johnny took a second look to see if she was the same person who had stormed the church. "I've brought someone with me—someone who knows how to pray." Sarah turned toward Johnny, fire returning to eyes tamed by a mist of tears. "You *can* pray, can't you?"

"Too late," came the labored reply. The woman coughed twice, then wheezed her last words. "I love you, Sarah." One last gasp and her hand slipped onto the bed.

Sarah stared. Then her eyes widened in horror. "No! Don't leave me! You *can't* leave me!" She scooped up the fallen hand and rubbed it along her cheek, sobbing. "No, please!" Her voice grew soft, pleading. "You can't." Then with an unearthly wail of distress, she fell forward onto the unmoving body.

Johnny tore his eyes from the scene when a commotion arose behind him. A man and two women stood in the doorway, gaping. The man removed his hat and clutched it to his chest.

The sound of shuffling footsteps in the next room told Johnny more of the curious were on the way. He scrambled toward the door, pushed past the onlookers and into the growing crowd, anger welling deep within. "Go!" He pointed, hand shaking, to the front door where more faces appeared every second. "GO!"

Wide eyes stared back at him. No one reversed course.

He flew at them, cane swinging. "Get out! Leave them in peace!"

Shooing and prodding, Johnny herded them through the door, past the porch, and into the yard where they scattered like birds. He stood resolute, eyes roving, daring them to come near again.

Moments passed while Johnny took long breaths, draining his anger. With his feelings back under control, he addressed them with newfound authority. "Stay here—please. She needs to be alone." He forced his voice lower still. "She needs your respect."

Then remembering his purpose, Johnny raced back to the bed where Sarah lay sobbing. He touched her arm and, after a moment, she raised her head to stare at him with red and puffy eyes. The agony on her face, the tears flooding down her cheeks—it was almost more than Johnny could bear. He'd never suffered a loss like hers. Nonetheless he felt her pain.

"Please." Johnny extended his hand. "Give me a minute alone with her."

Still shaking, Sarah narrowed red eyes on him and slapped away tears. "She's dead! Can't you see that? What right do you have telling me to leave?" She glared at him, lip quivering.

"Please, miss—Sarah." Johnny knelt and searched her eyes. "I know you're hurting. But you trusted me when you came to the church. Trust me now. I won't be long."

She stared back. The fire faded somewhat and her countenance softened. She cocked her head, then rose. "Not long," she said, then tip-toed the length of the room only to pause at the door where she held his gaze for an endless moment. Then after drawing a deep breath, she disappeared.

Johnny stared after her, thoughts swirling. Then he dropped onto both knees, clasped his hands before him, and shut his eyes. "Oh, God! Help me! It's just the way you showed me. Why did you call me here? This woman is dead."

Minutes passed while Johnny listened for what no ear could hear. Somewhere in the depth of his spirit a voice called to him. Faint yet unmistakable, the same voice that first spoke to him on the mountain called his name. It told him exactly what to do.

Johnny obeyed without question. He stretched out his arms over the corpse, and prayed.

* * *

"Sarah?"

The muffled question almost escaped her amidst the nervous chatter of those fellowshipping in the yard. She searched the crowd. Who had called her?

"Somebody's asking for you, ma'am." This from an older gentleman nearest the house.

"Who?"

"Sarah!" Unmistakable now, the voice emanated from inside. It didn't sound at all like the young preacher. Sarah's eyes grew wide. She bolted for the house.

In her haste she stumbled over the threshold, caught her balance, then hurled herself toward the bedroom door, a human stampede nipping at her heels.

"Mother?" Sarah rushed to the bedside, mouth open, unbelieving. She threw her arms around the woman who sat upright on the bed. "Mother!"

"Sarah!" The elder woman struggled to free herself. "Dear me, lass. Give a body the chance to breathe."

"Mother!" Sarah pulled back to look at her. "You're alive!"

"That I am. But if you keep squeezin' me thattaway, I'll soon be joinin' your dear father on the other side."

Sarah lifted a hand and stroked her mother's cheek. Her color had returned and her eyes shone bright. "I...I can't believe it."

Noises from the doorway drew both women's attention. A middle-age lady in a fancy new hat pointed straight at Sarah's mom. "She was dead."

"Yeah," confirmed an older man beside her. "I saw it with my own eyes."

Sarah's mother frowned. "What's this? Sarah—who are these people?"

Someone else yelled from just out of sight. "Reverend Jones did it! He raised her from the dead!"

Pandemonium erupted as the news rippled back through the crowd. "He raised her from the dead! It's a miracle!" Their cries filled the house, and soon, the yard.

The woman at the door ventured into the room. "Where *is* Reverend Jones?"

Heads turned every which way. "Where's Johnny? Where's Reverend Jones?" The question bubbled backward into the throng.

None had an answer.

Sarah hugged her mother and kissed her cheek. She had all she wanted. She could care less about any preacher boy.

Chapter Twelve

"Man, Trev, you look wasted!" Brent smiled in admiration as he met Trevor outside the main campus parking lot.

Trevor glanced down at his dirt-stained jeans and mud-caked hiking boots. He rubbed the stubble on his chin, and shrugged. It wasn't *that* bad. He had probably made a bigger mess of himself on a drunk sometime.

Kenny raced up from behind and thumped Trevor on the back of his head. "Where have *you* been, dude?"

Trevor lunged at Kenny, then punched him on the shoulder when he tried to duck. "I've been camping, toad face." He rubbed the sore spot on his head. "What's it to you?"

"I don't care what you do in the woods. That face, though— *that* bothers me." Kenny laughed, then grew more serious. "What did Lisa say?"

"Hmm?" Trevor swiped dirt from his jeans. "I dunno—I haven't seen her yet."

"Are you *serious*, man?" Brent grinned wide. "She's going to freak."

"Ooh, baby!" Kenny flicked Trevor's arm. "That chick's going to rip your head off!"

"Get out of my face." Trevor pushed Kenny away and sneered. "*She'll* think I'm sexy."

"Hah! I bet she won't talk to you."

"Twenty bucks says she will."

"Twenty bucks? Man, I'll put a hundred on it."

"A hundred? You're on."

Later that day, Trevor sauntered into English Lit alone. He flopped down in his seat to find Kenny eyeing him. Lisa stepped in a minute later. Trevor followed her with his gaze, but she looked the other way.

Kenny shot Trevor a knowing look and nodded at Lisa. Trevor scowled.

Professor Litchfield banged his desk and brought the class to order before Kenny could respond. "All right, everyone. Let's get started. Please turn in your assignments."

Murmuring and the sound of shuffling paper filled the room. The students crowded to the front and dropped their work in a heap on the teacher's desk. Trevor, last in line, flung his paper on top of the pile and turned away.

"Mr. McIntire—wait a minute." Professor Litchfield snatched up Trevor's paper and gave it a cursory reading. He shook it at Trevor. "This is hardly acceptable. When I let you choose this assignment—"

"What's wrong with it?" Trevor felt his cheeks grow warm.

"Would you please refrain from interrupting when I'm speaking?" Mr. Litchfield took Trevor's silence as agreement, and went on. "You don't have nearly enough facts to support your arguments. And it is quite obvious you paid little attention to spelling and grammar. This simply isn't acceptable." He shoved the paper toward Trevor. "Bring it back tomorrow and," he peeked over the rim of his glasses, a deathly serious look on his face, "be glad I'm in a generous mood."

Trevor snatched the paper and tramped back to his seat. Professor Litchfield prattled on. "Perhaps if you were to spend more time in class you would have a better understanding of my expectations. Also, I believe you owe me a signed excuse for your absence."

"Uh, yeah. I'll see what I can do about that."

Kenny snickered.

Professor Litchfield dove into his lecture, but Trevor turned him off. He daydreamed of the time he spent on the mountain until the last bell of the day brought him back to reality. Then he thought of Lisa. He had to talk to her.

Trevor packed his things and bolted from the classroom. Lisa beat him out the door but he caught her halfway down the hall.

"Lisa!" Trevor grabbed her arm and forced her to stop. She yanked free and shot Trevor a look cold enough to freeze water. He smiled in return. "Hey—let me tell you about my trip."

"Do I know you?"

"Come on, Lisa." Trevor forced his tone to remain upbeat. "You won't believe all the nuts that live on the mountain. There's this one guy—"

"Excuse me—are we back on speaking terms? I'm sorry but no one told me." She turned and stamped off toward the exit.

Kenny and Brent arrived at the tail end of the exchange. Kenny brayed like a donkey, mocking them. He and Brent both laughed.

"Hey, Trev—that sexy beard you're growing really knocked her dead." Kenny rubbed his chin. "I think I'll grow one and see what it gets *me*." He hooted, and Brent doubled over laughing.

Trevor kicked a nearby locker and cursed. "Why don't you two go play in the street?" He searched the hall for Lisa but she was nowhere in sight. He swore and gave chase.

"Ten bucks says she's mad all week," Kenny called after him

When Trevor reached the exit he banged through the door and poured on the speed. "Lisa, wait!" He neared the parking lot before he caught up with her. Even then, she kept moving, so Trevor changed tactics. He sprinted until he was in front of her, then blocked her progress. She sidestepped him, but he matched her move. Lisa tried once more with the same result, then pulled her books against her chest, huffed, and gave up.

"I'm sorry, Lisa—I was wrong." Though she wouldn't look at him, Trevor forged on. "I should have told you where I was going. I just went off on the spur of the moment without thinking. I tried to call but I never got a clear signal."

"Trevor…" Lisa turned toward him, frowning. She heaved a sigh, then her face softened. "You had me worried. I can't believe you ran off for a whole week."

She was putty in his hands. Trevor lowered his head to sweeten the pitch. "I know. I'm really sorry." He raised up just enough to catch her eye. "Will you forgive me?"

"A whole *week*, Trev? I still can't believe you went that long without calling. Why didn't you find a place with better reception?"

"Well…I don't know. I guess I just kept thinking I'd reach you on the next call. I'm *really* sorry."

Lisa shook her head. "Oh, Trev—sometimes I don't know what I see in you."

"So, we're on speaking terms again?"

"You're too much." Lisa sighed. "Don't do it again, OK?"

"Oh, no way—never. I promise." Trevor broke into a sly grin and sidled up next to her. "How about I make it up to you?"

"And just what is *that* supposed to mean?"

"I'll take you to the mountain and show you around. You'll love it. It's so peaceful, and so—well, just *beautiful*. You'll see why I lose track of time up there." His grin grew wider. "And the best part is at night. Just you, me, and a million stars in the sky."

Lisa raised her eyebrows and nodded. "Mmm—that sounds romantic. I think I just remembered what I like about you."

Trevor slipped his arm around her and pulled her close. "Great! Let's go tomorrow. I'll pick you up at nine."

She pushed away and locked eyes with him. "Tomorrow is Tuesday, remember?"

"So?"

"Um…school?"

"So take a vacation. You deserve it."

"I can't skip school—my grades will suffer."

"Get off it, Lisa. You're making all A's. Don't tell me a little relaxation will mess that up."

"This is crazy talk, Trevor." She shook her head. "Forget it. I'm not going."

"Seriously?" Trevor felt his cheeks grow warm. He tried to push back the feelings but knew the tension came through in his voice. "You care more about school than you do me."

"Trevor! Get a grip, will you? I'm not falling for a stunt like this. If you really want me to go we can leave after school Friday, but I'm *not* cutting class."

"Just this once?" He gave her the puppy-dog look.

"No."

This wasn't the happy ending Trevor had hoped for. But he could wait until the weekend if that's what it took. He nodded. "OK, you win. I'll suffer a little longer just for you."

Lisa brightened. She took his arm and wrapped it around her waist. "That's more like it. I knew there was a sensible fellow in there somewhere."

* * *

As it turned out, Lisa's sensible fellow agonized all week waiting for Friday. His heart simply wasn't in school any longer. Now, with their final class of the week over, Trevor grabbed Lisa by the hand and sprinted with her to the Explorer.

"I told Mom I was staying with Jennifer this weekend." Lisa giggled as she hopped into the passenger seat. "I can't believe we're doing this!"

Trevor shoved the keys in the ignition and laughed. "I didn't tell my parents *any*thing. They have my number if they need me."

The SUV soon roared out of the parking lot, tires squealing against Trevor's demands. Once on the highway, Trevor pegged the speedometer at eighty and held it there. The world whipped past in a blur.

"Tell me about the mountain." Lisa's eyes gleamed with excitement.

"Like what?"

"You know — what it looks like, why it's got you so fascinated." She waited until Trevor glanced at her, then added, "What's so special about it that you can spend a whole week there without me?"

"Well…to start with it's really quiet. Like, all the time. I mean, Winterville isn't exactly a roaring city, but the mountain makes it look like one."

"You said there would be stars," prompted Lisa, eyes closed and dreaming.

"Hmm…yeah. A little ways from camp there's a stream. I sat there on the bank doing nothing for hours. There's mountains for miles around, and at night there's so many stars it feels like you're part of the sky." Trevor sighed. "I don't know how to explain it. They seemed so close — like I could reach out and touch them." He thought back to the night he spent on the river bank alone. It would be nice to have company this time around.

"Could you see the sunset?"

Trevor snorted. "Are you kidding?" He glanced across the seat at her. "It's *incredible*. When the sun's behind the mountain, you won't *believe* the colors. There's nothing like it here in town."

Lisa breathed a sigh. She reached for Trevor's hand and squeezed it tight. "It sounds *wonderful*."

"Oh, it will be." He squeezed back. "You can bet on that."

* * *

The day played out like paradise. They strolled for hours, hand-in-hand along the bank of the babbling stream. A passing cloud pelted them with tiny droplets, and they laughed like children at their polka-dotted clothes. Then they lazed by the water and skipped rocks across the surface, sharing their wildest dreams. Trevor grabbed Lisa, tossed her into the grass, and kissed her like a madman.

Sunset broke across the sky in brilliant pink. Long stringy clouds stretched across the breadth of the horizon, stacked atop one another like stepping stones. It brought tears to Lisa's eyes, and Trevor admitted he'd never been more impressed.

When the last tinge of color faded from the sky, Trevor grabbed Lisa by the hand and pulled her upward. "Come on."

She drew back. "What's the rush?"

He brushed a kiss against her cheek. "I have an idea."

Lisa pulled Trevor close and whispered in his ear. "You were right—I like it here." Then she let him lift her to her feet.

Trevor dashed into the tent and came back with a blanket. He spread it on the ground beside the ring of rocks where he built the nightly fires. "Have a seat," he said, then sprinted toward the woods to gather sticks.

It took several minutes for Trevor to get a steady flame going, but once he did, Lisa tugged him toward her. He resisted.

"What are you doing?"

"You'll see," he called over his shoulder, already racing for the Ford. A moment later he returned, guitar in hand, and plopped down in front of her. He fingered random notes to warm up, then settled into a mellow tune.

Trevor hummed a few measures, then sang Billy Joel's "Just the Way You Are." When he reached the second verse, he noticed Lisa streaming tears. If a song could capture a lady's heart, he figured he'd just won first prize. He reverted to humming, then laid down his guitar.

Lisa scooted over and snuggled up to him. "That was *beautiful*, Trev. You never told me you could sing."

He pulled her close—very close. "Yeah, well. There's a first time for everything."

* * *

Saturday's weather didn't cooperate like the day before. It rained cats and dogs, with only an occasional break in the clouds. Trevor and Lisa spent most of their time snuggled together in the tent. It might be miserable outside, but nothing could dampen Trevor's spirits. He couldn't remember the last time he felt so good.

They dreamed together of the future. They confessed sins of the past and shared emotions of the present. They withheld nothing from each other.

As the evening light faded to dusk, the clouds finally rolled away. Rain turned to drizzle, and only a few lingering droplets pattered against the tent. The young couple lounged against each other, enjoying the orchestra of nothingness.

Trevor's dreamy grin faded. "Hey! Do you hear that?" He jumped up and darted outside, leaving Lisa in a heap.

A haze of clouds draped the moon. Trevor searched the sky, the mountain, and the woods as if by sight he might improve his hearing.

Lisa poked her head out of the tent. "What's up?"

"Shh!" Trevor glanced at Lisa, then back to the horizon. "Listen—it's music."

Lisa padded over to Trevor and cocked her head. "I hear *some*thing," she whispered. "Maybe just the wind."

"Nah, it's…I dunno—bagpipes?"

She followed his gaze. "Hmm. Maybe. But…different."

Trevor wheeled around, sprinted into the tent, and trotted back out with his guitar. He hummed what few notes he could pick out from the distant melody, then squatted to one knee and strummed them one by one, filling the gaps as best could. A definite tune emerged.

Lisa knelt beside him. "I think I know that song." She listened several more seconds, swaying to the beat. "Yeah—that's 'Amazing Grace'."

Trevor whacked the strings to silence and glared at Lisa. "'Amazing Grace?' Is that some kind of religious song?"

"Well…yeah, I guess so."

"Hmph." Trevor lowered the guitar. "It sounds like funeral music to me."

"They *might* play it at funerals. When I was a kid, though, we used to go to church on Easter. I'm pretty sure I heard it there."

Trevor plopped to the ground and swung his legs out in front of him. He pulled Lisa close. "That explains why it sounds so dreary." He barked a mild expletive. "I can't believe I was playing that stuff."

"Why not?" Lisa smirked. "You sound like a natural. Maybe good enough to be a priest!" A fit of giggling overtook Lisa. "I can see it now—Father McIntire and his holy choir! Where's your frock, Father?"

All Trevor's happiness drained. "I don't think so." He let go Lisa and stood, then sauntered over to the stream, kicking the occasional tuft of grass.

By now night had displaced day, and Trevor strained to find the mountain's outline. He cursed under his breath. Where was the music coming from?

Lisa tiptoed up beside him and rested her fingers on his shoulder. "I'm sorry, Trev. I didn't mean to hurt you."

He barely heard her. "I've got to find that music." He latched onto her hand and tugged her toward the woods. "Come on. Let's take a hike."

"Trevor!" Lisa pulled free. "We can't go on some wild goose chase tonight."

"Why not?"

"It's pitch dark."

"So? I've got a light."

"You're crazy. You'd get us lost and we'd never find our way back."

Trevor started to respond, but thought it through. It irked him, but Lisa was probably right. He felt confident he could navigate the entire mountain during the day. But in the dark? They probably wouldn't get very far.

Something in the distance tugged at Trevor's inner being. He swore. "I'll find you," he said to the mountain. Then his gaze drifted back to Lisa. "And I'll find that wizard, too. You wait and see."

* * *

"What are you doing?"

"It's getting late, Trev." Lisa shoved a handful of cosmetics into a duffel bag. "We need to think about heading home."

Trevor latched onto her shoulders and pulled her close. He whispered. "Stay with me."

Lisa's eyes went wide. "*Stay*? Another night?" She pulled away, frowning. "We have school tomorrow."

Not *that* again. Trevor couldn't decide which curse word to use. If it wasn't for school, he might have a decent life. "C'mon—just a few more days. There's so much more to see. Besides, I thought you liked it here."

"Trevor! Get a grip, will you? We can't skip school just to go running around in the woods." Lisa's face softened. "I had a great time—really. But life's not all fun and games. Like it or not there's a real world waiting for us. Now, come on and pack."

He had been down this road before—and lost. "Oh, all right. But," he winked at her, "I expect you up here again *next* weekend."

"Trevor McIntire!" Lisa giggled a curse. "What am I going to do with you?"

* * *

"Hey, hey, hey! Where's Mr. Romance?" Kenny, along with Brent, approached Lisa from across the hallway.

"Oh, no—you guys haven't seen him, either?"

"I haven't seen you *or* him since Friday. Imagine that—both of you missing the entire weekend." Kenny gave Lisa an evil grin. He nudged Brent, producing a smile. "I wonder what *that* could mean?"

Lisa blushed and turned away. She could guess where Trevor was—on the mountain again. "Trevor," she said under her breath, "what *am* I going to do with you?"

Chapter Thirteen

What are you supposed to do when God asks you to do something that doesn't make any sense? Well, I had to obey him. That's all there was to it—I had to obey.

* * *

"Father, I need your help." Johnny, kneeling, prayed while sweat dripped from his brow and splattered the floor before his knees. His forehead rested on top of the wooden pew in front of him, hands clasped over his neck. He'd come to Eatonton, Texas to hand out miracles, but he found his thoughts straying uncomfortably far from God.

"Lord, I can't concentrate. I keep thinking about…well, other things. Please, Father, help me keep my thoughts on things above. You know I only want to serve you. I don't want anything to come between us." Johnny sucked in a breath, and sighed. "I'm struggling, Lord. Please take this burden from me."

He lifted his head, opened his eyes and rubbed them. Then… Bang! He smacked a fist on the pew before him. "I can't get her face out of my mind, Lord! I've tried. I've honestly tried. But this isn't something I can do on my own. Please give me strength. Show me what I need to do so I can stay focused on your will."

Johnny bolted to his feet as if struck by lightning. He grabbed the back of the pew for support as his cane clattered to the floor.

The voice he heard came straight from God. It was his answer. He just couldn't believe what it told him to do.

* * *

First Baptist Church of Eatonton, just north of Amarillo, boasted the largest congregation in town. But that didn't say a whole lot. A big city church would have held much more than the hundred and sixty First Baptist was designed to seat.

Elegant lighting and stained glass windows adorned the structure—a step up from most other places Johnny had visited. Plush red carpet, new and unstained, rolled down the central aisle. For Eatonton, it was a fancy church. And despite the flashy decor, Johnny felt a sweet spirit in the place. In fact, he felt right at home.

First Baptist's pastor, Joe Roth, stood just under six feet tall and bristled with muscle. Tan, leathery biceps bulged from his short-sleeve shirt, a testament to years spent under a harsh sun. He had answered the call to preach only five years ago. Before that, he told Johnny that years on a cattle ranch had given him his alligator skin—something required to stand behind a pulpit, according to Joe.

Pastor Roth had invited the young Reverend Jones to First Baptist for a week of revival meetings—longer if all went well. It astonished Johnny to learn that people so far from his hometown knew about him. He had never asked for speaking engagements and he never advertised—he just went wherever the Lord took him. And, with each passing month, it seemed the Lord led him farther from home.

A white tent, large enough for a small circus, stood on the church grounds in anticipation of the upcoming gathering. Almost five hundred chairs begged, borrowed, or bought for the occasion lined the inside of the tent. Volunteers ran every which way, adjusting this, carrying that. Pastor Joe said every business in town sported a poster in the front window, inviting people to the big top that night.

"But Johnny, you can't just up and leave." Pastor Joe's Texas accent expounded every word larger than life. "I've been planning this for weeks. The whole town's expecting you."

"I know this is awkward, Pastor Joe. And I'm really sorry it puts you in a bind. I would never back out of a commitment if I could help it, but this a matter of obedience to God."

"Johnny," Pastor Joe wrung his hands, "you said it yourself—it's a commitment. You don't think God would ask you to break a promise, do you?"

It *was* a dilemma. Johnny hesitated. But there was no doubt what he'd heard. "God's ways are not our ways, Pastor Joe. I can't explain it any better. I've *got* to go home."

Pastor Joe laid a meaty hand on Johnny's shoulder. "I don't doubt you heard God, son. But maybe you interpreted what he said the wrong way. I mean, he didn't actually tell you to come home *today*, did he?"

Johnny thought it over. "Nooo…he didn't exactly say that. But he did make it clear I should go home. I don't think it would be right to put him off."

"OK, OK, I know you have to obey him." Pastor Joe released his grip. "But think a minute, Johnny. You can't start for home right this minute—it's too late. Why don't you preach tonight, get a good night's rest, then leave first thing in the morning? I think that'd be fairly prudent in God's eyes."

Johnny's wheels turned. It was true he might not get very far tonight. In fact, there might not be any more buses running at this hour. He formed a silent prayer, asking God what to do.

But if God had any opinions on the matter, Johnny couldn't tell.

"All right." Johnny sighed. "I'll stay tonight, but I'm leaving tomorrow at the crack of dawn."

Joe huffed a long sigh of relief. "Thanks, Johnny. This means a lot to me. And it's going to mean a lot to Eatonton."

* * *

"Johnny!" A vibrant fortyish redhead grabbed him by the neck and wrapped him in a bear hug. "It's such a pleasure to see you again!"

"It's good to see you, too, Mrs. O'Reilly." Johnny greeted her with a warm smile. "Thank God you're well."

"Thank God, indeed. And thanks be to you, Mr. Jones. I've no doubt my standing here this very minute is due solely to your kind intervention. Ah, but where's my hospitality?" Mrs. O'Reilly stepped away from the door and motioned inward. "Come in, come in. Rest your weary bones. I've just the thing for you—fresh apple pie." She flitted off toward the kitchen before Johnny could utter another word.

He flicked his gaze about the room. Not a thing had changed since his last visit. Same faded wood. Same sparse furnishings. But still, the place felt different—more inviting, more alive. Johnny sauntered into the kitchen.

"Uh, Mrs. O'Reilly. I, um...."

A plate of steaming hot apple pie clinked down on the table before him. The aroma brought back memories of Ma's incredible cooking. He studied the temptation but a moment, then seated himself and reached for a fork.

"Mrs. O'Reilly," he said between mouthfuls, "I've come to see Sarah. Is she here?"

The Irish matron cocked her head and raised an eyebrow. She stared at him that way until he squirmed.

"Oh?" She mouthed it soft. Then her eyes widened. "Oh! Ohhhh!"

Johnny wasn't so sure he liked the look Mrs. O'Reilly gave him. "So, uh, is Sarah here?"

"Well, now, I expect her any moment. She stepped out to—"

"I'm back, Mother." Sarah's voice sounded from the front door before Mrs. O'Reilly could answer. "Whose car…oh, hello Reverend Jones. It's good to see you're still with us. I thought surely an angel must have snatched you clear up to heaven the way you disappeared last time you were here."

"It seems the Reverend Jones has come calling on you, dear." Mrs. O'Reilly winked at Johnny.

Johnny pushed back from the table and stood, looking first to Mrs. O'Reilly, then to Sarah. "Oh, uh, it's not like that at all. I…" Well, what *should* he say? God had told him to go see Sarah but hadn't said a thing about his purpose in being here. Aside from that, Johnny couldn't concentrate. Sarah's beauty stunned him. Gone were the tears and the anger he remembered, replaced by bright eyes and a clear complexion. Silky red-blonde hair now lay in a long ponytail down her back, a far cry from the unruly mess of their last meeting. She had even been smiling—until she saw him, that is.

Sarah swept into the room, brushed past Johnny, and set a brown grocery bag on the table. "So, what brings you out our way again, Reverend Jones? If it's handouts you're looking for, I'm afraid you've come to the wrong place. Things have been a bit tight since Father's passing."

"Young lady!" Mrs. O'Reilly shot Sarah a menacing glare. "I'll not have you sassin' the minister right here in me own household."

Sarah's boldness rocked Johnny. He had never heard a woman speak to a man the way she did. While Sarah flitted about the kitchen, putting away groceries, oblivious to the nasty stare from Mrs. O'Reilly, Johnny prayed under his breath for wisdom.

"God told me to come, Mrs. O'Reilly. I don't know why. I was hoping...Well, that is..." Words just flat out escaped him. He exhaled. "Do *you* know why I'm here?"

At this, Sarah turned to Johnny and smirked. "Land sakes! The man who commands the very finger of God has come seeking wisdom from *us*? I think you're in trouble, Reverend, as I've not a ghost of an idea why God sent you here, and I'm sure Mother will say the same."

Mrs. O'Reilly smiled like a Cheshire cat. "Sit down, young man. Finish your pie." She nodded at Sarah. "And you have a slice as well, me lass." She looked from one to the other for a moment, then addressed them both. "I've no doubt the good Lord will make it all clear to us in due time." Mrs. O'Reilly took a seat across from Johnny and served herself some dessert. "Make himself clear, he will. All in due time."

* * *

Johnny and Sarah shared a picnic lunch under an aged weeping willow behind the O'Reilly farm. A breeze rustled through the trees while birds chirped in the distance. They relaxed on a red-checkered tablecloth spilling over with a cornucopia of home-cooked delights. Mrs. O'Reilly had provided the feast, insisting the two get out of the house for a while so she could take care of some cleaning without interruption.

They had started with awkward chit chat, Johnny stuttering his way through terse responses to Sarah's questions while avoiding eye contact. Thankfully, Sarah insisted that Johnny tell her how he became a minister. That, at least, he could explain without hesitation. She listened with rapt attention while Johnny relayed the tale of his mountain experience and the events that followed. He explained the vision, the voice, and his desire to give more than just the gift of healing.

Then he turned the tables on her. "I just don't understand. Your father was a deacon, you grew up in church, and you had a good home life. Just because he died, you're mad at God? Bad things happen to everyone." He raised a fried chicken thigh to his mouth. "I mean, look at me—I had polio. God even left me with a limp. But I don't hate him for what happened."

"*You* don't understand?" Sarah's face flushed red. "How *could* you understand? You've lived the perfect life, *Reverend* Jones!" She tossed the plate she'd been holding to the ground. "So you have a limp. Tsk, tsk. In the end, it all worked out like a fairy tale, didn't it?" Sarah's ire rose with every word. "You get sick, he makes you well. You fast a few days, he gives you the gift of healing. Look around you, Mr. Jones—*no* one else gets the same treatment you do."

Sarah rose, glowering at Johnny.

"You still have your mother *and* father. Why, you've never even had to worry where your next meal was coming from. You've never cried out to God, hurting so bad you wanted to kill yourself only to hear *total silence* in return. You've never been so much as *tempted* to wonder if God really cares, have you, fair Reverend?"

Johnny's tongue turned to stone. He'd asked the question in innocence. He meant no harm—only wanted understanding. How could anyone, having met God, turn away from him? But Sarah wasn't finished.

"I was thirteen when my father died." Sarah shouted now, berating him. "He was thirty-six years old—thirty-six, you hear? What kind of God takes a good man at such an age? What kind of God leaves a poor woman and her daughter alone in this world? Can you answer me that, Mr. Jones?"

Johnny wanted to respond, to defend the God he loved. How could he make her understand? How could he answer such a blind rage? Even if he had the words, Sarah charged forward like a raging bull.

"And don't get started about my mother. I'm thankful enough she's with me, but why would God heal her and let my father die? What kind of insane God plays with people's lives that way?"

Without warning, Sarah's anger turned to tears. She hid her face and sobbed, shoulders heaving. Johnny watched, helpless. He had healed every imaginable physical illness, but what could he do for a broken heart?

As she cried, Johnny's eyes misted over, her pain becoming his own. Even so, he knew he could never truly understand her loss. How could he comfort her? What words could he use to ease the pain?

Still uncertain, Johnny rose and placed a hand on her shoulder. "Sarah—"

"Don't touch me!" She jerked away.

Johnny withdrew his hand as if burned and lost his balance in the process. He plunged right into what had been their lunch, scattering food, plates, and utensils in every direction.

Sarah took flight, sobs echoing behind her. Johnny righted himself, grabbed his cane, and dusted off bits of chicken crust before starting after her. What he would do when he found her, he had no idea. But, he was determined to try *something*— anything to relieve her misery and anger.

"Lord God," Johnny prayed as he limped in the direction of the house where Sarah had fled, "I need help. You told me to visit Sarah, but this has been a disaster. I can't even talk to her without making her mad at you. And if that isn't enough," Johnny heaved deep breaths now as he hurried along, "I know this is crazy, but I'm attracted to her, Lord—every move she makes."

* * *

A knock sounded at the door of the old farmhouse. Sarah set aside the dishes she had been cleaning and wiped her hands on her apron. The evening meal had long since been served and only a few small chores remained before bedtime. At this hour, unannounced visitors were not expected.

Reverend Johnny Jones cowered outside, eyeing Sarah sheepishly, looking like he would rather be doing anything but standing on her front porch. They stared at each other a full minute as Sarah tried to conjure up the anger and resentment she had felt the last time they were together. But she felt only emptiness.

How could God entrust such a naïve young weakling with so much power? He healed the sick and, arguably, had even raised Mother from the dead, but knew nothing of the daily problems ordinary people faced. She hated him, hated all he stood for. She hated that he had made her weak again, even if it had been only for a moment. Life required strength. It crushed the weak—and she refused to be crushed.

Anger welled up and dissipated in waves. At first she despised him. Then that feeling melted into something she couldn't put her finger on. Maybe it was pity. No, not pity, but...*attraction*? No way was she attracted to him! The thought sparked anger again. And then nothing made sense. The see-saw of emotions was more than she could sort out. Was she going crazy?

"Well, you might as well come in, Reverend Jones." She stepped out of the way to let him by. "It wouldn't do to have you still standing there come morning, now would it?"

Johnny stepped inside, hands deep in his pockets, head low.

"Hello, Johnny." Mrs. O'Reilly gave him a cheery smile from the couch. "So good to see you again." She leapt from her seat and skittered out of the room before Johnny could reply.

"Mother!" Sarah stamped her foot. She huffed, then turned to Johnny, arms across her chest. "What brings you here this fine evening? Wait. Don't tell me—God sent you and you've no idea why. Is that it?"

She got her answer by way of a barely perceptible shrug and the hint of a grin.

* * *

Johnny visited the O'Reilly residence no less than once a week. Oftentimes he showed up several days in a row. There were plenty of speaking engagements to keep him busy, many of which kept him out of town for days at a time. But it seemed the Lord sent him back to the O'Reilly home every day he didn't have obligations elsewhere.

Mrs. O'Reilly always found an excuse to disappear anytime Johnny came calling. Sarah let him in and out like a cat, but otherwise ignored him. It wasn't always easy pretending he wasn't there, however, and he managed to suck her into an occasional discussion regarding scripture. Otherwise, he just sat on the couch and read his Bible, or prayed.

The pattern continued three full months.

As the weeks progressed, Sarah's attitude toward Johnny softened. She even made small talk with him periodically. To her surprise, after so many weeks of having him as an out-of-place fixture around the house, she began to look forward to his frequent calls.

"Tell me something, Reverend Jones." Sarah paused from her housework one day and eyed Johnny where he sat at the kitchen table. "What kind of miracles have you seen in your travels this past week?"

"Please, Sarah—call me Johnny. Reverend Jones sounds so stiff."

"Johnny, is it? Hmph. 'Tis no proper name for a man. People should call you John—Reverend John Jones." She nodded. "That has a much better ring to it."

"John?" Johnny scratched his head. "Nobody ever called me that before."

"It's well nigh time they did. You're not a boy any longer." Sarah lifted an eyebrow. "Don't you like it?"

"Umm..." Johnny searched the ceiling. After a moment, his gaze returned to Sarah. "I tell you what—you can call me John if you leave off the Reverend part. How's that?"

Sarah laughed. "Can't decide if you're a boy or a man, eh?" She gave him a most serious look. "You'd do well to accept the mantle the Lord has given you. A proper title goes hand-in-hand with the position."

He had no response for that.

What a funny little man.

Somehow he managed to make her laugh every time she saw him, whether through awkward speech or his too-innocent outlook on life. Her father had made her laugh, too—but not the way John did. Father had been a jokester, always ready with his quick wit. It was different with John. But even so, Sarah hadn't felt so light-hearted since before Father's death. She frowned. It angered her that such a simpleton could control her emotions.

I'm falling in love with this bumbling oaf and I'll never forgive myself for it.

John had changed, though. She'd first thought of him as a shy nincompoop—a very gifted nincompoop, but a nincompoop nonetheless. He couldn't even initiate a conversation back then, the little imp just sitting with a silly grin on his face until spoken to. Now he made casual conversation like an old pro.

"If you could be anything you wanted," John asked, interrupting Sarah's thoughts, "what would you be?"

The question surprised her, and it took a moment to answer. "You know, I've never given it any thought. All my time has gone to taking care of Mother, helping run the farm, just making ends meet. I never had time to dream." She pulled an ironing board from a corner near the doorway and laid a blouse across it. "Before Father died, all I wanted was to be a wife—just to have a place of my own." She giggled. "And lots of children. I never had brothers or sisters, so I always thought it would be nice to have a swarm of kids running around."

That she could speak of Father's death without crying astonished her—a first. John had brought her to this point over the past few weeks with his unending questions. Now the memories came without tears, and the pain had dulled. Truly, John was a miracle worker.

* * *

Johnny knelt in prayer beside his bed after a long day of visiting congregants with Pa. "Lord, I've enjoyed the time you've given me with Sarah. But I still don't understand why you've got me doing this. The more I see her, the more I think about her, and the less I think about you.

"I can't even remember the last time I left the county to preach. There are sick people everywhere, and plenty more work for your kingdom out there waiting for me. I'm ready to go, Lord. Why are you keeping me here?"

He paused to reflect, collecting his thoughts. "You know I'll always obey you. I'm not even asking you to change anything—I just want to know what's going on. Could you find it in your will to give me understanding?"

After listening for eternal seconds, Johnny collapsed to the floor.

"You want me to do *what*!?"

Chapter Fourteen

A half moon cast an eerie glow across the mountain landscape. Somewhere in the distance a coyote's howl echoed through the valley. A lone figure, backpack in tow, struggled to the top of a rock outcropping and surveyed the rolling hills.

Sitting on the edge of the cliff, legs dangling, the hiker unstrapped a guitar from his back. He strummed it, coaxing out soft notes of a forgotten melody. He wondered who else might be listening to the ballad he cast against the mountain walls.

No matter how hard he tried to play a different tune, no matter how hard he willed it otherwise, his fingers kept slipping back to the song he'd heard the first time not so far from this very spot. Lisa had called it "Amazing Grace." The title made Trevor gag. Religious music. Yuck.

Yet he was drawn to it. Inexplicably, it soothed him.

After picking at the chords for several minutes, he soon found himself no longer playing alone. The bagpipes—or whatever they were—moaned out matching notes in time to his guitar. He had fallen in step with the distant music without realizing it. The instant the other musician's haunting notes pierced his consciousness he stopped playing and set down the guitar.

Trevor strained to locate the sound, searching every possible direction. But the valleys and rolling hills played havoc with his sense of direction. It could be coming from anywhere.

"I'll find it. If it's the last thing I ever do, I'll find it."

* * *

"They call me Finch." A wad of tobacco juice smacked the ground at Trevor's feet the same time a hand stretched out in greeting. He had returned to the site of the camouflaged army tent after the allotted two weeks. Finch, it seemed, really was willing to talk.

"I'm Trev." Trevor took the hand and shook it.

"I 'preciate your help, Finch." Trevor imitated the man's country drawl as best he could. It wouldn't do for Finch to think him an outsider. "My sister—she ain't gettin' no better." Trevor couldn't help but crack a smile. He reminded himself of the *Beverly Hillbillies* reruns he had seen on TV.

With the afternoon sun beating down on them without mercy, Finch glowed with perspiration. "How 'bout we have us a little drink before we get started?" He spat another wad of tobacco close enough to splatter Trevor's boots, then squinted at the sky. "My mouth gets mighty dry days like this."

Trevor smiled. "Whatcha got?"

Finch stepped into the tent and Trevor followed. Finch lowered himself onto a fat, up-ended log, pulled a canteen off a nearby peg, and upturned it. He gulped twice, then swiped an arm across his mouth and handed the canteen to Trevor.

"Ahh." Trevor matched Finch's long swigs. "That's good stuff!"

"Oughtta be. Made it myself."

Trevor raised an eyebrow. He held the canteen at arm's length, and glanced from it to Finch. The old guy appeared healthy enough for someone imbibing homemade brew. Trevor made a mental note to hit him up for the recipe.

"Now." Finch stood. "Let's get started." He snatched the canteen away from Trevor and stepped outside, Trevor on his heels. He glanced at the sun and back. "We can make it before sundown— *if* you keep up." He cast a skeptical eye toward Trevor, then downed another swallow before heading toward the trail.

Finch set an amazing pace for a man his age. Even when the trail turned steep, Trevor couldn't tell any difference in his gait. Keeping up with him wasn't exactly a cakewalk, and soon Trevor found himself drenched with sweat.

Neither spoke as they climbed, the arduous pace making conversation an energy-sapping luxury. But the hike was far from silent. Crunching leaves, the occasional snapping twig, and birds chirping from both trees and underbrush kept monotony at bay.

Two hours later, Finch stepped onto a plateau, and stopped. "This is it—Wizard's Court." He leaned against a tiny pine that swayed under his weight and brought the canteen to his lips for a long swallow.

Trevor surveyed the scene—not that there was much to see. The clearing was perhaps a hundred feet long and fifty feet wide. The right side dropped off in a sheer cliff. A pile of large, flat stones sat in the center. At the far end, a well-worn path led upward past a cluster of trees.

"Wizard's Court?" Trevor searched Finch's face. "What's *that* supposed to mean?"

"This is where you get your answers, boy."

Trevor looked the entire area over again. Surely he'd missed something. "Uhh…" He turned back to Finch. "How's that?"

"'Course, you gotta follow the rules."

It struck Trevor that Finch might be toying with him. He brushed sweat from his forehead, and squinted. "What rules?"

"Well," Finch cocked his head, staring at the sky as if reading off a list amongst the treetops, "you can't come out on a full moon, and you can't come out on a new moon. You can't come out on a week that has a new moon or full moon in it. But you can't come out unless you can see the moon."

"All right, already! I want to know what I *can* do—not what I can't."

"Hey—I'm tellin' you the rules the same way they was told to me. You want to know how it's done, or you want to run your mouth?"

Trevor started to tell the old man exactly what he thought of his rules. Instead, he cursed. "Go on."

"You come out here on one of them nights—when you can see the moon, but it ain't full or new. You get here at ten o'clock, and you don't be late—and make sure nobody else is here 'cause there ain't no two miracles the same night. You put your gift on them rocks," he pointed at the pile in the middle of the clearing, "then you step back and—"

"What gift?"

Finch folded his arms across his chest. "You're about the most impatient fellow I ever met. I'll get to that. Now, hush up and listen." He spat. "You wait and you watch. If you wait long enough, and if the wizard is in the right mood, then he'll show up right in front of ya."

Trevor drew a breath to interrupt again, but Finch frowned at him. When Trevor closed his mouth, Finch scratched his belly, then went on.

"Now, then. When the Wizard shows up, he looks over your gift and, if it suits him, he'll ask you what you want. Then he works his magic on you. But," Finch shook a finger at Trevor, "you can't ask for just anything—you ask for healing. That's all he gives. Not money, not a new shotgun, and no curses on your enemies. All he does is fix sick people.

"Now, as for that gift, it can be most anything as long as it's something you survive on. You can bring food, or lamp oil, or even shotgun shells. You set it right on them rocks, and step back." Finch sniffed. "No money, though. He never takes money."

Trevor thought for a minute. "How much? I mean, how do you know how much to bring?"

"You bring what your heart tells you. Just make sure it ain't no skimpy gift. You don't want to go insulting the wizard." Finch squared eyes with Trevor. "That wouldn't be good for you or anybody else, understand?"

"Uh, yeah—sure. So why don't you just take things straight to him? He probably comes down that trail over there." Trevor pointed at the path on the far edge of the clearing.

Finch pushed away from the tree and stuck his finger in Trevor's face. "We can't have none of that. *Nobody* goes up that trail, you hear? Nobody. You're just as likely to disappear off the face of this here Earth as make it up that hill. You do just like I said—nothing more, and nothing less."

"Hmm. Sounds way too easy to me. I bet every time somebody sneezes, they come running to the wizard. Heh, I bet he makes a killing off this little operation."

"Shh!" Finch held a finger to his lips. His gaze darted to the trail, then all around the clearing and back. "Boy, you best keep your mouth shut. If the wizard gets wind of what you said, neither one of us might live to tell about it. Now let's get out of here before you stir up more trouble than either one of us wants anything to do with." He clipped the canteen to his waist and started for the downward trail.

"Wait!" Trevor ran after Finch and grabbed his arm. "Do you really believe this stuff? You really think there's a wizard?"

Finch looked him straight in the eyes. "'Course there's a wizard. I seen him myself. He's as real as you and me standing here, and you can bet your life everything happens just like I said."

* * *

"Yes, what is it?" James McIntire held his cell phone in one hand, pecked at his laptop with the other. Caller ID showed his wife on the line.

"I need your input on something, James. It's about Trevor."

"Can this wait, Olivia? I'm busy right now." He tapped a few more keystrokes on his computer and frowned at the result.

"I think this is important. None of Trevor's friends have seen him all week, and he hasn't been home, either. I'm afraid he's hurt, or—"

"You know how he is, Olivia." James shifted the phone to his left hand and tapped a few more keys with his right. "He's probably off doing something with Kenny. Those two love to horse around. We can talk more tonight, OK? I need to go."

"Wait, James—I talked with Lisa. She thinks he ran off to the mountains. There's no telling what might have happened to him up there."

James swore at her. "Listen, Olivia—I said I'm busy. Trevor knows how to take care of himself. Did you try texting him? Did you talk with Kenny and Brent? Use your head, OK? We'll talk later. I have to go now. Bye."

* * *

It didn't take a lot of thought to come up with a plan. Trevor set up his tent at the closest almost-level spot down the trail from Wizard's Court. He would simply hide in the bushes near the plateau and see what happened at ten o'clock. What could be easier?

Now, at ten minutes after ten, he drummed impatient fingers against the bark of an old pine. Clouds masked the moon, blanketing the land in darkness. Even if something happened, he wasn't convinced he would see it.

"Filthy liar." Trevor cursed Finch's name. "That old coot is probably laughing his head off right this minute." He scanned Wizard's Court once more, then glanced at the sky.

The moon! It has something to do with the moon! What was it Finch said? Nothing happens on a full moon or a new moon, but nothing happens unless you can see the moon.

There were too many clouds! No wonder nothing happened. What an idiot! He had been waiting here all this time when the night didn't fit the rules.

Wait a minute. Did I really think something would happen?

The thought disturbed him. But he didn't have long to reflect on it—the sound of "Amazing Grace" cut into the darkness. Bagpipes! They sounded closer and clearer than ever before. He looked all about, trying to determine their direction.

Trevor stepped out of his hiding place and into the Court. Music echoed all around him. Then he looked in the direction of the forbidden trail. Could that be where it came from?

He switched on the flashlight in his phone and jogged across the Court. Despite the light, the thick band of trees, and the brush and undergrowth made it near impossible to find the path. He took one step upward where he thought the trail should be and caught his foot on something. Pain jolted up his ankle. He dropped his phone and went down on one knee. The phone landed with the light pointing up and blinding him.

"Ee-oww!" He cursed the ground, his ankle, the clouds, and for good measure, the whole wizard legend.

He felt of his ankle. Tender, yes, but probably just sprained—if even that. Limping back to his tent, he noticed the music had stopped.

* * *

Hard-packed soil, scattered over with random bits of vegetation and leaves, marked the tiny path that snaked its way up through a mixture of hardwoods and pines. Trevor followed it upward with his gaze from the edge of Wizard's Court until it disappeared around a gentle bend a hundred yards or so away. He shifted his backpack, then ventured onto the trail and pounded upward, still favoring his ankle. Beyond the bend it turned right and continued for another couple of hundred feet to where the tree line came to an end.

Near the edge of the trees the ground dropped away at a sixty degree angle. Trevor peered over the brink to where the tops of pines stretched upward from far below. To his left, the narrow path hugged the mountainside, winding counterclockwise up and left around a rocky cliff. A single person, proceeding with caution, would just barely be able to navigate the dusty path without *too* much difficulty.

After following the trail upward a few feet, Trevor gave in to the overpowering urge to peek over the edge. Vertigo! A sheer drop of several hundred feet shocked him into hugging tight against the side of the cliff.

It took only seconds to regain his composure. He shouted an expletive at the depths, and chuckled when the sound echoed throughout the valley. Then, with childlike curiosity, he scooped up a pebble and tossed it toward the abyss. Many seconds later a distant pattering noise reached his ears. Not a place to make a mistake.

The path switched back and forth as it wound its way up the mountain until several minutes later it opened into a plateau that was a miniature of the Wizard's Court below. The mountain rose in a sheer wall on the left and straight ahead. To the right, earth met sky at a scraggly edge. The trail he'd just climbed appeared to serve as the only way down.

A tent nestled against the mountain face at the farthest section of the clearing, its flap making lazy passes back and forth in the breeze. A small animal roasted over a spit a few feet away from the waving canvas. Trevor edged closer to the tent, and was taken aback by a white-haired mountain man snoring away on the ground behind the fire. The old guy woke with a start when Trevor's shadow fell over him.

"Hey!" The old man jumped to a sitting position. "What are you doing here?" He rubbed his eyes, squinting into the sun over Trevor's shoulder.

"Just looking around. Didn't mean to spook you."

"You should know better than to come up here. What's gotten into you?" The old man rose, leaned back and steadied himself against a tent pole. He raised a hand against the sun's glare and studied Trevor with piercing eyes.

"Take it easy, old fellow. I was just exploring. No harm done."

"You're not from around here, are you?"

OK, time to try the country drawl again. "Why, sure I am. Been on the mountain my whole dang life."

"You're lying, boy." The old man stepped toward Trevor. "Why are you here?"

Strange—the old guy's accent sounded nothing like the rest of the local yokels. Trevor switched to his regular voice. "Yeah, OK. I live in town. But I'm just hiking, that's all—you know, enjoying the scenery."

"This is private property." The old man nodded toward the trail. "How about you head on back to wherever it is you came from?"

"You're not from around here, either, are you?"

The old man's eyebrows went up. "Boy, I've been living here longer than you've been alive."

"Then you should be able to tell me about the wizard."

The man's mouth dropped open and his eyes went wide. "Wh...What do you mean, the wizard?"

"Don't give me that—you're living on *his* mountain."

The old man became furtive, shuffling foot to foot, eyes roaming. "Who told you that?" he said, staring at the ground.

"Everybody knows it. In fact, they say he comes down that same trail that leads to your tent." Trevor waited until the old guy glanced up at him. "I don't suppose you know anything about that, huh?"

That old man stiffened, then glared at Trevor. "You're poking your nose in places best left alone, young man. Now, you've worn out your welcome. It's time for you to go."

"Uh-uh." Trevor shook his head. "You're hiding something."

The old man's response was like a volcanic eruption—a low rumble in his throat, followed by a growl and a shout. "Get out of here!" The old man pointed toward the trail, cheeks red. "Now!"

"All right, all right." Trevor stepped back and raised his hands. He cursed, then turned heel and stomped off toward the trail but paused at the edge and turned back. "This ain't over, dude. Sooner or later, somebody's going to talk."

* * *

A cool mist settled over the clearing, twisting and shimmering in the moonlight. Trevor peered through the bushes at the end of the

Court, straining to see the pile of stones that the mist alternately covered, then revealed. A peek at his phone showed almost ten o'clock. Not so much as a cricket had chirped in the past half hour.

Trevor grew restless. His legs cramped, but he dared not move for fear of making a sound. Something would happen tonight—he could feel it. According to Finch's instructions, all the conditions were exactly right.

What's that?

A shuffling sound to his right near the end of the trail. Seconds later a shadowy figure came into view, the form of a small human working its way into the Court with obvious caution. Trevor figured it must be a woman—or maybe a boy.

"She" lifted some sort of bundle from her side and placed it on the stones, then stepped back and waited.

Five minutes passed, then ten. Still the woman stood motionless. Then Trevor heard her gasp—definitely a woman's voice. He peeked further past the bushes and searched for what had startled her. She seemed to be looking at the trail Trevor had climbed earlier in the day. He flicked his gaze in that direction.

His heart skipped a beat. Something darker than night—darker even than the woman's shadow—glided from the path into the Court. Approximately the size of a man, the thing had no arms, no legs, no distinguishable features.

The silhouette drifted across the ground with a curious motion. Stop-start. Stop-start. Stop-start. It headed straight for the pile of stones where the woman stood frozen.

Ignoring the smaller figure, the apparition halted in front of the package. Trevor couldn't tell for sure, but it seemed to be studying the contents. Then it spoke, and Trevor strained to hear. The words, gentle and soothing, and just audible across the plain, tickled his ears.

"Thank you for the gift. Now tell me, what can I do for you?" The voice sounded human. It sounded like a man.

"It's my tooth, Mr. Wizard, sir." The woman, speaking in the curious lilt of the mountain folk, raised a hand to her mouth. Her voice trembled over every word. "It's rotted—almost gone. And...and it hurts. I...I can't take it no more. C...can you fix it? P...please."

No way she's old enough to have teeth falling out. I bet she's never even seen a toothbrush.

Something reached out from the shadow toward the woman. Hands appeared past the edge of the blob and came to rest on the woman's chin. For a moment, two figures in the clearing stood as one.

It's a man in a cape!

Trevor sorted it all out in his head. The man wore a long, flowing cape that covered him head to toe. With the light so faint, he looked like a featureless ghost. From a distance, no one would ever guess he was human.

"Aihhh!" The woman jumped back, stumbled, and flailed to keep her balance. She raised a hand to her mouth after steadying herself. "It's there! It's there! It's *all* there!" She danced a little jig. "It don't hurt no more!"

What a hoot. Trevor snickered, covering his mouth to suppress the sound.

"Thank you, Mr. Wizard..." The woman's voice trailed off. She searched every which way, but she stood alone in the Court.

Trevor stepped clear of the bushes. Branches covering the upward trail blocked the moonlight, obscuring his view. Looking back toward the woman, he noticed her package had disappeared.

"Whoohoo!" The woman pranced and yelped, excitement building. "It worked! It really worked!" She skipped over to the path that led down the mountain, singing a nameless tune.

Trevor approached the rock pile, then made his way to the far end of the Court. He desperately wanted to head up the trail, but the painful memory of his twisted ankle damped his enthusiasm. Even so, he made the effort. Using the light from his phone, he took the first few steps and...

The phone dimmed, flickered, then dimmed some more. Trevor tapped the screen and found the battery near depleted. No way. He shook it, but to no effect. So he cursed, and cursed again. With the path so narrow and the ground so precarious, he dared not rely solely on filtered moonlight—that would be suicide. It pained him, but he would have to wait for morning to resume his quest.

"I've got you now," he muttered, turning back toward the downward trail. "It's just a matter of time."

Chapter Fifteen

I don't know how to explain it. For the longest time it was just me and God, and I was plenty happy that way. Nothing compared to falling in love, though. I experienced a range of emotions I didn't know were possible. But even that was just the beginning of changes to come.

* * *

"I declare, Johnny. I believe you're the handsomest man I ever did see." Ma's eyes twinkled. "But don't tell your pa I said that."

John—Ma and Pa were about the only ones who called him Johnny any more—darted his gaze about the room while Ma fussed with his tie. He thought ahead to the day's festivities and wondered what it would be like. A day to remember, that's for sure. He just hoped he lived through it.

I can't believe I'm doing this. I know it's your will, God, but I'm still scared to death.

"All right, now. Stand back and let me look at you." John retreated a single step and stared back at Ma as she looked him over head to foot. Thank goodness *she* still had her head on straight. What would he ever do without her?

John wore the new pin-striped suit Pa had bought for him. The three piece affair had been tailor made—the fanciest set of clothes John had ever seen, much less owned. Gold-plated cuff links with a matching tie tack, a bright red tie, and black leather shoes polished within an inch of self luminescence completed the outfit. He felt like a king.

Ma adjusted his tie and took a long last look at him. "Oh, I guess you'll do." She sniffed, then wiped her eyes and stooped to retrieve her purse.

"Gonna be a hot one today, don't you think, Ma?"

Ma smiled. "Nervous, Johnny?"

He turned away. "Well...maybe a little." Limping, he made his way to the front door, legs more stiff than usual. "Ready?"

She joined him at the door and took his hand. "I'm ready."

Arm in arm, the pair strode to the '48 Studebaker Champion John had purchased only a couple of weeks prior. He reached to open the door for Ma, but paused. "Ma?"

"Hmm?"

He let his gaze roam the length of the property, the house, the woods, the yard he'd once thought so large. Then he faced her, barely able to choke out anything above a whisper. "Thanks."

Ma nodded, eyes moist. "You're welcome, son. Now, we best get to church."

* * *

Mt. Carmel's new organ belted out hymns one after the other, the organist flailing at the keys like a prize fighter. The resulting sound, somewhere between too loud and painful, drowned out all but the most determined conversations in the sanctuary.

John had stationed himself on the platform just right of where the pulpit normally stood. He stole glances at the crowd every few seconds. As usual, the place was packed.

Skip Jefferson waited next to him in a loose-fitting suit likely handed down from his father. A couple of high school buddies positioned themselves stiff as tin soldiers beside Skip, testaments to the many, many souls converted by John's power-packed sermons over the past couple of years.

To John's right, on the other side of the dais, a mixed array of young women angled toward the congregation. The first, a pudgy girl with light brown hair, forced a smile that ballooned her pimpled cheeks into cherry balls. A freckle-faced young lady stood next to the pudgy girl, dabbing tears. An attractive blond occupied the last position, rivaling the young men for height. The three women all sported French braids woven into elaborate buns atop their heads. Peach chiffon dresses, identical except for size, made them look like an aspiring gospel band.

August heat poured through open windows, weighing heavy on every soul. Sweat dripped from John's forehead. Not just nervous, he felt lightheaded.

The current hymn came to an abrupt halt, exposing murmured conversations, then picked back up a moment later in a spritely familiar tune. Over a hundred bodies rose on cue—and turned away from John. He followed their gaze to the rear of the church where double doors swung wide, revealing a man and woman making their first appearance at Mt. Carmel as a couple.

Pastor Joe Roth—all the way from Eatonton, Texas—beamed ear to ear. The most beautiful woman John had ever seen draped his arm. Her white home-made dress, passed down from her mother, swished along behind her in a short train. A radiant smile brightened her face and, in John's mind, she outshone the sun.

With the wedding march wailing from the church organ, Pastor Roth ushered Sarah O'Reilly step by step down the aisle. Smiles and nods followed the pair. The groom marveled.

This is not happening. There's no way a woman like that would marry me.

Beautiful. Gorgeous. Angelic. John couldn't decide on the proper words to describe her. And if the summer heat affected her in any way, John couldn't tell. She was as perfect as any human could be.

And still, she drew closer.

Oh, Lord! She's incredible, but...Is this really what you wanted? What if I made a mistake? What if...

The last thing John remembered before fainting was the red-haired angel's smile.

* * *

"It's not much, but at least the price is right."

"It's a fine place for a start, Mrs. O'Reilly." John gave her a quick hug. "We're more grateful than you'll ever know. Being a traveling preacher has its rewards, but money isn't one of them. Sarah's room is perfect for us."

"He's right, Mother. Like we told you before, we're proud to live under your roof. This is the best wedding present you could have given us. Now, don't give it another thought."

Mrs. O'Reilly welled up with tears. "I knew you had a heart o' gold, me dear. And now you've found your match." She grabbed them both in a bear hug and cried on John's shoulder. "You'll be the son I never had. May God bless you both."

"Now that's enough." Sarah pulled away. "Sit down, Mother. I'll tell you about our honeymoon. John couldn't have picked a more beautiful place."

"Aye, lass." Mrs. O'Reilly dabbed a handkerchief to her cheeks, then led the newlyweds to the couch where she sat next to John. "I only regret your father's not here to share your joy. He'd be right proud of his girl, he would." She turned to John, a gleam in her eye. "He'd have taken a shine to his new son-in-law as well."

"I'm sorry I never met him, Mrs. O'Reilly. Sarah's told me so much about him. I only hope I can be half the man to Sarah that he was to you."

"Don't be silly." Mrs. O'Reilly frowned. "My Tom was as good as they come, he was. But you'll be that and more. Of that I'm certain."

"We went camping, Mother." Sarah's eyes danced with excitement.

"Camping!" Mrs. O'Reilly tore her gaze away from John. "You've not spent a night outdoors in all your life. Tell me more."

"It was wonderful, Mother! We went to the very spot where God gave John the gift of healing. I never imagined such a paradise existed on earth. And it's just a few scant miles away. We can go back any time we like!

"There's a river—with fish jumping out of it. And the air is so cool and fresh. Oh, and I just can't begin to describe the sunsets. They were so gorgeous they made me cry. It was like God painted a portrait just for the two of us every single night."

"I'm happy for you, dear. It sounds like you had the time of your life."

"Yes, Mother. We even talked about building a cabin up there. It's the perfect spot to settle down."

"Oh?" Mrs. O'Reilly's smile faded. "Plan to leave me by my lonesome, do you? I knew it would come to this sooner or later."

"There's no rush, ma'am." John patted Mrs. O'Reilly's hand. "We'll live right here for a while. Besides, we have to get back to God's business. There's no time for house-building any time soon."

"Mm—yes. You'll be going back to the pulpit, I expect, draggin' me Sarah all over creation."

John shifted in his seat. "That's probably true, but we don't know anything for sure just yet. God brought us together and that's all that matters right now. I might pick up where I left off, or God might have something new in mind. He'll let us know when he's ready. And when he does," he glanced at Sarah, "we're going to obey."

* * *

"Well hello, son! How's my old married man?" Pa beamed at John and Sarah, and wrapped them both in a hug. Ma added a peck on the cheek for each.

"We're doing fine, Pa—just fine." John grinned ear to ear. He patted Pa on the back, and returned Ma's kiss.

Sarah smiled at her new in-laws. "It's so good to see you. Thanks for inviting us over."

"Don't stand there like a couple of strangers." Pa stepped aside and swept his hand toward the living room. "Come on in."

John grabbed Sarah's hand and pulled her inside. He led her to the couch and flopped down at one end, making himself at home. Sarah settled in beside him and fanned her skirt over her knees. Ma and Pa took positions across from the young couple on a love seat. For a few awkward seconds, four pairs of eyes stared at each other.

"Ahem." Ma focused on Sarah. "I'm glad you two found time for a visit. I've been looking forward to getting to know you, dear."

"I'm sorry, Mrs. Jones. It's been a whirlwind." Sarah laughed. "It's funny, isn't it? John and I spent so much time together, and neither one of us realized we were falling in love. But it's a new life we're starting now. I can't wait to spend time with you—and to make you part of my family."

Pa piped in. "We always dreamed of having a daughter. That's one prayer God never answered—until now. We're glad to have you, hon. And we're glad Johnny has you, too."

Sarah leaned forward and clapped her hands on her knees. "I should like to call you Aunt Ida and Uncle Jeremiah. Would you mind?"

John gave her a quizzical look.

Ma furrowed her brow. "Well, I—"

"You call us whatever you like, hon." Pa nodded first to Sarah, then to Ma.

"Good! Mr. and Mrs. Jones sounds so stodgy, don't you think?"

"Yes, I...I suppose." Ma managed a smile.

"Well." Pa patted Ma's knee. "These kids must be hungry. How about serving up that delicious chow you've been slaving over all afternoon? There'll be plenty of time to talk when our bellies are full."

"Goodness!" Ma brought a hand to her chin. "I forgot all about supper." She rose and headed to the kitchen.

"That's a hanging offense, dear!" Jeremiah laughed, and the newlyweds chuckled with him.

An overflowing banquet greeted the newlyweds at the kitchen table. Ma had set out a mound of chopped steak covered in thick brown gravy, fresh tomatoes, sliced cucumbers, steamed chopped carrots, and creamed potatoes. A huge boiler full of green beans weighed down Ma's corner. Plates filled with three different types of peas sat in a row down the center. The aroma of peach cobbler drifted through the room from a steaming dish resting on the stove.

Pa said grace, and the various dishes made their rounds until everyone's plate heaped to overflowing. John and Pa ate like horses. Sarah put in a good showing for a young lady her size. Ma grinned through the entire meal, saying little and eating less.

"Mrs. Jones—ah, Aunt Ida—this is the best food I've *ever* eaten. And I've never seen such a full table before."

"Thank you, dear." Ma blushed. "I'm glad you enjoyed it."

"Ida," Pa winked at her, "how about serving up that cobbler that's been tempting me all day?" He turned to John as Ma rose. "Son, what's God put on your heart for the coming days? Any chance you'll do less travelling now that you're a family man?"

He shoved his plate aside to make room for the cobbler. "It'd sure be nice to have you settle down somewhere close."

"I'm really not sure, Pa. We don't have any plans right now. We're just waitin' to hear from God."

Sarah pushed her plate out of the way as Ma set dessert in front of her. "God put us together for a reason, Uncle Jeremiah, but we've yet to figure out what that is. We'd both appreciate your prayers on the matter."

"You can bank on that, little lady. I've seen God's hand at work in Johnny for a long time now. He wouldn't have set you two up if he didn't have something incredible in store for you."

After the meal everyone retired to the living room. Pa pulled a dusty accordion from a nearby closet and fastened its strap over his shoulder. He stood in the middle of the room and belted out a mini concert of popular hymns while the other three clapped in time to the music. Pa grinned, tapping his foot and swaying.

"Uncle Jeremiah?" Sarah asked at the end of the latest song, "Would you mind if I tried?"

"Of course, dear." Pa unstrapped the instrument. "I didn't know you played."

Sarah chuckled. "I don't." She rose to receive the awkward bundle. "I've just never seen one of these things. It's quite the oddity."

She ran her fingers over the keys, getting the feel of them. Pushing and pulling each end, she pressed every button within reach. Everyone, including Sarah, laughed at the cacophony she produced.

"What about you, John?" Sarah turned to him. "Do you play?"

"Mmm…not really. I never quite got the hang of it."

"Don't be so shy, son. You're better than you let on."

"Aw, Pa. I never was much good with that thing."

"Please?" Sarah gave John the puppy dog look. "For me?"

John shook his head in defeat. He relieved Sarah of the instrument and pressed a few buttons and keys to bring back the memories. Then he made an earnest effort but, at first, he sounded little better than Sarah had. After a few minutes, however, he managed a recognizable version of "Amazing Grace," albeit with quite a few foul notes. His audience laughed and clapped when it was over.

"Fair enough, John." Sarah's eyes twinkled. "But I think it best you spend your time behind the pulpit and leave the music to Uncle Jeremiah."

John shrugged. "I warned you."

When the sinking sun's last shadows faded into darkness, John and Sarah exchanged heartfelt hugs with the older Jones' and waved goodbye. The couple stepped off the porch and headed toward the Studebaker. A voice from behind stopped them halfway to the car. They both turned back.

"Johnny—I almost forgot. Your Uncle Matthew sent you a letter. It came while you were on your honeymoon. Just a minute and I'll get it." Pa disappeared into the house and came back a moment later with a small envelope. He jogged across the yard and placed it in John's hand.

"Uncle Matthew? He's never written me before. What does he want?"

"I have no idea." Pa grinned. "It's probably an apology for missing the wedding. Maybe even a little gift." He winked. "Good night, now. Take care on the way home. We'll look to see you Sunday if not before." He waved once again and headed for the house.

John opened the door for Sarah and helped her in. He glanced at the envelope, slid it into his front pocket, and promptly forgot about it.

Chapter Sixteen

One thing after another thwarted Trevor's plans. It rained the day after the Wizard sighting—and kept raining. When he tried to charge his phone, he found the power adapter in the truck had stopped working, so he had *nothing* to occupy his time during the downpour. If that wasn't enough, every last scrap of food was gone, and he couldn't very well hunt during the flood.

It stunk, but the Wizard would have to wait. At first light the next day, with it still raining and the path turned to mush, Trevor put the truck in four-wheel drive and headed toward home.

He caught up with his friends during lunch at the college cafeteria. Brent saw Trevor first when he glanced up from a wilted slice of pizza, cheese hanging in a string from the corner of his mouth. "Hey, look—it's Trev!"

"Hey, guys." Trevor plopped down beside Brent.

"Whoa-ho!" Kenny jumped out of his seat and clapped Trevor on the back. "It's the mountain man!" He sat back down, chewing and talking at the same time. "Bring me anything from the mountain—like some moonshine?" He laughed, then wrinkled his nose. "Say...What's that smell? Oh, man, Trev—that's *you!*"

Trevor told Kenny what he could do with the smell, then dared him with a nasty look to say anything about it. He turned to Brent. "Hey, listen—I'm looking for Lisa. Have you seen her?"

"I think—"

"You mean that cute brunette with the hots for bearded strangers?"

Kenny pinched his nose when he spoke. Any other time the resulting nasal tone might have amused Trevor. Not now.

"She's been scarce, man," said Brent. "You left her high and dry."

"Yeah," said Kenny. "She's probably somewhere crying her eyes out. But dude, really—you're going nowhere with that girl 'til you to take a *bath*."

Brent burst out laughing, spewing crumbs on the table.

Someone put a hand on Trevor's shoulder, and he turned to find himself looking up at Lisa. His friends' antics must have masked her approach.

"Lisa! I—"

"What is that *smell*?" Lisa stepped back and made a face.

Kenny held up both hands, improvising puppets. He mocked the exchanged between the two lovebirds with lewd gestures that drew the attention of passing students.

When Trevor caught on, he stood and took Lisa by the arm. "Come on. Let's go talk—alone."

Lisa followed him outside the cafeteria's entryway to a long metal bench. "Lisa," Trevor began, caressing her hand, "I've been doing a lot of thinking. School isn't where the action is. It's...I dunno—It's just not real life." He entwined his fingers in hers. "I want us to live on the mountain together."

She blinked. "You...you *can't* be serious."

"I couldn't be *more* serious. Let's leave the whole stupid world behind and get off the grid. You know—live life the natural way, the way it was meant to be lived."

"Trevor!" Lisa yanked her hand free. "I can't believe I'm hearing this. You—you've flipped. You can't just throw your life away. I'm certainly not throwing *mine* away. Besides, it's just plain weird." She stared at him hard. "Have you been drinking?"

He shook his head. "Bone dry sober—I swear. Haven't had a drop all day." He pulled her close and whispered. "Come on, Lisa—say yes."

Tears welled in Lisa's eyes. She laid her head on Trevor's shoulder until dampness soaked through his shirt. "Trev...I love you."

"So, you'll come?"

She lifted up and pushed away, then held him at arm's length. "If you love me, you'll stop this nonsense."

"If you love *me*," came the calculated reply, "you'll forget this rat race and come live with me on the mountain."

* * *

The Wizard's Court lay another hour or so up the trail. Trevor paused from his journey and took in the scenery, breathing deep as a cool breeze played with his hair, causing it to tickle his ears. A few of the hardwoods already hinted at autumn colors, thousands of acres fanned out before him, dotted with yellow, orange, and specks of purple. He drank it in, lips curling into a smile.

Ahh. This is the life. Those old mountain hoots may not be much on brains, but they've sure got the right idea about how to live.

With a bit more spring in his step, Trevor resumed his hike. Soon enough, just a short distance from the Court, his campsite came into view.

Lisa doesn't know what she's missing. Homework, deadlines, responsibility. Nothing but freedom up here. Why would anybody choose college over this?

Trevor plodded past his camp until he reached the Courtyard. Once there, he searched the sky. Far to the west, menacing dark clouds covered the horizon, changing shape and moving fast. He estimated no more than an hour before the storm rolled in. "Not again." He cursed, then kicked the rock pile, his gaze moving toward the upward trail. "I *will* get to the bottom of this."

A rumbling in his stomach forced Trevor to examine his priorities. He unstrapped the old hunting rifle—a gift from his grandfather—from the side of his backpack, and checked to make sure it was loaded. The gun's age, and its long history of use, had long ago worn off all indication of its place of manufacture. Whatever the brand, Trevor favored it over the Winchester shotgun he had left at home. The old relic felt good in his hands— and it brought back one of his few good memories with Dad. They had gone hunting when Trevor was twelve, and he had surprised Dad by bringing down a deer with this very gun.

He swung the rifle into a barrel-down position and set off for the lower mountainside. Two minutes hadn't passed before he caught sight of a white-tailed rabbit in the center of the trail not thirty feet away. The rabbit hunched tail-high, chewing on something, but lifted its head and sniffed the instant Trevor raised the rifle.

Trevor sighted quickly. Crack! The shot rang true, and the hapless creature fell without a twitch. He had never eaten rabbit before, but today was as good a day as any to try. Besides, he would be relying on the land from here on out if he wanted to survive. For this part of the world, dinner had just delivered itself to his door.

Preparation of a wild animal proved messy, but Trevor didn't mind. It felt good taking care of himself for a change. It made him feel like a man. If skinning a rabbit was his biggest challenge, mountain life beat the city any day.

Soon flames licked upward over the spit as the first hesitant droplets pattered the leaves. Trevor's thoughts drifted back to the man he'd met just up the trail from the Court. It might have been a rabbit the old guy had been cooking when Trevor first found him. *He* certainly knew how to live off the land. In fact, if he'd lived here as long as he said, he probably knew everything there was to know about the area.

That old codger. He knows something about the wizard. There's no way he could live this close to the Court and not know what's going on.

Rain threatened to extinguish the flames by the time Trevor pulled the rabbit off the spit. He retreated into the tent just as the heavens broke loose. He plopped onto the ground, and pulled out his pocket knife. Then he cut a hunk from the rabbit and tossed it in his mouth. Hmm. Not bad. It could use some seasoning, but at least he wouldn't starve to death.

While eating, he schemed of how to get in good with the old mountain man and extract the truth from him. Nothing obvious sprang to mind, so Trevor finished his meal, licked his fingers, and set his guitar in his lap. He strummed a few chords, hoping music would help him think.

Soon after Trevor began playing, bagpipes wailed a new tune that competed with the steady rain. Trevor banged the strings to a halt and strained to hear. As always, the sound seemed to come from every direction at once. Here and there he plucked a matching note until the bagpipes quit, then listened a moment longer until he satisfied himself there would be no more music.

He laid down his guitar, and cursed. "Bagpipes, wizards, and crazy old mountain men." He cursed again, then furrowed his brow in thought. *Are they connected?* It was an interesting thought. He puzzled over it until he fell asleep.

* * *

A cool, damp wind tousled Trevor's hair the way his mother did when he was a kid. It interrupted his dreams and roused him from sleep.

As he gathered his wits, remnants of dreamland flitted through his mind. He saw himself dressed in a black cape, laughing hysterically while hoards of invalids begged for healing. He shouted at them, cursed them, urged them to leave him alone. They pressed him, suffocating him, then banded together and emptied their lungs, creating a wind that hurled him into the clouds, leaving them far, far below.

Wind picked up, beating against the side of the tent. It whisked away what remained of the fading images and ushered in reality. Trevor eased into a sitting position and rubbed sleep from his eyes.

Judging from the position of the sun, he had slept most of the morning away. He took perverse pleasure in it. With a drawn out yawn, Trevor pulled a snack bar from his backpack and munched it to crumbs. He tossed the plastic wrapper aside, and a baby dust devil near the tent coaxed it outside.

Trevor exited the tent and stretched with an exaggerated motion. He caught site of the wrapper as a playful wind tumbled it in the direction of the upward trail. Recalling his mission, an idea took shape as the crumpled plastic veered off into the trees. With only a moment's consideration, Trevor rushed into the tent and grabbed his guitar, then set off for the higher plateau.

The trail remained slippery from all the rain, so Trevor took his time. Eventually he reached the top where gusts of wind, unimpeded by trees, threatened his balance. He scanned the area while resisting the gale. The mountain man's tent jittered crazily in the wind, but there was no sign of anyone. Perfect.

Without a proper place to sit, Trevor plopped down on the ground in front of the tent, crossed his legs, and pulled the guitar into his lap. Sounds of the haunting melody—"Amazing Grace"— soon challenged the howling wind.

He started soft with single notes on individual strings. On the second chorus he added chords at strategic intervals. Then, strumming full chords on every beat, he plucked individual strings on strategic notes for accent. Soon he lost all consciousness of his surroundings as more and more complex variations flew from his fingers.

"You play beautifully."

The voice startled Trevor so much that he dropped his pick and blurted a choice expletive. The old man stood over him, staring. Trevor swore again. "Don't *do* that. I almost wet my pants."

"Hmph." The old guy frowned. "Your speech leaves a lot to be desired."

"What...?" Trevor rose, guitar in hand. Was everyone on the mountain a mental case? Oh, well—it would get him nowhere to make snide comments. He shifted the guitar to his left hand and extended his right. "Hi. My name's Trevor." He forced a smile. "Sorry, I didn't see you." The old man ignored the proffered hand, but Trevor kept rolling. "Listen—I'm sorry about the other day. I really overstepped my bounds."

"Mmm." The old man seemed to stare without blinking.

"What was your name again?" Trevor lowered his hand. He felt his confidence fading under that piercing stare.

With the old man unresponsive, Trevor took time to study him. A tad frail compared to the other mountain folk. And he seemed to stoop, his eyes dead even with Trevor's. A shaggy white beard fell to his chest, stray hairs bristling in the wind. Wrinkles marked a sunburst pattern over each cheek. A dirty black hat that would have been at home on a Swiss yodeler sat cock-eyed on his head.

"John." The old man broke his silence so softly Trevor wasn't sure he'd heard anything.

"Wha—?"

"You can call me John." The voice, stronger now, carried no trace of emotion.

"Well, John, it's a pleasure to meet you!" Trevor tried once more for a handshake, but John wasn't having it.

"What are you doing here, boy?"

"Well, uh, I need help. I mean, my sister does. She's real sick, you see, and I heard people around here—"

"What's wrong with her?"

"She has, uh…an incurable disease. The doctors can't do anything." Trevor smiled. "She needs a miracle."

John narrowed his eyes. "You're a liar. Now, get off my mountain." He spun around and tramped toward his tent.

"No, wait! It's true." Trevor chased after him. "I have to meet the wizard. My sister's gonna die without him."

By this time John had retreated all the way into his tent. He stuck his head back out and stared daggers at Trevor. "Even if there *was* a wizard, I'm sure he wouldn't waste time on a liar like you. Now," John poked a finger in Trevor's chest with every word, "Get. Off. My. Mountain."

Trevor felt his temperature skyrocket. He burst out an expletive. "Who do you think you are? You can't tell me what to do!" He kicked the ground, sending dirt all over John's pant legs.

John flung his tent flap closed and disappeared inside. Trevor shouted a continuous stream of insults and obscenities at the opening. His tirade came to an abrupt halt, however, when the tip of a shotgun poked him in the belly. An ominous click sounded, and Trevor flung up his hands.

* * *

"Well, that's two for the old man, and zip for me." A cloud of defeat hung over Trevor as he traipsed back down the path. He muttered curses as he went. "That old fool will *not* get the best of me."

Back at camp, he filled himself with leftover rabbit and thought about his next move. He searched the tent for ideas but came up blank. With the rabbit gone, however, there was nothing left for the next meal. So, needing food and hoping to find inspiration, he gathered his fishing gear and headed down the mountain. It took a good hour of hiking to reach the nearest branch of the stream.

As luck would have it, the fish didn't cooperate any more than John had. Trevor fished the entire afternoon without so much as a nibble. But just as he decided to pack it in, he landed a good-sized trout. Encouraged, he cast the line again, and a few minutes later was rewarded with a second fish.

He strung his catch on a line, gathered his equipment, and whistled a merry tune back to the campsite. An idea bubbled to the surface of his thoughts as he sliced and cleaned the fish. He dumped the fillets in a plastic container and shoved it in his backpack along with a few more supplies, then strapped on the guitar and headed up the trail toward John's place.

The sun shone low over the horizon when he reached the plateau. As before, John was nowhere in sight.

Good.

Trevor unlimbered his load and got to work. He started a fire in John's pit with a handful of kindling he found lying nearby. Then he pulled the fish and a frying pan from his pack, dashed it with spice, and positioned the pan over the budding flames. Soon the sizzle and aroma of frying fish announced itself throughout the plateau. Trevor breathed deep. It smelled *great.*

Guitar in hand, he retreated about ten feet from the fire and lowered himself to the ground. Glancing right, the first brilliant colors of sunset near blinded him as it spread across the sky. He squinted, turned from the light, then began to play the same enchanting melody the bagpipes favored. But Trevor had christened it with a new name. He called it "The Song" because he didn't like "Amazing Grace." At first he played low and gentle.

Then as before, he worked his way up through increasingly complex moves to a thundering crescendo.

* * *

Unknown to Trevor, his music echoed around the various parts of the mountain and into the valley below. As the music grew louder, the mountain folk quit what they were doing and listened.

"Is that the wizard?"

"Must be. That's his song."

"It sounds different."

"Yeah. It's different all right."

"What's it mean?"

"It's an omen. Things are changin'."

"I don't like it."

A pause, then. "Me, neither."

* * *

John peeped out of his tent, shotgun in hand. He planned to run that pesky boy off the mountain once and for all. But there was something about the way Trevor played that gave John pause. He didn't just hear the music, he *felt* it. For the first time in years, the song stirred pleasant memories. He watched a bit longer as Trevor, engrossed in his own music, rocked back and forth to the beat.

An idea popped into John's head—something that just felt *right*. He disappeared into the tent, then returned sans gun and with a different bundle in his hand—a contraption that appeared very much like a burlap bag with baseball bats sticking out of it. He held the device under his arm and blew into one of the sticks protruding from it.

A new sound filled the air—the sound that mountain folk knew from years of nightly concerts. This was the sound Trevor had heard during his first weekend on the mountain. It mingled with the notes from the guitar and, for a brief moment, the two instruments played as one.

Mere seconds passed before Trevor slapped his strings to silence and jerked his head toward John. The guitar slid to the ground and Trevor stared at John for the longest time as, staring right back, John continued to play.

Sweet, clear, and crisp, the eerie sound not so much pierced the air as blended with it. Nowhere else on Earth could music like this be heard—the sound of bagpipes transposed down a full octave. Mellow and mournful, haunting and soothing.

Trevor snatched his guitar and tossed it back into position, then joined with John, turning the performance into a laudable duet. Though an odd combination, John thought the two instruments complemented each other well, and the mountain had never heard such a moving rendition of the famous hymn. For a few mystical moments, the stars shown brighter, the air smelled fresher, and John felt at peace.

The feeling didn't last.

Out of nowhere John felt the urge to cry, a mixture of sadness and loneliness that he'd suppressed for a great many years. The old controls kicked in, though, and he suppressed all emotion.

When the song drew to a close, Trevor banged down the guitar and sprinted over to John. "I can't believe it! You're the musician! I just *knew* you had something to do with all this!" He moved in close and ran his hand over the bagpipes. "Where did you get these? I've never seen anything like them."

John inched back enough to remove Trevor's fingers from the bag. He shrugged. "I made them."

"No, way! That's *way* cool." Trevor cocked his head. "Can I try?"

John took another step back and narrowed his eyes. "Don't tell anyone you were here. And don't say anything about the bagpipes, either. Understand?"

"Why not?"

John reached over and grabbed Trevor by the arm. He squeezed hard enough to show he meant business. "Promise me, boy. You'll regret the day you were born if you breathe a word of this to anyone."

"Hey!" Trevor yanked once, then harder until he broke free.

"Promise?"

Trevor shrugged. "Yeah, sure."

John stared into Trevor's eyes, probing. Trevor returned an innocent grin.

Chapter Seventeen

Uncle Matthew had always been a distant figure—someone I saw at Christmas every few years. And then he drops this thing on me out of nowhere.

* * *

Saturday morning a cool breeze blew through the open window, enticing home-made curtains to dance. A lone figure lay curled in a fetal position on the bed beneath the window, just out of reach from the sun's gleaming rays.

"John!" A shout from the kitchen. "John Elijah Jones!"

The bed's warmth lulled its occupant, its softness enveloped him. He twisted and moaned, then lay still.

"John—time to get up!" Sarah stamped into the room. "What's gotten into you, sleeping half the morning away?"

"Hmmm?" John raised his head and rubbed his eyes. "What time is it?"

"It's well past nine, you lazy man. Now, get up–I didn't marry you just to have you lie in bed all day."

John closed one eye and turned the other up to where his bride stood over him, hands on hips. "But I was sleeping *so* good." He stretched both arms above his head in a long, drawn out motion. "I guess I just needed a little extra rest."

Sarah wore a look that reminded John of Ma the few times he had displeased her. She tapped her foot. "It's a wonder you slept at all. If you snored a wee bit louder, we'd be re-shingling the roof."

"Again? I'm sorry, honey. You should have poked me."

"What use is that? Once I'm awake, I'm awake. Besides," she slipped him a grin, "what sort of gossip would it be if people heard the preacher's wife beat her husband?"

John laughed. She teased him that way all the time, and it was one of the things he loved about her. "You're the best wife in the world."

"Sweet talking your way to forgiveness, is it? You should be ashamed of yourself, playing with a poor girl's emotions that way."

John shook his head. "I love you."

"Ha! And a fine way you have of showing it, snoring me right out of my own bed." Sarah stepped toward him, eyes narrowed and mock-menacing.

"How *would* you like me to show you?"

Sarah plopped down on the bed next to him. She leaned close, voice going soft. "You could start by holding me."

John wrapped his arms around her, soaking up her scent and the delicious feel of her flesh. She tilted her chin toward him, eyes closed. Their lips brushed, then...

"Ahh!" Sarah's eyes popped open.

John had goosed her. Before she could retaliate, he tossed her to the bed and tickled her without mercy while she yelped like a puppy.

"Make fun of *my* sleeping habits, will ya?" He poked her again, then went for her knees.

"Stop it, you monster!" Sarah wriggled and spasmed under the onslaught, wholly without defense.

"Sleeping late on Saturday is a deadly sin, is it? I'll just have to make sure you never tell." John grabbed her feet and pawed until she convulsed.

He had gone too far. With force that surprised them both, Sarah kicked John square in the chest. The blow sent him tumbling.

"Ooof!" He hit the hardwood floor with a thud, bare feet sticking straight in the air.

"John!" Sarah peered over the edge at him. "Are you OK?"

"What's all the fuss in here?" Mrs. O'Reilly poked her head through the doorway. "Is everyone all right?"

John glanced up at her and grinned. "Uh, we're fine, Mrs. O'Reilly." He shot Sarah a conspiring look. "Just a lover's spat. No need to worry." He reached over and swatted Sarah on the behind. She grabbed her bottom and squealed.

"Sometimes," Mrs. O'Reilly shook her head, "I don't know what to think of you two. A preacher, for goodness sake. No dignity. " She pushed away from the door and disappeared.

Sarah frowned at John. "Just what do you mean, embarrassing me in front of Mother that way?"

"Hey—look what I found." John rolled into a sitting position and waved an envelope in the air, the top of which had been torn open. "Somebody's been reading my mail."

"Oh, that. It's the letter from your uncle. I found it in your shirt while I was cleaning—and *you* were sleeping."

"You read my mail?" John tried to look stern.

"It was addressed to Mr. *and* Mrs. Johnny Jones."

John wagged his head, then peered into the envelope and found it empty. "OK, so what does he have to say, *Mrs.* Jones?"

"Ah," Sarah's eyes twinkled, "that's a matter that needs discussing. God just may have an answer for what we're to do next."

She stood, then tugged John's arm until he rose. He followed her to the kitchen where she handed him a single folded sheet of paper. Sitting at the table, he flattened the note in front of him. Sarah leaned over his shoulder and rested her hand on his back. He read the handwritten message aloud:

Dear Johnny,

Congratulations to you and Sarah on your wedding. Please accept my apology for not attending the ceremony. I find long journeys too taxing now that I am getting on up in years.

Jeremiah tells me you found yourself a good woman. I never expected anything less from a Jones. I can't wait to meet her.

My brother also tells me of the astounding works God has displayed by your hand. The things he said are quite incredible, but Jeremiah never was one to exaggerate, so I have to believe every word.

You may have just what my church needs. I won't burden you with the details in this letter, but I simply ask that you consider paying us a visit as soon as you are able. Your new bride, of course, is welcome as well.

In Christ always,
Uncle Matthew

P.S.: I have enclosed a gift to help you get settled into married life.

John turned the letter over and back but found no attachment. He examined the envelope a second time and satisfied himself it was empty.

"Looking for this?" Sarah held up a ten dollar bill.

John reached for the money but Sarah yanked it away. "Hey!"

"I'll just put this away for safe keeping." Sarah disappeared into the bedroom, then returned a moment later empty-handed.

Mrs. O'Reilly lugged a basket of clothes in through the back door. The O'Reilly house didn't have the luxury of an electric washing machine or dryer. She hand-washed their clothes and hung them out to dry on a line between two trees in the back yard. Mrs. O'Reilly turned to John after lowering the basket onto the table. "What's this news from your uncle that Sarah's been keeping from me?"

John glanced up at her. "He wants us to come visit."

"Hmph. 'Twould be the proper custom for *him* to visit *you*."

"Yes, well, he said it's getting hard for him to travel. I think he's a good bit older than my pa."

Sarah seated herself next to John. "So, what do you think? Is this the answer we've been waiting for?"

John shrugged. "I dunno. I can't see how it would hurt to pay Uncle Matthew a visit, though. We have a couple of commitments in the next few weeks, but I don't see why we couldn't head out there sometime next month."

"And just where does this Uncle Matthew of yours live?" Mrs. O'Reilly leaned close, peering at the letter.

"Winterville—South Carolina." John tapped his fingers on the table. "It's a good three days drive from here."

"Mmm-hmm, just as I feared—taking away me only kin to go traipsing all over the country. I'll be all alone in me old age."

John clasped a hand over Mrs. O'Reilly's arm. "You're a very capable woman. I think you can manage without us a few days. Besides," he patted her hand, "God will take care of you."

Mrs. O'Reilly snatched the envelope and swatted John on the head with it. "See that you bring her back safe and sound. You two are all I have left in this world."

"God will watch over us, Mother." Sarah placed her hand beside John's on Mrs. O'Reilly's arm. "He always has. Even when it was just you and me, and even when I thought he didn't care."

"Don't you go preaching to me, young lady. Take your message to the heathens where it belongs."

John shook his head, grinning. "OK, enough you two. We have more important matters at hand. Like, where's my breakfast?"

"Hmph." Sarah whacked his belly. "You'll be having it cold this morning, sleepy head."

* * *

"There it is—Number 407." Sarah pointed across the street to a white mailbox with bold black letters on the side.

The Studebaker slowed to a crawl. Its big black hood swung across the road and onto a gravel driveway where a small, but charming cottage came into view. Forest green shutters accentuated the cheerful white wood siding. Hanging plants lined the eve of a tiny front porch, sporting vibrant blooms of red, yellow, purple, and white. Two rows of small fir trees lined the driveway on either side. A wall of shrubs hugged the exterior of the home.

Rose bushes dotted the yard, boasting red, white, and yellow petals. A huge pink blossom of some exotic species floated past Sarah's window as the car crept by. Two lines of alternating red and white azaleas angled away from the house at forty-five degrees, appearing as welcoming arms. Daffodils formed a dotted path around to the right, disappearing into the back yard. Four-foot chrysanthemum bushes displayed their wares at each of the two front corners of the home. Every plant, every tree, and every shrub displayed meticulous planning and care.

"Oh, John. This place is beautiful!" Sarah turned every which way, trying to take in the kaleidoscope of color while bouncing to the rhythm of the car's aging suspension. "Is your uncle rich? He must have his own gardener to keep up with all this."

"I don't think Uncle Matthew has more money than anyone else. He lives on a pastor's salary, you know." John's head also swiveled back and forth, absorbing the beauty as he eased the car toward the front of the house. "If I remember, gardening is a hobby."

The car rolled to a stop next to a late model Chevrolet sedan. John wrestled the column shifter into first gear and killed the ignition. "Well, here we are." He reached for the door handle just as a plump woman with graying hair stepped onto the porch, face radiating an energetic smile that belied her years.

John stepped out of the car and waved. The woman on the porch wiped both hands on her apron, then bounded down the front steps and made a bee line toward her visitors. A man appeared behind her at the front door. He followed at a more dignified pace, his burly body rocking gently side to side, a most serious expression on his face.

Before John could shut the car door, a husky set of arms engulfed him and squeezed until he gasped. "Johnny!" The woman squealed with delight.

"And you must be Sarah!" The woman let go John and peered through the front glass. She danced around the front of the car, yanked open the passenger door, and leaned inside. Sarah found herself the awkward victim of the same crushing embrace that had stunned her husband.

"Sarah, this is my Aunt Martha." John peered around the woman and into the car. "But, ah, I guess you two have already met."

The giant arms released Sarah. She blinked up at the smiling face of Aunt Martha. Ruby red lipstick, costume jewelry hanging from her neck and arms, and horn-rimmed glasses with three jewels in each corner. Aunt Martha made quite the first impression—and that was before her perfume billowed into the car and made Sarah cough.

"Johnny." The deep, bass voice would have been at home on a grizzly bear. A gigantic hand clamped down on John's shoulder. "I'm glad you came."

John turned to greet the newcomer. "We're glad to be here, Uncle Matthew." Then, gesturing at the car, "I'd like you to meet Sarah."

The abundant presence of Aunt Martha, standing there with a silly grin on her face, hid much of Uncle Matthew from Sarah's view.

"Martha, stop crooning and step aside. I want to have a look at the latest member of the Jones family."

"Oh, Matthew." The big woman put a hand to her mouth and giggled. She winked at Sarah, then stepped out of the way.

"Hello, young lady. It's a pleasure to meet you."

Matthew extended a hand but just brushed Sarah's fingers before pulling away. He spoke in such a prim and proper tone, and his movements were so controlled and restrained, that Sarah wasn't sure what to make of him. She studied him as she would a potential enemy. Her response was measured. "It's a pleasure to meet you as well, Uncle Matthew."

"Johnny, get your bride out of the car." Matthew sounded like a drill sergeant. "Do you need help with your luggage?"

"No thanks, Uncle Matthew. I can handle it." He reached for Sarah's hand and helped her onto the ground.

Martha wrapped a heavy arm around Sarah's shoulder and herded her toward the house. "I'm so glad you're here, hon. We wondered if Johnny would *ever* find a proper wife. But now I see it was worth the wait. Why, I just know we're going to be good friends..." She babbled on as the two made their way toward the porch.

Sarah couldn't loose herself enough to see if John had followed. She hoped her knight in shining armor had sense enough to recognize a damsel in distress when he saw one.

Once inside, Aunt Martha released Sarah and pointed her toward a couch. "Can I get either of you something to drink? Some tea, maybe?"

John appeared beside Sarah. "I'd love some, Aunt Martha."

"And you, dear?"

"Um...yes, please."

While Martha hurried off to the kitchen, Sarah studied the room. The incredible organization of everything in sight struck her as almost bizarre. A Bible sat in the center of the coffee table with two commentaries placed on either side at matching angles. Family pictures hung on the wall in a perfect pyramid structure. A glass curio cabinet displayed tiny porcelain figures in matching sets, exactly as they might appear in an upscale retail store.

"Have a seat, you two. Make yourselves at home." Coming from Uncle Matthew, it sounded more a command than an invitation. He remained standing, waiting for his guests to comply. Sarah found herself developing a distaste for his curt and regal manner.

John flopped onto the Queen Anne sofa and pulled his bride down beside him. She ran a finger over the bright floral patterns and wondered what it would be like to have anything so beautiful in her own home. Uncle Matthew relaxed opposite the young couple in a well-worn armchair. Sarah felt the comfort of John's arm as it came to rest on her shoulder.

"I see an ordinary young man." The odd statement from Uncle Matthew drew Sarah's attention like a magnet. His gaze bored holes into John. "Is it true that you're a miracle worker?" Uncle Matthew narrowed his eyes. "And if so, where do you get your power?"

Sarah raised her eyebrows. She knew her own reputation for being direct, but Uncle Matthew took it to a whole new level. Perhaps he had been a military man at some point? She glanced at John, but his uncle's gruff manner didn't seem to faze him.

"First of all, Uncle Matthew, the only power I have comes from God. I wouldn't be anything without him. As for the miracles, I can't deny them. God gave me a gift. I share it freely wherever I go."

The old man stroked his chin. His brow unfurled, and a satisfied grin spread across his face. "You are your father's son. And a man of God, I believe, as well."

"Of course he is, Matthew." Martha returned from the kitchen holding a small tray with four full glasses on it. "There's never been a question about that." She passed the containers around, then sat next to Sarah. The couch lurched under the sudden load, and the newlyweds scrambled to keep from spilling their drinks.

John gulped from his glass and made a face. "Whewee! That tea is *sweet*!" He shook his head, then after licking his lips took a more reserved sip.

Curious, but wary, Sarah raised her glass and let the barest hint of liquid touch her tongue. It wasn't enough to indicate why John made such a fuss over it, so she sipped a little more. The flavor was definitely different than she was used to.

Martha rested a hand on Sarah's leg. "Not too sweet for you, dear?"

"Hmm." Sarah tried a full swallow this time. "No—it's, ah, quite good actually."

"Enough chatter, Martha." Matthew scowled. "I have a more questions for the boy."

"Matthew!" Martha shook a finger at him. "Stop badgering these kids and let them relax. They've had a long trip. There'll be plenty of time for your questions later." She turned to Sarah. "Now, tell me about your family, dear."

Uncle Matthew harrumphed, but held his tongue.

Sarah sunk back on the couch and nestled up to John. "It's just me and my mother—and John, of course. My father died when I was young, and I never had any brothers or sisters. There's no other family nearby, so I'm not used to all the attention. It's been a nice change, though." She gave Aunt Martha a cautious smile.

"And how's your walk with the Lord, hon?" The question sounded natural, unobtrusive, coming from Aunt Martha.

"Truth be told, I held God at a distance after my father died. I suppose I blamed his death on God. John helped me work through the pain, though, and now I'm discovering every day what a wonderful God we serve."

"Devotion to God shouldn't depend on circumstance." Uncle Matthew leaned forward, searching deep in Sarah's eyes. "We serve him through the good, and the bad."

Sarah matched his stare. "I won't deny I was wrong, Uncle Matthew. I asked God to forgive me, and now I'm moving on."

The big man sank back in his chair. "I'm sorry, Sarah. And you forgive me too, Johnny. I know that I have been quite forward with you. I need to make sure, you see." His eyes roved back and forth between them. "I have to be certain that you both are the right people for the job."

"Matthew! Good heavens! I told you to leave them alone." Martha planted both hands on her hips, one elbow jabbing Sarah in the side. "There's no reason for you to rush at them like this."

"It's OK, Aunt Martha." John gave her a reassuring smile. "We believe God sent us here. There's nothing we'd like better than to find out why."

"Well said, young man." Matthew clasped the arms of his chair. "If you will, let me give you some background information." He didn't wait for permission.

"Martha and I have been in Winterville for nearly twenty years. We started with nothing, and worked hard to get the church established. Most of the people around here are backwards, and they don't trust outsiders. We had to prove ourselves, become part of the community. There are those who would not even speak to me in the beginning. It was almost five years before we had twenty regulars on Sunday mornings.

"But we showed them God's love. Martha took meals to families in need all over the county. I volunteered a helping hand every time I saw someone working in their yard. Slowly, we earned their trust, and they let us share Jesus with them.

"Nine years later we built a new building and filled it to capacity. But then things changed. We stopped growing for some reason. Things stagnated, then went downhill. Today we have anywhere from forty to fifty show up any given Sunday. Those who are left seem to come because of habit rather than any real love for God. I feel like I'm preaching to bumps on a log most of the time." Matthew stared thoughtfully into the distance when he finished.

John jumped in. "That's why you asked us here, to bring life back to the church?"

"Exactly. The people need more than I can give. I want you to consider stepping in to make things right again."

"I'd be glad to, Uncle Matthew. I've seen just what you're talking about at dozens of churches. We'll have the whole town bubbling with excitement in less than a week."

Aunt Martha's expression turned uncharacteristically serious. "Oh, uh, goodness." She tapped nervous patterns on her legs, eyes on Matthew. "Please pardon me." She pushed up from the couch and scampered away to the kitchen.

Matthew watched her go, then turned back to John. "I don't think you quite understand what I'm trying to tell you."

"Don't worry, Uncle Matthew." John gave a dismissive wave. "God will take care of everything—no matter how bad it seems."

"It's true." Sarah nodded. "I've learned so much about how God watches over us. Let me tell you what he did for my mother—"

"Please." Uncle Matthew held up a hand. "I apologize for interrupting, Sarah. I really want to hear that story sometime. Right now, though, I need you both to listen carefully."

John drew a breath to speak but Matthew shook his head and silenced him. "What I have tried to tell you is that it's time for me to retire. I have been searching for my replacement, and now, I think I have found him."

Chapter Eighteen

"Mom, I am *not* going back to school." Trevor pulled up into a sitting position inside the tent. He held the cell phone to his ear, frowning.

"You can't quit," said the voice inside the phone. "My family has *never* had a dropout, and we're not going to start now. I'd be absolutely mortified to show my face in public again."

He swore at her. "You think I care about that? I found a place where your petty social status isn't worth a dime."

"Your father is going to be *very* upset."

Trevor cursed again. "So what—he probably won't even know I'm gone. In fact, tell him…" Trevor made several rather unpleasant suggestions regarding his father.

"You aren't going to abandon Lisa, are you? I have trouble believing that."

"Let me worry about Lisa." Trevor swatted at a mosquito, missed, and frowned.

"Trevor, you're throwing your life away. I thought you were smarter than this."

"Ha! Maybe I'm a lot smarter than you think. I found a way out of the rat race *and* out from under your thumb. I'm way ahead."

"You can expect a call from your dad."

"I won't lose any sleep over it. Bye, Mom."

"Trevor—"

Click.

He tossed the phone onto his sleeping bag and crawled out of the tent. One problem down, one to go. Time to pump more information out of the old mountain goat.

Ready or not, John, here I come.

It had been a couple of days since he'd climbed the trail to John's place. Maybe the old guy had cooled off by now. Trevor dropped his peace offering—a spicy grilled trout—into a plastic bag and placed it in the shoulder pouch he had fashioned from a rabbit's hide. He slung the pouch and a canteen over his right shoulder.

The old guy had softened up a little when Trevor played "The Song." So, Trevor figured it made sense to play a little music while he was up there. He grabbed his guitar and tossed it over his left side.

With his load swinging and bumping, Trevor started up the trail to the hermit's lair. "Nice day for a stroll," he told a passing bird. Moments later, he bowed and extended a hand in mock cordiality to a zigzagging dragonfly. His load shifted forward when he made the gesture, and the guitar swung around, bopping him in the ribs. He lost his balance and slipped on some loose gravel that lay on the hard-packed soil.

One knee hit the ground, but he caught himself in time to prevent further mishap. His knee hurt, though—and his side, too. Pulling himself up, he rubbed his leg with one hand and his rib with the other. He cursed while looking himself over. No blood. Maybe a couple of bruises. He pushed his cargo back into its proper place and resumed the ascent, but with subdued aplomb.

His recent decision to abandon school had felt like a weight being lifted and, without intending to, he whistled while he climbed—nothing in particular, just a few merry notes thrown together at random.

After a few minutes he realized his tune had transformed itself into "Whistle While You Work." In his imagination, he marched with the Seven Dwarves on their way back home from a day at the mines. He felt of his lengthening beard and glanced down at his dirty attire and jangling accessories. "Ha! I bet I *look* like one of the Seven Dwarves."

He guffawed from deep in his throat and swung his arms back and forth. "Look—I'm an idiot! I can do anything I want— nobody'll even know. This is awesome!" He tucked his guitar tight against his side and danced a jig, swaying and prancing within the miniscule confines of the trail.

Just ahead the path narrowed, hugging the mountainside. To his right the trees thinned out and a drop-off loomed.

Time to get serious.

Stomp, clomp, crunch became the steady rhythm from his Redwing hiking boots, spotless when he first set foot on the mountain, now sporting a dozen rips and scratches from their recent harsh adventures. Nevertheless, they did their job—they propelled him steadily upward.

Bump, scrape, bump, scrape. As the trail narrowed further, the neck of his guitar struck the side of the cliff and scrubbed the dirt and rocks with each step. The noise grated on his nerves. Trevor twisted sideways, backside to the mountain, in order to keep the guitar from banging. He side-stepped upward. A little awkward, perhaps, but only half the trail remained.

The swinging weight of the guitar, his clumsy sideways gait, and the steep slope of the narrow trail made progress difficult. It also made his leg muscles ache from the awkward positioning. His head twisted sideways toward the incline, the leafless branch resting partway across his path lay below his line of sight. He discovered it by stepping on it.

When Trevor placed his full weight on his left foot for another step upward, the branch rolled and his boot skidded. His left leg slipped down and slammed into his right ankle. Both legs went sideways, feet pointed down the path. There was no time to curse.

He flailed, one-armed, on the way down, an involuntary motion. The sudden movement flung the guitar down and around his back where it landed under his outstretched arm. This caused his center of gravity to shift away from the mountainside and toward the drop-off.

Plunging sideways parallel with the trail, he slammed the ground and banged his head. "Oomph!" Air rushed from his lungs, the world jittered, and all sense of bodily control flew the coup. The guitar, now under him, dug into his armpit, metal strings ripping away skin.

He slid.

Too fast. Way too fast the mountainside receded, the guitar a surf board. Trevor's face dragged the dirt, bobbing and banging, dust and debris stinging his eyes.

He accelerated before having the first thought of stopping himself. Ever downward, he inched closer to the edge until his feet flew out into nothingness. Then, too stunned to take rational action, he simply flailed the ground, fingers clawing in desperation. But the hard-packed surface provided no handhold.

The weight of his legs became the driving force behind his motion. Having regained his senses, Trevor fully realized the danger of his predicament. Eyes wide, adrenaline slammed his heart into overdrive and sent him into a full panic.

He had to get control! Hands clawed the ground until blood seeped from his fingertips. His shirt slid up, baring his torso, and hundreds of tiny rocks dug tiny craters in his skin. He couldn't find a grip anywhere.

His boots! Maybe he could sink them in the ground and stop the alarming momentum. That *had* to be it.

When his hips reached the edge, he swung both legs and kicked. The loose, rocky surface crumbled under his feet. He slowed, but did not stop. Now, he cursed.

Something jolted him to a stop. It felt like the guitar strap caught on a rock or clump of grass. Trevor didn't care what had happened. He was safe.

His breath came in quick gasps while blood pounded in his ears. For the longest time he made no movement other than the heaving of his chest. Then as panic faded and relief set in, he whistled a long sigh and took stock of his situation. His legs dangled over nothing. His hands now trembled uncontrollably. Think. How to get back on the trail?

Could John hear him from this distance? Probably not. Then again, what choice did he have? Trevor gulped air and tried to yell, but managed little more than a hoarse whisper. Plenty of curses raced through his mind, however.

He lifted his head just enough to search either side for a handhold. It was his undoing. Something snapped and the guitar sprang from its resting place. Trevor smacked both hands on the ground, but instead of arresting his motion, it launched him from the cliff with greater force. His feet dropped downward and his hands closed on empty space. Free-fall. Nothing but blue sky and bright sun filled his vision. The light blinded him so he closed his eyes. His mind raced, and he thought of the fate waiting for him below. Terror filled his heart.

"Aiiiihhhhh!" The sound echoed for long seconds across the valley.

* * *

Shadows danced against the cave walls in conflicting patterns, fueled by the flickering light of four glass oil lamps. Paraphernalia from a lifetime of solitary mountain life hunched in semi-neat rows along both sides of the cavern. A hundred or more books lay in stacks of tens on the left. Dozens of crudely-carved wooden animals jutted from the floor in a tangled pile to the right. Cylindrical wooden tubes of various lengths and diameters poked out here and there from among the pile of carvings.

A mixed bag of metal and hand-made wooden utensils hung near the ceiling from pegs driven into a tree branch wedged between opposing walls. Three large coils of hemp rope hung on the last few pegs in the branch. A few beaten pots and pans stood in columns on the floor under the rope, and a shotgun sat propped against the wall near the pans with several fresh shells scattered on the floor around its stock. Other miscellaneous bric-a-brac, some stacked neatly and some not, occupied various portions of the cave floor. A damp, musty smell filled the air.

John squatted on an old wooden milk crate in the middle of the collage. He wielded an eight-inch hunting knife by the blade, which he weaved back and forth across a block of wood roughly six inches to a side, squinting as he worked, brow furrowed in concentration. Periodically he leaned toward the nearest lamp and turned the carving back and forth, studying it at different angles.

"Hmm." John rubbed his chin, then shook his head. "No, that's not right, either." The carving sailed through the air, clattered down the pile occupied by its peers, and rolled into the middle of the cavern floor. John slumped back against the wall and frowned at his latest failure.

The cliff.

His eyes went wide. It had just been a whisper—a thought, not an audible voice. Yet it carried enough power that it shocked him off his perch. He stumbled to the ground and the crate went with him. He searched the cavern but found no other signs of life which, deep in his soul, is what he expected because that was no human voice he'd heard. However, he *did* know that voice, no matter the years that had passed since he last heard it.

The hair on the back of John's neck stood on end. Sweat beaded his forehead. Hands shaking, he righted the crate and eased onto it, hand over his mouth, thoughts racing. Maybe his mind had played a trick on him after all these years.

No. The Lord spoke to him, all right. But, why now—or at all? He couldn't remember the last conversation they had together. Well, maybe he could. But he didn't like to think about those days.

"The cliff?" What was that supposed to mean? The cliff beside the trail, maybe? "All right, let's check it out."

John stood, stepped toward the cave entrance, paused, then turned back. "I might need you," he said, grabbing the shotgun from against the wall. He trekked to the cave entrance, paused again, and sent a questioning look heavenward. Retracing his steps once more, he propped the gun against the wall in its original position.

Hurry.

The voice again! He grabbed a five-foot walking staff from the mouth of the cave and rushed to the tent. Pushing the door flap aside, he hobbled onto the plateau and limped toward the downhill trail, progress slowing as the incline grew steep.

Every few steps he stopped to look and listen. Nothing here, nothing there. No sounds except the occasional calling bird. He reached the woods just above the Wizard's Court and stopped, confused. No more cliff. OK, back up and try again.

Now he squinted over the edge every so often. He must have missed something on the way down, his eyes not being quite what they used to be. This time he took extra care staring at the depths and the ground along the way. Still, nothing but the tips of green pines greeted him beyond the rim.

Just a minute. Something telltale on the ground ahead. He quickened his pace for another twenty feet and then stopped before a set of freshly etched ridges from the midpoint of the trail to the edge. Skid marks? John dropped to all fours and peered over the side. Nothing obvious down there. Nothing left, nothing right...Wait!

"There!" He squinted, shielding his eyes from the sun. At least fifty feet below, a ledge jutted from the side of the mountain. Something, no some*one* lay sprawled on the ledge—an unmoving someone at that.

"The rope. I have to get the rope." John scrambled to his feet and limped up the path all the way home. When he reached the plateau, he leaned over, hands on knees, wheezing. Precious moments later, he stood, swallowed hard, then huffed over to the cave. He pulled all three rope coils from the overhead branch and tossed them over his shoulder. "This better be enough."

John rushed back outside and looped the longest stretch of rope around the base of a tree at the mouth of the trail. Fixing it with a triple knot, he pulled against it with his full weight and assured himself it would hold. Back down the trail he went, unwinding rope behind him along the way.

About a third of the way down the path he ran out of line. He unlimbered the second coil and, in less than a minute, had it tied to the first and was on his way again. When he reached the skid marks he tossed the rope over the side then leaned over and peered below.

"Darn!" John pursed his lips. The rope didn't reach halfway to the ledge. The last coil—the shortest one—dropped from his shoulder and landed in his hand. He hauled up the second rope and added the short one to it, then threw the lot of it back over the edge.

A quick glance over the side brought additional disappointment. "Hang it all!" He could tell the rope didn't reach the ledge, but he couldn't see how far off it was. "These old eyes just aren't what they used to be. Ten feet...five feet...twenty?" He just couldn't tell. What now?

Trust me.

The voice again. He glanced at the sky. "I darn well guess I'll have to. I sure can't figure it out on my own." He lowered himself to the ground, grumbling.

With a glance toward heaven, and a shake of his head, John tossed his walking stick to the side and grabbed the rope with both hands. He swung his legs over the edge and, inch by inch, lowered himself down the bluff.

At first, the cliff face provided few footholds. He relied solely on arm strength—a strength that weakened with every move.

"Dang...fool...crazy," he grunted through clenched teeth.

About ten feet below the path, John found enough solid rock and tiny outcroppings to support him. He paused to catch his breath and afford his arms a measure of relief. "Whew. Thank you, Lord."

After catching his breath, John continued the descent. A quick glance upward gave a sense of finality to the situation—the edge of the cliff was no longer visible. Then, a few more feet down, he grasped the frayed end of the rope. OK, so how far off was he? A tiny outcropping just below his feet prevented him from seeing any part of the ledge, so he felt with one foot for solid ground. Nothing. A gust of wind upset his balance and set him swaying.

"Dear Lord. What are you doing to me now?"

Craning his neck, John just barely caught sight of the ledge below.

About ten feet appeared to separate him from solid ground. What to do? Wait a minute—ten feet from his eyes meant maybe half that distance from his feet. He could manage a five-foot drop, couldn't he?

This sure ain't going to feel good, Lord. Please don't let me break anything.

Gritting his teeth, John let go the rope and clawed dirt to slow his descent. His boots smacked the ground hard enough to throw him off balance, and he fell flat on his backside.

"Ee-ouch!" He rolled over and rubbed his behind. "Land sakes!" He glanced heavenward. "The Lord chastises those whom he loves, eh?"

No time to dwell on the pain. John pulled himself up and limped over to the motionless figure. It was that fool of a kid that had been pestering him lately. What had he done to end up down here?

Trevor lay on his back, spread-eagle, his head cocked sideways at an odd angle. Both eyelids hung half open, pupils rolled back in his head. Shards of glossy wood littered the ground around him. What in the world? On closer inspection, John recognized the splinters as the remains of Trevor's guitar.

John knelt and put an ear to Trevor's mouth while watching his chest for signs of life. No sound, no motion. Nothing. John seized a wrist with one hand and grabbed Trevor's neck with the other. No discernible pulse.

Would CPR work? He'd only heard of it, but never seen it demonstrated. He had to try something, though. John pressed down on Trevor's chest a few times, then blew some air in his mouth. No response.

"OK, God. You brought me here for a reason. What do you want me to do—use the gift?"

Hands over Trevor's heart, John looked heavenward and waited. And…nothing. Something wasn't right. He tried again, this time praying under his breath. Still nothing.

"What's going on, Lord? This hasn't happened since…" Bitterness, and then anger, replaced John's confusion. "Is that it?" He stood, and his voice rose with him. "Is that why you brought me here—to remind me of my failure?" He shouted now, voice directed at the sky. "Well, I don't need any reminders, thank you very much. My memory is fine—just like it has been every day for the past forty two years!" He shook his fist, then looked back down at Trevor.

Darn that boy. John kicked the ground and sent a cloud of dirt and dust over Trevor's body. "Why should I care about *you*, you stupid heathen? You're going to burn anyway." He kicked the ground harder, showering Trevor with pebbles and dirt. Then he kicked Trevor.

For endless moments afterward, he just stared and seethed.

One more time. The right way.

That voice! John fell to his knees from its power. And it told him to do things the *right* way. For forty years, he'd done things *his* way. Forty years of parlor tricks for ignorant hillbillies. Could he do anything the right way anymore? Maybe it was time to find out.

He laid an open palm on Trevor's chest, then bowing his head, he prayed aloud in the simple manner he'd abandoned decades before. "Young man, I command you to wake up—in the name of Jesus."

Trevor lay still.

John jumped to his feet, swung around, and kicked the mountain. "I can't take any more of this!" He fell against the cliff and buried his head in his arms. "I don't have anything left to give."

A different voice—a human voice—shocked him upright.

"Hey, old man—what are you doing here?" A slight pause. "What am *I* doing here?"

Chapter Nineteen

And so we had a decision to make. Of course, I had always jumped at the first sign of God's voice. But, now I had Sarah. And she had different ideas on how to go about things.

* * *

"Serving God has been fun so far," Sarah whispered, "but this is *serious*."

John also spoke in hushed tones, not wanting to wake his aunt and uncle. "Sarah, this is how it works. God calls, and we answer. We never know what he might ask, and that's not important. All that matters is for us to obey."

"That's just fine and dandy for *you*, Mr. Jones, but you're not the one leaving your mother to fend for herself, now are you?"

He couldn't see her very well in the darkened living room, but he knew her cheeks were flushed and there were flames in her eyes. "Sarah, God will take care of your mother. He always has and he always will. You've just got to have faith."

"What about *me*? Does God care how I feel? Do *you* care?" Sarah shifted position, voice rising. The springs in the rollaway bed squeaked. "I'd be leaving behind everything I've ever known."

"Shh—you'll wake them." John stilled himself and listened to make sure there were no sounds from Uncle Matthew's bedroom. "Sarah, it's not about you or me. It's about what God wants. And you know what? Here we are arguing about something that may not even be his will. We should pray about it."

"But what if it is? Are you going to just pack me up and move me away without another thought?"

"Sarah." John reached for her hand. "Let's seek God before we jump to any conclusions. We can spend the day tomorrow praying and seeking his will. Then we'll decide. For tonight let's just forget about it and get some rest. OK?"

"That's easy for you to say. I doubt I'll sleep a wink."

He leaned over to kiss her but she pulled away. The reaction didn't come as a surprise. In the short time John had known her, he'd learned she didn't like change—and he knew from the first time he laid eyes on her how easily she got in a huff when things didn't go her way. What he didn't understand was why she couldn't just turn it over to the Lord.

Now John found himself torn between God and the wife God had given him. He loved them both and didn't want to disappoint either one. What should he do?

Dear Lord, grant me wisdom. Open Sarah's eyes so she sees your truth. Help her to accept your will.

At peace, John drifted off to sleep.

* * *

"Sarah, are you sure you're all right?" John paused from their walk through the field at the back of Uncle Matthew's property. He searched her dark-circled eyes. "You look terrible."

"Thank you for those kind words of encouragement." Sarah frowned, then looked away. A playful breeze whipped her skirt to and fro, then sent it billowing behind her. Long stems of wild grass danced about her legs.

"I didn't mean it like that, hon. It's just that...well, you look like you either didn't sleep, or you're sick or something."

Sarah sighed. "I suppose you're a prophet as well as a healer. I hardly slept at all last night."

John pulled her face toward his. "Talk to me."

"It's you and your just-obey-God attitude, always brimming with excitement. It's not the same for me." She pulled away. "I don't want to move."

"I prayed for you last night." John let the words sink in, then reached for her hand and gave it a reassuring squeeze. "Everything is going to work out just fine. You'll see."

"It's not *whether* it works out, but *how*. I don't want to leave the only home I've ever known. A week here and there is fun, but to just up and move away for good isn't the same thing."

"Sarah—"

"Let me finish, John Jones." Sarah furrowed her brow. "What happens if God *does* tell us to move? The people may not even like us. And where would we live? We don't have money, or a place to stay, or anything. Not only that, you'd be giving up your calling to go out in the world and heal people."

John stared across the field at his uncle's house, wind rustling his hair. "I don't have all the answers." He turned back to Sarah, expression serious. "I just know I can trust him."

"What do you *really* know about trusting him? I used to trust God, too. I trusted him to keep my father alive, but he died in spite of my prayers. You've never had to face anything that truly put your faith to the test, have you?"

"I—"

"No, you haven't. So it's easy for you to trust. But my life hasn't always been a fairy tale."

Where is this anger coming from? Is it all about losing her father, or is there more?

"I thought you put all that behind." John lifted her chin, brushed her cheek with a kiss. "God's given us a new life now, and he *will* take care of us. Even with your father gone, you never went without food or shelter—"

Sarah started to protest.

"Hear me out, hon. I know it was tough—and sometimes it still is. And I know things didn't go the way you wanted. I'm not trying to make light of what you've been through, but I *am* saying things could have been worse. And there are people in the world who *do* have it worse. You don't get mad at God just because you got dealt a bad hand."

"I..."

Fire faded from her eyes, and tension drained from her face. She huffed. "I hate it when you're right."

John smiled. "Just trust him, OK?"

Sarah leaned into his chest. It wasn't long before he felt her sobs. "I wish I could, John. I really wish I could."

He tightened his arms around her, and for the longest time they held each other.

* * *

"And where have you two lovebirds been?" Martha looked up from her knitting as the newlyweds came through the door. "I was beginning to think Matthew scared you off."

John eased the screen door closed, then ushered Sarah to the couch. "We've been outside talking, Aunt Martha." They both sat down, and John picked up the morning paper.

"You have such a lovely place." Sarah shook her head in wonder. "I imagine the Garden of Eden must have been like this."

"Well, thank you, dear. I'm not sure it's *that* special, but we've been mighty fortunate to call it home. I'll sure miss it when we're gone. But it'll help knowing that the right people will be looking after it."

Sarah's eyes widened. "You've already sold it?"

"It is not ours to sell, young lady." Uncle Matthew appeared at the end of the hallway, a Bible in one hand and a cup of coffee in the other.

John glanced up from the paper. "I didn't know you rented, Uncle Matthew. I thought you owned the place."

"The house belongs to the church." Matthew passed them by on his way to the kitchen. "Part of the package," he called over his shoulder.

"Hmph." John resumed reading.

"You mean..." Sarah absorbed her surroundings with fresh eyes, mouth open.

Aunt Martha leaned forward. "Sarah, dear—are you all right?"

John glanced sideways and caught the faraway look in Sarah's eyes. "Um, Sarah?"

She raised a hand and partway covered her mouth. "Do you mean," she said in a dreamy voice, "if we accepted the position, this place would be mine? Ah—" Sarah lowered her hand. "I mean *ours*? Free and clear—no rent or anything?"

"That's right, dear," said Aunt Martha. "Isn't it a wonderful blessing? God always has a way of taking care of his children."

"Heh." John resumed reading. He spoke from behind the paper. "See there? I told you, hon."

"Oh, my." Sarah clutched John's arm, drawing his attention from the paper yet again. "Do you think this could this be God's way of confirming what he wants us to do?"

Long ago, John heard Pa say something that made little sense at the time. Pa had told him that you can't understand women—you just have to love them the way they are. Sarah now showed signs of that strange disease.

"Uncle Matthew?" John called toward the kitchen. "I think we have an answer for you."

* * *

"Johnny, this is Bull Tankersly. That's his real name, by the way—Bull." Uncle Matthew turned from one to the other. "And Bull, this is Reverend Johnny Jones—and his wife, Sarah."

It took John a moment to absorb Bull's features. The man stood about six feet tall and appeared to have about two hundred and fifty pounds of pure muscle clinging to his bones. His big bald head contained a toothy grin, and freckles covered the high points of his cheeks. The biceps poking out from his short sleeves reminded John of coconuts.

"Nice to meet you Reverend Jones. You too, Mrs. Jones. Sorry I didn't get to see you last month." Bull extended a meaty hand that looked like it belonged on a nine-foot giant. John grimaced under his grip.

"Bull is my right-hand man." Matthew patted the big guy on the shoulder. "He knows everything that goes on in the church. I have already told him why you are here, and he knows that I am leaving. If you need anything, Johnny, Bull is your man." Uncle Matthew gestured toward the building. "Now, shall we pray?"

The foursome made their way up the front steps, then down the aisle to the altar where they dropped to their knees. Bull went right to praying before the others got their eyes closed. "God Almighty, thank you for sending Reverend Jones to us. If he's the man for the job, please make that clear to the whole congregation. I ask that you give him the words we need to hear, and open our ears to listen. Most of all, God, I pray that you have your way in this church. Amen."

John opened one eye and peeked at the big man. There sure weren't any words wasted in that little talk with God, he thought.

Uncle Matthew started up a prayer that sounded much like one of Jeremiah's. A good while later John and Sarah got their turn. It wasn't long afterward that the church organ signaled the approaching service, and John found it hard to believe they had been kneeling almost an hour.

The four rose as one, and Uncle Matthew led John to the small pew behind the pulpit. From his place of honor, John studied his surroundings. It felt a little surreal that God would set him over such a fine place as this.

The sanctuary contained seating for a couple of hundred people. A balcony had room for forty or fifty more. Centered above the aisle, a golden chandelier hung from the thirty-foot ceiling. Gilded fixtures perched between stained glass windows on either side of the room. John figured it was one of the top ten fanciest places where he'd ever stepped foot.

Despite the size and grand furnishings, only enough people to fill a quarter of the seats showed up. From there the service read like a script from any of dozens of churches John had visited in recent months. An introductory song, announcements, a few more songs, and then time to preach. John felt the slight twinge of nervousness that always accompanied him when he spoke.

The crowd quieted, all eyes to the front. "God loves you." The words echoed, bouncing back in a curious way. John examined their faces, and a wave of compassion washed over him. A familiar voice told him not to wait until the end of the sermon.

He stepped from behind the pulpit and, leaning on his cane, down onto the green-carpeted aisle. He singled out a white-haired lady sitting alone on the second row. Leaning toward her, he stared deep into her eyes. "God loves *you*." Warmth coursed through him. He reached further and spread the warmth to the woman in a heartfelt hug.

The lady wailed, sending eyes wide all over the sanctuary. She lifted a quaking hand to the sky. "Glory! Glory, glory, glory!"

John found Bull, and every eye centered on his approach to the big man. "Bull, God loves you." He reached over the side of the pew and brushed the oversized man's shoulder with his fingertips.

"Unh!" Bull jerked sideways, his right hand springing to his left shoulder. His gaze followed the young reverend's retreat to the pulpit, mouth wide.

John dove into his sermon. He preached about the Father's unfathomable love, and explained that God wanted them free from every disease. Holding their undivided attention, he relayed the story of his own divine healing on the mountain so many months ago.

"And now I want you to exercise your faith." John searched the room. "The first person who comes to this altar for prayer," he pointed to the space below him, "will be healed."

John stepped down from the pulpit and waited, facing statues. At last a frail old woman with curly gray hair rose and shuffled out of her pew. She hobbled to the front, bent nearly double. John leaned down to hear her whispered request, then faced the crowd, smiling.

"In the name of Jesus," he ran his fingertips across her back, "stand up straight!"

A shriek pierced the air and every person in the building jumped at the sound. The old woman whooped, hollered, and stamped her feet, then stood up straight and tall. She pranced back and forth in front of the pulpit, speaking the name of Jesus again and again.

John faced the crowd, ready to speak, but the old woman tackled him. She threw her arms around him and squeezed with the strength of a young buck. "God loves you," he repeated, for her ears alone.

When she released him, he peered back at the congregation. He saw the skeptics. A rickety woman with a cane, the middle-age man in his expensive suit, and the farmer in overalls on the back pew. But the believers far outnumbered the doubters. A spontaneous ovation erupted. John shook his head, pointing heavenward.

Later, at service end, a line formed from the sanctuary to the foyer. Everyone—including the skeptics—wanted a closer look at the young preacher. John and Sarah stood beside a beaming Uncle Matthew. They greeted each person in turn as excitement bubbled throughout the room. Smiling faces blurred, hands numbed, and small talk lost its meaning. John turned to Sarah and clasped her hand.

"You know, it kind of feels like home."

* * *

"He said the vote was unanimous." John sat with Sarah, Mrs. O'Reilly, and his parents in the living room of the elder Jones' home. Each held a saucer with a slice of tea cake. The aroma of fresh-brewed coffee filled the air.

"That's wonderful, son. Absolutely wonderful. I'm so proud of what God's doing. I know he has a lot more in store for you, too—for both of you." Pa grabbed Ma's hand and clasped it tight.

"Well I, for one, am not looking forward to it." Mrs. O'Reilly set her saucer on the coffee table. "I just got used to having a man around the house again. Now here you two go gallivanting off halfway across the country." She huffed. "Why, Sarah and I barely scraped by before John came along. How will I make ends meet all by me lonesome?"

"Oh, Mother." Sarah heaved a deep breath. "You're in better health than ever before, and you have a new church family to watch over you. You'll be fine."

"You can be sure of that," Pa piped in. "And I'll keep an eye on you. Just make sure you do your part—trust God."

"I'll miss you, Johnny." Ma's lip quivered. A tear ran down her cheek. "I knew this day would come, but I never knew how hard it would be."

Mrs. O'Reilly turned to Ma, saw the look on her new friend's face, and lost all control. She moaned aloud, then broke into a series of staccato boohoos. Pa wrapped an arm around Ma, and John soon joined him. A moment later Sarah burst into tears, leapt from the couch, and ran to her mother.

"I'll...never...see...you...again!" Mrs. O'Reilly huffed between sobs.

Sarah cried louder.

"Ladies, please." Pa patted Ma's cheek. "Ida."

What could John do but wait for the clatter to die out on its own? Fortunately, the worst of it passed soon enough, leaving the women sniffling.

"Come on, everyone." Pa showed a toothy smile. "This is a happy occasion. John and Sarah are starting a new life—the life God chose for them. We'll miss them, but we can't keep them under our wings forever."

Dabbing tears, Ma faced Pa. "I know he has to leave. It's just hard, that's all."

John let go of Ma and hobbled over to Sarah. "I thought you were excited about moving. You're not having second thoughts, are you?"

"No, I—I *am* excited." Her red eyes met his. "But I'll miss Mother. I didn't realize how hard it would be."

"Sarah." John stroked her cheek. "This isn't the last time you'll see her. We'll be back for Thanksgiving, and Christmas, and we'll try to have visits in between, too." John addressed the others. "We want all of you to come see us whenever you can."

A smile returned to Sarah's face. "Mother, you *must* see the house. It's like a little paradise. You'll love it."

Ma's tears dried and Mrs. O'Reilly's sniffles disappeared. The mood in the entire room lightened. John breathed a sigh of relief.

"There!" Pa's grin broadened. "Much better. Now let's enjoy the time we have left together."

Sarah snuck off to the kitchen and returned with another piece of cake. She sank down on the couch and munched in earnest. Mrs. O'Reilly frowned at her. "You'll ruin your supper, dear."

"Oh, Mother. I'm grown and married. I think I'm allowed a little extra cake. Besides, I'm famished."

Mrs. O'Reilly started to respond, but just cocked her head and blinked. She cut her eyes toward John, then back to Sarah. One eyebrow lifted, but she said no more.

* * *

John determined he would visit every person who had ever darkened the doors of Winterville Chapel. It might take weeks— maybe months—but he felt it important to know every person who had ever been connected with the church. Perhaps such face-to-face meetings, mixed with genuine love, would draw those who had drifted away back into the fold.

Any other day Sarah would have gone with him. She had blossomed in their new setting, enjoying the experience of meeting new people even more than John. He suspected Sarah might be trying to fill a void created by her isolated existence back in Arkansas.

Today, however, she had begged off, saying she had errands to run in town, leaving John to his own devices. And quite a day it had been. John had made a good dozen contacts in his journey around the foothills. Now, he eyed the sun hanging low over the Goodman sisters' house as he prepared to head back home. With a wave to Edna Goodman, who stood on her porch watching him go, John settled into the Studebaker and cranked over the engine.

The car lurched into gear and soon John was well on his way down the winding country road. He imagined Sarah's petite features as he drove, and could almost smell the sweet scent of her dime store perfume. Miles passed, and in what seemed like no time at all he pulled into the driveway of the splendid little cottage that brought his wife so much joy.

Sarah rushed out the door and met him halfway to the house. "Oh, John!" She wrapped him in a hug. "I love you so much."

"Well, I love you, too." John kissed her proper on the lips, then cocked his head. "Someone must have had a pretty good day."

She pushed away from him, still holding his hands, face lit with a smile. "I wanted to do something special, but I just can't wait any longer!"

"Wait?" John gave her a puzzled look. "For what?"

She squeezed his hands, grinning ear to ear. "I'm pregnant!"

Chapter Twenty

As Trevor tried to regain his senses, he watched John sink to his knees and search the sky. "He's alive," said the old man.

"Who's alive? What's going on?"

"You did it." John shook his head. "You really did it, but..." He nodded at Trevor. "Why *him*?"

Trevor rolled onto his knees. "Hey! What's *with* you? Are you sick or something? I asked you what we're doing here."

John flopped down on the ground and stared.

Cursing, Trevor rose and surveyed his surroundings. He stood in the middle of a ledge about ten feet wide and twenty feet long that jutted from the face of a sheer cliff. Polished wood shards and twisted metal strings lay in heaps all around him. "My guitar!" Trevor dropped to all fours and picked through the wreckage.

Uttering curses in earnest, Trevor rose with the G-string and a dangling bridge in hand, and walked the ledge end to end. Scratching his head, he searched right, left, front, and back. The ledge tapered into the mountain at each end, and the ground dropped away at a sixty degree angle over the side. Above him, the mountainside rose vertical fifty feet or so, ending in what appeared to be another ledge. He caught site of the rope, but it was as high as a basketball goal overhead.

It made no sense. He couldn't remember coming here, and he didn't see any way in or out. "John." Trevor waved both hands at the old man. "Hey—I get you're having your own little moment right now, but," Trevor cursed most pointedly, raising his voice with every word, "I could really use some help figuring out what's going on!"

John looked away and doodled in the dirt. "Yeah, I can relate to that."

"You're crazy, old man. Can't you answer a simple question?" Trevor drew a deep breath and emphasized every word. "How... did... we...get here?"

John blinked. "You don't remember, do you?"

"Ha!" Trevor slapped his forehead. "Somebody *is* home. That's what I've been trying to tell you."

"Hmmm." John stared up the mountainside, then turned back to Trevor. "Apparently, you slipped."

Trevor squinted at the rope as it twisted in the breeze. His gaze followed it upward to where it disappeared beyond the overhead ledge. "Umm..." He frowned, straining to remember, then turned back to John. "So, were we climbing down the mountain or something?"

"Mm. Let's talk about this later. We need to find a way out of here."

Trevor switched mental gears. "Why don't we just go back the way we came?" He looked around the ledge again. "Which was...?"

John eyed the rope. "I'm not so sure that's possible." He stood and dusted himself off, then ambled over to the cliff's edge and peered over the side. "That doesn't look very promising, either."

The rope held Trevor's attention. "You know, I think I can reach that..." He backed up and got a running start then sprang toward the dangling line—and missed by a good two feet. A couple of more tries brought him no closer to his goal and, each time, he thudded into the dirt and slid back to the ledge, accumulating a nice set of scratches and bruises for his efforts.

John scratched his beard. "You're going to break something if you keep that up."

"Give me a boost, will ya?"

"You've got to be kidding. You're too heavy."

"No—get down on your hands and knees and I'll stand on your back."

John folded his arms and gave one exaggerated shake of his head. "Uh-uh. Not happening."

"Do you have any better ideas?"

Eyeing each part of the area for the umpteenth time, John conceded that the boy had a point. He heaved a sigh. "I really don't think this is a good idea..." But with one last glance at the rope, he knelt down and made himself a human footstool. "Take it easy, OK?"

Trevor placed one foot on top of him, started to lift up and...

"Hey!" John swatted Trevor's leg. "Get those boots off."

With a disgusted huff, Trevor stepped back and wrested off his boots, then climbed onto John's back. After wavering a bit to get his balance, he stretched his arms upward and found the rope still out of reach—but just so. "I'm gonna jump."

"What? No you're—"

Trevor pumped hard, sprang upward, and came down with a thud on top of John.

"Unh!"

The two tumbled into a pile, John grabbing his ribs.

"You lunatic! Are you trying to kill me?"

"I almost had it," Trevor said, pulling himself up. "One more try and I'll get it for sure."

"No you don't, you nincompoop! I'm lucky you didn't break my ribs."

"No, really—" Trevor motioned for John to get back in position. "Just one more time and I'll have it."

"No!" John winced as he pulled himself to a sitting position.

"Well..." Trevor stared at the rope. "What if you stand next to the cliff and I'll climb on your shoulders?"

"No."

"Come on, at least—"

"No!" John shook his head. "You already clobbered me once, and it ain't happening again." He stood, sucked in a deep breath, then tramped over to the far end of the ledge. For several seconds he stared at the drop-off. "There's got to be another way."

Trevor came up behind John and looked over his shoulder.

The ledge blended into moss-covered rock that dotted the mountain face. Both rock and moss continued up and down as far as the eye could see. Sporadic crevices and flat spots might have provided support for climbing, but this wasn't the movies—playing this game without proper equipment meant certain death.

John turned to step away and nearly ran Trevor over. "Would you move? You've caused enough trouble for one day." He pushed past Trevor and trudged to the other end of the ledge.

"Doesn't look very promising over here, either." John tapped his fingers together as he continued studying the slope.

Trevor busied himself lacing up his boots, then came up beside John and joined him in his scrutiny. The mountain sloped away into a cluster of trees about twenty feet below. At the base of the trees, the ground seemed to level off a bit.

By this time John had given up and limped back to the center of the ledge, shaking his head and muttering, one eye on the rope.

"Um, John?" Trevor glanced over his shoulder. "John! Come here."

"Why?" John's tone conveyed more than a little irritation. His eyes never left the rope.

"I have an idea."

"So? What is it?"

"Come see." Trevor motioned, and John, frowning, ambled toward him. Trevor pointed. "That level ground isn't all that far down. I think if we kind of lowered ourselves off the ledge, we could slide down and let the trees break our fall."

"'Break,' is a pretty good description of what those trees will do to us. You're crazy, boy."

"No, really—I don't think it'll be that bad. I'll go first." He dropped to the ground and dangled his legs over the edge.

"Hey! Don't do that—you'll get yourself killed!"

John grabbed for Trevor's arm, but it was too late—he had already let go and started down the slope. Fast. A flurry of arm waving and leg flailing did nothing to slow him. He tumbled into the trees full tilt, and they did, indeed, break his fall.

"Are you OK, boy?"

Trevor shook himself and rolled over just in time to see John's face appear over the ledge. A smile split Trevor's lips. "You're turn."

"Wha—?" John's eyes grew wide. "Oh, no. You *are* crazy." He disappeared from the brink.

"Come on—I'll catch you."

"You're out of your mind." John's voice sounded muffled over the ledge. "I didn't get this old by living like a daredevil."

"Yeah, well what's *your* plan?"

Seconds passed, then a minute or more. Finally a pair of boots appeared over the ledge, moving in slow motion. John muttered something before taking the plunge, but it was too low for Trevor to hear.

* * *

"All right—enough stalling. What were we doing climbing down the mountain?" Trevor set his coffee mug on the ground and tossed off the blanket John had draped over his shoulders. He leaned forward on the makeshift stool and gave the old man a penetrating stare.

John slurped another mouthful of stew. He glanced at the ceiling, the cave entrance, and back to his stew—everywhere, that is, but at Trevor.

"Well?"

Another bite of stew found its way into John's mouth, then he set his spoon aside. He stared at the floor for the longest time before answering. "So...you don't remember anything, huh?"

"How many times are you going to ask me that!" Trevor swore. "The last thing I remember is leaving camp. And the next thing I knew, we were sitting on that ledge. What happened out there?"

John chewed his lip. "Um, you fell."

"I *know* I fell, Einstein!" Trevor cursed again, face contorting in a furious frown. "Why were we climbing down the mountain? And why did I have my guitar with me?" He shook his head. "It just doesn't make sense."

"Hmm. Sorry about your guitar." John looked away again. "I really did enjoy hearing you play."

Trevor felt his face flush, but the word *guitar* jogged his memory. He calmed himself, and focused. Thump, thump, thump. The guitar bumped against the hillside. He had been hiking up the trail—going to see John. But...Trevor rubbed the lengthening stubble on his chin.

"Hey, wait a minute! I was going *up* the trail, and...I was by myself." He closed his eyes in concentration. Sliding, grabbing, falling. The mountain spinning away, and then blue sky. Panic. Screaming. The flood of memories jolted Trevor's heart into overdrive. He stared at John.

The old man met his gaze for the first time, rocking back and forth, waiting.

"I fell off the trail and you came and got me, didn't you?"

John continued to stare.

"I was…just lying there. I remember looking down at myself…like I was floating over my own body." A thought struck him. Trevor jerked a hand to the back of his head and felt under his hair. Then he flung both arms in front of him and examined the length of them. He reached under his shirt and felt the spot where he had landed on the guitar.

"I'm not hurt at all—I'm not even bruised!" He stared at John, incredulous. "I fell sixty feet off a sheer cliff and there's not a scratch on me. That's impossible, unless…"

John shifted and looked away.

"Unless I was *healed*." He pointed a finger at John. "You did it! You healed me just like that woman with the toothache. You're…you're the Wizard of Winterville!"

"Now hold on, son." John faced Trevor again. "Don't go jumping to conclusions."

"Ha! It fits." Trevor leapt to his feet and paced. "You live right next to the Wizard's Court, he comes down the same trail that leads to your place, and I'm the only person besides you who's not afraid to go up here. I fall off the cliff, and you use your magic to heal me." Trevor smacked a fist in his palm. "You're the wizard!"

"Hold on. That was quite a spill you took out there. I believe it's got you thinking a little bit sideways."

"Don't give me that. I'm not some mountain moron you can yank around—I know what happened." Trevor kicked the ground in glee. "Man, I can't wait to tell the guys about this."

"You won't tell *any*body!" John jumped from his seat, hands waving. "You have no right to say things like that. I just want to be left in peace, and I've had nothing but trouble since the day you showed up. If you tell people that nonsense, I'll never hear the end of it." He shook a finger in Trevor's face. "So just keep your mouth *shut*."

Trevor shrugged. "Why hide it? Hey—you could be rich and famous. But here you are working for peanuts—literally." He snorted at his unintentional pun.

John turned three different shades of red. "How *dare* you say such a thing!" He pointed at the cave entrance. "Get out of here!"

"Take it easy, old man." Trevor's feeling of triumph faded.

"I will *not* take it easy." John got in Trevor's face. "I've taken all I'm going to take from you. Get out of here—and don't come back!"

Not again. It took two whole days for the old codger to cool off the last time he got this riled. "OK, I'm going. Thanks for the stew. See you around, all right?"

"Out!"

* * *

A dark figure approached the front door of a two-story brick home that America's lower class would have considered a mansion. The stench from days of perspiration exuded from the apparition's body. A torn shirt and dirt-covered blue jeans announced to the upscale neighborhood, "I don't belong here!"

A hand reached out and pressed the doorbell.

Footsteps sounded behind the door. A face appeared in the sidelight, then quickly retreated. Another stab at the doorbell, then another. Heavier footsteps approached. The door cracked open and an eyeball peered through the crevice.

"Can I help you?" asked a man's voice.

"It's me, Mr. Dawson—Trevor. Is Lisa here?"

The door swung wider. "Trevor? What happened to you?"

"Well, it's kind of a long story. Lisa can tell you about it later. Is she here?"

"Uh, just a minute…"

The door closed and Trevor ran a hand through stringy hair. He heard a muffled conversation, words indistinct. Soon the door swung wide and Lisa stood before him.

"Trevor? You look *awful*."

He glanced down and back up. "Yeah, well, I prefer to think of it as the rustic look. But listen—you'll never believe it." He grinned. "I found the wizard."

Lisa cocked her head. "Um, exactly what is that supposed to mean?"

"You know—the magic wizard. Up on the mountain. I found him."

Blank stare. It wasn't exactly the reception Trevor expected. "I mean I *found* him—I know where he is." He smiled, waiting for congratulations.

"You mean there really is somebody claiming to be the wizard? Huh." She shoved her hands in her pockets. "I guess that means your little, um, *excursions* have paid off. Can things get back to normal now?"

Trevor heaved a sigh. "Can I come in? I've got a *bunch* of stuff to tell you."

Lisa looked him up and down. She wrinkled her nose. "Trevor, do you think…well, maybe it would be best if you went home and got cleaned up first."

Trevor blinked. Then it hit him.

"Ha!" He slapped his thigh. "Sure thing, babe. I guess I smell like a mountain goat, huh? Baths are kind of scarce where I've been." He took a half-step backward. "Sorry. I'll go de-slime myself. But after that…how about dinner tonight? It's been a while."

Lisa's eyes brightened. "Sure. Get yourself cleaned up and it's a date."

He pivoted on one foot and started toward the Explorer. "Six o'clock," he called over his shoulder.

"OK, six. See you then."

* * *

"Aaahh!" Mrs. McIntire slung her coffee cup on the kitchen floor where it shattered, hot brown liquid splattering her legs. She uttered a curse.

"Mom, it's me." Trevor stepped back and raised his hands.

She stared hard, eyes wide, then heaved a sigh. "Trevor? Omigosh. You scared me half to death." She made a face. "What in the world happened to you?"

"Nothing a bath and change of clothes won't fix." He shrugged. "Everybody looks like this on the mountain."

"Do they *smell* like that?"

Trevor rolled his eyes. "I know, OK?"

"You deserve a beating. Are you *ever* going back to school?" She pulled a dish towel from a drawer beside the oven and knelt to clean up the coffee.

"Mom, college is for kids who don't have a clue what they want out of life. That's not me." He sighed. "There's a big world out there. I've learned things they don't teach in school."

"Trevor McIntire, this is ridiculous. Do you know what my friends at the club are saying?" Mrs. McIntire rose and tossed the towel beside the sink, then opened the refrigerator and pulled out a dark green bottle. "Would you like some wine, dear? It might help clear that mixed-up head of yours."

"Actually, yeah." Trevor padded over to a barstool and took a seat.

Mrs. McIntire retrieved a couple of wineglasses from an overhead cabinet. She poured half a glass of dark red liquid into one, glanced at her son, and doubled the portion. "Here." She eyed him up and down. "You look like you could use it."

"Thanks, Mom." Trevor finished the drink in two gulps. "Ah! Man, that's good. I haven't had anything but water in days." He made a mental note to work some kind of deal with Finch for his special recipe. A couple of swigs now and then would come in handy when dealing with John.

"Don't give up on college, Trev." Mrs. McIntire filled her glass halfway and set the bottle on the marble countertop. "There's plenty of time to see the world after you earn a degree. I spent a year in Europe with a couple of friends after I graduated. Some of my fondest memories come from that time."

Clink. Trevor's glass wobbled to a rest on the counter. He frowned. "I'm not going back to school, Mom." He drew a deep breath. "I found the Wizard of Winterville—I actually talked with him. He's for real."

Mrs. McIntire shook her head. "Your father will have a fit."

"Did you even hear what I said?" Trevor leaned toward her. "I found the Wizard of Winterville. He used his magic to heal me."

"*Heal* you? Heal you of *what*?" Mrs. McIntire shook her head. "Oh, Trevor. I thought we taught you better than to get involved with that kind of stuff."

"Mom!" Trevor felt his cheeks flush. "Oh, good grief. What's the use?" He shot her a dirty look and stomped up to his room.

* * *

"I'm serious, Kenny. He really exists." Trevor paced his room, phone in one hand, gesturing with the other.

"I know he does, Trev. In fact, he just left my house. He said something about having tea with Santa Claus. You *did* know Santa moved in next door, didn't you? My dad's already called a lawyer about all the reindeer poop in our yard." Kenny laughed so hard Trevor yanked the phone away from his ear.

Then for three full minutes Trevor fired off every foul word and phrase he had ever heard, accusing Kenny of moral crimes and questionable ancestry. His face grew warm as he closed the verbal tirade with a suggestion that Kenny move to a much hotter climate. Then Trevor hung up and slung his phone on the bed.

"Who needs him!" Trevor kicked a pile of magazines and scattered them across the floor. Then he trudged off to the bathroom for a shower, head filled with darkening thoughts.

* * *

"Well! That's more like it."

Trevor stood at the door of Lisa's house, red Polo shirt and khaki shorts clean and neatly pressed. He had even trimmed his beard and tied his lengthening hair into a man-bun. A winning smile brightened his face.

"In the flesh, baby. Come on—let's go." Trevor reached for Lisa's hand, but she pulled back.

"Maybe I should smell of you first." Lisa gave him a sly grin. "Just to make sure you're really back to normal."

"You're a real riot—not. But hey—sniff all you want." Trevor returned a mischievous smile. "That kind of turns me on."

Lisa chuckled. "A cold shower would turn *you* on." She took Trevor's hand and stared into his eyes. "I love you."

"What's not to love, babe? Now," Trevor pulled Lisa close and wrapped an arm around her waist, "let's get some grub." He guided her to the waiting Ford.

"What did you have in mind?" asked Lisa once they were both seated.

"I have a lot of things in mind." Trevor shot her and evil grin. "We can talk over dinner."

Trevor started up the Explorer, slammed it in gear, and roared out of the driveway. Once in the street he gunned the engine, causing the truck to fishtail. Lisa yelped in surprise, then giggled. Trevor glanced across the seat. "How about seafood?"

"Ooh, that sounds good. Captain Kid's?"

"Exactly. I've got a righteous craving for shrimp after all the rabbit I've been eating." Trevor glanced at Lisa to see what kind of reaction he'd get from the rabbit remark. If it registered, Lisa showed no sign of it.

They made good time through the town center, then turned left at the first intersection onto Grist Mill Road. Seven more miles brought them to Captain Kid's Seafood on the right. Judging from the number of cars in the gravel lot, the place was packed.

The minute they stepped out of the truck the delicious fragrance of fried seafood set their stomachs rumbling. A thirty minute wait ratcheted up their appetites to near-starvation levels. Trevor imagined a plate piled to overflowing with hot, fried shrimp. He planned some serious damage against the steep entrance fee.

A waitress in black shorts and red-and-white-striped shirt led them along a convoluted path to their table near the back of the cavernous dining room. The dim interior, modeled after an ancient pirate ship, sported heavy ropes and decayed fishing nets hanging from brown columns shaped to look like masts. A buoy, a ship's anchor, and hundreds of other sea-related artifacts covered every inch of the walls, with additional paraphernalia hanging from the twelve-foot ceiling. A line of hustling, bustling customers jockeyed for position at the buffet, three deep at the favorites. Trevor and Lisa soon joined the fray, and brought heaping plates of shrimp, catfish, crab, and other goodies back to their seats.

"So," Lisa raked another bite of catfish onto her fork, "the quest is finally over?"

"I found the wizard," Trevor said while munching. "But I don't have his secret yet."

Lisa's fork stopped halfway to her mouth. She rolled a question and statement into one. "You're *not* going back."

Leaning back in his chair, Trevor stabbed lazily at his remaining shrimp. "You don't understand. I fell off a sixty-foot cliff and this guy, John, was standing over me when I woke up. I didn't have a scratch on me. He's *got* to be the wizard." Trevor eased forward and poked the last shrimp in his mouth. "I want to find out what makes him tick."

"Omigosh, Trevor—listen to yourself. You *can't* seriously believe there's a wizard. I mean, you didn't actually see him do anything, did you?"

Trevor sighed. He focused off in the distance, remembering. "I was flat on my back, staring at the sky. My guitar was under me, smashed to a thousand pieces. The fall should have killed me." He held out both arms. "But look—not even a bruise."

"Trev—"

"I *did* see him heal somebody—a girl with a toothache. He was sneaking around in a black cape, and she gave him a present, like she was sacrificing to a god or something. Then he healed her."

Lisa shook her head. "I can't believe what I'm hearing. A man in a cape? Seriously? That's just...I mean...were you *drinking* when this happened?"

"I saw it with my own eyes!" Trevor punctuated his outburst with a curse. "Why can't you believe me?"

Heads turned at a nearby table. Trevor scowled at the onlookers.

"Trev—hold it down." Lisa gave the nearby patrons an apologetic shrug then turned a warning look on Trevor. "How can you expect me to take this wizard nonsense seriously? Besides, even if it was true, what do you care about mountain voodoo?" She leaned forward and spoke just above a whisper. "I want my old Trevor back."

"There's a wizard up there!" Trevor banged the table and cursed, drawing stares from multiple directions. "I found something better than gold and nobody gives a rip! What's it going to take to open your eyes?"

For a moment, Lisa only stared. When she spoke, it was in a soft, measured tone. "What I really want is for you to tell me you love me, and," Lisa locked eyes with Trevor, "to stop talking about the wizard."

Trevor pushed away from the table and swore. He stamped to his feet and glared, then whirled and elbowed his way through the crowd, and finally out the door.

Chapter Twenty-One

I was happy, excited, and nervous all at the same time. I didn't feel ready, but I knew God was in control. He had never failed me—I trusted him completely. The problem was, like Sarah said, except for the polio, my life had been a fairy tale. And fairy tales don't test your faith.

* * *

"Do you have indigestion, hon? Indigestion means that baby's going to have a head full of hair. When I was pregnant with Jonathan, I had so much indigestion I lost ten pounds. And when that little bugger popped out, he had hair down to his eyeballs." Mrs. Picket, the youngest mother among Winterville Chapel's congregation, prattled on. Sarah glanced away, hoping to catch John's eye.

Mrs. Picket and a host of other ladies encircled Sarah in the sanctuary before the Sunday service. News of the baby had anointed the pastoral pair with celebrity status beyond even that of John's healing exploits. While John received plenty of congratulatory remarks, Sarah bore the brunt of the extra attention.

"How far along are you, dear?" Emma Tankersly, Bull's wife, placed a gentle hand on Sarah's shoulder.

Sarah turned to Emma and forced a smile. "About three months, I think."

"Are you carrying low?" Mrs. Picket butted in. "If you carry low, it'll be a boy. Girls always sit high."

Reverend Jones, standing just a few feet away and surrounded by his own group of well-wishers, finally caught Sarah's desperate look. After an unsuccessful attempt at extricating himself, he gave Sarah a weak smile and mouthed, "Sorry."

Bull Tankersly strolled up and peered over the wall of femininity surrounding Sarah. "I haven't seen this much excitement since we caught the deacons' kids smoking cigars in the basement!" His booming voice and subsequent laughter captured the attention of every woman in Sarah's entourage. His wife, Emma, frowned then motioned for him to leave.

John appeared beside Bull just then and reached through the crowd for Sarah's hand. When he found he couldn't wrest her free, he peered up at Bull. "I can't believe this commotion. How are we ever going to start the service on time?"

Bull looked from John to Sarah, and chuckled. "Welcome to parenthood, folks." He slapped John on the back so hard it knocked the wind out of him. "It's a lot like life—never quite what you expected."

* * *

"Oh, John. I've never been this excited before." Sarah's face glowed and her eyes twinkled.

The car door clanged shut, and John looked over at her. "I think I can safely say I've never *seen* this much excitement." He started up the old Studebaker and held down the gas pedal just enough to smooth out the idle. "I just don't understand it. They make a bigger fuss over one little baby than the mightiest miracles of God."

Sarah's smile faded. "I thought you were excited about the baby?"

John reflected a moment before putting the car in gear. "You know what? I haven't had a chance to really think about it. To start with I was just plain shocked. After that...well, with all my work, and the big fuss everybody's been making...I don't know. Maybe I'm *still* in shock."

"You're not jealous, are you?"

"Jealous?" John wrinkled his brow. "No—"

"Are you telling the truth, Reverend Jones?" Sarah gave him a mock frown.

"No—I mean, yes, I'm telling the truth." John shook his head. "And no, I'm not jealous. I just need time for it to sink in."

Sarah formed a half-smile. "I love you. I just want you to be happy."

"I love you, too, hon. And I *am* happy. Just...give me some time to adjust, OK?" A moment later, with the car puttering down the road, John glanced Sarah's way. "I don't think it would be hard to get excited about being a father." He grinned. "But right now I think our friends are excited enough for both of us."

"I'll say. I thought the advice would never stop. Make sure you do this. Don't ever do that. I don't know how I'll *ever* learn to take care of a baby if it's as complicated as they make it out."

"Hmm. I'm sure we'll figure it out." John gave Sarah a quizzical look. "That reminds me—do you have any cravings?"

"Cravings?"

John shrugged. "You know—something special to eat. Alice Potter said I have to take care of your cravings. If I don't, she said the baby won't be happy and won't sleep right."

"*Alice Potter?*" Sarah rolled her eyes. "I wouldn't put stock in anything *she* says. You know what she told me? She said if the baby gets thrush—that's white spots in the mouth—that I should put whiskey on its lips. Whiskey! Can you imagine? I can just see myself waltzing into the nearest pub and asking for a bottle. Me, the preacher's wife, for heaven's sake." She shook her head. "They would kick us right out of the church—maybe out of town."

"She told you that?" John scratched his head.

"She sure did. You've really got your work cut out for you with some of these folks."

"Well, that's why God called us here." John looked from the road to Sarah and back. "Let's remember to say extra prayers for the Potter family tonight."

* * *

"John?"

The voice called to him out of darkness, the only sound in the little white cottage on the edge of Winterville. A slice of moonlight pierced the bedroom window, dispelling a fraction of the night. Was he dreaming?

"John!"

An elbow to the ribs chased away any remaining doubts the voice had been an illusion.

"Unh!" John's eyes flew open. "What? What's going on?" He rubbed his side and blinked hard at the drowsiness still fogging his brain.

"Some...something's wrong," Sarah said with a shaky voice.

John shifted toward her. "What?"

"It's hurting." Sarah sucked in a deep breath. "Something's not right."

Rubbing his eyes, John shook himself awake. Dark outside. He reached for the bedside lamp and switched it on, winced at the sudden brightness. The clock on his nightstand showed eleven p.m.—still Sunday night. He couldn't have been asleep more than an hour.

"Want me to rub your back?" John pulled into a sitting position and leaned toward Sarah. They had been through this many a night of late. Even as he reached for her, his eyelids felt like concrete, and his head drooped lower. Never would he have guessed the toll all the little inconveniences of pregnancy would take on him.

"It's not my back—it's the baby. Down low. Deep inside." She grabbed his arm. "It *hurts*."

Oh? Now *that* was new. "Do you want me to rub your stomach?"

"I...I don't know. Ow!" Sarah yelped as John caressed her belly. "That makes it *worse*." She pulled away. "Oohh!"

John reached to comfort her, but she stiffened at his touch before yanking away again. Maybe something really was wrong this time. But how would he know? He'd never been around a pregnant woman before.

"Maybe if you try lying on your side?"

"Unh. I did already."

"Your other side?"

"I...OK, I'll try." The bed jostled and squeaked as Sarah turned. "Ow! I can't—I can't move."

"We should pray."

"Ooh! John?" Sarah's breathing came in short bursts now, punctuating her speech.

"Yes, hon?" John forced his voice to remain calm despite his rising anxiety.

"It's time."

John frowned. "Time? Time for what?"

Sarah moaned. "It's time for the baby."

"The baby?" John's mind whirled. "You're not due for another two months. It *can't* be time."

"It's time, John—I know it is." Another quick breath. "It feels...*different*."

John reached for Sarah's forehead. Hot and sweaty. Maybe a fever. "Hon, I need to pray—right now."

She heaved another deep breath and whispered, "OK."

"Fever, be gone." Short and to the point, but said with authority. John rubbed her cheek. "How is it now?"

Sarah grunted through clenched teeth. "It...still...hurts."

What now? Should he pray the pain away? That wouldn't be right if it was really time for the baby—there had to be pain for it to work right, didn't there? But was it really time? Seven months *couldn't* be right. Or could it? Yet, what if this was part of God's plan?

John lifted his eyes toward heaven. "Lord, what should I do?"

"Unh! Call the...unh...doctor." The bed shook when Sarah trembled.

The doctor! Of course—he would know if there was a problem. "OK. Right away." John jumped out of bed and banged his toe on the nightstand. "My *word*!" Just what he needed at a time like this. Limping on both sides, he walked like a monkey to his chest of drawers, grabbed his cane, then made his way into the living room.

Ring. Ring. Ring. Ring. Why didn't he pick up?

"Hello?" A groggy voice sounded from the other end of the line.

Thank you, Lord.

"Doc Binder, this is John Jones—Reverend Jones. I need your help."

"Yes, Reverend?" The doctor's voice lost its crabby edge. "What can I do for you?"

"It's Sarah. She's hurting real bad and I don't know what to do." He paced, clenching and unclenching the phone cord.

"What kind of hurt?"

"Um, she says it's the baby."

"She's only six months along, isn't she?"

"Seven."

"Right. Well Reverend, I know you're concerned, but this is fairly normal. She's going to have little pains along the way. That's just—"

"It isn't the same, Doc. We've been through the little stuff before. This time she's really hurting. I've never seen her in so much pain."

"False labor can be pretty scary. That's normal, too, about this time. I can come over first thing in the morning, if you want, and check her out."

"Doc, she said it's different—that it's time for the baby. I really don't think it's false labor—I think something may be wrong." John waved his free hand frantically at nothing. "I think she has a fever, too. Well, at least she had one. I prayed, so I guess it's gone, but I didn't check again to see."

"A fever, huh?" The doctor paused. "It *could* be something else. I'll come on over and have a look. Give me a few minutes, Reverend. I'll be there as quick as I can."

"Thanks, Doc." John breathed a sigh of relief. "I really appreciate it."

John slammed down the receiver and scrambled back to the bedroom where a blood-curdling scream greeted him at the door. He flicked on the light to find Sarah's contorted face staring back at him. He couldn't imagine what kind of pain she must be going through—she hadn't shed a tear the time she cut her finger nearly to the bone with a kitchen knife.

With a sudden jerk, Sarah rolled into an upright position against the headboard, covers pulled tight under her chin. Head quivering, she white-knuckled the comforter, breathing erratically and in sharp gulps.

Adrenaline kicked John's system into overdrive and he began to shake. "Sarah," he said, running to her, "let me help you lie down." He knelt beside her. "I called the doctor. He's on his way."

"Johhhnnnn! Hurry!" Sarah groaned, slurring the words until they were near unintelligible.

John slipped one arm under her neck, the other under her legs. She screamed louder. "It's OK, hon. I'll be careful."

As gently as he could manage, John slid her down from the headboard. Her body heat was flames licking at his arms. She screamed again.

A sense of helplessness settled about John—an odd feeling he'd never experienced before. He reached out a hand and stroked Sarah's cheek. Seconds later something tickled his elbow. He withdrew his hand and found his arm dripping with...blood! It ran down his wrist, dripped from his elbow, and onto the covers. John stared in disbelief. Where had it come from?

"John!" Eyes clinched shut, Sarah croaked out a different sort of scream—one that set alarm bells ringing throughout John's system.

He yanked back the covers and found blood everywhere—splattered along her legs and soaking the bottom of her nightshirt. A dark stain surrounded her on the bed like a shadow.

"Oh, Lord!" He recoiled, eyes wide in horror. He sank to his knees and covered his eyes, trembling so hard he fell flat on his face.

John found himself studying the random grain patterns of the wooden floor. He swallowed, tried to think. OK, so he had a problem—a big one. And it was a shock. But his wife needed him, and God could make right whatever was wrong. He reached for the bed and pulled himself up.

The sight of bright red streaks on his arm slowed him. He swiped his bloody appendage along the edge of the bed. Instead of ridding himself of the offensive substance, it smeared. John tore his gaze from it, breathed deep, fought the pounding in his ears. Sarah needed him. This was no time to lose control.

He dragged himself from the floor and onto the bed next to Sarah. She yelped and whimpered with every breath, a pitiful sound like an injured puppy.

Don't think about it. Just pray.

He placed both hands on her stomach, bowed his head, and closed his eyes. "Father God, I need you. I need you now more than ever. I don't know what's wrong with Sarah, and I don't understand why this is happening. But I know you can heal her. I need you to show yourself strong and make her well.

"You've given me power to heal every kind of sickness. I call on that power now." He looked straight into Sarah's agonized eyes. "Sarah, I command you to be healed, and to be whole."

An ear-piercing scream rebuked him. John opened his eyes and gulped. Sarah's face was ashen. She appeared surreal, a ghost.

"Father God..." John tore his gaze from Sarah and gathered his thoughts. "If this is a test of faith, I accept it." He closed his eyes and prayed that much harder. "I committed myself to follow you and I'm not backing down. I know all healing power comes from you and I trust you to provide. So, in the name of Jesus, I ask for Sarah to be made well, and that all the power you've given me would manifest itself in her right now. Glory to your name. Amen."

Another round of screams filled the air, less forceful, though, as Sarah struggled to breath.

This can't be happening!

"Lord, I don't understand. What am I supposed to do? What do I need to say? You've never failed me before."

Sarah writhed on the bed and John watched the contorted movements in horror. He felt her pain.

Something broke inside John, and he wept.

He didn't cry from defeat, but he cried from a broken heart. Here lay the love of his life, mortally wounded for all he knew, and nothing he did made it better. He hated seeing her in such pain, yet he felt as helpless as an invalid to do anything about it.

"Dear God," John lifted his gaze heavenward, "let me take her place. Take my life, Lord—I don't care. Just let her live. Please, make her well again."

Tears streamed down John's face. They splattered onto the bed, and mixed with Sarah's blood.

* * *

A late model pickup truck made its way down the driveway of 407 Hedgemont Road. The headlights bobbed up and down, attracting a steady stream of eager moths.

Doc Binder rubbed sleep from his eyes as he pulled up beside the aging Studebaker and shut off the truck's engine. With a practiced motion, he grabbed his bag from the seat with one hand and swept a derby onto his head with the other. As he stepped from the truck, he began whistling a jaunty tune, then strolled toward the front door.

At six feet tall, and topped with a hat, plenty of folks had told Doc he looked like Abe Lincoln. He rather liked the comparison, and had even grown a beard to exaggerate the resemblance.

Skipping up the front steps two at a time, Doc quit whistling as soon as he knocked on the door. After a moment with no answer, he knocked again—louder. Still, no answer.

Strange.

Side-stepping to the front window, he peered inside. A faint light shone through one of the doorways, but otherwise darkness blanketed the interior. "Hmph. Wake a fellow in the middle of the night, the least you can do is open the door when he shows up."

Drawing himself up tall, Doctor Binder stepped back to the door, balled his hand into a fist, and made it count. Other than rattling windows, only silence answered. He stamped his foot.

"Darn it, if I come to make a house call in the middle of the night, I'm not leaving until the job is done." He tried the door knob and, finding it unlocked, swung open the door. "Reverend Jones?" He said it loud enough that he wouldn't be missed.

When no one answered, he stepped over the threshold and fumbled for the light switch. An empty house greeted him. "Hello?"

Doc slid off his hat and headed toward the doorway where the only other light in the house shone bright. Upon reaching it, he poked his head inside. The word "Reverend" formed on his lips, but the sound never made it out of his mouth. It took several seconds for the scene in front of him to register.

Reverend Jones lay sprawled across the bed, face-first, in the most awkward way, with Sarah beneath him and staring at the ceiling. Neither responded to Doc's arrival at the doorway. He stepped back, not quite sure what he had stumbled into.

"Ah, Reverend Jones?" Doc alternated between averting his gaze, and stealing quick looks at the couple.

He tiptoed into the room—and caught sight of the blood. His heart beat faster. The dark red liquid covered everything—Sarah, the reverend, the bed, and the floor. There were even splotches on the wall. Doc hadn't seen anything like this since the battlefields of the First World War.

"Reverend Jones!" Doc rushed to the bedside and shook the young pastor but received no response.

Reaching for John's neck, he felt for a pulse. It was there—and strong. That much was good. He tried to reach Sarah, but the reverend's body blocked him. He tapped John on the back, then the shoulder. Receiving no response, he tugged John's arm. The young preacher slid off the bed and hit the floor with a thud. He moaned once, but otherwise remained as still and silent as a rag doll.

Doc felt for Sarah's pulse. He tried her wrist, then her neck. If she had a heartbeat, it was too faint to detect.

Doc's attention returned to the blood. Sarah floated in a pool of it. He glanced down at John, back to the blood, and then to Sarah. Though her eyes were open, they did not blink.

Then Doc knew what had happened. He was too late.

Chapter Twenty-Two

"John!" Trevor yelled across the plateau where he had first found the old hermit, his voice blending with a light breeze that danced across his path. He marched forward, calling John's name every few steps. When he reached the tent, he yanked the flap aside and stomped in. The mouth of a cave lay before him. Trevor stared. He didn't remember a cave the last time he was here. A glance upward showed that the back wall of the tent had been rolled up. It must have been down before, veiling the dark opening.

John rushed from the gaping hole. "Get out!" He poked Trevor in the gut—hard—with the business end of a double-barrel shotgun.

Trevor stepped back but the cave sucked his attention away from the gun and the angry man threatening him with it.

"I told you before to get out, and I'm telling you now! Get out and stay out!" There was fire in John's eyes. He shoved Trevor with the gun barrel.

As if seeing the weapon for the first time, Trevor raised his hands. "Whoa there, old fellow. I just came to visit a friend." He backed through the tent at John's prodding until he was outside in the sunlight.

"*Friend*?" John poked hard with the gun. "Friends treat each other with respect. They must not teach that where you come from."

Trevor lowered his hands partway. "Listen, John—I'm sorry. I don't even know what I said to upset you."

John squinted at him, gun wavering. "No—you wouldn't, would you?" The gun fell to John's side. He turned, shoulders drooping, and shuffled back inside the tent. "Go on home, boy," he called just barely loud enough for Trevor to hear.

"Wait—I need your help." Trevor followed John inside where he found the old man leaning against the cave entrance, face buried in his arms.

"Why can't you leave me alone?"

"I need your help. Nobody believes me."

"Nobody believes what?" John mumbled the question through his shirtsleeve.

"They don't believe you exist."

John turned just enough to peek one eye at Trevor. "Boy, you're not making any sense."

"My friends. I told them what you did but they don't believe me. They think I made the whole thing up."

John turned both eyes on Trevor. "And just what did you tell them?"

"About falling off the cliff and not being hurt—and how you were there when I woke up." Trevor narrowed his eyes. "I told them I found the wizard."

"Darn it, boy!" John bolted upright and stamped his foot. "What did you do that for? Why can't you keep your trap shut?"

"Because there's no way I could fall off that cliff and live to tell about it. You did something. I don't know what, but I'm going to find out." He pointed a finger at John. "And I *know* you're the wizard."

"Stop it! Enough of that wizard talk." He raised the shotgun but stopped short of pointing it. "Go home. Forget what you've seen."

Trevor stepped closer. "Are you the Wizard of Winterville?"

John whistled a long sigh. "I'm no wizard, boy."

"Seriously? It was just the wildest coincidence I walked away from that fall without a scratch. You had nothing to do with it, huh?"

John met Trevor's stare. He ran a hand down his beard.

"That's what I thought." Trevor nodded. "You don't like lying, do you? A little smoke and mirrors maybe, but no outright lies. Good. We're getting somewhere."

"What do you want from me?"

"Come meet my friends. Show 'em I'm not crazy."

"You *are* crazy! I'm not leaving this mountain!"

"What's the big deal? Just say hello to a couple of my friends, heal some little something so they know I'm not crazy, then I'll leave you alone—forever. You can rot up here for all I care."

"I don't want anything to do with your friends. I don't want anything to do with *you*." John stuck a finger in Trevor's face. "Now, go away."

"OK." Trevor shrugged. "I'll leave. But, I'll be back."

"Yeah? Well maybe I won't be here." John turned his back and disappeared into the cave.

Trevor smirked. He left the tent and started down the trail with a smile. The old geezer was softening. He'd be off the mountain soon enough. It was just a matter of time.

* * *

Trevor pulled out his cell phone and dialed Lisa's number. It rang and rang with no answer. When it went to voice mail, he tried again. And again. Finally, she picked up.

"What do you want?"

He sighed. "Listen, I didn't like the way things ended the other night. Do you think we could get together and talk? I'll make sure to take a bath."

She chuckled. "Oh, Trevor. Maybe. But on one condition."

"Uh-huh?"

"No talk about you-know-who. Not a single word."

"Well—"

"Not one word or you can forget it."

Trevor ran a few scenarios through his head. "OK, it's a deal. See you at seven?"

"All right. And Trevor?"

"Yeah?"

"I still love you."

"You know it, babe."

* * *

"What's all that stuff in the back?" Lisa nodded toward the rear of the Explorer before climbing into the passenger seat.

"Eh, just some things from my room. You know—to make roughing it a little less rough." Trevor flashed a smile.

Lisa frowned. "You mean you're going back to the mountain?"

"I like it there. In fact,. I thought we could spend another weekend together." He reached over and stroked her arm. "You had fun last time, didn't you?"

"I don't exactly like the idea of supporting your bad habits." She shut her door then turned to Trevor, a wary look on her face.

"Just come for the day Saturday. If you want, you can spend the night. If not, well, that's OK. Either way we'll have a blast."

Lisa wrinkled her brow. "I don't think so, Trev. I'd love to be with you—but not on the mountain. Besides, I have a paper due."

"It's just a day trip. Besides, you can't keep your nose stuck in a book all the time—it's not good for you. And even bookworms need a little recreation."

"Mm-hm. Recreation and taking it easy—that seems like all you've been doing lately. How do you expect to pass with all the classes you've skipped?"

Trevor crossed his arms. "I'm not going back to school."

"Don't be ridiculous. You can't throw your life away just to become a backwoods hippie. What do your parents have to say?"

"Ha!" Trevor slapped the seat. "Dad's not around long enough to have a clue what's going on. Mom, well she wasn't exactly thrilled. But what can she do? I'm old enough to make my own decisions."

"Trevor." Lisa shook her head. "If you won't listen to anyone else, will you listen to *me*? You're acting like a fool. If you want our relationship to go anywhere, you need to think long and hard about what you're doing. Who wants to spend their life with a half-crazed hillbilly?"

He winced. "I'm not crazy. Give me a chance and I'll prove it. Come with me Saturday and you can meet the wizard yourself."

"Hey." Lisa pointed an accusing finger. "I told you not to mention that again. You need to make a choice—are you going to chase after the wizard, or me?"

"Lisa!" Trevor slammed a fist on the steering wheel. "Don't do this. Why does it have to come down to—"

"I want an answer, Trevor!" She locked eyes with him. "Do you want *me*, or do you want the wizard? Because I'm telling you— you're *not* getting both."

Trevor brooded under Lisa's unwavering glare. What was he supposed to say? He *did* want both—and that's exactly what he intended to get.

Lisa kicked open her door and jumped to the ground. "When you make your decision—and if it's the *right* decision—give me a call." She slammed the door and cursed him through the open window. "Until then, don't bother!"

* * *

John whittled away at a tiny wooden statue, the results of which—so far—looked like something a six-year-old might be proud of. He perched on a hand-made wooden stool just outside his tent, sunlight warming one cheek. Trevor advanced in full stealth mode to within inches of him.

"You are without a doubt the stupidest person on Earth," John said without looking up or pausing from his work.

"I think of myself as persistent."

"Hmph." John made a few more passes across the statue with his knife, then set tool and wood alike down beside him. He cocked his head at Trevor. "What's it going to take to get through to you, son? I'm a little tired of the battle. Heck, I was tired when I moved up here forty years ago. I don't have the energy it takes to keep fighting with you."

"Why *did* you come here?"

John shook his head. "That's *my* business. Not up for discussion."

"I'll tell."

"Tell what?"

Trevor crossed his arms. "I'll tell everybody on the mountain I know where the wizard lives."

John snorted. "You're probably fool enough to do it, too. Well, say what you want about the wizard. For one thing they won't believe you. For another, they might just shoot you for bringing it up. They have some pretty strong beliefs around here, you know." He retrieved the statue and made several delicate slices down the side of it.

"I'm not giving up. I'll keep coming back until you tell me what I want to know."

John looked at him again. "What *do* you want? What's it going to take to get you off my back?"

"I want the truth."

"Truth? Ha! You wouldn't know the truth if it bit you in the backside. What do *you* care about truth?"

"I..." Trevor had a flippant answer ready as usual. But for some reason the question stirred him deep inside. His own truth eluded him, however. "I can't explain it. I just know I *have* to find it. That's all."

"So, let's say you find your wizard. What are you going to do with him—show him to the world? Sell tickets so folks can come see the circus freak? What?"

Trevor searched the sky. "No... I just want to know. I wouldn't tell anyone—I promise." He lowered his head. "Besides, my friends don't believe anything I say."

John stroked his beard. "Suppose I told you all about the wizard. Would you promise to go away and leave me alone—forever?"

Trevor raised his eyebrows. "Really?"

"I asked for a promise."

"You bet!" Trevor loosed a happy curse. "I won't tell anybody."

"You'll go away and never come back?"

"Absolutely!" Trevor clasped his hands in anticipation.

John sighed and scratched his head. "Your promise probably ain't worth two cents, but maybe it's time." He motioned to the ground in front of him. "Have a seat."

Trevor flopped down and crossed his legs, eyes locked on John.

John rested his chin on his hand, one finger aside his nose, and stared off into the distance so long Trevor thought he might have gone to sleep. "There's no wizard," he finally said, turning back to Trevor. "There's a man. He doesn't work magic. He gets his power from God."

Trevor made a face. "Not one of those religious stories. I don't need any tall tales about some non-existent God. I'm looking for facts."

For long seconds John said nothing. Then he jerked just like someone had poked him in the ribs. He turned his gaze heavenward, maintained that pose for a moment, then mumbled, "Oh, all right." He turned back to Trevor with a frown.

Searching the sky, Trevor produced his own frown. He found nothing up there worthy of his attention. "Well?" he asked, turning back to John.

"I'd appreciate it if you wouldn't interrupt again. If you want to hear what I have to say, then keep your opinions—however wrong they may be—to yourself. Agreed?"

Trevor shrugged.

"Agreed?" John emphasized this time.

"Yeah, all right."

"So," John shifted on his seat, "like I said, there's a man who has the power of God to heal people. He lives here on the mountain, and he helps folks in need. They give him food and other gifts to show their appreciation.

"Like me and all the other folks around here, the healer likes to keep to himself. The last thing any of us need is for some outsider to go meddling in our business. And that," said John, shifting again, "is all there is to it." He sat up straight and stretched his back. "Satisfied?"

Trevor scoffed. "No."

"What do you mean, 'No'? I gave you what you wanted. Now," John jerked a thumb toward the downward trail, "keep your side of the bargain and head on out of here."

Trevor shook his head side to side. "You're still not telling the truth."

John heaved a deep sigh and tapped the ground with his boot. "Sure I am. What don't you believe?"

"I don't believe the part about God, for one thing. I never did believe that silliness, and I never will." John started to speak, but Trevor pre-empted him with a wave. "But I'll let that ride for now. What really gets me is what you *didn't* tell. You didn't tell me who the wizard is."

"He's a healer, not a—"

"*You're* the wizard—or the healer. Or whatever. I don't really care what you call yourself. Your *him*." Trevor set his jaw. "I want to hear you admit it."

John turned away. "You did this, didn't you?"

"Did what?" Trevor frowned.

"You sent him here," John said, still gazing at the mountain.

"Sent *who* here? What are you talking about?" *This guy is nuts.*

John sighed. "It's been a long time, but I guess I could do that."

"Hey!" Trevor waved a hand in John's face and snapped his fingers. "Anybody home?"

John's gaze moved back to Trevor. "I'll make you a deal, son."

Trevor wagged his head. "I hope it's better than the last one."

If the barb had any effect on John, he didn't show it. "I'll tell you the story about the wizard—the *whole* story. But I have some conditions."

"Sure. No problem."

"Don't take it lightly. My conditions are serious, and they won't be easy."

"Try me."

"OK. First, I don't want any whining about anything I tell you. If you don't like it, or if you don't believe me, then that's your problem. I'm going to shoot straight, and I don't need any back talk when I'm done."

"You got it." Trevor rubbed his hands together.

"Second, I want you to leave me alone when I'm through. No more of this wizard business—just go away. If you learn to mind your manners, I might let you come back and visit every now and again. But, I'm not going to say anything else about the wizard after today."

Trevor shrugged. "OK."

"Third, I don't won't you running your mouth. I told you before we don't need any curiosity seekers around here. I can make sure the mountain folk give any newcomers a proper sendoff—including you." John raised an eyebrow. "I'm sure you know what *that* means."

"Hmm." Trevor thought back to a few of his run-ins with the locals. "Yeah, I'll keep it quiet."

"Finally, I'm not saying another word unless you let me tell you about God and his plan for your life."

Trevor shook his head. "Now, wait—"

"No, *you* wait. I'll keep it short and to the point, but you're going to listen. And I want you to listen with an open mind, or I won't tell you anything about the wizard." John folded his arms and waited.

Trevor thought it over. There wasn't much he hated worse than listening to superstitious religious garbage. But if the old man truly came clean about the wizard it might be worth it. "OK," he said. "You've got ten minutes—max—for your little sermon."

John's eyes twinkled. "I can do it in five unless you have questions. No limits in that case."

This might not be so bad. Trevor smiled. "All right." He pulled out his phone and checked the time. "The countdown begins."

John leaned toward Trevor and stared him square in the eyes. "Regardless of what you've been told, God exists. He's a loving God, and he wants you to know him. In fact, he wants you to come live with him in heaven after you die."

Trevor rolled his eyes and John gave him a warning look. When Trevor shrugged, John continued. "There's a problem, though. You can't live with God if you have sin in your life because he can't stand to be around sin. So even though he loves you, he won't let you into heaven.

"Now you might not think of yourself as a sinner, but the Bible tells us *everybody* has sin in their life—even the holiest person in the world. So God came up with a plan to wipe away all our evil. He sent a part of himself—named Jesus—to Earth. Jesus taught people about God and showed them how to live a holy life.

"More important than that, Jesus let himself be killed as the ultimate sacrifice to God. That sacrifice paid the price for all our sins. All we have to do is believe in Jesus as God's son, and accept him as the Lord of our lives, and then we get to go to heaven when we die."

John squirmed a bit, but kept his eyes on Trevor. "If you're interested, you can accept Jesus right now. That's all it takes to erase your sins. Or, if you have any questions, I'll do my best to answer them. Otherwise, I'm done."

Trevor smiled. "OK. Now, let's hear about the wizard."

"Mm-hmm." John nodded as if expecting that answer. "All right—your decision. I'll keep my end of the bargain, but don't forget—I expect you to keep yours."

"Yeah, yeah." Trevor dismissed John with a wave. "Let's talk about the wizard. And this time, don't leave anything out."

John drew a breath. "Very well. It's a long story, though, and I tell it exactly the way I want. You either get the whole story, or you don't get any story at all." He poked Trevor in the chest. "And no interruptions. OK?"

"Get with it already."

Hunching, John rested his elbows on his knees and his head in his hands. He scratched his chin, then looked at Trevor.

"My story starts some sixty years ago. I know that's a crazy long time, but you need to understand what happened back then so everything else will make sense..."

Chapter Twenty-Three

Trevor pondered John's story for several minutes, trying to absorb it all. It was an incredible tale. Maybe, a little *too* incredible.

John simply stared at the ground. The evening wind tickled his beard, and the setting sun cast an eerie glow on his face. Whether the old man couldn't continue, or had just said all he planned to say, Trevor couldn't decide.

"So that's when you moved up here—after your wife died?"

Several seconds passed with no answer. Maybe John was lost in the ancient memories. Trevor was about to prompt him when he spoke again—subdued, without emotion.

"It was a boy."

"Huh?"

"The doctor said it was a boy—I had a son." John chewed the inside of his lip while staring at nothing in particular.

Trevor had no idea what to say. He searched for some way to connect. "Yeah, well, I always wanted a little brother, but I'm an only child. I guess I kind of know how you feel."

"You don't know *any*thing!" John shouted through clinched teeth. He stomped the ground, then glared at Trevor.

The force of the old man's anger caught Trevor off guard. He held up his hands in surrender. "Take it easy, dude—I didn't mean anything by it. We don't want get your blood pressure up."

"Are we done now?" John turned away.

"Well...no. Why are you still up here? I mean, I guess I understand wanting to run away, but forty years is a long time."

"The memories still hurt, boy. Up here I don't have anything to make me think about it—except *you*." He shot Trevor a dirty look.

"So what's the difference? I mean—you heal the mountain people. Why can't you heal the rest of the world?" Trevor barked a mild curse. "There are *tons* of people that could use somebody like you."

"I told you it hurts too much. I'll never leave this mountain. I'll die here." John closed his eyes, then buried his head in his hands. "Now can you leave me alone?"

Trevor chewed a fingernail. "Umm—just one more question."

John's shoulders heaved upward once, then down. "What?"

"Why the wizard game? It sounds like that goes against your religious beliefs. Or did all that go out the window when you couldn't heal your wife?"

"It's not what I wanted." John looked up and huffed. "I never intended to heal again—didn't know if I could. So I found this cave and hid in it. I only came out for food, or when I needed something I could only get through trade.

"One day I was bartering for shotgun shells in a nearby village when I heard somebody scream. A bunch of people ran by, and someone said a little girl had been bitten by a snake. They would never make it to the hospital in time, and I couldn't stand the thought of anyone else losing their baby, so I went to help.

"I tried to do it without anyone knowing. But when I touched her, she quit crying immediately and told everybody I made her better. The village went nuts. Everybody started screaming and yelling, saying I used magic on her. I told them it wasn't magic, but they wouldn't listen. It wasn't long until they started calling me a wizard. They were scared to death of me, but at the same time they looked up to me like a...well, like a god."

John hung his head and shook it side to side. "After a while we worked out the arrangement we have today. They bring me little gifts because, well, that's their way—they won't accept something for nothing. So I go along with it. Since they wouldn't believe me anyway, I figure at least they're better off than they were before I came along."

With that, John slapped his knees and stood up. "That's it, boy. That's the whole story. I'm not proud of it, you understand, but that's just how life is these days."

"So it's true—you really are the wizard." Trevor paused. "You healed me when I fell off the cliff, didn't you?"

"Yes, I did. Now, can that be the end of it?" John shoved his hands in his pockets. "Are you going to keep your end of the deal?"

Trevor nodded slowly, thinking. "Cool. Thanks, man." He stood to go. "See you around, OK?"

"Eh, no, I don't think so. I'd rather just forget this ever happened and let you get back to your own life. All right?"

"Um, sure." Trevor gave John a quick nod, then headed back toward camp.

Lisa has got to meet this guy. I'll get her up here if it's the last thing I do.

* * *

"Woo-hoo! It's the mountain man himself." Kenny banged a fist on his desk in appreciation.

Trevor acknowledged him with a slow wave as he stepped into Professor Litchfield's class. Then he made a beeline for Lisa. He leaned on her desk with both hands and waited for her to acknowledge him.

"Trevor?" Lisa raised her eyebrows. "What are you doing here?" A wavering smile made its way onto her face.

"I'm back, doll."

"For good?" Lisa's face lit up. "No more mountain madness?"

"I got everything I needed." Trevor hoisted his book bag in the air and patted it. "It's all right here."

Lisa's mouth dropped. "You actually wrote your report?"

"Hey, hey, old buddy!" Kenny interrupted the conversation with a slap on Trevor's back. "Is it really you? I heard you turned into a ghost so you could get inside the wizard's castle. Haw-haw!"

"Such a riot—not." Instead of getting angry, Trevor smirked.

Kenny threw a punch at Trevor's arm but wasn't quick enough. Trevor jerked sideways to avoid the blow, then reached out and popped Kenny on the back of the head. Kenny frowned, and the two exchanged shoves. By now Trevor was smiling. It felt good to get back in the ring with his old friend.

"Quit acting like kids, you two."

"Yes, master." Kenny put on a serious expression and gave Lisa a mock bow. Then he rose and shuffled back toward his seat, but not before getting in one last slap at Trevor.

"You picked a weird day to come back," said Lisa. "The last day before Christmas break? Why didn't you just give up and start over next semester?"

"I have this paper I wanted to turn in." Trevor gave her a mischievous wink.

The class bell rang. Trevor noticed Professor Litchfield's eyes on him, so he put on his best smile, sauntered down the aisle, and took his seat.

"All right, everyone." Professor Litchfield shuffled the papers on his desk. "I know you are all ready to get out of here and start your holiday, but first we have some unfinished business." He waited a few seconds for the residual noise to quiet, then his gaze wandered to Trevor. "Mr. McIntire. Nice of you to join us. I expect you have a written excuse?"

"Absolutely—but I left it at home." His response elicited a few chuckles from around the room, not the least of which originated with Kenny.

"You will not be issued a final grade for this class without that excuse. Understood?" Professor Litchfield drummed his fingers on his desk.

"No problem, Teach."

"I suppose you have your project ready?"

"Sure do." Trevor rose and strutted to the front of the class. He dropped a single sheet of paper on the professor's desk. "Here you go."

Professor Litchfield's gaze dropped to the paper, then up to Trevor. "I hope you don't think this is funny, Mr. McIntire." Then he spoke in a more measured tone. "Because *I* certainly don't."

"No, sir. This is no joke—that's my project in its entirety. I think you'll find it's some very interesting reading."

The professor drew a deep breath. "Have a seat, sir. We'll discuss this after class."

Trevor returned to his desk while Kenny fake-clapped for him. A few incredulous looks followed his return. Kenny laughed and gave Trevor a thumbs-up. Lisa's face showed anything but approval. She shook her head, then ignored him the rest of class.

* * *

"Hi, babe." Trevor waved, and flashed a smile as Lisa hurried from her desk at the end of lecture.

Without so much as a glance, Lisa swept by Trevor's seat and weaved her way through the crowd of students heading toward the classroom door.

"Lisa!" Trevor scrambled together his belongings and dashed after her. "Hey, wait up!" He jostled past his lingering classmates and shoved his way through the myriad crowd streaming down the hallway. Lisa reached the exit just before Trevor caught up with her. She stepped through the door and let it swing back in Trevor's face. Once outside, she marched on without slowing.

"Hey, Lisa—what's up with you?" Trevor caught up and jumped in front of her, blocking her path. She wasn't having it. Shoving him aside, she continued on toward the parking lot. Trevor chased after her and grabbed her arm.

"Get away from me!" Lisa shook him off and kept moving.

"Come on—this isn't fair. What did I do?"

When Lisa reached her Miata, she unlocked it with the remote and swung open the door. Trevor grabbed the door and held it open. Lisa spun on him.

"Leave me alone, will you?"

Trevor felt his face grow warm. "All right, enough is enough. What's your problem?"

"What's *my* problem?" Lisa shouted the question. "What's *your* problem? When are you ever going to grow up?"

"Um," Trevor managed a sly grin, "I thought we've all been trying pretty hard to avoid that."

"Get serious, Trevor. You're about to fail out of college and all you can think about is clowning around. That was real cute, turning in a single page for your project."

"All this is about my project?" Trevor's anger drained, replaced by confusion. "You lost me somewhere."

"It's *not* about the project—it's your attitude. I'm through wasting my time on a loser. So, if you'll excuse me..." Lisa plopped down in the car and tugged at the door, but Trevor refused to let go of it.

"Wait." Trevor forced a softness into his voice. "You used to like it when I goofed off. If you're still mad about me spending so much time on the mountain, I told you that's over. I'm back for good."

Lisa shook her head. "I don't know if I believe you anymore. But even if you're telling the truth, the rest of your life is a mess. You act like you're still in high school, and I'm over that. Now, would you please quit acting like a child and get your hands off my car?" She pulled on the door, but still Trevor held it open.

"Can't we talk this out? I'll take you somewhere nice."

"Yeah, well that worked out *so* good last time, didn't it? Besides, I have an appointment. Now, get out of my way—I don't want to be late."

"I'll call you later, OK?"

Lisa yanked hard on the door and it slipped from Trevor's grasp. She slammed it shut, started the car, and threw the shifter in reverse. Tires squealing, she zoomed out of the parking lot and into the street.

* * *

"Hello?"

"Hi, Mrs. Dawson. It's Trevor. Is Lisa there? She's not answering her phone."

"Mm. She's here, Trevor. Hang on—let me see what she's doing."

Soon Trevor heard a muffled conversation in the background. Moments later Mrs. Dawson came back on the line. "Trevor?"

"Yeah?"

"Lisa doesn't feel like talking right now. She's locked herself in her room and won't come out. Why don't you give her a little time? I'm sure she'll be over it in the morning."

"Um, OK. Tell her I called, all right?"

"She knows."

"OK. Well, thanks."

Trevor slipped his phone back in his pocket, frowning. Something odd had gotten into Lisa. He'd seen her steamed before, but never like this. He ran through their last few conversations, searching for what had triggered her. The mountain. The paper. Skipping school. Maybe something unrelated that wasn't his fault. There was no telling what was really eating her. And for now, all he could do was wait.

* * *

"Honestly, Trevor, I've never seen Lisa act this way. She wouldn't even come out to eat. Did something happen between you two?"

"Well..." Trevor tapped a finger against his phone. "She got mad at me for skipping school, but I don't know why she'd lock herself up over that."

"Hmm. I have an idea—why don't you come over and talk to her? It might do her good to hear your voice."

"Uh, well, sure. Is right now OK?"

"Now is fine."

Trevor shoved his phone in his pocket and rushed out of the house. He kicked the Sunday paper off the porch on his way to the Explorer, then made record time to Lisa's house.

Mrs. Dawson opened the door before Trevor could ring the bell a second time. "Hi, Trevor. Come on in."

He didn't waste time on social graces, but brushed past Mrs. Dawson and ran up the steps to Lisa's room. "Lisa!" Trevor banged on her door. "Open up."

"What are you *doing* here?" Lisa sounded hysterical. "Get out of my house!"

"We need to talk. You can't avoid me forever."

"You're the *last* person I want to talk to. Go away."

"I'm not leaving until this is settled." Trevor paused when he thought he heard sobbing. "What's going on in there? Are you OK?"

When she didn't answer, Trevor wracked his brain for a new approach. After a moment it hit him. "All right, *little girl*, who's acting immature *now*? You jump all over *my* case, but *you're* the one who needs to grow up and act like an adult."

"What do you know about maturity, you jerk?"

The curses that followed brought a smile to Trevor's face. He had hit a nerve. Good. "Adults talk through their problems. Children hide from them. I always thought of you more like an adult. But maybe I was wrong."

"How *dare* you accuse me of being immature!" The door swung open to reveal Lisa's teary-eyed face.

Trevor reached out to dab her tears, but she slapped his hand away and swore. "Don't touch me, you ape!"

"Lisa—why the tears?"

Using words that would have made her mother blush, Lisa accused Trevor of various moral discrepancies. Her whole body trembled during the tirade.

Trevor relaxed. At least she was talking. "Yeah, that's all well and good, but I was hoping for something a little more specific. I know I've been running a little wild lately, but I have no idea what made you *this* angry."

Lisa's face twisted in anger. She shoved the door but Trevor stuck out his foot to keep it from closing. He forced his way into the room, then grabbed her arm and pushed her toward the bed. She lost her balance and toppled onto her pillow.

"I'm sick of these games." Trevor cursed her. "You're going to talk, and I'm going to listen."

She stared up at him, bottom lip quivering. The tears started again. "Not here."

"Fine. You name the place."

She heaved a sigh. "Let's go for a ride." Then, wiping tears, "I need a minute to get ready."

"OK. I'll be downstairs." Trevor backed away. "If this is a trick, I swear I'll break down that door. I'm not putting up with any more crap."

"I just want to clean up first, OK?"

Trevor frowned as he trudged out of the room. At the doorway, he glanced over his shoulder one last time, then clomped downstairs. Mrs. Dawson gave him a questioning look which he answered with a shrug. She left him then, and he dropped onto the couch and brooded.

A bit later, Lisa startled him out of a catnap with a whisper. "I'm ready."

It took a second for Trevor to gather his senses. When he did, he found himself looking at a different person than he'd left upstairs. "You look, uh, better."

"Mom," Lisa directed her voice toward the back of the house, "we're going out."

"OK, hon. See you later."

Trevor followed Lisa to the door. They walked in silence to the Explorer and climbed in. He started the engine then looked over at her. "Where to?"

"Just drive." Lisa stared straight ahead.

He shrugged, then drove to the end of the subdivision, looked both ways, and turned left away from town.

"Let's go to the park—the one past Thunder Road." Still, she avoided his eyes.

"OK." Trevor pressed hard on the gas pedal. "Want to give me a clue what's up?"

Lisa sniffed back tears. "Not yet."

Soon Trevor found himself whistling a light-hearted tune as they drove past the northern edge of Winterville and turned left onto state route sixty-four. The country two-lane turned into the stretch called Thunder Road just a few miles away. Trevor kept the speedometer somewhere north of seventy—a good twenty-five miles per hour over the limit.

They passed the spot where he'd crashed the Honda, and the truck picked up speed in the straightaway. Trevor glanced at Lisa. She looked as though she would burst any minute.

"I know you're hurting." Trevor spoke with as much tenderness as he could manage over the roar of the road. "What's going on?"

"Trevor." Lisa drew a deep breath. "I'm pregnant."

It didn't register. Trevor ran the statement through his mind, trying to connect it with meaning. He cocked his head. "What?"

Lisa never got a chance to reply. Trevor, having ignored his father's instruction regarding the worn-out tires, found out what happens when radial belts separate from aged rubber.

BOOM!

The explosion shook the vehicle and jerked it to the right. Trevor lost his grip on the wheel. His hands found their place again, but by that time the truck had lurched onto the shoulder, momentum sending it sideways on two wheels. What was left of the front tire dug in to the soft dirt and caught enough traction to flip the back of the truck upward, then into a lateral roll.

The air bag detonated in Trevor's face, spraying hot gases down his neck and blocking his forward vision with billowing fabric. On either side, trees, sky, and ground spun at a dizzying rate. With each rotation, Trevor's head banged against the window until the glass shattered, ragged edges lacerating him and sending weeds and dirt showering into the cockpit.

After a dozen rolls, the truck crunched into a ditch just below the road, twisted a hundred and eighty degrees, and slid to a stop in a grassy field, landing on the driver's side. Steam and hot antifreeze spewed from the mangled radiator and rained down all about the truck. The offending front wheel wobbled to a stop just as a small fire sparked beneath the hood.

Trevor's vision of the world continued to spin several seconds after the commotion ended. He drifted in and out of consciousness, sights and sounds of the last few seconds replaying in random sequence during his wakeful moments. In a detached sort of way, Trevor realized every inch of his body was complaining.

Then the pain stopped, and the world went dark.

Chapter Twenty-Four

Sound everywhere. Loud noises, soft noises, buzzing and humming. Why? What? And people—blurry, fuzzy people, rushing this way and that, appearing and disappearing at random. They seemed to be talking but the words made no sense. Someone—or some*thing*—jostled him and a face appeared with a halo of sunlight in the background. Then the face disappeared. An angel? Where was he?

Thump, thump, thump, thump. Thor beat the ground with his hammer. Blinking lights. Wind. Oh, no—a hurricane! He had never felt such a wind.

Mercy, what a headache! Why did his head hurt so bad when he didn't remember drinking?

A motorcycle—or maybe a chainsaw—revved its engine just a few feet away. The small-engine buzz grated his ears as the thumping and wind faded. A high-pitched metallic screech magnified the headache. Trevor turned his head to yell at the guy on the stupid motorcycle but he blacked out from the pain.

The next time Trevor's eyes blinked open he had the strangest sensation of movement, of floating on a choppy sea as he lay flat of his back. A bearded guy he'd never seen before leaned over and mouthed something. If he was talking, Trevor couldn't make sense of it.

After a few minutes—hours?—reality began to coalesce. Over the bumpy, bouncy sense of movement, the bearded man's words connected with meaning.

"Take it easy, buddy. You're going to be all right. Just keep still."

Red, white, and yellow flashing lights. The bearded guy mumbled meaningless words to someone out of sight. A voice blared from a radio. Pain. Trevor hurt all over, but mostly his head. Where was he?

Then the strangest thing happened. After more bumping and jostling, Trevor found himself in a tiny room—or perhaps a massive metal box. The man who had talked to him earlier leaned over again, this time peering deep into his eyes. Trevor wanted to laugh, but his head hurt too much. Then everything went into slow motion.

A door slammed. Something rumbled. A siren sounded both near and far at the same time. Motion. Either there was an earthquake or the little room was moving. Trevor wanted to vomit.

He tried to sit up so he could ask the man what was going on. But everything disappeared again.

* * *

"Trevor!"

He grimaced. When he tried to move something held him down. A voice that sounded like anything but his own croaked from his throat. "Mom?" Trevor blinked, but his eyes wouldn't focus.

"Trevor, thank God you're all right."

Blurry objects filled his vision, sharpening slowly. He seemed to be in another small room, but larger than the last. A TV near the ceiling flashed images too fast to comprehend. To his left, a curtain formed a temporary wall. A hospital?

"WhereyamI?" The words tripped over a tongue shot with Novocain.

"You were in an accident, hon. You're lucky to be alive."

Accident? He didn't remember any accident. Trevor wiggled his fingers and toes, shifted his arms and legs. Everything seemed to be present and accounted for, though most of it hurt like the dickens.

"Whad happen—happened?" Trevor's senses wakened slowly. He swallowed a bad taste, and wriggled his tongue to bring it back under control.

"You were in a wreck—and you have a concussion." Mrs. McIntire leaned in close. "There weren't any other cars around. Don't you remember anything?"

He thought for a minute. Bits and pieces came back—loud noises, flashing lights, and the man leaning over him in the tiny room. The images must be related to the accident, but Trevor couldn't piece them together.

"I, uh..." He tried to raise his arm, but it wouldn't cooperate. And everything around him was still a bit fuzzy. "I don't know. I don't remember an accident."

"It's OK. Don't strain yourself. Just get some rest."

Rest. That sounded like an excellent idea. Trevor closed his eyes and drifted off to sleep.

* * *

"How are you feeling, son?"

Dad's voice. Trevor's eyelids fluttered, then opened. The hospital room. The accident. So it wasn't a bad dream after all. He cursed, then told his dad in no uncertain terms how he felt. "What happened? Did somebody hit me?"

"The sheriff hasn't finished the investigation yet, but he said you must have been going pretty fast. There weren't any skid marks, and there doesn't seem to be any other cars involved. Their best guess is you lost control, but for now it's still a mystery."

Trevor strained to remember. He had been driving on Thunder Road and there was an explosion. The world rolled and spun, and then just noise and confusion.

Wait. He hadn't been alone…

"Dad, where's Lisa?" Trevor tried to rise but his head pounded so hard he almost blacked out.

The look on Mr. McIntire's face said a lot.

"She's OK, isn't she? Dad?"

"She's alive, Trev."

That didn't make Trevor feel any better. "Alive? Come on, Dad—how is she?"

Mr. McIntire looked away. "I don't know, son." He hesitated, then turned back to Trevor. "She was life-flighted to Greenville."

The news hit him like a brick. What could possibly be so wrong they had to fly her to another city? She was fine the last time he remembered seeing her. In fact, she was…pregnant? Did she really tell him she was pregnant, or was his banged-up head playing tricks on him?

He had to get out. He had to go to Greenville. "I've got to see her. When can I leave?" Trevor again tried to rise, again went woozy.

"I'm afraid that'll have to wait. The doctor wants to keep you at least another night to make sure the swelling goes down."

Trevor made a last valiant effort to pull himself into a sitting position. Pain shot through his head and down his neck. He sank into the pillow, room spinning, no choice but to wait.

* * *

Trevor slammed the rental car's door and hobbled toward the front of the hospital as fast as his aching body would go. Up the garland-decked stairs, into the lobby, and around the giant Christmas tree, he headed for the front desk. A quick check with the receptionist showed Lisa Dawson in the critical care wing. He found the elevator and punched the button for the fifth floor.

A red phone hung on the wall outside the restricted double doors. He picked up the handset and asked for Lisa. "She already has two visitors, and that's our limit," said the voice from the phone. "Wait there until someone comes for you."

He slammed the phone back in place and cursed, then peered through a rectangular window set in the double doors. Two nurses stationed at a desk a few feet away pointed at a computer screen and scribbled notes. Trevor schemed how he might get past them.

Leaning against the wall, Trevor diddled with his phone. The longer he stood there, however, the angrier his headache became. Closing his eyes wasn't helpful. He needed to sit, so he sauntered down the hall in search of a more comfortable resting place.

Fortunately, a small waiting room appeared on the left, not fifty feet down the corridor.

Trevor stepped inside and scanned the room. A preschooler sprawled on the floor, eyes glued to a TV playing cartoons at low volume. Two elderly couples stood in a corner, chatting. Of the several empty chairs, Trevor picked one as far from the TV and conversation as he could get, then poked through the magazines littering a glass-top coffee table. Nothing interested him. He eased into a seat and held his head in his hands, wishing the headache away. He stayed that way a good half an hour, fidgeting and shuffling his feet.

"Trevor?"

"Huh?" Trevor looked up, then rose. "Hi, Mrs. Dawson. How's Lisa?"

Mrs. Dawson's countenance dropped. "She's going to be fine. Everything's going to be OK." Her tone didn't sound convincing. She glanced at Trevor's head. "How are you? I'm surprised you're here."

"Oh, I'm OK. Can I see her?"

Mrs. Dawson drew a deep breath. "Yes. But, Trevor…" She reached for his arm. "You need to prepare yourself—she really took a beating. You may not…" Mrs. Dawson choked. Tears came to her eyes. "You may not recognize her."

Not recognize her? That didn't sound like "Everything's going to be OK." Trevor searched her face a second longer, then dashed out of the room and down the hall. This time, the nurse let him in. She guided him to where Mr. Dawson stood at the door to Lisa's room, blocking the entrance.

"Trevor, I'm glad you're all right. I heard you had a concussion."

"Yeah, still do. But that wasn't gonna keep me away." Trevor moved to squeeze into the room, but Mr. Dawson stood firm.

"We saw the sheriff's report." He caught Trevor's eye. "I just wanted you to know we don't blame you for what happened."

That stopped Trevor cold. "What *did* happen?" He searched Mr. Dawson's face. "Nobody told *me* anything."

"Your front tire blew out—the one on Lisa's side. It pulled you off the road and, according to the deputy, there wasn't anything you could have done."

Trevor remembered the explosion. So *that's* where it came from. Memories of spinning came back to mind. He grabbed the door frame and leaned against it.

"Are you OK, son?" Mr. Dawson reached out a hand and steadied him.

Trevor exhaled. "I'm fine." He sucked in a deep breath then stood taller. "I want to see Lisa."

"Are you sure you're up to this? She looks pretty bad right now."

"I have to see her." Trevor stepped forward, and this time Mr. Dawson moved aside.

The thing on the bed wasn't Lisa. It didn't even look human. Deep purple, yellow-green, and black splotches covered the head—the part not hidden by bandages, anyway. Blood, scabs, and stitches matted the one visible patch of what once had been beautiful hair. Cheeks, eyes, and neck had swelled to twice their normal size. Tubes protruded from the mouth and nose, and wires and sensors ran everywhere. One leg hung in the air, suspended from thick cables, and covered in a cast. A rasping sound accompanied irregular shallow breaths.

Trevor felt sick.

"She's going to be OK." Mr. Dawson had joined Trevor beside the bed. "It looks bad now, but they're taking good care of her."

Trevor turned away. "What, uh...what exactly's wrong with her?"

Mr. Dawson crossed his arms. "Well... She has a fractured skull, three broken ribs, and her right leg is, well, shattered. One of her lungs collapsed—it's better now—and she ruptured her spleen. Also," he gestured toward the bed, "the swelling is pretty bad." He heaved a sigh. "We don't have the results of the brain scan yet, but she's breathing on her own. That's a really good sign."

The mechanical recitation of injuries lent a surreal aspect to the visit. How could Mr. Dawson stand there discussing things so calmly while just a few feet away his daughter looked like a zombie? Trevor studied Lisa again. "Do the doctors really think she'll get better?"

"Well...they didn't exactly say for sure. But you know how doctors are—they always give you the gloom and doom talk. We can read between the lines, though. She'll be fine."

"Did they say anything else about, um, her condition?"

"Hmm? I'm sure I forgot some of the details—it's been pretty hectic. But that's all the big stuff."

Trevor ran his fingers through his hair. Apparently no one else knew about the little announcement yet.

"Oh, man."

* * *

Sweat poured from his brow and dripped into his eyes despite the constant swipes at his forehead. Back during the heat of late summer and early fall, Trevor had never gotten so winded on a climb up the mountain. The accident must have affected him more than he thought.

He paused to catch his breath, and to swear. Another mile lay between him and the Wizard's Court. He leaned against a tree and again wiped away perspiration. Every muscle begged him to stop, but he would not give in. He had to keep going.

One exhausting step followed another as he trudged up the trail. An endless number of those steps later, the Court came into view. Almost there, but the hardest part loomed ahead at the cliff. He took a deep breath and started the climb. And now, winded as he was, the steep incline really began to take a toll when...

"Ahhh!" John bumped into Trevor.

"Yah!" Trevor yelled in response, scared more by John's cry than the unexpected impact. He teetered for a moment, but John had the presence of mind to grab his arm until he regained his balance.

"Good gracious, boy." John sucked in a deep breath. "You nearly gave me a heart attack."

"Yeah, well, I think I need to check my pants after that blood-curdling scream of yours." Trevor eyed John up and down. "Where ya going?"

"I need fresh water." John jangled a canteen in Trevor's face. He motioned with it back the way Trevor had come. "Want to head back down? I'd never be able to squeeze past you."

"Whew. You bet—down is definitely better than up."

"You look rough, boy. What's going on?"

"I...well, it's a long story. Can we sit down somewhere and talk?"

"Eh, I suppose—as long as you behave yourself."

The two hobbled down the trail and, at the Court, John plopped down on one of the stones. He beckoned Trevor to do the same. "What's on your mind?"

Trevor squatted on a rock and gulped a few breaths, waiting for his heartbeat to slow. When it did, he squared eyes with John. "Lisa's in the hospital. She's hurt really bad and needs your help."

John stiffened, then rose. "I told you no more wizard stuff."

"I'm not talking about the wizard." Trevor's tone escalated. "I'm talking about somebody who's hurt and needs...needs what you can do. I'm not asking for anything you don't already do for your hillbilly friends."

"You've got doctors and medicine where you come from— good ones. They don't have that here. Couldn't afford it if they did."

"It's been three days and she's not any better. She needs *you*." Trevor stood to face John. "Listen—I'll pay you, or give you food, or whatever. Just help her."

John stared until his features relaxed. "Oh, all right. Bring her up here and I'll see what I can do." He glanced away, then back. "Oh, ah, no need to pay me—that's just for the mountain folk."

"No—you don't get it. She can't move. She's hooked up to all sorts of wires and machines. I can't even remember everything that's wrong. You have to go see her."

"Oh, no." John held up a hand. "You just hold it right there. I'm not leaving this mountain."

"You're not...?" For a moment Trevor wasn't sure he'd heard correctly. "How can you say that? If I could get her up here, she'd be here now." He felt his face grow warm. "I'm not asking you to give up your stupid mountain. All I want is five minutes of your precious time, then for all I care you can hide here the rest of your life. What's so hard about that?"

"I'm not leaving, boy. Not for you, not for her, not for anybody. Get that through your thick skull, OK? Now, if that's all you wanted, I have things to do." John turned and walked away.

Trevor went after him, swearing. "You scumbag! I thought you wanted to help people, but that's a lie, isn't it? Just like your game with the stupid mountain yahoos. Well, thanks for nothing." He punctuated the tirade with a poignant curse, then stooped down and picked up the first rock that came to hand, which just happened to be a small one. He launched it at John and hit him square between the shoulders.

If John noticed, he gave no indication. He just kept walking.

* * *

Mr. Dawson paced the family waiting room near the critical care ward, crossing back and forth in front of his wife, who sat with her face buried in her hands. Trevor approached Lisa's dad from the side.

"How's she doing?"

"Mm—Trevor'" Mr. Dawson's jaw muscles flexed. He glanced down at his wife then stepped closer to Trevor and spoke in a hushed tone. "Not good. Nothing's really changed since you left and…" Mr. Dawson choked back tears. "They had to restart her heart." He hung his head. "That was this morning. They haven't let us back in yet."

Trevor's eyes widened. "This isn't happening."

Mrs. Dawson burst into tears. Her husband moved to her side and draped an arm around her. "It's OK. She's going to make it." If the reassuring words had any effect on Mrs. Dawson it was only that she cried harder.

Trevor had heard enough. He ran from the waiting room and headed straight to the double doors. "I want to see Lisa Dawson," he demanded of the red phone.

"I'm sorry, sir. She's not ready for visitors."

"Then let me talk to her doctor." Trevor scrubbed his fingers over the grain of the wallpaper.

"The attending physician is busy at the moment. If you're a member of the immediate family I can give her your name and she'll speak to you in the waiting room when she's available."

Trevor's face flushed. He screamed at the phone. "Then get me her nurse! Get me *some*body who can *do* something, you freaking imbecile!"

"Sir, I'm one of her nurses. You can speak with me."

"In person!"

A muted conversation bubbled out of the receiver, then the door clicked. "Come on back, please."

Trevor banged down the phone and stepped forward the instant the doors parted. Two nurses blocked his path. He drew up short just short of bowling them over. "I've got important information about Lisa Dawson. Get out of my way."

Both nurses stood their ground. The larger one eyed him with suspicion. "What's your relation to Ms. Dawson, sir?"

He cursed her. "I'm her boyfriend, and—"

"I'm afraid we can only discuss medical issues with the immediate family. Now, if you would step back—"

"She's pregnant!" Trevor's shout echoed throughout the wing, drawing stares and raised eyebrows from the various staff milling about. "Have any of you Einstein's checked on the baby?"

The nurses hovering over Trevor gave each other questioning looks. "Just a minute." The larger nurse scrambled back to her desk and tapped away on the computer. Then she leapt from her chair and made a bee line for Lisa's room. An excited discussion spilled out into the hallway, followed by a hurried exchange of personnel.

Satisfied he had made an impact, Trevor exhaled deep and leaned against the nearest wall, eyeing the commotion with a mixture of disgust and relief. His head hurt, and he was glad a major confrontation hadn't been necessary. Several minutes later the big nurse returned.

"Thanks for letting us know about Ms. Dawson's condition. She's being well cared for." The nurse's expression darkened. "You can go back to the waiting room now—please."

Trevor pushed away from the wall. "When can I see her?"

"Maybe in an hour or so."

"Can I just peek in? I'll stay outside the room."

"I'm sorry—no."

Trevor crossed his arms over his chest and narrowed his eyes. "I *demand* to see her."

The big nurse matched his pose. "Then I guess my next call will be to security so they can escort you out. And if they do that, you won't be allowed back in this facility as long as she's here." The nurse paused just long enough for it to sink in. "But if you'll just head back to the waiting room..." She gestured toward the double doors.

Trevor glanced across the hall toward Lisa's room, weighing the risk. Probably not worth it the way he felt. But if he didn't see Lisa soon, no nurse or orderly in the world would keep him out of that room.

* * *

Trevor found it harder to make the climb this time. The long drive back from Greenville, and the nighttime hike with no rest in between, sucked every bit of energy out of him. Sweat oozed from his pores, felt like ice on his forearms in the chilly night air. Heart pounding in his ears, a splitting headache raked pain across his forehead. His body begged him to rest even as his dogged determination drove him on.

Just visible in the beams of the crescent moon, miniature clouds of condensation curled out of Trevor's nostrils with each labored breath. Every step he took weighed heavier than the last as the winding path grew steep. Soon his body reached its limit. He collapsed in a heap on the forest floor. Sleep overtook him in an instant, bringing with it sweet relief.

The first rays of morning sunlight played over Trevor's eyes and woke him. Sensation returned with consciousness. He felt stiff and hungry, and he shivered from the cold. His head hurt. Groaning, he rolled into a sitting position. When he didn't pass out from the pain, he stood. What a night.

Studying his surroundings, he determined he couldn't be more than a few minutes from the Court. But, rising, the lethargy of the night before returned. Thoughts of Lisa, however, drove him to motion. Up the trail he went, past the Court, around the winding pass, and onto the plateau, all at a weighted pace, and with his stomach screaming for nourishment.

Now John's tent stood before him.

"Hey." Winded, Trevor croaked out his words. "John?"

When no one answered Trevor ducked under the tent flat and shuffled toward the cave. "John?" He managed a little more volume this time.

It took a minute for his eyes to adjust. When they did, he moved on into the cave where he found a lump in the vague outline of a man, curled on a mat, snoring.

"John!" Trevor rushed over and shook him.

"Yah!" John twisted, then jerked away. His hand shot out beside him, grasping air.

"John, it's me—Trevor."

"Huh?" John pushed partway up, leaning on his hands. "Trevor? What are you doing here?"

"I need you. Get up."

John groaned, sat up straight, and rubbed his eyes. "You're starting to be a real pest."

"Hey—this is serious! She's going to die if you don't help her!"

"What? Wait a minute." John slicked back his remaining hair, and stood. "I need coffee. Let's go to the tent."

Retrieving his staff from against the wall, and a coffee pot hanging overhead, John limped out of the cave with Trevor right on his heels. John snagged a match from somewhere within a pile of junk along the wall which he used to start a fire in the pit once they were outside. Then he hung the pot from a stick jutting over the fire and marched back inside where he plopped down on a stool and rubbed his hands.

"A bit chilly, eh?"

"John!" Trevor swore. "Forget the weather—you have to *do* something!"

"Now," John held up a hand, "you just hang on. There's nothing so urgent it can't wait 'til after coffee." He narrowed his eyes and poked a finger in Trevor's belly. "You come barreling in here like you own the place, then expect me to jump at your every command? Well, it doesn't work that way. You can just hold your horses a few minutes while I get my wits about me."

Trevor gritted his teeth and held his tongue. He knew from experience it would get him nowhere to fly off the handle at the old buzzard. The pompous jerk was really starting to get on his nerves.

After a few minutes of Trevor fidgeting in silence, during which John pulled on his boots and a coat, Trevor jumped up and ran outside. He grabbed the pot from the fire, hurried it back into the tent, and thrust it in the old man's face. "Here. It's warm enough. Let's talk."

John felt the bottom of the pot and frowned, but poured himself a cup anyway. He glanced at Trevor. "Want some?"

Trevor started to curse, but the ache in his stomach told his brain a cup of coffee wasn't such a bad idea. "Sure." He relaxed, if only a little, as John sat a spare mug in his hand.

It took a painfully long time for John to finish his elixir—long after Trevor gulped his mug dry. After upending his cup, John poured himself another round, a smile now brightening his face. "Now, what's the fuss?"

"It's Lisa—she's worse. They had to restart her heart!"

"Hm." John downed half his cup. "Sounds like they have things under control."

Trevor's cheeks flushed red hot. He jumped up and threw his cup to the ground. "You stupid fool! Her heart stopped!" A long stream of expletives echoed through the cave. "She could have died. And here you sit in your comfy little cave, all cut off from the world, pronouncing judgment on somebody you've never seen. She's black and blue all over! She doesn't even look human!

"What's it take to get through to you? I'll give you anything—*anything*! Just come see her long enough to do your thing. Why is that such a big deal? Why don't act like a...a *Christian*, for once?"

John rested his head on his hands, watching Trevor's tirade without expression. Every few seconds he took another sip.

"You do your piddling good deeds for these worthless mountain morons, but you won't lift a finger for somebody who *really* needs you. Lisa's a smart girl—she makes A's in college. She deserves to live! Don't you have a spark of compassion somewhere under that callous hide of yours?" Trevor planted clinched fists on his hips. It took everything he had not to punch the old guy right in the nose.

"You know what, boy?" John spoke with his head still resting on his hands. "I feel sorry for your girlfriend. I really do. But there's a whole world of problems out there, and I can't solve them all. I do my part up here on the mountain. The rest of the world, well, it can take care of itself. Like I told you before—bring her up here, and I'll see what I can do."

"You idiot!" Trevor kicked the ground. "Get it through your head—I can't move her. I *can't*. It's absolutely impossible."

"I dunno." John shrugged. "Maybe you're not desperate enough."

Trevor glared at him. Then on a whim he jumped past John and dashed into the cave. After some clattering and clicking, he returned a moment later with a shotgun in hand. He shoved the barrel into John's cheek.

"The game's over, old man. You're coming with me."

John didn't bat an eye. "Nope—don't think so. Besides, that one's not loaded."

Trevor swung the shotgun right and pulled the trigger. Boom! A ragged hole the size of a football appeared in the side of the tent. He swung the muzzle back toward John and pointed it right between his eyes.

John met Trevor's stare. "Go ahead, son—pull the trigger. It won't help your girlfriend, but it'll sure put an end to my misery."

Trevor's finger tightened around the trigger. Something screamed for him to go through with it, to get rid of this selfish mule once and for all. But, John was right—it wouldn't do a thing for Lisa. He lowered the muzzle.

"You're a real nut case." Trevor threw the gun at John's feet. "Is this what believing in God is all about? Well, I'm glad I'm not that stupid." He paced back and forth as he debated his next move, casting an occasional glance John's way.

John followed Trevor's movements with his eyes.

"She's pregnant." Trevor's tone ratcheted down, took on a note of pleading. "There's more than Lisa's life at stake here."

"Pregnant?" John's eyebrows went up. "So I should put my stamp of approval on your sin by healing her, eh? I hardly think so." He shook his head. "The wages of sin is death. Fair pay in my opinion."

"*Fair?*" Trevor made a face. Then he shook his head. "I should have expected that from a church-goer—selfish and hypocritical. Happy to help as long as it doesn't inconvenience your petty little routine. It's pretty obvious all you really care about is yourself, and playing God. Makes you feel good, doesn't it, deciding who lives and who dies?

"Well let me tell you this—if Lisa dies I'll be back to tell you about it." He pointed a finger in the old man's face. "I want you to feel the guilt—that is, if you're capable of feeling anything but your self-righteous pride. And you know what else? I might just kill you to get even.

"But if she lives, well, you won't ever see me again. I guess that'll make us both happy. Either way, though, I want to thank you for something. Thanks for proving religion is a farce. I mean, if anybody ever has a question about whether or not God is real, all I have to do is send them to you. You're living proof that man invented God just to gratify himself."

With that Trevor spit in John's face, whirled, and marched from the tent.

Chapter Twenty-Five

John hunched by the side of a broad mountain stream, an ancient rod and reel extended over the water. Fish nipped at the surface here and there but, so far, nothing took his bait. His thoughts traveled back to his conversation with the unruly kid. Some of it stung.

"What does *he* know about pain?" John asked the stream. He wiggled the rod mindlessly up and down. "Might do him good to hurt for a change."

The slightest tug at John's line brought him back to the present. He cranked the reel until the hook broke water, part of a worm wriggling on it. John stared. Why did death always have to be so ugly?

"What do *I* care if she dies? Happens every day. She's nothing but a hussy, getting pregnant out of marriage like that."

Trevor's words echoed in his head. "I should have expected that from a church-goer ... all you really care about is yourself ... playing God..."

John dropped the rod and covered his ears. "Stop it! I don't need some heathen ruining my life!"

I love him, just like I love you.

The voice! John jumped to his feet and stomped the ground.

"So?" John scowled at the heavens. "He doesn't even believe in you. I'm sure she doesn't either."

John reached for his pole and another worm. Hands trembling, he fumbled with the bait and snagged his thumb on the hook.

"Ee-ouch!" The pole hit the ground and rolled away. John squeezed his thumb until a thin trail of blood dripped to the ground.

Red, life-ending blood. That's how it was with Sarah—one big bloody mess. He clenched his damaged hand into a fist and thrust it skyward.

"I begged you! I *trusted* you. Why should an unbeliever get something you wouldn't give *me*? What did I ever do to deserve that?"

The heavens remained silent. John dropped back to the ground and kicked dirt with his good leg. He closed his eyes and buried his head in one hand. "Pregnant," he mumbled.

A few seconds passed then John's eyes flew open. He slammed a fist into the ground. "Pregnant! Sarah was pregnant, too! Why didn't *she* live? That boy doesn't deserve to be a father! He didn't even have the decency to marry the girl. Why should a sinner's baby live when my son died?" He raised two trembling fists overhead. "Why?"

Eventually, John's hands came down. And like a thousand times before, he broke down, and he cried.

* * *

Trevor hunched in a chair beside Lisa's hospital bed, stroking her hand. Mrs. Dawson slept in the poor excuse for a recliner in the back corner of the room. They had been there for hours—long past the last call prompting visitors to leave.

The nurses left them alone. They seemed to know.

"Don't leave me, Lisa. Life won't be the same without you." He ran a finger down the side of her swollen face, then stroked her hair.

"I don't care what the doctors say—you can make it. We both have something to live for now. You *have* to pull through."

Trevor leaned close to Lisa's ear. "I'm sorry I couldn't tell you before. It's just that… well, because I didn't know. I still don't know what it means, but I'll tell you anyway. I think I love you, Lisa. At least, the best I know how."

He pulled back and searched for a response, but his only answer was the mechanical slurping of the life support system and the heart monitor's incessant beeping. He rubbed his eyes. Too many hours without sleep. How long could he keep this up?

Giving in to the fatigue, Trevor sank to his knees. He leaned into the bed and lay his head as close to Lisa's pillow as he could reach, then hummed the haunting melody he had first heard on John's bagpipes so many weeks ago. He still didn't understand what attracted him to the tune, but somehow it seemed appropriate.

The melody lulled him to sleep.

* * *

A lone figure in black crept through the deserted hospital corridors. It made its way to the fifth floor undetected. Pausing at a set of double doors, the figure knelt on the floor in prayer.

Fingers reached from under the dark cloak and pressed the right-hand door. It swung open. A nurse walked past without glancing up and disappeared down a secondary hallway. The dark form moved with a curious up-down gait and clip-clop sound along the perimeter of the critical care unit, pausing to examine the name posted by each door.

When it reached Lisa Dawson, the apparition halted and peered into the room.

John's heart skipped a beat. Trevor lay face down and motionless over the body of something that might once have been a young lady. John's thoughts raced back through the years. In his mind's eye he saw himself in the same position, Sarah lying under him. The doorframe seemed to sway as John leaned against it, legs turned to rubber.

The memories had their way with John for a while, but he finally pushed them aside. Then he steadied himself, drew in a deep breath, and limped to the bedside. There he took up a position opposite Trevor and gripped Lisa's arm.

"Father God," he said, voice bold and certain, "tonight I obey your calling. According to the gift you placed inside me, I command this body to be made whole."

Trevor stirred. He slid halfway off the bed, eyes opening on the way down. John glanced at him, but quickly turned back to the work at hand. Lisa hadn't moved a muscle.

"Lord, I'm asking you to show yourself strong—" John stopped in mid-sentence and cocked his head sideways.

Trevor pulled himself halfway up, elbows planted on the mattress. "Hey—what's going on?"

"You!" John pointed. "You were trouble before and you're trouble now."

"Yeah, nice to see you, too."

"Leave me. Get out of the room."

"What for?"

"You're hindering my prayers."

"*I'm* not doing anything." Trevor stood and crossed his arms. "Go ahead—heal her."

"Not with you here."

"Why not?"

"I told you. Your unbelief is in the way."

"That's crazy. What did I do wrong?"

"You have to believe." John raised up tall and clacked his staff on the floor. "It's the only way."

"You're kidding. I haven't seen anything that tells me there's a God at work here."

"You...?" John furrowed his brow. "How can you say that? You've seen his miracles with your own eyes."

"Who says it was God? It could be...I don't know—anything."

"Listen to me, young man. You lectured me earlier and gave me some things to think about. Now it's your turn. I'm telling you my power comes from God, and unless he heals her," John nodded at Lisa, "she's not going to make it. And everything depends on you.

"I'm here, and I'm willing to do my part. But God let me know it's not going to happen unless you do *your* part. If she dies, it won't be me who's guilty—or God. So what's it going to be?"

Trevor narrowed his eyes. After a moment he said, "Well, I believe you can do it."

Once again John banged his staff on the floor. "That's not good enough. You have to recognize where my power comes from, and I'm telling you it comes from God through the name of his son, Jesus Christ."

Breathing a curse, Trevor's gaze fell on Lisa. Then he scanned the lights and numbers on the monitoring and life support equipment. A moment passed, then another. He sighed, then turned back to John.

"You've got something, old man. I don't know what it is, or how it works. I don't even see how a normal human can do what you do." Trevor glanced at Lisa and back. "You say your power comes from God. Well, I have a hard time believing that. I've never believed in God—I never had a reason to.

"Maybe there *is* a God, and maybe there isn't. If there is, well, I guess it's as good an explanation as any where you got your power. But I don't know." Trevor shook his head. "I honestly don't know."

John stared into Trevor's eyes for the longest time. Did he detect a change? If so, it certainly wasn't to the level he expected. He huffed. "If nothing else, at least now you're being honest with me." He closed his eyes and whispered toward the ceiling, "Is it enough?"

Seconds passed. Eventually, Trevor interrupted. "Well?"

John opened his eyes. "He says you're moving in the right direction." He leaned over Lisa once again. "Now, if you're not sure God *is* real, hold onto that thought that he *could* be real. Then close your eyes and believe with all your heart that Lisa will be healed."

With a shrug and a last look at John, Trevor closed his eyes.

"Now, witness the power of the Almighty God!"

Trevor's eyes popped open.

At the same time, Mrs. Dawson woke with a start. "Wha—?"

"In the name of Jesus, young lady, I command you to be healed." John extended his staff over the bed and, for the briefest moment, it seemed that the room brightened ever so slightly and a warm glow appeared to settle over Lisa. If the lighting had changed at all, it faded so quickly there was no way to be certain of it.

Trevor leaned over Lisa, and gasped. The swelling in her face disappeared and her proper color returned. She stirred, and her eyelids fluttered open.

"What's going on here?" Mrs. Dawson, eyes wide as saucers, rose from her chair, gaze moving from John to Lisa.

John lowered his staff. He rested a hand on Lisa's stomach. "In the name of Jesus, be made whole."

"Trevor?" Lisa's eyes flashed between Trevor and John. "What's happening?"

"John! You did it! Look at her!" Trevor jumped up and down, pointing.

But John was already halfway to the door. He glanced back at Lisa, then lit out into the hallway. He heard Mrs. Dawson call after him.

"Who in the world was that?"

* * *

Multi-colored Christmas decorations hung from every light post in downtown Winterville. A red and black toy soldier, white snowflakes, a red and white Santa, all wrapped in green garland and surrounded by flashing lights. The pattern of ornaments repeated at an alarming rate as Trevor's car zipped down the main boulevard.

"So," Trevor glanced over at Lisa, "do you want to talk with your parents tonight?"

She took a moment to answer. "Uh, Trev...I've been thinking about that. There's really no reason to get my parents involved. I mean, we can just go take care of it ourselves."

Trevor backed off the accelerator and let the rental car coast. He looked across the seat at her. "What are you saying?"

"We can solve this ourselves. I don't want my parents involved."

The car eased to a stop, pointing at the curb. Trevor took his hands off the wheel. "You don't want the baby?"

"I can't go to school and raise a child at the same time. And I certainly don't see *you* being ready to support a family."

"But, Lisa—this is our chance. It's the perfect excuse to leave everything behind and move to the mountain. We can start a whole new life together."

"Trevor! I can't believe you! You said you were through with the mountain."

"I was. But this changes things."

"It doesn't change *anything*. You've got to face reality, Trev. Running off to never-land won't solve this problem."

The car had landed near a hardware store in the downtown shopping area. Trevor frowned at the tools on display, then tapped the gas pedal enough to ease the car into a parking space. He keyed off the engine, then turned his full attention on Lisa.

"Don't you want to have kids?"

"I don't know...I mean, someday, I guess." Lisa closed her eyes and shook her head. "But now is not the time."

Trevor huffed. He pressed his nose to the window and tried to think, watching the passersby along the sidewalk. An old man with a limp caught his attention. He thought about John.

"Hey!"

"What?"

"That's John!" Trevor pointed at the retreating figure. He pushed open the car door and leaned outside. "Hey, John!"

If the old man heard, he gave no indication.

"Come on, Lisa—you've got to meet him."

Trevor jumped out of the car and leapt onto the sidewalk. He glanced behind to make sure Lisa followed. She hesitated, then unbuckled and joined him.

Trevor ran on ahead. "Hey, John—wait up!"

The old man slowed. He looked over his shoulder, then halted, a pleasant smile made his face appear to glow.

"Lisa's with me," Trevor said, gesturing back up the sidewalk. "I want you to meet her."

A moment later Lisa joined them.

"John, this is Lisa." Trevor shuffled side to side, grinning.

"Hello, young lady." John smiled and extended a hand. "It's a pleasure to meet you."

"Nice to meet you, uh, John." She shook his hand. "I've heard a lot about you." Lisa raised an eyebrow. "In fact, it's hard to believe everything I've been told."

"Hmm, I—"

"But it's true," Trevor cut in.

"So...you're really the Wizard of Winterville?" Lisa pulled her coat tight as a gust of wind whipped past.

John chuckled and shook his head. "I may never live that name down. It's what the mountain people call me...but I'd much prefer you stick with John."

"What are you doing here?" Trevor found his teeth chattering when he spoke. "I thought you'd be holed up in your cave."

John pointed to a building a block down the street. "That's Winterville Chapel. I haven't been there in over forty years. I thought I'd have a look around."

"Did you really heal me?"

John's attention returned to Lisa. He gave her a most serious look. "Young lady, God healed you. He just used me as the instrument of his healing."

"Um...then, I guess I owe you my life. How could I ever repay you?"

"You owe your life to God—not me. As far as repayment goes, how about you show up at Winterville Chapel next Sunday morning?" John lifted his staff and poked Trevor with it. "And bring that boyfriend of yours with you." He winked. "I'll be there, and I'll be looking for you."

Lisa hesitated.

"That's nuts," said Trevor. "We really appreciate what you did, but that doesn't give you a right to force your religion down our throats."

"Hey, now—hold your horses, boy. I'm not forcing anything. I just asked you to go to church, that's all." John turned to Lisa. "Is that too high a price to pay for your life, young lady—going to church just once?"

"John—"

"We'll go," said Lisa.

Trevor made a sour face. "I don't—"

"I owe him something, Trev. If all I have to do is go to church one time, he's letting me off easy."

Trevor growled. He shoved his hands in his pockets and kicked the sidewalk.

"In the mean time," said John, "I believe you two have some talking to do." He tapped Trevor's leg with his staff to get his attention, then gave them both a serious look. "Don't make any rash decisions, understand?"

* * *

By Sunday morning the temperature had dropped and the clouds looked desperately like snow—perfect weather for the weekend before Christmas. Inside Winterville Chapel, warm air and an even warmer spirit contrasted with the outdoor weather. Red ribbons, green holly, and innumerable lights adorned the pews and walls. A freshly cut ten-foot pine stood in the corner left of the pulpit. Adults and children alike milled about, chattering and laughing.

Peering down the aisle from the back pew, John noted the changes that had been made over the years. The seats had been upholstered in crushed red velvet, and matching carpet covered the floor. A sound system had been installed, with huge speakers hanging from the ceiling. Even the overhead lights seemed different. Despite the changes, the place still gave John the same feeling it had forty years ago. It felt like...home.

When the organist fired up with an instrumental version of "Joy to the World," the crowd dispersed in patches to their seats. A few children continued to run around the sanctuary until called down by their parents.

Attendance must be down, John thought. Holidays usually drew the largest crowds, but there probably weren't a hundred people in the room when the song leader stepped behind the pulpit.

"Turn in your hymnals to number one forty-two."

Everyone stood and belted out a reasonable rendition of "The First Noel." John joined the merry chorus, but stole glances toward the foyer every so often.

As the song wound down, Lisa crept into the sanctuary wearing an expensive-looking new dress and bright red shoes that contrasted with the uncomfortable look on her face. She took a seat near the back—on the opposite side of John—and stared straight ahead without noticing him.

The pastor, a man who looked to be in his fifties, delivered a traditional Christmas sermon. He spoke of the birth of Christ, telling what it meant at the time and how it related to people today. Bits and pieces of a salvation theme popped up here and there throughout his talk.

John kept glancing Lisa's way at various points during the service. She sat stiff and unmoving. John couldn't read anything from her expression.

"If you don't know Jesus," the preacher said, "then now is the time for you to meet him." He motioned to the organist, and she eased into "Amazing Grace."

"You can know him personally, and he can live in your heart. If you want to make that decision, come on down front and let me pray with you."

Lisa stood. She turned to leave but after slipping into the aisle she noticed John. They watched each other for an eternity. A single tear formed under one eye and made its way down her cheek. It splattered on the crimson carpet.

John rose and limped toward her. He wrapped her in a one-arm hug and whispered in her ear. "Would you like me to go down front with you?"

Tears flowed in earnest as Lisa nodded affirmative. John walked her down the aisle.

"This is my friend, Lisa," John told the pastor. "I think she wants to talk with you." Then he stepped aside and let the minister take over.

The pastor leaned toward Lisa and listened for a moment, then spoke so only she could hear. Every so often Lisa nodded. Twice she said something back. All the while, her shoulders shook and she continued to weep.

"I have an announcement," the pastor said minutes later, addressing the congregation. "We have a new sister in Christ. Her name is Lisa Dawson." He beamed at her and gave her a reassuring pat. "She's going to need a lot of support in the coming days, so I'd like you all to introduce yourselves after the service, and make her feel at home. Now, let's pray..."

John slipped out the back and waited in the foyer. Ten or fifteen minutes passed before Lisa appeared. When she did, she ran to him, smiling, and smothered him in a hug.

"Oh, John. I never knew." Tears lined Lisa's cheeks, but she wore a smile. "I had no idea what church was really about."

"Heh. Now that you know, it's time to tell others."

Lisa's countenance fell. "Trevor should have been here. I couldn't get him to come."

"You tell him what you found. He wouldn't listen to me, but maybe he'll listen to you. After all, I think you have something that interests him." John gave her a knowing grin.

"I will, John." The smile came back. "I can't wait to talk to him."

* * *

John relaxed on a park bench, watching people come and go. He smiled wistfully at the children, wondering what it would have been like if Sarah hadn't died. A pair of hands reached around him from behind, covering his eyes and interrupting his thoughts.

"Guess who?"

"I hope it's not my mother. I forgot to brush my teeth."

Lisa giggled as she came bounding around the bench. She plopped down next to John and pecked him on the cheek.

"How did it go?"

"OK, I guess." Lisa's smile faded. "To say they were disappointed would be the understatement of the century. Mom cried a lot, and Dad was pretty quiet. They said they would support whatever decision I made."

"And that is...?"

"I—" Lisa looked away. "I haven't made up my mind yet." She turned back to him. "I'll probably have the baby, but I don't know if I'll keep it. I'm not ready for motherhood right now."

"Hmm. What does Trevor say?"

"He still wants us to move to the mountain." Lisa followed a passing stroller with her gaze. "To tell the truth, I think he's more interested in the baby than he is me. It's weird—I never thought of him as the fatherly type."

"He's a wild card, all right. There's no telling what's going on in that head of his."

"Yeah, I'm realizing that more all the time." Lisa looked thoughtful. "Say—what happens to you? I mean, are you staying in town, or are you going back up to the mountain?"

John laughed. "I have some unfinished business down here that goes back quite a few years. I expect you'll see me around more often than not."

"That's good. Because I'm going to need help with Trevor. He still doesn't like talking about God or religion. How do I get him to see the truth?"

"God is pretty patient," John said, smiling. "After all, he waited forty years for me to come around. So, you just keep praying for that boyfriend of yours." He patted her hand and winked. "I have a feeling that God isn't finished with him yet."

End

About the Author

I have a story to tell...

Robert Quattlebaum is a committed Christian, husband, and father of six children, three of whom are adopted. He is an honor graduate of the Georgia Institute of Technology, and has enjoyed a successful career in computer science. Mr. Quattlebaum enjoys reading, writing, music, and automobiles.

Connect with the author at robertquattlebaum.com.